# How Green Were My Mountains?

# How Green Were My Mountains?

LEONARD I. LINKOW

**To order additional copies of this book, contact:**
Xlibris Corporation
1-888-795-4274
www.Xlibris.com
Orders@Xlibris.com
16788-LINK

# Contents

TO MY BELOVED FRIEND, COMPANION AND CONFIDANT, CECILIA.

# PROLOGUE

*Create like a god, command like a king and work like a slave—*
Constantine Brancusi

*It may almost be a question of whether such wisdom as many of us have in our mature years has not come from the dying out of the power of temptation, rather than as the results of thought and resolution.*—Anthony Trollope

I have been a world traveler for more than forty years, but remain a native of New York City. Humans have made no more cosmopolitan place. New York society, primed by old money and the new, lures every form of international business. Ambition soars above the vast grid of buildings; those seeking the power of fame and the glory of fortune (or vice versa) are certain they are the goals of the game and act accordingly every day. The cream and the bastards, as the saying goes, rise to the top. In about equal numbers, I think. For the wizards and the wicked, a misstep followed by a fall in New York can be more traumatic than the upward struggle because it often occurs much more quickly. Which is another way of saying, the higher they rise, the harder they plunge. I have struggled to remain at the top of my profession since I began in 1953.

Almost from the start I lived and worked according to the credo of the New York business and personal jungle. I played by the rules and have tried to write a few of my own. If I was head of a law firm or a high finance empire, I would be likened to "the old lion," or thought of as a living time capsule for having contributed to a golden age. Momentous eras have passed in these five decades; virtually every nation on earth has been transformed by politics, war, technology and finance. During all, I, a Depression-era child, born in the heyday of Babe Ruth and Charles Lindbergh, worked doggedly to establish a worldwide reputation for innovation, to improve the huge catalog of methods that I developed and to hone my skills in their application. And then I worked even more relentlessly to prevent what I had labored to create from being disparaged, co-opted or ignored. There were, I knew, countless thousands of people around the world who would benefit from my tools and techniques. Wherever there was a community, there was a patient, or dozens, or hundreds; the supply was and remains potentially boundless. People, often in pain, need help. I, of course, cannot provide it for all of them. But I have taught many others at seminars held at institutes and universities around the world. (Some of these institutes bear my name, erected as a result of my unstinting effort to be the main messenger of a new technology domain, and as a consequence, its king.) I have done so because, basically, I intended to thrive among the leaders at the top rather than sink to the followers nearer the bottom.

I am an implantologist. That's a rather inadequate and perhaps even a misbegotten term. A foreign visitor not keen on the convolutions of the English language might well take the term for something else–a gardener, a jeweler, a silicon surgeon for the bosom, perhaps even a consultant on factory design. But many Americans (in recent years totaling nearly 500,000,000 annual visits) who sit in the dental chair–the leather-and-steel recliner that would look equally at home on the bridge of a warship–to have their teeth examined, cleaned, drilled or removed would know that I am a specialist, a doctor with expertise in a variety of exotic, high-grade materials and

their exacting utility in the human jaw. Because of the nature
of dentistry–full, sometimes bloody, and often intimate contact with the most multi-purpose orifice of the human body–
we are often denigrated. (Even I am among the last to call it
glamorous.) What is more, many people, even my colleagues,
tend to lump general practitioners, oral surgeons, orthodontists and so on together in the facile, all-inclusive and, I think
disagreeable rank of 'dentist'. (A word I am, for lack of a better one, obliged to use throughout this book.) We are not
thought of as medical doctors, at least not in the same way one
considers, say, a cardiologist or an orthopedic surgeon. Nonetheless, when in dental school students are required, as are all
future doctors, to submerge themselves in studies on the structure and function of the human body, to become rote experts
on anatomy, biochemistry, physiology, and a broad range of
other subjects which would by and large play only a supporting
role in whatever dental specialty we eventually came to adopt.
It is of course all for the noble purpose of higher learning.
Generally speaking, the more factual knowledge a doctor (or
anyone at all) has, the greater the chance that s/he will become highly competent and successful. If we are lucky and
persevere through the long ordeal of dental school and the
trials of life, we might gain true wisdom in the bargain.

My uphill trek towards the distant, flickering light of wisdom is a long one, by no means over, and anything but direct.
I have traveled six continents and worked literally countless
hours in my pursuit of professional perfection, to learn more,
to be more useful to the patients and colleagues who relied
upon me. This journey is five decades long and, much like
anyone's life, it is filled with an abundance of joys and sorrows,
triumph and dejection. These extremes may perhaps be wider
for leaders in their fields, magnified as they are against ordinary, daily human life in a slow-motion cyclone of great change.
This change, inspired by innovation, gathers momentum and
soon threatens to leave many behind. Sometimes, I fear, the
evolution comes full circle and obscures its pioneers.

I have been a leader in a challenging and demanding domain of my profession, helping to sustain cycles of invention,
application and refinement without pause since 1954. Institutes in Germany, Italy, Romania, Japan, Colombia, and the
U.S. bear my name. My reputation runs the gamut: I have been
celebrated, vilified, feted, demeaned, adored, sued, hailed and
scorned. Sometimes all in the same week. My designs, often
among the first of their kind–and granted over 30 patents–
have been deemed by many to be revolutionary and ingenious.
By now they are a conventional fixture (so to speak) in the
profession, a common tool rather than an exotic experiment
or a last resort. Nevertheless there are others who, even after
all these years in a world of accolades, with designs that are
verifiably effective, believe my work is nothing but a hustle, a
misguided attempt to complicate the issues of dentistry, to introduce new and seemingly strange methods when treatments
centuries old had long sufficed. (In my view, this status quo
view has been and is driven by explicit fear of change and ulte-
rior money motives; or, more bluntly, greed.) I have adamantly
insisted–and repeatedly proven–that it is in fact quite the contrary.

I have simplified the lives of thousands of men and women
by restoring their appearance and their confidence. They can
once again happily perform those functions that nearly everyone else unthinkingly takes for granted: smile, eat, speak, kiss.
Through this I have made my living and, on balance, a good
one. Guided by my rigorous training, which effectively began
in the days of my curious boyhood and continues to this day, I
have performed a service that until the late 1970s was provided by relatively few specialists worldwide. I have conducted
cutting-edge research, applying the results to the precise and
wondrous architecture of the human mouth, jaws and skull.
(And more than once, experimentally, on packs of anesthetized dogs.) By taking procedural and scientific risks, and by
adhering to my sorely tested principles and professional be-
liefs, I have developed a wide variety of devices which allow for

the permanent, that is, non-removable, emplacement of per-fectly functional, attractive although fabricated teeth. Not den-tures. Not removable bridges. Not caps. Implants by any mea-sure are much more feasible and far more convenient than these half-measure substitutes. What I have devised is the next best thing to nature's original and optimal design. Statistics prove my case: implants have a 90% rate of success over the long-term of ten years or more. People exasperated with their inconvenient removable prostheses, or in great pain, or ashamed of their appearance, undergo the procedure and find themselves reborn, grateful to have availed themselves of my work. Many of them have previously visited other dentists, but their problems remained fundamentally uncorrected, or even exacerbated, by inadequate or poor treatment. Implants restore their entire self-image, their ability to fully enjoy life. That is the ultimate goal and, once attained, makes me deeply proud.

Despite my deep misgivings about where the technology and business of the field has been headed, I am remarkably privileged to have been engaged in this work since my late twenties. I aim to relate the story of my work and the place it has held in my life. Indeed, this work *is* my life. Unremarkable it may seem to some in the greater scheme of things, in a world that spins from tragedy to crisis to terror, where stark choices of life or death are daily issues, where nations have been de-stroyed by war, where calamity or an epidemic may strike at any moment. Mine is not a whodunit nor an exposé nor a tale of jet set celebrity, scandal, sex, or sensation. But a life–like mine–lived to its limits has high drama and a wealth of lessons to impart. Not least of all, to myself. My past behavior, when it comes to wives and women, may seem offensive, vain, foolish, or worse. But it is me. Or *was* me. Some of it, most of it, seemed proper or inevitable at the time. My busy romantic life as a young man, several tempestuous marriages, occasional affairs, and epic, ugly battles with my peers do not always conjure pleas-ant memories or illuminate me as a hero in my own drama. I have regrets–very few of us don't–but the balance of my accomplishments, the nature of this international profession, and the sheer weight of time inspire and compel me to share my story with you, its heart and soul, the naked truth.

# One

## MY ITALIAN RENAISSANCE

A slight drizzle strayed from the moonless, pitch-black sky. I was in, but couldn't see very much of, Reggio Emilia, Italy. It was 1969, fifteen years after my entry into dentistry. I had become somewhat renowned and was in increasing demand on the lecture circuit as more practitioners around the world clamored to learn about the techniques I had developed and continued to improve. Little did I know when I began that I would fight many mighty battles, in my personal and professional life, before my work finally became largely accepted. This trip to Italy occurred at the end of the first phase, sort of like when the main booster of the Apollo rocket that in those days was launching men into space would burn out and the second stage took over.

I undertook this initial trip to Italy at the invitation of Professor Bertolini, a luminary in the emerging field of tooth transplantation. He had become aware of my growing reputation in the United States. Several of my articles on implantology had been published in respectable (now extinct) journals like "Dental Digest Magazine," drawing the attention of those who would help to make my career. Bertolini was eager for my visit to Italy so he could introduce my techniques to the dental profession there, and in so doing promote himself as a patron of an emerging market. The itinerary called for me to begin a lecture series in Reggio Emilia, a small city midway between Bologna and Parma which, in theory at least, was about four hours from Rome by car. But it would be seven hours before myself and the entourage of American dentists with me arrived there by train, just after 1:00 a.m. The station was deserted. No red cap was available to help with our luggage.

Searching about we found a large pushcart on the platform; we loaded all our luggage into it and I shoved it down the road. We walked. And we walked. We had no idea of our location, and simply headed towards the dim city lights, stopping a few late stragglers to ask directions, in English, and of course receiving answers in Italian (or silent, common-language shrugs). At first it seemed like an adventure, but it soon grew strange to be walking along, in a foreign land, very late at night. At last we reached our destination, a wretched excuse for a hotel, a dingy old-world affair with short, narrow beds and no carpets on the cold floors. More than likely, none of us would get much sleep during what remained of the night.

Nevertheless, in this inauspicious beginning I was on the verge of launching my career in Europe, and from there, throughout the world. The time was ripe–I was forty-one years old and certainly felt ready.

Later that morning I arrived at Professor Bertolini's office on what must have been the main street in town. Bertolini appeared to be in his early or middle sixties, a stern and craggy academic, peculiar in nature. He spoke very little English but was cordial and made himself understood with gestures, a half-smile and a translator. The three-day seminar, he said, would begin at about four o'clock that afternoon. When that hour arrived Bertolini came to the hotel and escorted me several blocks from his office. He owned the small theater in which he gave his own lectures and courses, for which he charged a fee. He promoted himself as a leader in the field, and made a tidy profit doing so. A good deal, I thought. I wished for a similar set-up.

This was my first lecture in Europe and I was quite excited. My adrenaline was flowing. For the moment the world outside this room ceased to exist for me. My American colleagues were in the audience, as well as my friend Hans Grafelmann, from Bremen, Germany. Drinking it all in for the first time, I realized the milestone at hand. I, a Jewish American from Brooklyn, New York, was in Italy, where one must complete medical school before dental training. I was about to present my techniques to over two hundred medical doctors who had specialized in dentistry, some with many more years of experience than I.

By the end of the first lecture, at about ten o'clock in the evening, it was obvious that I wasn't alone in my excitement. The message I had brought of an innovative implant procedure had electrified the audience, and I was delighted to deliver it. Their many questions kept me on the podium until after midnight.

Elated by my success, I returned on the second day with confidence that the response would be equally enthusiastic. But as I began to show my many slides which depicted the theories and procedures of implantology, Grafelmann hastened to the podium. I sensed he wanted to interrupt me, but had not determined how to do so unobtrusively. Something was obviously wrong, but I had no clue. Though the lecture was going splendidly, Grafelman was clearly agitated. He whispered that I immediately stop speaking and accompany him to the back of the room. I was not to ask any questions. I was embarrassed and confused; two hundred people were watching me. Us. What had gotten into him? I quietly but firmly refused. But he insisted and latched on to my hand, tugging me off the dais. Deprived of a choice, eager to quickly quell the disruption, I followed Grafelman's lead. He guided me through a small door at the rear of the hall and up several steps to a second door which he pushed open to reveal two young men who until a few moments before had been videotaping my lecture.

They had aimed the camera through a hole in the back wall and attached it to the recorder resting on the table. No one had bothered to inform me that my lectures would be taped, much less sought my permission! The cameramen seemed barely phased to learn that this was a violation of the law. They put up no resistance when Grafelmann confiscated a completed cassette and demanded that they surrender the one in the recorder. Once I was satisfied that we had terminated the taping, I returned to the podium, pretending that nothing had happened. But something had — and I knew it. These men certainly would never have dared to tape my lectures on what they obviously knew in advance to be my new techniques and implant devices if they hadn't been sanctioned by Bertolini himself. I was not accustomed to being manipulated and immediately lost a great deal of respect for the sly old professor.

I nonetheless continued with the seminars. On the third day I decided to illustrate my techniques in a most dramatic manner by performing implant surgery on seven doctors among the audience. I even did one procedure for the girlfriend of a colleague, a fact I note for a simple purpose: more than three decades later the implant remained in her mouth and intact.

The next day my compatriots and I were scheduled to return to Rome, where I was to give another seminar, this one to include numerous surgical demonstrations. The seminar was arranged by my friend, colleague and kindred spirit, Dr. Giorgio Gnalducci, and by Mr. Raoul Beraha, who owned a large dental supply business in Milano.

But before we departed Reggio Emilia I visited Bertolini's office. And was assailed on entering. Bertolini began yelling and, to my bewilderment, pointed to a magazine on his desk. Through an interpreter he demanded, "What is the reason for all this publicity?"

It was an awkward moment. Instead of me browbeating him for his cunning videography, I was the berated one. I didn't know what he was talking about, but I sensed he was attempting to turn the tables on me. I was shocked at his rationale. *Oggi*, the popular Italian weekly magazine, had just published a profile of me. The writer, however, had not felt obliged to observe a journalistic custom. Namely, the facts. Indeed, I had never exchanged one word with the *Oggi* reporter. Not that the piece wasn't flattering: I had been deemed a great inventor, designated the leading implantologist in the world, and even dubbed the "Einstein of the dental profession." But the writer also said that I had performed implant operations on Elizabeth Taylor, Frank Sinatra, and Neil Armstrong, the first human to walk on the moon. According to the reporter, who was nothing if not fanciful, Armstrong was afraid that his removable denture would fly away from him "because of weightlessness if Professor Linkow did not give him the benefit of his miracle operation."

I was mortified. I tried to explain that I had nothing to do with these blatant fabrications, but Bertolini seemed unconvinced. I suspect that he was actually trying to humiliate me because Grafelman and I had exposed his video flimflam.

It's true that I have had some notable patients, among them Broadway genius Alan Jay Lerner, Misha Auer (the Mad Russian), opera tenors Jan Peerce and Richard Tucker, New York radio talk show host Barry Farber, legendary radio and TV talk show host Joe Franklin–on the tube for a record-setting 43 years, and on radio even longer–the actor Harry Guardino, Eddie Fisher, John Gotti, and Sam (the Bull) Gravano (who later squealed and dealed on Gotti, then was a star in the FBI witness protection program, and then sentenced to jail for drug trafficking), and nearly worked on renowned film director Otto Preminger. But certainly not Elizabeth Taylor, Frank Sinatra or Neil Armstrong.

I was raised on homespun American virtues of honest work and strong ethics, of professional pride and personal reputation. Thus I told Bertolini that in light of this controversy, I would telegram Giorgio Gnalducci to cancel my lecture in Rome. And that is exactly what I did. Later that day I phoned

Gnalducci to explain how worried I was that the celebrities named in the article would sue me.

Gnalducci laughed convulsively. I was taken aback. Was he laughing at me or at the situation? There was no reason to worry, he assured me. It was ridiculous to fret about lawsuits in Italy, he said, because virtually anything goes. A rag like *Oggi* could publish whatever it liked without fear of repercussions. (In America we call it tabloid journalism.) After some deliberation, I decided that maybe there was no reason for concern after all, and renewed my plans to go on to Rome. Gnalducci, I later learned, had been the culprit of the *Oggi* article.

What I couldn't know was that, far from being over, my troubles were only beginning.

The following morning we departed for the Eternal City. My seminar was scheduled at the Cavallieri Hilton Hotel, located on the outskirts of Roma. Seeing what a splendid hotel it was, compared to the dive in Reggio Emilia, I was immediately confident that the trip would go far more smoothly than it had so far.

The next morning, at about 9:30, I began my lecture in the hotel's main ballroom, more than large enough for the audience of nearly four hundred Italian dentists. My lecture lasted until nearly ten that evening, allowing for the Italian custom of a three-hour lunch break. The second day went even better than the first. The audience was attentive, and deeply inquisitive during the question and answer session. I was elated. An appreciative and intelligent assembly of one's peers, eager to heed your expertise, is an honor. They would return to their practices, applying what I shared to the benefit of countless patients, and that is quite a thrill. This is the compelling dream of anyone who imparts ideas and knowledge, for in doing so, the profession, and hopefully society, is improved.

Thus there was no reason to expect anything to be amiss on the third day when I was to perform surgical procedures on several patients supplied through local doctors. This time the demonstrations would be taped with my permission and simultaneously piped into the closed-circuit system monitors. The requisite dental equipment had already been set up in the front of the grand ballroom; all I had to do before proceeding was to check that all was working to my satisfaction.

I had successfully completed three operations and was about to begin the fourth when I heard a commotion near one of the ballroom doors. A knot of dentists were pushing against each other and against the door. Were they trying to get out, or to prevent someone from entering? In my peripheral vision, I saw several others gesturing frantically in my direction. At me. Dr. Gnalducci pleaded with me to follow the group and refrain from asking questions. For a moment it seemed like Reggio Emilia in déjà vu! In true madcap comedy fashion I was hustled to the rear of the ballroom, out the back door and into a waiting taxi with Gnalducci. I repeatedly asked what was happening, but Giorgio's repeated reply was, "Hurry!"

Only after our taxi had gone several blocks from the hotel was I told the purpose for this scene. If I hadn't left when bidden, Gnalducci said, I might have been arrested. Arrested? For performing implant surgery? I was incredulous. But apparently I had technically run afoul of Italian law by engaging in operations without the necessary permission. My allegedly illegal activities were taken so seriously that police officers had been summoned and were waiting to grab me right outside the ballroom. It seemed likely, said Gnalducci, that they had been tipped off by a Dr. Tambura de Bello, at that time the leading pin implant dentist in Italy. Once a close friend of Gnalducci's, he now considered himself his rival—and by extension, mine as well.

The upshot was that I was prohibited under pain of imprisonment from performing any surgery on Italian soil. I became— to say the least—very angry. Furious. Why hadn't anyone told me this before? My friends explained that in Italy, any ruse is valid if one is cunning enough to get away with it. I quickly noted that the rules so integral to American professional society (which is not to say that it abounds in integrity) do not apply in Italy. They, in perverse fact, are sometimes bewilderingly turned upside down. I think that I was equivalent to Gulliver, the picaresque traveler of the Jonathan Swift classic who finds himself oddly out of place in several strange lands. I wasn't wise to these customs or games, and was vulnerable to those who were.

My compatriots did not satisfy me with their answers. Especially not when I had been forced to desert a large audience in mid-lecture, as well as a patient — on whom, fortunately, I had not yet started surgery. It was humiliating. By my standards I had not committed any transgressions.

I was rushed to a train bound for Switzerland, the traditional refuge of people, villains and heroes alike, on the lam in movies and in real life. It was best that Jean had remained home. I imagined the quandary of being "on the run" with a partner, who also happened to be my wife. It was bad enough that on my own I resembled a World War Two expatriate, trapped in high-stakes drama, reduced to low-grade farce, and lacking an Ingrid Bergman to ease my woes.

It wasn't the first time I had gotten into trouble for ruffling the haughty peacock's feathers because of my pioneering work in dentistry. And it occurred to me as the Zurich-bound train began its ascent into the spectacular Lombardy countryside that it wouldn't be the last.

# TWO

## AS FAR BACK AS I CAN REMEMBER

Peering into the past can lead down many blind alleys. Time casts a haze over events; people cannot fully "see" even the most important events in their lives, or are willing to only selectively remember. But I am over seventy years old, "in the twilight of my youth," as I like to say, and am sincerely trying to recall my humble beginnings, to pick up the thread that, pulling it back through time, will lead me back to where I began. And with such a rich but stormy life over so many years–spanning several social eras but a virtual millennium in the practice of dentistry–what I should include or omit poses a real conundrum, a testament to my faith in honesty.

My earliest memories are jogged when I gaze at family photographs. In nearly anyone's life these personal artifacts some times elicit wonder and joy, and at others a sweet sadness for irrecoverable moments. In one, a cracked black and white frame yellow with age, I see a little fair-haired boy, three or four years of age, wearing short pants and a blissful smile. In another, he stands by a rock about four feet in diameter, little more than three feet high. At my tender age that rock may have resembled a mountain. I would repeatedly climb atop it, holding a little girl by the hand. Did I, even then, need to be king of the hill?

These photos were probably shot during the first summer vacation I remember taking with my parents. The hotel where we stayed was located somewhere in the Catskills, the "borscht belt" as it was commonly known. I think it was called The Pioneer. How appropriate!—as a harbinger of the revolution I helped to initiate in the field of implantology, now recognized around the world as an essential (but at one time radical) development in the dental profession. All right, maybe it's not on a par with the discovery of penicillin or sending men to the moon, but it represents a breakthrough, and it has many relative merits.

*"Little Lenny" at the Pioneer Hotel — around 1928 when I was about 2 ½ years old.*

*A little lady friend*

The Pioneer was a big world of rooms, surrounded by acres of trees and land. To a child, it was vast playground, a land without borders. That little girl and I found our hiding place. The empty closet – as big as a room – was enclosed on one side by a bank of windows. The sun streamed in, creating a secret solarium. We would retreat there, away from the adults we didn't understand, to play out our giggle games and pretend to be at home.

I have another memory of a young lad who let me to peer into the tiny eyepiece of his picture viewer. As I rotated the small photo disc inside, the vistas of other, faraway places were brought into view. Even then, nearly forty years before the fact, I was a world traveler. I recall finding this gadget a day or so later, abandoned in the fields. Rather than return it to the owner I was tempted to keep it. I must have felt guilty, though, because I finally gave it to my mother and told her to whom I thought it belonged. After that I never claimed or kept anything that wasn't mine. In that era innocence was a virtue. Integrity and honesty were among my early traits. My trusting soul, alas, later venturing into the business jungle, was bound to be scarred by the slings and arrows of outrageous practice.

I see myself, age six, at a summer sleepaway camp nestled near the Adirondack Mountains. And one special day. From atop a hill overlooking right field I watched my first baseball game, played by our camp's seniors and those from another camp. My camp won in the last inning, when the son of one of my dad's friends hit a home run. I didn't know him very well, but at that moment he became my hero. I vicariously felt the freedom, the exhilaration—the thrill—that he and his teammates must have experienced after delivering that telling blow.

I desperately wished I had been the one who'd hit that ball. From that moment I knew what I wanted to be—a great baseball player! Every day for the rest of the summer I counted the minutes until it was time for baseball. I was only a little boy, but I tried so hard to be a big slugger. I was still too young, though, and could never hit the ball past the pitcher's mound. Watching the other boys swat the ball much farther than I caused me great frustration. I wanted so much to excel, and I kept trying. Although I never became the slugger of my imagination, baseball did become a very important part of my young adulthood. The path of my life would bring me into the orbit of some Hall of Fame players, and briefly into flirtation with the major leagues.

Two or three weeks before summer camp season ended I fell very ill and was confined to the infirmary. It seemed that the camp had kept my illness a secret from my parents for some time—especially my Dad, because he was a world-class worrier. If he'd had any intimation of my state he would have come and retrieved me in a flash.

In late August, the day before the season ended, the camp

HOW GREEN WERE MY MOUNTAINS?      27

owner and the camp doctor drove me home. The entire time
I lay in the back seat, shivering even under the blankets they
had wrapped around me. I remember the shock and fear on
my parents' faces when we reached home, then in the Flatbush
section of Brooklyn. I soon learned that they had already been
informed I was ailing, just not how much.

I was immediately put to bed. But it wasn't the bed I had
left in June. It had a strange-looking structure over it, an oxygen tent. There were two windows, made out of some transparent material, which allowed me to see what was going on in
my room-world: one at the foot of the bed and another on my
left. From the latter I could look into a full-length mirror hanging on a closet. My father later told me that he used to watch
me study my reflection in the mirror and have long, intense
conversations with myself.

He told me that whenever he asked how I was feeling, I
would tell him, "Oh, I'm feeling great! I just hit a home run
and we won the game." Or sometimes just, "Great, pop! We're
winning!" I was delirious, of course. I had pleurisy and was
running a very high fever. This was in 1932; there were no
antibiotics. Most details of those days are a blur, but my parents
must have been scared witless.

I pulled through–only to get hit again less than a year later
with double pneumonia. I conquered that too, none the worse
for wear, although that first baseball summer had been marred.
I was a stubborn kid. Not much could scare me. I believe that
youngsters don't fear death; probably because the concept of
dying doesn't cross the mind. At the age of say, eight, life seems
to be a very long road. Neither of the grave illnesses I contracted seemed at the time to have anything to do with death,
though I learned later how close I had actually come to it.

That same absence of fear, or fearlessness, led my friends
and I to do some pretty dumb things.

After school on snowy days, for instance, our sleds at the
ready, we would wait for an automobile to stop at a red light.
Back then, in the event of a blizzard, the streets were not plowed

regularly, if at all. Sneaking up behind the car, we lay supine on our Flexible Flyers and grabbed the rear bumper for a free ride. If the car, even moving slowly in the snow, had come to a sudden stop we would have skidded underneath the car or been smashed into the back end. We sure did live dangerously!

Most of us were good kids. Mandatory virtues were respect for our parents, our teachers, and the rights of other people. Violence of any kind was almost unheard of. In my innocence I believed that everyone was honest and that people would never deliberately harm others. What a beautiful world! Maybe we all see the days of our childhood as a better, purer time, no matter the era. Then we grow into our skin and our selves, trying to deal with the world on its inequitable terms. Adulthood is complicated, weighted with responsibility, choices, conflict. When one is young, such abstractions have no relevance.

I'm told I retain some of that youthful innocence–or naivete–to this day. On the other hand, maybe I just suffer from chronic stupidity. (Which, for the record, I define as willful denial or oversight of evident facts.) After all, it's a well-known human malady, even among the accomplished. Or, given my experience, perhaps especially among them.

Another photo, now resting on my office desk, shows Harold and Rose Linkow, my parents, a handsome couple, peering off into the distance, perhaps at some Utopia known only to them, or maybe just adopting a serene expression at the photographer's direction. The composition captures that hazy aura of 1930s black and whites, slightly worn by the years but freezing the love and respect my parents had for each other and for life, a strength they joined forever on their wedding day in April, 1924. My memories of them are complicated and ambivalent, but I believe all children feel this way about their parents. My father, for instance, had a negative or pessimistic streak. Perhaps in part it was his overweening sense of obligation to appropriate behavior, or impatience in his affairs, or a need for things to always be perfect, or . . . Well, of what use, really, is this form of psychoanalysis? What truth or insight do I ultimately derive? Even a brilliant key to the puzzle of his or anyone's psyche is to no avail. My father is with God. I'm still here, trying, hoping to put it all in perspective. But I do know this. He fed me, clothed me and loved me deeply as best he could. And in those Depression days, in an era of real and nation-wide deprivation, that was quite a bargain.

Still, his anxiety could be stifling. He was a traveling jewelry salesman, and often away. If anyone in our family ever fell ill, we would go to great lengths to conceal it on his return. My Dad simply could not abide ailing people. Even a head cold would be cause for a rebuke. In his view, illness meant that you weren't taking proper care of yourself. That you were weak or lazy. Perhaps he felt that only the strong survive, and illness was a sign that maybe you wouldn't, at least not without someone to hold you up. But even then I knew that the most robust people get sick. And, needless to say, sometimes there is no way to hide a malady, especially when it's pleurisy or pneumonia.

I must admit that some of my father's negativity rubbed off on me, too. After all, just like the physical resemblance, we often cannot help adopting some of our parents' personality, no matter how much we disapprove of or disclaim it. I remember how I would lie awake the night before a baseball game I was going to play in, too anxious to sleep. Not because I was excited, or felt inadequate to the sport, but because I was worried. What about all those clouds I had seen in the sky? There was no question in my mind that rain was on the way and the game would be cancelled. I needed to play; baseball had quickly become part of my identity. Not playing would further delay the demonstration of my worth to the world. Damn the clouds, real and imagined. These sleepless nights as a kid may account for why I suffer from insomnia even to this day.

I can understand my father's attitude, though. His life had not been easy. Although he was a very bright student at Seward Park High School in Manhattan, which at the time was the only three-year high school in the city, he was compelled to

start working full-time early on to help support his mother
and three sisters. No one else in the house could do it; his
father had died young, of double pneumonia. So my Dad
signed up for City College night school and worked during
the day as a pharmacy delivery boy for $5 a week and no tips.
In time he did better. Hired as a clerk by a leading Manhattan
jewelry firm, he specialized in the manufacture of fine diamond and other rare stone mountings and worked his way up
until he became the most successful traveling salesman the
firm had ever employed. Several top jewelry merchants com-
peted for his services. Consequently, he was able to make important changes in his career and in his family's lifestyle. We
were never rich, but it didn't require much to be secure and
content in those years.

While he could be hard on his household my father was a
prince with almost everyone else. All my friends adored him.
And he could be the most generous of men—sometimes too
generous. Every Sunday, for instance, we would visit my Aunt
Flo, one of his sisters. She was married to Sam, a mailman who
had a well-deserved reputation in my family for laziness. He
was so lazy that I did not meet him more than once or twice;
most of the time when I accompanied Dad to their house Sam
was upstairs in bed. (Obviously, he was not too sociable either.)
My father would insist at every visit on giving Aunt Flo money.
It didn't seem to have occurred to him that she and her indo-
lent husband were probably better off than we were. Later on
it struck me that this might have been my father's way of playing God, or of making himself feel less guilty for having more.

But even if he was prone to that illusion, he never made
any attempt to influence my life. He took what we now might
call a libertarian approach. Water sought its own level. Whatever I did was all right with him. And he would do anything to
help me, selflessly staying up late to lend me a hand with my
homework or driving me and my buddies back and forth to
the baseball field every weekend (which entailed a good deal
of driving since I'd often play in as many as five games over

Saturday and Sunday). But what a worrier he was, what a skeptic. It wasn't until my second and third implantology volumes were published–in 1970–that he finally acknowledged the possibility that I would be a success, and not end up in prison for doing this "dangerous" work. All that said, to me he could do no wrong. I loved him very much.

And my mother, Rose? She was born Rose Sandler, in Manhattan, the youngest of five children, in 1901. She lived her happy and healthy young life in an East Harlem brownstone on East 114th Street near Pleasant Avenue, a fairly affluent neighborhood near what is now (or was even then) Jefferson Park. She grew into a gracious and beautiful woman. Insightful. Patient. Elegant. Traits that no doubt attracted my father, a World War I Army veteran, traits that are ideal as a wife and a mother and that I later held out as a model for a companion of my own. She was a dedicated housewife, fond of her small kingdom and loving everyone in it. And she was quick. By the time dessert was served Mother was nearly done with the dinner dishes. Everything was good if all was in good order. Efficiency was vital. Mother would not let a moment of neatness go to waste. If I inherited insomnia and negativity from my father, I think I learned speed from my mother. Always be on the move, improving and, simply, proving.

My mother's industriousness–some would call it compulsiveness–had its downside, though. She would never let my younger sister Enid do anything, for example, not even a task as mundane as clearing the table or washing the dishes. Through this need to be in control, to run the house to her specifications, she succeeded, however unwittingly, in turning her daughter into a virtual invalid for years to come. Enid could not have learned to become a good home manager (back when that was the exclusive province of wives) and possibly in the process come to an inferiority complex that is very difficult to undo. Still, I don't favor the conclusion that all of Enid's problems could be attributed to my parents. In spite of my father's honest efforts to steer her right she later experienced enor-

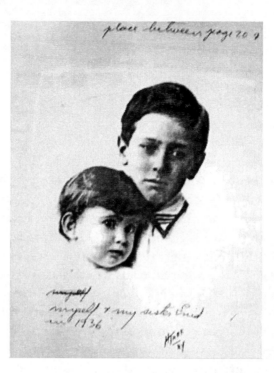

*Myself and my sister Enid in 1936.*

mous difficulties in relationships, especially with men. Reaching adolescence she developed a hatred for my parents that
caused a rift in our family for years to come. She was never
abused in any fashion, so it's hard for me to guess where her
anger came from. I was grateful when she put it behind her
and reconciled herself with Mom and Dad before they died. I
suppose I shouldn't have been surprised when she entered a
bad marriage–to a dentist no less, who resented my success
and was inclined to blame me whenever his career faltered.
But when the marriage mercifully came to an end Enid coura-
geously resolved to take matters into her own hands, going
back to college for the Masters degree she needed to get a
decent job. I gave her money to tide her over, understanding
how hard it was for her to juggle work and school and the
needs of two children. One day Enid phoned me to say that

*Dad, Mom and I — about 1968, at Grossinger's Hotel in Liberty,*
*N.Y. I had just completed Jenny Grossinger's mouth reconstruction*
*supported by my own self-tapping screw implants, and she invited us*
*to remain at her hotel for the weekend.*

she was earning enough and no longer needed my support. I
was gratified to learn that she had finally made it on her own.
Attaining true independence is like finding sweet honey in
the rock.

I see another photo: it is Saturday morning, February 25,
1939. I'm walking to Temple Ahavath Shalom, Avenue R and
East 16th Street in Brooklyn. This was the day of my Bar
Mitzvah–the day I was to become a man. I was with my father
and his best friend, Dr. Joseph Danoff, a dentist who would
later play a significant role in my life. I was understandably very
nervous; shaking, cold and petrified, my stomach felt as though
it had been filled with fifty pounds of wet cement. I had never

performed before a large number of people. Even in school, when I was called on to answer a teacher's question, I was scared stiff. This was an exaggerated shyness, I suppose. Or fear of failure. I was expected to stand on stage and read several portions of the Torah and Haftorah. I had studied Hebrew diligently, tutored by both the rabbi and the cantor for this once-in-a-lifetime occasion. My anxiety, however, fed by my lack of self-confidence, created such fear in me that the closer I drew to the Temple, the less interested I was in becoming a man. I wanted to flee Temple Ahavath Shalom, go back home, and remain a boy. For just a little longer.

But then a strange thing happened. After the first few sentences emerged from my mouth–as if they were spoken by a stiff, stuttering stranger–I began to feel at ease. Layers of inhibition dissolved. I discovered a flair for self-expression and even performance that perhaps I had denied and suppressed. Eureka! A star was born. I went on to do a great job. I particularly enjoyed concluding the ceremony with a speech in English, written for me by the rabbi. The words were intended as an extended thank you to my parents for their love, teachings and kindness. The fact is, quite opposite to my terror not two hours previously, I was a bit sorry to bring the ceremony to a close.

The entire congregation repaired to the "Linkow catering hall" to partake of a great feast my parents had set out on the ping pong table, draped with an ornate tablecloth for the occasion. It was one of my life's happiest events, even if it did spell the end of childhood. But that is life. Ages. Stages. Snapshots of phases.

My neighborhood was a very small, insular world. Everything we knew was contained in a few square blocks of Flatbush. The neighborhood was a kingdom of small one—and two-family houses, each with its own garden and garage. My friends and I made our hangout a nearby stretch along King's Highway between Coney Island Avenue and Ocean Avenue. And Coney Island, a long walk or a short bus ride away, had no shortage of amusements. Though there was little crime, not every social interaction was free from tension. I lived but a short distance from St. Edmond's, a Catholic school on Ocean Avenue. Students streamed back and forth on Avenue T past my house. They often hurled anti-Semitic taunts at me and, inevitably, I got into fights. Still, upsetting or insulting as it often was, it never got ugly. This was America, not Nazi Germany. And I knew that these insults were foremost a test of my character, not a threat. I was able to keep secret from my parents the real reason for any bruises or scrapes I sustained, explaining them away as sports injuries. If they ever suspected differently, not a word was said. All in all, the days of my youth were happy ones, and I lived months and years of grand adventures, sometimes never going more than three blocks in any direction. And though I have since circled the globe many times, I will cherish that place and those years forever.

On fall and winter weekends we usually went to either the Avalon movie theatre on Kings Highway at 18th Street, or the Kingsway at Kings Highway and Coney Island Avenue. A double feature cost all of 25 cents. Like millions of others filmgoers, I vicariously lived the screen lives of heroes embodied by Tyrone Power or John Garfield, and, of course, usually fell in love with the gorgeous and idealized leading ladies like Hedy Lamarr and Rita Hayworth.

Most of my friendships naturally revolved around baseball. Leo was the catcher. He bravely played without a mask because his family couldn't afford to buy him one. Luckily, he was never badly nailed by a foul tip or a poor pitch. And he was quick enough to evade those that might have. (But he had a hard head, too.) Bruce did most of the pitching. As team captain, I assigned myself to first base and the clean-up spot in the batting order. Ken, on the other hand, the lover boy, didn't play sports that well. He tried, but we understood and didn't invite him to join our team. Ken had other interests, namely girls. He could hit and catch, alright, but it wasn't a baseball. Some guys can't concentrate with all those hormones shooting through their bloodstream, and Ken was Exhibit A.

When I entered seventh grade I was considered anything but an outstanding student. The smarter students were in Class 7A. To my mild shame, I was in the lower ranks of Class B, the pool of those not known for a distinguished academic record. This was my reward for having spent much more time playing than reading. Although I never failed a subject, on occasion I came too close. Reminiscing over my junior high school report cards I see that in June, 1939 I soared in Geography and Drawing and Foreign Language. And wallowed in Reading/Literature and Self-Control. For the latter, I was given a D. As in Disinclined. Or Dense. Anyway, I wasn't so much interested in 7A's reputation for scholastic achievement, just a beautiful girl in its ranks. I fell in love with Meta at first sight. Wherever she was, that was where I wanted to be. However, I never said a word to her. It was infatuation, puppy love, and my first encounter with the mysteries of women.

If I wasn't to be an academic luminary, impressing Meta or other girls with my brains, I would be a super-jock, doing it with brawn! (Perhaps one eternal purpose of athletics–besides, say, perpetuating the macho ethic and proving the wisdom of teamwork–is to give men an excuse to prance and strut for the women. A mating ritual by any other name.) I became captain of our softball team, and of the stickball and touch-football teams. My class was the champ and I was often the star. I pitched and was the clean-up hitter, swatting many home runs.

Despite my growth to manhood through athletic success, I remained a shy, well-mannered boy. I tried hard, in my own lame fashion, to get Meta's attention, but I was just spinning my wheels. In a problem common to many adolescents, I simply didn't know how to be direct.

Unwilling to give up the idea of winning Meta's affections, I chose another tactic. I focused my attention on a fellow we nicknamed "The Gawk," an odd fellow a few years older than most of my teammates. He lived directly across the street from Meta. I deliberately befriended him and put him on our sand-lot baseball team, even though he seldom got a chance to play.

But with him on the roster I was better able to carry out the rest of my plot: I arranged for the team to assemble every Saturday and Sunday morning on his stoop, right in front of Meta's house. We wore our sparkling white uniforms, trimmed in royal blue, with our name, Saracens, emblazoned on our chests. I thought we looked terrific, and I hoped it would impress the hell out of her.

In spite of my clever maneuvers, however, I don't know that Meta ever even looked out her window. For all my conniving I had failed to take into account the simple possibility that, because it was so early, around *7:00 a.m.*, Meta was likely asleep and oblivious to us strutting about in our gorgeous uniforms.

Meta's best friend was Phyllis, who lived just a few houses away from her. So I tried yet another method. During most of the parties I attended–many of them at Phyllis's house–I spent a lot of time with her, hoping she would like me enough to recommend me to Meta. I sought sort of a personal reference, to network my way to true romance. Stupid me. I may have done better to summon the nerve and just approach Meta directly. But fear of failure manifests in a curious way: if you don't try, you can't fail.

A curious situation unfolded. Phyllis developed a crush on me. So as not to hurt her I forfeited the opportunity to seek out Meta. So, in a way, I exploited the attentions of someone who cared for me in a futile effort to get close to someone who was barely aware of me. It was just puppy love, no physical contact besides holding hands. But that meant a lot, like your first kiss or the first date. Beginnings are often delicate.

Phyllis was a young daughter in an affluent family. They soon moved to a new home in Great Neck. That might as well have been Missouri, so seldom was I out of Brooklyn except during the summer. Not long after Phyllis departed, she invited me to spend the night–just an innocent sleep-over–at her new residence. I declined the invitation unless I could bring along a buddy or two. As companionship, as diversion, even a kind of security detail. Bruce, Leo and Ken Rudman

accompanied me, brave Romeo, on the outing. It never occurred to me that I was greatly stretching the terms of the
invitation! We took the subway to the Long Island Railroad
station and there bought tickets for Great Neck. We felt like
big shots, going all the way out of New York City for a social
event! Phyllis's brother picked us up at the station in a new,
fancy, expensive Packard. We arrived at the house and carried
our valises up the stoop to the open front door. Open for us.
Like an invitation-only to the Waldorf or something.

I was first in and looked across the foyer and up a high,
winding stairway. Phyllis's mother stood there, gazing down at
this crew invading her house. What an expression! Confusion,
dismay, even a bit of contempt. I immediately felt uncomfortable and quite out of place. Where was Phyllis? She sheepishly
appeared. We weren't there long. There was no food. No party.
No fun. No sleeping over. In retrospect, I wasn't such a good
invited guest, bringing along my troop of pals for protection
from the wiles of a female admirer. The mini-trek to suburbia
soon climaxed at her mother's glower.

It was nearly one o'clock in the morning. Time to exit stage
right. We reached Brooklyn through a combination of hitch
hiking, subway and plain old marching. The first person home
was Ken Rudman. It was nearly 3:00 a.m.: the perfect hour for
some breaking and entering. He lived next to a big garden on
the ground floor of an Avenue T and East 17th Street home.
He didn't want to awaken the family so he aimed to sneak in
through his bedroom window. Leo opened the window and
we lifted Ken the couple of feet to the windowsill and shoved
him through. Seconds later we heard a surprised, then angry
and kind of scared-stiff scream. We took off. (Next day we
learned that Ken's uncle had stopped by for a visit and, staying
late, had gone to sleep in Ken's empty bed.) Bruce, who lived
on East 24th between Avenues S and T, went home on his
own. I took Leo home with me. By now, it was well after 3:00,
later than I had ever been up, the dead zone of time. We gam-
boled to my house on Avenue T between East 21st and 22nd

Streets. I very carefully opened the front door, straining to be silent. The least noise is amplified greatly in total quiet; a squeaky floorboard or a rustle of clothing not heard in the daytime seems like a claxon in the wee hours. But my Dad was a light sleeper. The hallway light quickly flicked on and off. "Who's there?" he demanded. I didn't respond. Dad was scared. I was mortified. "I'm going to call the police!" he threatened. I had to sheepishly confess, inviting his wrath on me so he could calm down. I was upset and ashamed. He was furious but relieved.

Baseball was my passion. But I didn't merely aspire to be a great ball player like Ted Williams or Joe DiMaggio. I was more ambitious than that! I also wanted to be a great singer like Enrico Caruso, Mario Lanza or Benjamino Gili. There were even times when I wanted to be a pilot. Or a great band leader, like Glenn Miller or Jimmy Dorsey. Or even a movie star. Thinking back on it now, like other young men, I spent a good deal of time in daydreams and fantasies. All in all, I guess I just wanted to shine–to be admired and recognized as someone of distinction, a fellow who mattered. In a few years, this trait would play a major role in setting stage for the rest of my life.

At fifteen, despite the dire state of world affairs, I was still an unabashed idealist. The Nazis had conquered most of Europe and, even though they had been badly bruised in the Battle of Britain, were poised to strangle the island nation. Many expected hostilities between the U.S. and Japan. I heard people say that FDR was angling, at Churchill's behest, to get into the scrap in Europe. Then it would surely be called World War II. I didn't understand the grave implications of these events. I knew the situation was deadly serious, to be sure, but as an innocent, head-swimming romantic my primary interest was not world affairs, but simply affairs, of being in "love." Or was I, even at that age, unwittingly seeking perfection? I must admit that this pattern persisted throughout my young adult life. I continued searching for that perfect woman, though in candor she was perhaps more real in my brain more than in the world.

I got the shock of my life one afternoon while hanging out in Meta's neighborhood. A friend of mine told me how my father and mother, or any man and woman, made love. Had sex. I could have killed him when he used a stream of dreadful earthy words to describe The Act. But I soon realized that he was speaking the truth, however crudely. And I saw my yearning for Meta in an entirely new light. Learning about the fundamental nature of sex is surely a defining moment in anyone's road to adulthood. Rather quickly one begins to acquire more perspective. Grown-up responsibilities somehow, eventually, emerge from the daydream-and-dancing realm inhabited by youngsters.

In those years I spent the summers mostly in Fleischmanns, New York, at Camp Ta-Ri-Go (The Hills of Health). They were the greatest summers of my life. I was overwhelmed by a sense of freedom. There was adventure, sports, the open fields, sunshine, long days, an idyll I wished would never end. I became friends with many boys my age. My popularity was largely due to my athletic prowess. I always won the coveted "All Around Athlete" trophy. I almost came to expect it, such was my vigor. And I had an appetite to match. A milk fanatic, I gulped down as many as eight glasses at each meal so I could be really strong when the time came to be drafted by a major league baseball team. I never cared how much I ate, certain that I would burn up extra calories in the rigorous training of an aspiring athlete.

I was far less enthusiastic about the Saturday night skits and scenes from plays we volunteered to perform. Most of them were morals and fables, but none of them good models of high drama.

What I remember most from those fabulous summers at the Hills of Health were the baseball, basketball and tennis games we played, and the hearts and souls so freely energetic in these great sports. The competition was keen and the fun boundless in this little corner of paradise. Obligations? Work? Peer pressure? School? What were those? I remember vividly a summer of clear and cool nights; we gathered around camp-fires and ate frankfurters and laughed. And the next day, or soon, before or after our sports activities, we set out on won-drous hikes in the green, wooded hills. On the way along a trail to a chosen summit, groups of us would rest in an open meadow beside a creek, basking in the sun. None of us had–at least I didn't have–any thoughts of an end to childhood. It was taken for granted that summertime, this free, easy living of gambols and revelry, would last forever.

# Three

## BASEBALL BLUES

I was dismayed on my first day in high school in September, 1941. First, I wondered if I would ever be smart enough to graduate from the vast, imposing James Madison High School. And second, I wondered if I would ever make the varsity baseball team. I wanted to play football too, but in junior high I had broken an ankle and a wrist at the game, and my father had forbidden further participation in that sport.

But between my first day and my last at Madison there were countless classes, a lot of baseball, and many pretty gals. All through that summer before high school, I shrank from the prospect of ever more demanding classwork, but I was on fire to try out for the high school baseball team. To get on the latter, I would gladly take the former! At last, September arrived. I quickly sought out the baseball coach, but by the manner in which he eyed me, crusty Coach Wunderlich did not take me as seriously as I thought he would.

Then he crushed me. The Coach pronounced that no one was eligible to even try out for the varsity team until the completion of at least one academic year. I was devastated. My vivid dreams of impending glory collapsed into despair. I would sit dejectedly in the stands almost every day watching the team practice. I even attended some of the intramural games; I thirsted for even the vicarious thrill of baseball, of wanting to be near such an enterprise.

Madison's first baseman was an outstanding player named Lefty O'Haye. He was good–but I thought I was better. During some of the games I heard the students next to me praising Lefty: "Boy, he sure is great!" "What a fielder and he can hit too!" It tore me up; there was no fielder of my caliber on this team. I could scoop the ball like Dolf Camilli of the Brooklyn Dodgers. He's not exactly a household word? So what? Even today I think he was the greatest, the classiest fielding first baseman of all time. Anyway, for an endless, frustrating year I had to keep my mouth shut and not make waves. I knew my day would come.

Sure enough in September of 1942 I at last got my chance. Lefty O'Haye was a senior and naturally was expected to be the starting first baseman. I was still a nobody, a wanna-be who had warmed in the bleachers. But one day early in my sophomore year, when I was eligible to tryout, O'Haye was late for practice. I saw my opportunity. Seizing the initiative, I ran to first base. Coach Wunderlich started hitting balls to me. He kept me hopping for at least fifteen minutes–fielding hot grounders, throwing to the other bases, and catching return throws. I knew he was carefully appraising my skills.

The Coach had himself a new first baseman from then on. When O'Haye finally arrived, he was sent to right field where, somewhat baffled, he finished out the season. I batted .356 that season, second only to one other player, a graduating senior. My future as a baseball player seemed assured.

The following year Wunderlich named me team captain. I felt like the lord of the manor. After a great season, we lost the city championship by 1-0 in eleven heartbreaking innings. And we were robbed! Three of our men, myself included, slid across home plate during that game, only to be called out by the umpires–who were all, not so coincidentally, from Staten Island, the home of our opponents. It was the first time I ever

*I was the captain of the James
Madison High School team in 1944,
playing first base. We won the
championship that year.*

saw Mr. Wunderlich, a quiet, levelheaded man, snarl at the
umps.

My life then was always baseball–I ate, slept, dreamed and
lived the game. I was devoted to my high school team, but I
also played on assorted sandlot teams, and served as captain of
most of them, too. I led the Rebels, the Saracens, and the Senators; I also played with the Betsy Head Cardinals, a team from
Betsy Head Park in Brownsville. Brooklyn in those years was
full of sandlot, semipro and amateur baseball teams; every organization and every neighborhood fielded its own team. One
was even called the "House of David," a contender in a respected semi-pro league: all the players wore beards to look
Jewish though, oddly enough, none of them were.

Curiously, despite my passion for baseball I seldom attended
any major league games. I went to Ebbet's Field only a few
times to watch the legendary Brooklyn Dodgers. In truth, I
found the semi-pro games to be of greater interest. Watching
a game was highly frustrating for me; I would much rather be
actively involved in it.

Baseball did not, of course, consume my *every* moment.
The basement of my family's house turned into a hangout for

*During those high school years I played for and captained many sand-lot baseball teams.*

my friends and teammates. They were drawn by the prospect of carefree carousing on the pool and ping pong tables. Having spent many hours there, often competing with my very capable father, I became an excellent player at each.

One of my casual acquaintances from those days was a fellow named Irwin Roth. Irwin wore the same light gray flannel pants every time we saw him. He had a high, big ass, so we dubbed him, none too poetically, "Roth's Ass." He wasn't a good pool player compared to most of my friends and certainly not compared to me. But he never wanted to play "straight" pool, which is strictly a game of strategy and skill. Instead, Roth's Ass often talked us into playing "pill pool," a game of dumb luck. He carried fifteen small, numbered "pill" balls, about an inch in diameter, in a leather bottle. Each player picked a ball and put it into his pocket, keeping the number secret. If the ball on the pool table matching your "pill" number was knocked into a pocket you automatically lost the game. The game continued until only one player was left. The balls had to be hit in numerical order, however. All one had to do was touch the proper numbered ball with the cue ball, and then whichever ball fell into the pockets counted. It was ninety-five percent luck. And Roth's Ass had ninety-seven percent of that. No wonder he never wanted to quit.

One fine summer day, after he had yet again won the jackpot, all of forty-five cents, we conspired to give him the business. One of the guys dashed to the side of our house and retrieved the garden hose. He opened the valve and trained the nozzle through the basement screen, aiming it straight at Roth's Ass. He was surprised and quickly saturated with cold water from head to foot. His light gray flannel trousers turned a much darker shade. Then we ganged up on him, tearing off his damp pants and underwear, turning Roth's Ass into "bare ass."

My mother heard the commotion and suddenly appeared in the drenched room. Everything was soaked: Roth, the pool table, the furniture cushions. Roth's Ass was sorely humiliated. My mother was furious, and for only the second time in my life, she really bawled me out. "What kind of a boy did I bring up!?" she shouted repeatedly, with many variations. I got the message. Her wrath was understandable, though. Several months previously, another one of my friends had hosed down "the Gawk" through his bedroom window while his mother was out shopping. All the Gawk had to do was close his window, but I guess he panicked or was too dumb; instead he had hidden beneath the bed while the room got drenched. Since I was the acknowledged leader of our gang, his mother automatically assumed that I was responsible and phoned my house. That was the first time my mother had raised her voice at me. I was made to feel as if I had committed a heinous crime—even though, on that occasion, I was innocent.

My mother gave Irwin Roth a dry towel, and lent him a pair of my own pants while she dried and ironed his flannels. I couldn't believe it–my own pants on Roth's Ass! I don't know how in hell he got into them as his backside was far larger than mine. But by this time my mother had me so rattled that I did not look closely.

I ended up feeling sorry for him, too–as I always did when things had not gone well for someone I knew–and I tried to befriend him after that incident. He was a pretty good sport. Every gang needs a butt (no pun intended) for gags. But Roth soon disappeared from our scene.

Even with these monkeyshines most of us were good kids. Our pranks on Roth's Ass and the Gawk was the extent of our deviltry. Unless you count our summertime antics of shooting water hoses at people passing in the streets. We were performing a public service, right? It was hot. Or hurling rocks at the nighttime street lights to see how accurate our throwing arms were. I would get a thrill watching the light bulbs flare up and then explode, like a miniature version of the Coney Island July 4th fireworks. This mischief–well, in this case, vandalism–was hardly angelic, but our adolescence was certainly a far cry from the drug abuse, random violence, despair and suicides that mark the lives of so many teenagers today.

In fact, our pranks weren't much different from the kind my own father had pulled. He related a game he played as a kid which was called, suggestively, "I did it, lady!" He and his friends would blindfold one of their cohorts under a ruse, then walk him up to someone's front door, deposit a dead rat by his feet, and instruct him to mumble "I did it, lady!" They would ring the bell and then quietly slip away. Meanwhile the victim would remain stranded at the door when it was opened, repeating the words, "I did it, lady!" It sounded completely senseless, but also like loads of fun.

During my adolescence the shyness that had bedeviled me grew less problematical. I began to molt from that skin. My confidence grew along with my popularity in school and the neighborhood as the captain of the varsity baseball team. Much more dynamic than didactic, I seldom studied, but I never failed any subjects either. Despite my initial dread of high school academics, many of my marks were still in the nineties. My keen memory proved very useful when I finally decided to crack the books. And I began to develop some study habits that, quirky as they may be, proved invaluable in only a few years.

When I say that my confidence grew, I mean my confidence with girls. I became a bit more aggressive and open, and when I wore the black-and-gold sweater my mother knitted for me, the one with the big letter "M" sewn on the front, I felt like a king announcing his status, just in case someone had forgotten. In those days, young men behaved more out of the simple pride of belonging than any brazen bragging. I began to get lucky with girls, although I never progressed beyond necking. Even with Florence, my first real high school sweetheart, there was never more than kissing and a bit of exploration.

*My black and gold sweater that my dear mother knitted for me with the big "M" for Madison High School.*

I was seeing a number of girls, but rarely one-to-one. Instead, parties were thrown at someone's home so that all the groups of friends could be there. Most of us lacked the funds to go on a real date. And when we went out it was invariably in formation–I was still reluctant to leave my buddies, just like on the expedition to Great Neck. We had a kind of pact that even kept us together on weekends. Nothing could break up the unit.

Romance, naturally, was helped by music. We danced to the vibrant Big Band sounds–some of the greatest music ever created–of Glenn Miller, Tommy and Jimmy Dorsey, Vaughn Monroe and Harry James. Many of the songs were about falling in love: ballads with simple, sometime sugary lyrics sung by the fine likes of Bob and Ray Eberly, Dick Haymes, Helen O'Connell, Helen Forest, and Frank Sinatra. (Nothing like that in our $21^{st}$ century; only noise!) The girls, of course, swooned, and what they liked, we played, as it was just another arrow from Cupid's quiver. On any number of occasions the music fostered my illusion that I was in love. But I went from one girl to the other like a bumble bee buzzes petunias. Once I got confused and fell for two girls almost simultaneously!

This happened only a few months before the high school prom–no minor mistake, as you might imagine. Eager to impress and curry favor, I had already asked Beverly to the prom. But that didn't stop me two months later from asking Annette, with whom I was even more smitten. The only problem was that I didn't have the heart to break my date with Beverly.

With the evening of the prom rapidly approaching I became increasingly desperate to find an exit from my dilemma. I appealed to all my friends–Bruce, Leo, and Ken, among others–for aid. At last we brainstormed the solution.

One of our pals, Connie–Conrad Mardenfeld–did not have a date. So we conspired for him to accompany me to the prom and run interference. (Even my love life had an pass-action game terminology.) That way all four of us, including my two dates, would go to the prom together. In theory, each girl would be under the illusion that she was my real date, and that Connie and the other girl were just tagging along.

Well, I was favored by luck or fate or some psychosomatic trick. The day before the prom I contracted severe laryngitis. Perhaps I summoned it up as a defense mechanism. Coward that I was, the ailment became an excuse to stay home on prom night. My good pal Connie gamely escorted both girls to the event. He somehow convinced each one that he was acting as my surrogate so they wouldn't miss the once-in-a-lifetime event. The only trouble was that Connie simply could not dance a step, so he was not a roaring success. But at least we got points for ingenuity and a measure of consideration.

We pals shared and shared alike, combining generosity with an impulse for pranks. My pal and teammate Bruce was unfamiliar with the charms of women. He looked, ogled, but had never been lucky. One night I hit upon an idea to help him out.

Myself and several other guys had gathered at the house of a friend of Lynn, my liaison for the evening. While everyone gathered downstairs, Lynn and I were in her room, responding to our heightened hormones. Giggles, kisses, some petting. Well, we got to a certain point. Decorum dictated a break in the action. I stepped into the hall. All the lights were off; in this part of the house it was pitch dark. I walked downstairs to see what the others were up to. Bruce was sitting there alone. What a great time to give my buddy a thrill, I thought. I told him that Lynn was in her room, waiting. He should go in, but not say a word; just sit on the bed with her and do what was natural. Bruce was a bit reluctant. I had never done this before and he may have suspected a prank. But he took me at my word. Here was a chance that Bruce couldn't get for himself. He shuffled upstairs. I heard the door open and close. It was completely dark. His identity was a secret. A few moments went by. She thought he was me. Gee, I thought, this is working out pretty good. But something about his style no doubt gave away the game.

The silence was shattered by Lynn's long, unhappy scream. The impostor didn't stop to explain. He whipped open the bedroom door, raced down the stairs and past me out of the house. I was right behind him!

\* \* \*

I graduated from high school In January 1944 with a commendable scholastic record and the highest athletic honors one could achieve at my age. A single athlete from the borough was chosen by the coaches of all the Brooklyn high schools to receive the All-American High School Athletic Education Award. I was to be the recipient. On graduation day, when all the academia award-winning students were called to the stage the Athletic Award winner was summoned last. (Tellingly, even then America put more emphasis on athletics than scholastic achievement.) I was so nervous that I, Mr. Sports, tripped over the microphone wire and nearly fell on my face. I was mortified. This drew rousing applause from my classmates; I had become a pratfall entertainer by default!

February 1944. I turned eighteen years old. The British and American armies, bound for Rome, had locked with the Wermacht at Anzio and then Cassino. Italy had been dubbed "the meat grinder" by American general Mark Clark. The U.S. Marines, Army and Navy continued to engage and roll back the Imperial Japanese in the Marshall and Solomon Islands and other tropical Pacific fields of slaughter. The Red Army was eviscerating the Germans' Eastern Front. It was anticipated that sooner rather than later the Allied Armies would invade Europe from the west. Then the war would wind down. I wanted to see some action.

I contacted the draft board, prepared to do my patriotic duty. But that wasn't the only reason I chose to enlist. War may have been hell, military service perhaps almost as bad, but I was mesmerized over the excitement of becoming a member

of the armed forces. Maybe I also thought that war was like
sports; the prospect of distant competition on a much larger
scale made it more alluring than a down-home Brooklyn baseball diamond.

One of my several ambitions, you may recall, was to become a pilot. So the Army Air Corps (the separate Air Force
branch did not yet exist) seemed a logical choice. I visited the
Manhattan draft office in May, and there was obliged to take
several written tests. Not long afterwards I received word from
the Air Corps induction captain that I had passed the tests.
The physical examination, however, had disclosed a deviated
septum, something I wasn't aware that I had. Without informing my father of my real reason for seeking to have the condition surgically corrected–perhaps he never deduced–I persuaded him to take me to an Ear Nose and Throat specialist,
Dr. Mayor, who had several beds in his clinic. What he led me
to believe would be a minor operation requiring one day of
recovery turned into a near-fiasco. Three days later I emerged
from the doors of Dr. Mayor–whom I might charitably call a
butcher–with a head that had ballooned well beyond its normal dimension. Since then my nose has never been quite right.
But, I told myself, at least I had met all the requirements to
join the Army Air Corps.

Contrary to my expectations, however, I wasn't immediately summoned. So I called the draft office, demanding to
know why. Someone passed on the message to a captain, who
had probably heard similar words from quite a few gung-ho
guys, and may have been very wise in the ways of gearing up
for war. He phoned a few days later. I was not home; speaking
to my mother about my complaint he said that enlisted men
do not necessarily get called at the click of eighteen, but only
when they are needed.

This was the first my mother knew of my plans to join up,
and she didn't take it well at all. It prompted one of those rare
occasions when she lost her temper. She couldn't fathom why
I was in such a hurry to join up.

In my head and heart, baseball, not bombs, was the goal. I was unable to divide myself into enough parts to see each girl at least once a week. On the other hand, I never wanted to hurt any of them by my absence. It was not, as some might think, a question of ego; I simply had a knack for choosing demure, sensitive girls who craved attention. My father had put the notion into my head that it was wrong to let people down. He was not mistaken, but the rules of young romance are written in a different code. Not until I was older did I realize the effect this mindset would have on my life and the guilt it elicited about issues of love and business.

As it turned out, when I finally did enter the Army Air Corps, I left behind perhaps a half-dozen girlfriends, many of whom may have been under the impression that she was my true love. Notwithstanding this bevy of admiring young women, I entered the service a virgin. For many teens of the era, despite a lot of talk and wishful thinking, sexual restraint was a bylaw. There was only one sure way to remedy an unwanted pregnancy: and a shotgun wedding is not exactly a bar mitzvah.

But I'm ahead of myself by several months. I had been thinking seriously about pursuing a career in professional baseball. This way I could match my boyhood dreams to inevitable adult realities. I made my first attempt at this revered brass ring in June 1943. The Brooklyn Dodgers announced they would conduct tryouts for their minor league teams during my first year of varsity ball at Madison. I decided to attend although the competition would surely be very stiff; a lot of bigger and older guys would be there, too. At five-feet-ten, one hundred seventy-five pounds I was a little above average size, and at a mere 16 years old, well on the tender side.

The tryouts were held at the home field of the Bay Parkways, at Avenue U and McDonald Avenue in Brooklyn. I executed the fielding drills with ease and confidence. But at bat, I was nervous and way out in front of the ball, fouling off most pitches. When the tryouts concluded the coaches culled the best prospects. I was not among them.

I spoke hopefully to the man in charge, who told me bluntly that I was not big-league material. Once again I was bitterly disappointed to be denied a baseball opportunity. My only real aspiration was the Major Leagues. I was talented; I knew it. And unusual; I threw southpaw and batted righty. Moreover, with so many professional ball players in the service, the leagues needed men to fill up the teams. I felt like a castaway reject for not making the grade, the forgotten hero of a great battle.

That summer, determined to succeed, I returned to Camp Ta-Ri-Go and practiced batting left-handed almost non-stop. I induced a number of campers to play the outfield and recruited pitchers during every spare moment we had. I practiced immediately after each lunch, during our free periods, during the rest hour, immediately after dinner and before the evening activities. Four and five times a day. I must have been obsessed.

Several of the bunkhouses sat just beyond right field, about 300 feet from home plate. More than once I swatted baseballs through the windows. Sometimes they were open, and the ball would sail in and rattle around inside. Open or closed, my drives broke glass. Once some campers were taking showers and a shattering pane cut one of them. No longer was I allowed to bat left-handed at Camp Ta-Ri-Go. Fortunately the summer was nearly over.

That fall the Dodgers held another tryout, this time on a Yonkers diamond. Yonkers? Where was Yonkers? I traveled on trains and buses to get there. It seemed to take forever. I was eager to have another go. I batted left-handed. Fortunately, the coaches from the previous tryout did not remember me. This time they were impressed. I was invited to one of the Dodger camps the following spring, for placement on a minor league team. Hallelujah.

Time elapsed to the early spring of 1945. U.S. Marines were engaged in truly horrific combat on Iwo Jima. American and British troops had penetrated Germany, passing the Rhine to the heart of Hitler's lair. And the world first heard the reports that the Nazis had operated "death camps" for the mass murder of civilians.

Oblivious to these horrors, I was busy as could be captaining my high school team and trying to pass all my classes so I would remain eligible to play. Someone had tipped off George Mack, the head scout of the New York Giants, about me, because he attended one of our varsity games. Afterward he quietly took me aside to ask several questions, among them, "How do you stand with the Armed Forces?"

I was enlisted in the Army Air Corps. But I lied, telling him I was 4F. "That's great," he said. "We need more guys like you."

*I had a contract with the N.Y. Giants to play for the Springfield, Ohio minor league team.*

For the first time in Giants' history, spring training was not going to be held in Sarasota, Florida, but in Lakewood, New Jersey. About a dozen prospects would be put up at the Monterey Hotel. I felt guilty for lying about my draft status, but as much as I wanted to join the Armed Forces and fight for my country, I wanted to play baseball even more.

In March I reported to Lakewood. The first thing I saw at the training camp were machines blowing the snow off the field. I was a little startled, never having seen blowers before. Nor was I accustomed to playing baseball in winter; this was a game of green grass and dog days. Roger Kahn, a great sports writer, wrote a 1972 book about the Brooklyn Dodgers called "The Boys of Summer." That title was exactly right; the hotter it was the more I thrived.

Carl Hubbell, the Hall of Fame Giant pitcher, had just been promoted to head of the Giants minor league system. I pitched in high school some but I loved the game much too much to stick with that position. A pitcher plays, at best, only one game in every four. I wanted to be on the field all the time, so I told Mr. Hubbell that I played the outfield and first base.

George Mack, however, had told Hubbell that I was a fine pitching prospect and, since, like Hubbell, I was a left-hander he commanded me to take the mound. I remember the scene as if it were yesterday: Mel Ott was the New York Giant manager, big Ernie Lombardi was the catcher, Phil Weintraub was at first base, Billy Jurges played either shortstop or second, and a fellow by the name of Reye was at the hot corner.

That first day of spring training in early April felt more like January. I couldn't warm up. Lombardi had to bend for a few of my low pitches and he complained about it.

They were undecided about my pitching, but at the end of the two-week tryout, Mr. Hubbell was sufficiently impressed to want to sign me up with the Springfield, Ohio, Class B minor league team.

I sure didn't know how to tell him that I had received notice from home that I was to report to Camp Upton, on Long Island, for my induction into the Army.

This was a complete dilemma, far beyond my complications with girls. That, ironically, was why I had enlisted in the first place! I had no solution. I didn't have the courage to tell Hubbell I had lied to Mr. Mack, so I compounded the lie by concocting another one. I told him that I would lose my job back home if I didn't get back to Brooklyn at once. He replied, quite logically, "Your job from now on will be with the New York Giants."

I was desperate. Finally, I using a ruse I obtained twenty-four hours' leave with the excuse that I had to go home and get more clothes.

Life can sure be a long strange trip. Those twenty-four hours evolved into twenty-seven months.

# Four

## IN THE ARMY NOW

On my first day in the U.S. Army, May 15, 1945—one week after the surrender of Nazi Germany—I reported to Camp Upton, Long Island, near Yaphank. It was a gray, dreary Sunday, full of rain. The maintenance department was closed until the following morning, so all the drenched inductees had no choice but to spend the day in wet clothes. It was a miserable way to begin my military interlude. But the next day I was decked out in new khaki, wearing boots that seemed the weight and flexibility of cinder blocks. The rain never abated. We were soon shipped to Keesler Field in Biloxi, Mississippi where there was at least the benefit of sunlight. If you've seen the film *Biloxi Blues* (based on Neil Simon's play) I can attest that everything in it is true, except the depiction of basic training was not half as rough as what we were forced to endure.

God knows, Biloxi was hot enough, but it didn't matter if the sun was beating down or not. We dogfaces-to-be could invite the rain. It became a pattern: another long-distance march, another downpour. And whatever the weather, our drills were relentless. The platoon sergeant was a tough Southerner who made it clear that he wasn't fond of Yanks. He worked us hard, from dawn to dusk: a grueling regimen of drills, long hikes with heavy packs, push-ups. The gamut. Every time someone messed up or fell down he would explode in rage, screaming incomprehensibly, contempt oozing from every pore. It was as if Sergeant McHugh had the illusion that it wasn't human soldiers he was breaking in, but wild, mindless broncos that needed nothing but the equivalent of a whip.

When we weren't out in the fields scrambling over obstacle courses or crawling in the mud beneath barbed wire and gasping through gas masks, some of us were on KP duty–"kitchen police." Obstacle courses, I soon learned, were far more pleasant than this odious ritual. The standard *eighteen hours* of KP was the one thing about Army life I totally loathed. I abided the rest of the physical and mental duress quite well. But placing a towel at the foot of my cot as a signal that I was to be awakened at three in the morning, when I would quickly dress and march into the mess hall's ugly kitchen, singing (you were expected to sing), "She Wore A Yellow Ribbon," was so depressing that I'd have done anything–even cleaned the latrines– to get out of KP.

The smells, the filth, the slime — those eighteen-hour stretches seemed like purgatory. (Well, I'm Jewish, so purgatory, a Catholic idea, may be a misnomer, but the general principle–stuck in the void and no easy way out–remains the same.) We found out, too, later on, that only the unfortunate young men of the Army infantry and Air Corps were required to perform KP duty. The Navy boys had specially trained personnel and prisoners of war for the awful task. The problem was that there just wasn't very much else for we Army boys to do on the base.

All of us wanted to be either pilots, bombardiers, or navigators, but as the war was nearly over we had no chance to obtain these prestigious action positions. It was expensive to train us for such jobs so we had to be satisfied with the duties of flight engineers or radio operators. After completing this training some of us might be sent on to gunnery school to become tail,—belly, or waist gunners on B-17s.

I said goodbye to Biloxi when I was shipped to Scott Field in Illinois for training as a radio operator. My initiation into this task was not what I had expected. We were herded into what appeared to be a radio room and given headphones. The earpieces emitted a dissonant babble of dits and dahs, a bizarre new language all its own. The experience scared the hell out of me, especially when the supervisor told us we would soon decipher this stream at the rate of eighteen words a minute. Who wants to learn this crap?, I thought.

But, to my surprise and satisfaction, I learned it very quickly, ahead of anyone else in the unit. The high-pitch pulses of Morse code, I grasped, had identifiable tones, and by the end of the six-week course I was deciphering code not at eighteen words per minute but at twenty-five, near the upper limit of what anyone could "read." I was written up in one of the St. Louis newspapers for making the honor roll.

Though I took to Morse code like a bird to the air, it wasn't so easy for many of the others. Almost each day I would see several of my fellow students fling off their headphones or slam them against the wall out of sheer frustration.

Scott Field was really an okay place. The food was decent and we were treated quite well, including frequent and easily obtained weekend and late-night passes. The base was not far from St. Louis. Like Chicago, St. Louis was considered especially hospitable to members of the armed services in this wartime July. The passes held a special benefit for me: courtship with the ladies. A USO in downtown St. Louis attracted me for no other reason than that many beautiful girls volunteered to work there. But it had another advantage, too: a bulletin board listing all kinds of special occasions and events. There were notices inviting five nice Jewish boys to a party, or another asking for eligible young men to join the graduating senior girls of a local high school for an evening on the "Mississippi Queen," a beautiful old steamship that embarked on nightly cruises on the mighty river. These voyages were a good excuse for a festival of dancing, drinking, talking, and a fabulous amount of kissing and necking.

I met some very lovely girls who livened my evenings, but I was still a virgin. This was another basic training I wanted, another code to decipher, certainly one of the vital challenges in adulthood. The twin riddles of sex and love befuddle nearly everyone. For the moment, then, in this summer of 1945, much of the world was preparing to heave a collective sigh of relief. Here in the heartland of the most powerful nation on earth, good times were stirring, and my main interest was fun with females. But the lack of opportunity was beginning to bother me. What were these hormones for?

Then I met a magnificent, long-legged, shapely girl. "Laura", two or three years older than myself, lived somewhere in the countryside near St. Louis with her mother. One sultry night while Laura's mother was out we sat on the back steps and soon started kissing. She wore no stockings beneath her skirt; silky smooth skin greeted my fingers as they stroked up and down her thighs.

Shortly Laura stood up, grabbed my hand and began leading me upstairs to her bedroom. This, I thought, was going to be it–at last!

Everything was sweet and cozy. She didn't seem reluctant at all. And then . . . then nothing. Because whatever I did, or didn't do, or was starting to do, I must have really flubbed it. Laura jumped up from the bed, crying "No more, no more! Please go home!" What had I done wrong? Or had she changed her mind even as I did right? I was baffled and dismayed. There was no gentlemanly way to rectify the situation. And that was the end of that.

Of the war, too. Japan surrendered in August. The free world could joyously wipe the sweat from its brow, but with sorrow too. What a horror.

Shortly after VE Day I was shipped out to Yuma, Arizona for training at the air-to-air gunnery school. I learned how to use fifty-caliber machine guns, first on the ground and then in the air, where I was trained to become an upper-turret gunner. After 14 months in the Army Air Corps, this was my first experience of actual military flying.

While I was in Yuma, "The Very Thought of You," sung by Al Bowlly with Ray Noble and His Orchestra, was a hit song. I heard it again while writing this book. It's amazing how a fifty-year-old song can summon back the time and places and people you knew when the song was popular. (The song was in a movie of the same title, with Eleanor Parker, and this time sung by Dennis Morgan.) I can almost smell the blooming flowers of that Arizona spring, the perfume-scented letter received from a girlfriend. These things all come back each and every time I hear select melodies. When Perry Como sings "Till the End of Time," I see myself in a canteen in Austin, Texas, sipping ice-cold Seven-Up, my mind filled with dreamy thoughts of my latest enamorata.

By the time I reached Yuma, after so long in the service, I was more than ready for my first furlough. I was in great physical shape and raring to return home to see my parents, and, naturally, some of the girls I had left behind, especially those who had been writing to me. Unfortunately my furlough came through just as I was stricken with a terrible bout of the flu. Nonetheless, I was determined to go.

I endured a three-day train ride, with a high fever, all the while slapping mustard plasters on my chest in a desperate bid to get well. It was terribly tedious, believe me. Even though I might have been ill and dog-tired, I couldn't and didn't sleep sitting up like everyone else. I figured I was smarter than that and instead slept on the dirty floor beneath my seat. I was lucky that no one stepped on me.

I arrived at Grand Central Station around eleven at night and nearly straight away caught the BMT to my old station, Avenue U, in Brooklyn. It was December and chilly outside, but all I had on was the summer outfit I had worn in the Arizona desert. Stepping out of the station, still suffering from the malady, shivering violently, I hefted my duffel bag and

*My sister, Enid, and I on my first furlough — 1946 on the stoop in front of our house.*

*On furlough from the Army Air Corps in front of my house in Brooklyn, NY.*

started trotting along the avenue, sure that with the chill I would become more sick than I already was. But before I ran far I was halted in my tracks. My dear, devoted father, responding to an intuition that I would arrive that night, had waited nearby in the car. The moment I saw him as if by magic my flu disappeared.

I spent much of my furlough making the rounds of grandparents, aunts, uncles, and cousins, and visiting some of my baseball buddies, but I was really interested in seeing my old girlfriends.

As luck would have it, a girl I knew from high school–"Vivian"– turned up at a neighbor's house. I had scorned Vivian when in school because she had a reputation as a tramp; I spurned every advance she made in my direction. Now, however, I saw her with different eyes. She looked pretty good to me. Frankly, I was so frustrated by my failure to maneuver other women into the sack that I thought Vivian might be okay after all.

Thus far in my young life I had secretly subscribed to the notion that a beautiful girl was to be admired, even adored, never touched. I believed that the lovelier she was, the more angelic. Surely, she would never engage in lustful carnal encounters. I admit this was at odds with my own promiscuous, gadfly nature, but in those days many men thought in this double-standard way. Look, fantasize and desire, was the unspoken code; just don't touch. If you were a brute she might break or scream and your reputation could suffer.

Notwithstanding this Puritanical morality, Vivian became my target. I arranged an assignation at the Hotel Victoria on Manhattan's West Side. Why the Hotel Victoria? Because some friend of mine had told me it was a safe place where no questions were asked.

The following morning, around eleven o'clock, we arrived at the hotel. My plan was to enter alone, sign in as "Mr. and Mrs.," then sneak Vivian into the hotel a bit later. But this scheme didn't work out exactly the way I had envisioned. So far, what had?

Wearing my Air Corps uniform, I strode up to the front desk, affecting a confidence I certainly didn't feel, and shakily inscribed Mr. & Mrs. Leonard Linkow in the register. Then the casual clerk gave me a key and led me a short distance—very short—to my room. The room was located directly behind the reception desk! I was too dismayed, guilt-ridden and nervous to request a different room.

I sat miserably in the room trying to figure out how I was going to smuggle my "wife" past the reception desk. I finally went outside to Vivian, who had grown annoyed at the delay. I proceeded to brief her on our tactic: "Here's the key. All you have to do is walk directly past the reception desk and to the room. If anyone asks you any questions, tell them your husband will be back in just a few minutes—say that I'm not feeling well and went to get some Alka Seltzer." I was only eighteen!

Well, I thought, the big payoff had finally come. After waiting a few minutes, I stepped back inside the hotel and walked into the room, avoiding eye contact with the clerk. On entering I saw that Vivian had prepared for the encounter and was nearly naked under the sheets. Not very romantic, but it was direct! I tore off my clothes and pounced into bed beside her. Suddenly I was making love to the girl I once thought of as a tramp, a girl who still claimed to be in love with me.

Then, as if the god of love or the cruel fates had decided to intervene, something happened that I thought could only be an episode in slapstick comedy.

The bathroom door, only several feet from the head of the bed, was ajar. There we were, in the throes of passion, when we heard an enormous crash from the john. We sprang up in alarm. Running naked or nearly so to the bathroom we discovered the source of this dreadful disturbance: an enormous hole had been punched through the wall. Two construction workers were staring expectantly back at us. Who's to say which party was more surprised? But the Men In the Hole were definitely more amused. Of course, the bubble had burst. What I was certain would be my first real sexual encounter had been ruined at the outset. It's a wonder we both didn't die of embarrassment!

The workers had been instructed to break through the wall behind the reception desk as part of the plan to renovate the hotel lobby. The clerk who assigned us our room had not been aware of the renovation schedule.

That, at any rate, was the last time I saw Vivian.

But Florence! It was during this furlough that I renewed my acquaintance with Florence, and fell head over heels in love with her. I guess she was truly my first love. She was a gorgeous, dark-eyed beauty with black hair and bore a striking resemblance to the actress Maureen O'Hara. We had our first date before I went into the service, and it began under unusual circumstances. On my way to her house I ran into Jerry, a classmate who would later become a good friend. He had just left Florence's house and whatever had happened, his expression implied that it wasn't very good. He'd been dating Florence, too, only to be informed just minutes before that she no longer wanted to continue the relationship. So that was the scene when I, her very next flame, walked into her life right on cue.

Here I was more than a year later. I couldn't imagine wanting anyone else. I spent a lot of my furlough with her, rather than home with my parents or gallivanting with my buddies. At the time it didn't matter to me that she was very spoiled. I think it ran in her family; her older brother took a lot for granted, too. He always seemed to be asking his father for money—ten dollars, nineteen dollars—so he could take his girlfriend on the town. It angered me that money came so easily to him, or that the family could afford to subsidize his love life. And I resented that he had never been in the service. He wouldn't be such a wise guy if he had ever slaved for eighteen hours in KP!

I was quite unhappy to leave Florence when my furlough came to an end. I remember Mother and Dad waving to me, with Florence beside them, as I got on the plane to take me away from home once more. But I wasn't certain that our relationship would endure past the term of my enlistment. She had left no doubt that she was anxious to be married, but I, not yet twenty years old, was understandably reluctant to make that commitment just yet.

I was transferred to Westover Field in Massachusetts to team up with my first flight crew. Our plane was the B-24 bomber, the "Liberator," often called the "flying box car." I was assigned as the radio-gunner.

Although I did my best to hide it, I detested this bucket of bolts. This wasn't like the movies! Squeezed into the cockpit, nearly overcome by the stench of fuel and the intensity of the heat, the rocking and rumbling of the plane in flight was preceded by nausea each and every time we took off. Curiously enough, though, I've since flown all over the world without any ill effects at all, although of course in vastly better conditions.

It also began to seem like our training was really an exercise in futility. No sooner would we learn how to fly in the B-24 then the crew would be broken up and teamed with other men in the B-17 "Flying Fortress." The fact was that, with the war over, there was no need to keep new crews intact for actual military service.

Despite my antipathy to flying in these rattle-traps I really enjoyed my time in Massachusetts. It was close to home, so whenever I could get a weekend pass I caught the train to New York. Naturally, I spent most of my free time with Florence. By this point, however, I was starting to think differently about beautiful women with angelic qualities.

All women, whether beautiful or not, I realized, must certainly have the same womanly desires. If a plain-looking woman wants to make passionate love to some guy, then why shouldn't a gorgeous gal have the same yearnings? (What seems so obvious to a mature man is revelation to a young stallion.)

To test my new theory, one evening I borrowed the family car and took Florence to a parking area where couples com-

monly went to neck. A passion pit. We were locked in a fever-
ish embrace when I was blinded by a light. I looked around
into the intrusive, almost painful glare of a flashlight and behind it, a large police officer. An instant later the door flew
open and I was dragged from the car with my pants around my
knees. What an awkward situation! (Another one . . .) Luckily,
the officer turned out to be a decent fellow. Which is to say, I
wasn't arrested. After taking Florence aside to give her some
fatherly advice he offered me some of the same and then let
us go. However, our night was ruined.

I detect a pattern in these vignettes . . .

I was transferred again, to Bergstrom Field in Austin, Texas.
Bergstrom was a great place even if it temporarily took me far
away from Brooklyn. Most of the men in our two-story barracks
spoke with Southern accents; many of them, also, were regular enlistees intent on making a career in the Army. My buddy
Nicholas and I were the two youngest guys in our barracks, and
we were both from Brooklyn. I was now a full sergeant in the
Air Corps. But I had no crew. I wanted desperately to fight an
enemy, but in early 1946 the war was already history.

While stationed in Texas I met two beautiful sisters, Eileen
and Marlene. I began to date Eileen, the younger one. We
were becoming quite intimate until the day she invited me to
join her family for dinner. They were very gracious and hospitable, but I couldn't ignore the several pointing and cutting
remarks they made about "the Jews." It surely embarrassed me
but, moreso, it drove home the spike of anti-Semitism in a way
that the taunts of the St. Edmond's kids or other slights had
not. In some strange way these casual insults bruised me more
than what I had read about Hitler's genocidal racism. Perhaps
I was unprepared for its expression in such a friendly domestic
context, or its expression by grown, responsible adults who
should have known better. Hadn't they heard my name? Does
it sound Anglo-Saxon, or Italian? But I just didn't have the
courage to speak up and assert that I was Jewish. It would have
made everyone uncomfortable. Instead, I just stopped calling

Eileen. When she phoned to ask what had happened I merely told her that the Army had kept me very busy, no free time, then, perhaps out of guilt at the white lie, I quickly added that I remained eager to see Eileen and her sister. Again, that trait of being reluctant to hurt anyone's feelings, to speak my mind.

When next we met I finally mustered the spunk to tell Eileen how hurt I was about what had transpired several weeks earlier. I was Jewish, I told her. Whether the dinnertime remarks had been deliberate or inadvertent, they scalded. The sisters, so embarrassed that their faces blushed to match their auburn hair, obviously felt terrible and sincerely tried to atone. But I knew my feelings were hurt beyond repair. The relationship had no future.

Some weeks later my luck seemed to change for the better. Early one evening, hanging out at the USO in Austin, I noticed a blond girl with a spectacular hour-glass figure dramatically clad in a clinging dress. Her body was svelte, her breasts lovely and ample. And because it was so warm in Texas she wore no stockings; her exquisite legs looked alabaster-smooth. The only flaw in this stunning impression were her thick glasses; but in my opinion, poor eyesight is not a drawback. Since she was sitting alone I didn't hesitate to walk over to her, flashing my main weapon, The Smile. What I said was something like, "How are you? What are you doing here? May I dance with you?" Her polite but cool answer was along the lines of, "I'm very fine, thank you, I'm waiting for my boyfriend, and no, I'd rather not dance, thank you." Pretty good, eh? I was really doing great.

My pride was hurt. The Smile. The Uniform. My Easy Manner. All ineffective. I slouched away and quickly directed my attention to a few other girls. But an hour later I noticed that the beautiful blond was still sitting alone. I approached again and inquired, "Where's your date, and why won't you go with me since I'm here now and he isn't?" "I don't talk to strangers," she replied firmly. This time I persisted. "Well, if you would allow me to introduce myself and chat with you a while we won't be strangers any more."

That logic softened up her defenses a bit. But it still took a great deal of persuasion because she seemed very shy. I had the impression she was inexperienced with boys—or at least with boys who were strangers. I finally succeeded in getting Betty to dance with me, and although she was timid, her warm body against me was an exquisite sensation. Behind the lenses of her glasses—she must have been quite nearsighted—I saw very lovely eyes.

I asked if I could escort her home. "No," Betty said, "I'll go home by myself on the bus. I live with my uncle and aunt and they don't like me coming home with any boy." I suggested a compromise. "What if I just go with you on the bus and leave you when we get near your house?" Very reluctantly she consented.

The bus ride lasted about an hour. We made small talk about our families, about my tour of duty, or sometimes were mum. The rickety vehicle left us on a darkened street with few houses, at the boondock border. Betty wanted to go right home. But I said, "Let's walk around a while so we can become better acquainted." By this point I suppose she had a little more confidence in me and agreed. As we walked I took the liberty of putting my arm around her waist. She didn't resist. I was glad; the firm curve and strong, supple sway of her hip was arousing. I don't know what she may have been thinking, but I sure knew what my thoughts were: I wanted to remove every stitch of our clothing and make wild love.

Thinking quickly, I noticed a school nearby, surrounded by a huge grassy field. I don't exactly know how—I think we both may have been in a kind of trance—but I guided Betty around to the darkened rear of the school. We lay down on the soft summer grass. She muttered not one syllable of anxiety, which I of course took as a form of approval. I began to unbutton her dress. The silky swells of her body were prettier than I had imagined. And I had imagined them quite vividly on that bus ride. Betty said nothing, but seemed to make sounds of encouragement. I deliberately made love to her and she was compliant. This sexperiment, as it might be called, was my first consummated encounter. Blissfully pleasurable, boldly triumphant. No wonder younger men were obsessed by the conquest and the sensation. I was, at last, a Casanova among them.

It was so phenomenal, in fact, that I immediately began to picture her as a steady date I could look forward to seeing and loving every week. I was in a fog, atingle, dazed. These thoughts and desires, however, were quickly shattered—like a pair of glasses when stepped on. Which is exactly what happened.

The sickening crunch of glass and plastic alerted me. That was no cricket. Betty heard it too. "You broke my glasses, you broke my glasses!" she screamed. I reached down in the darkness, groping to find the mangled monocles. She started to cry. Her aunt and uncle would kill her, she said, when she came home with broken glasses. How was she supposed to continue working as a typist without them? Moreover, they were the only ones she owned. She was nearly hysterical. I felt terrible, and terribly guilty. When I started walking her home and realized she could hardly see, that I had to lead her like a goat, I felt even worse. I told her to buy another pair tomorrow and I would reimburse her. It was only an innocent accident, I said to myself, a moment's lapse between two new lovers. But she was inconsolable, and sobbed all the way home.

The next day I phoned to say that I was sending the money for her new glasses. But despite my pleas, Betty refused to see me again. Maybe it was more than the mishap of the eyewear. Perhaps she was feeling guilty about her surrender to a man she hardly knew. Nevertheless, it was a shame, this disastrous end to a relationship that had scarcely begun. My first woman, on a night that should have been full of magic, was relegated to a blip on my personal radar only a few hours after I first set eyes on her.

From that point on time moved painfully slowly.

One day an officer entered our barracks with a "contract"

that, he said, we could sign or not as we pleased. The contract stated that since the war was over and thousands of servicemen would be discharged, the ones who had been in the service the longest would (naturally) be the first to go. On the other hand, the reward for renewed enlistment was a ninety-day furlough. (The old bait and switch technique.) The older guys told Nick and me that we would be crazy to not re-enlist, pointing out rather disingenuously that we might remain in the service for three more years anyway, bureaucracy being what it was. Why not at least get the long furlough? So Nick and I put our signatures on the contract.

But I soon felt very uneasy about it. That evening I telephoned my father for a little advice. He was irate when I told him what I had signed. He urged me in no uncertain terms to get my name off that damn piece of paper, asserting it was a ploy to retain men for the post-war Army. He was certain I would be discharged long before that three-year hitch was up. He was right, of course.

Nick and I returned the next day to tell the officer who had presented the contract that we wanted it nullified. He brought us to another officer, a rare bird female captain. She was cold and tough, calling us two wise guys, trying to verbally emasculate us, warning that she would personally see to it we would have nothing but misery ahead.

We soon grasped the meaning: that day we were placed on KP duty. This time, with further chores assigned, it seemed to last *all* day. We were awakened at three in the morning, and made to work till nine at night. Eighteen hours work, six hours sleep. Nothing else. Madness. Punished for a crime or an infraction we had not committed. Wasn't this America? Weren't there laws against slavery and cruel and summary punishment? American servicemen had died defending legal rights. Didn't we get the benefit of them?

Three full weeks had elapsed in this deadly routine–which of course was a sentence for rescinding on our agreement–when Nick received new orders. He was headed for

Washington, D.C. That didn't sound bad at all. I wondered how he could be so lucky. Was there a lottery, or did he have some pull I didn't know about? No, it was just plain dumb luck. Within days, my Brooklyn compatriot in Texas was gone. Soon after he mailed a postcard, proclaiming that he'd been assigned as the radio operator on a C-47 used solely to fly the "big brass" around. He also wrote that he managed to get home to Brooklyn almost every weekend. What a break he'd gotten! I was happy for Nick, yes, but my heart sank.

Three endless months of KP dragged by. I was demoralized. My energy, enthusiasm and perseverance were being pounded right out of me. I grumbled that I was the only sergeant ever chained to KP. No one had mercy. In retrospect, there must have been a factor in my personality that invited this treatment, sort of like a carcass attracts flies.

Finally, thank God, I received orders sending me to Fort Benning, Georgia. To clarify my new assignment I went to the officer in charge, again the lady captain. "Isn't Fort Benning a paratrooper base?" I asked. And she replied, "You have two choices: you can remain here pulling KP or you can quietly 'volunteer' to go through jump training school at Fort Benning. We need to augment the dwindling number of volunteers we've gotten since the war ended." At least she was honest.

I had always been a gutsy kid and even when scared I acted as if fearless. I believed very strongly in fate, even if mine seemed to move in slow motion. So I said okay. Anyhow, anything was better than KP.

The basic training at Fort Benning, including jump training, lasted almost eight weeks. In that time I lost twenty-seven pounds and my waist shrank from thirty-two to twenty-nine inches. The rigorous regimen consisted of long hikes each morning, exercise, drills, instructions on sliding down various jump-training contraptions and how to break the momentum of the fall by hitting the ground and rolling. We were exhorted—no, required—to jump off 200-foot towers. Dangling on a steep conveyor pulley like captives of a perverse Coney Island ride, each man was transported to the top and then released. Our chutes would automatically open. Over and over again we took this rotisserie circuit, while the training masters admonished us to bend our knees and keep our boots together.

A few days before our unit was to make its first jump from an actual aircraft, we heard a rumor about the training group that preceded ours. Apparently one paratrooper's shroud had been chewed by the propeller of the plane behind his–one of the two rear planes comprising the typical triangular three-plane flight formation. Although I didn't learn all the details, it seemed that his emergency chute had also failed or been damaged beyond repair. The poor fellow never had a chance and plummeted to the ground like a Roman candle. Certainly, this scuttlebutt only added to our dread.

At last our turn came. On the last three days of our jump training we were to make five jumps from C-47s. We were expected to perform two jumps on each of the first two days; on the third would be a night jump. And the night jump was the one in which the paratrooper had been killed.

The target landing zone was a strip of grassy land near the Chattahoochee River that forms the Alabama-Georgia border; although fairly flat, the designated area was surrounded by hills and trees. The trees were a hazard for men who missed the site.

There were twenty-four paratroopers per plane, twelve of us–a "stick"–occupying each side on long metal benches. The jump master, a kind of a bar bouncer, or a trail boss, was stationed by the open door. His job was to kick out anyone who "froze" at the exit because each "stick" had only seven seconds to clear out to avoid dropping onto the trees.

Just prior to the jump, each trooper hooked the line connected to his pack to a heavy wire running the length of the fuselage above our heads. (Numerous war movies portrayed this moment of truth. My favorite is "Objective: Burma," a hard-nosed World War II actioner with Errol Flynn commanding a

*My waist shrunk to 29 inches as a result of demanding paratrooper basic infantry training program in 1947.*

paratrooper unit in the jungle.) As the jumper plunged out, the strap, snapped taut, would automatically yank the parachute chord. If the main chute didn't open, each of us could manually operate an emergency chute affixed to our chest. We just hoped that the trailing plane wasn't too close, and allowed sufficient time for us to clear. No one had deduced that since the military (snafus aside) had recently defeated two powerful enemies, there must have been some reliable procedures in place to guard against the one mishap we had convinced ourselves was about to occur.

The morning of our first jump we lifted off in the rickety, rattle-trap C-47. None of us knew what to expect and plenty of bad jokes made the rounds, but I don't believe that anyone was nervous. However, from the instant I stepped out of the plane–just a vulnerable bag of flesh and blood–to hurtle through the air at some horrific speed, it was certain that this would be totally different from the jump tower training. After several seconds I was petrified to realize that, in a spin, I had completely lost my orientation. One moment the earth was below me, then above or to the side. And whither the parachute's break of my rapid descent? Wasn't the chute supposed to pop immediately? Then, to my great relief, I registered a hard pulling sensation between my legs, caused by a near-instant reduction in free fall while the mushroom-shaped canopy blossomed and my harness took the brunt of my weight against gravity. I swooped to earth; or it rose to greet me as if I had jumped from a fifteen-foot garage roof. I tucked and rolled, just like they taught us. Nonetheless, the wind was knocked out of me.

When we went up that afternoon for our second jump we all knew that this was no picnic. No amusement park ride. No one cracked jokes, or made believe we were D-Day heroes. Silence reigned. During two more day adventures, some of the men froze and had to be booted out, others sustained injuries, mostly scratches and several fractures. By the night jump, we were veterans, of a sort. When it was over, we all knew this had been an unforgettable experience.

Our social nights during this intense training were equally memorable. I wonder now which was really the toughest part of the program–jump school by day or Phenix City, Alabama, by night.

We spent most of our evenings off base. After chow, we took the bus into Columbus, Georgia and then walked over a small bridge to the hamlet of Phenix City, Alabama. The entire main street of Phenix City consisted of four or five bars and several stores, including a grocery store that was sandwiched between the two most notorious saloons. The saloons were always filled with men from the infantry, the Air Corps, and many paratroopers, all served by some of the toughest looking young women I had ever seen. I couldn't stand beer, but I would always order one to keep in front of me as camouflage– a man in the service has to maintain a certain image–while I scarfed serial colas.

We paratroopers were brainwashed by our commanding officers and training personnel to believe that we were the roughest guys in the armed forces, that nobody was meaner. Every night one of the paratroopers set out to prove these claims. They would pick on some infantryman–and before you could blink two or more men were out in the street smashing each other senseless.

If the fight was particularly exciting the curious Phenix City crowds would swell. These disturbances would most often occur directly in front of the grocery store, and frequently concluded with one or the other combatant being pushed, punched or thrown through its window. And if peace ever broke out in a bar one of the waitresses would quickly rectify that by baiting some paratrooper, declaring that the infantry man she was pointing to had just called him a son of a bitch or a pansy. Another fight would erupt in the bar, then flow outside, like a tide, to the poor grocery man's window–which would be smashed again. I cannot say how many times the MPs called the store owner to tell him his window was shattered. I wonder if the proprietor billed the Army, or if the perpetrators were docked for the damage. I would see the poor fellow shaking his head in bewilderment. Finally the town was declared off-limits to servicemen.

Years later, in the mid-50s, long after I was discharged from the Army Air Corps, Hollywood made a small movie called "The Phenix City Story." It wasn't very good, but I relived those Army training days and fist-fighting Dixie nights all over again.

I had written my parents a letter after the last leave the Army would ever give me. In it, I heartily apologized for hardly being at home with them during the furlough–I was on the town almost exclusively with Florence, of course, stockpiling a year's supply of female charm in about ten days. Returning to base on a train out of Penn Station, I felt like a heel. "I can't tell you how sorry I am, folks, but please believe me when I say that you both mean more to me than anyone else in this world," I wrote. "When I get out of the Army we will have many wonderful times together. I'm the luckiest fellow in the world to have such wonderful parents as you." Soon after my last return to Fort Benning, a notice was posted announcing that my unit's discharge would be pending by May 1.

In my final letter from the Army, May 9, 1946, I wrote my parents: " . . . there were many times when I enjoyed myself in army clothes. I learned a lot too. Mostly that if you want something you must go out and get it yourself and not depend on the next fellow to get it for you." I believed that this new life philosophy might mean my favorite sport. Baseball, not women.

I had played ball for several camps while stationed in Ft. Benning. One of the players on my teams was Bill Rosen, a major leaguer from the Cleveland Indians. Many others were minor leaguers. Playing with them, and getting to know a few, I realized that even as a professional ballplayer it was possible to end up a bum for a good part of one's life. They made not even a fraction of the enormous salaries the men draw today. Minor leaguers worked for peanuts, traipsing from town to town by bus–not by airplane, like the stars in the big leagues. And they were obliged to layover in ratty flea-bag hotels with a minuscule meal allowance, or sometimes none at all. It was quite a lesson: that could be my fate if I didn't make the pros. There was no real job security, no preparation for other professions. Make it or sink. Opting for such a life had distinct drawbacks.

By this point, after excelling in Morse code training at Scott Field, I had gained some confidence in my intellectual abilities. I understood the meaning of discipline and had grown self-reliant. And I knew that now I would have to decide how to make a living. No more high school or summer camp indulgences. After the Army, boy, nothing looks so simple as home cooking and a carefree July.

My discharge from the Army became official on May 16, 1946. Mere words could not express my happiness. I kissed the ground on the other side of the camp fence when I realized it was finally all over. No more KP, strange towns, decrepit planes, KP, bad food, parachute drills, .50 caliber machine gun tests—or KP!

I had several tempting choices. The first was to report to the New York Giants spring training camp in Sarasota, Florida. While I was in the Army I had written to the New York Giants Baseball Association, to the attention of Carl Hubbell. I told him the truth about why I hadn't returned after the twenty-four hour pass he had issued me. Hubble responded, and I was relieved that he bore no hard feelings. I had only done my duty, he said. Several months later I received a short letter from the Giants organization stating that when I received my discharge, they would welcome my visit to Sarasota.

My second option was to attend New York University in September on a baseball scholarship.

The third was to immediately begin summer classes at Long Island University. The summer session started on June 10th. I had only a few weeks to make a decision and prepare. What would be the best investment of time, the one most likely to quickly yield good returns?

I had some difficult decisions to make at this, the proverbial fork in the road of life.

The Army had knocked out a lot of my boyishness and forced me to think more seriously about a practical, reliable career. As much as I dearly loved baseball, that route posed a substantial risk. What would happen if I got hurt? Or was lost in a flood of professional players returning from tours of duty? Or I struggled in the minor leagues and never made the bigs?

I chose Long Island University. I decided that I was ready—at least I thought I was ready—to make up for the twenty-seven months I had spent in the Army.

Logic prevailed. Or, anxiety about whether the game of an uncertain future could be won in the ninth inning.

# Five

## COLLEGE DAYS

I was back home in Brooklyn. It saw a strange new old world through my culture shock, of readjustment to the impulsive rhythms of the city and of childhood stomping grounds after more than two years of rigid Army discipline in rural digs. I was and remain amazed at how men who had served, especially in combat, coped with reintroduction to the workaday domestic world they had fought to protect. I am certain it was very difficult. They had longed for home, but although it had remained largely the same, the men had not.

There was much to be done before the first day of summer classes on May 10th, 1946. I had to register, read the rules and regulations of the University, and work out a course schedule. First and foremost, I realized that If I was going to make progress I would have to get a grip on the new life before me–the life of a college student. That was sure to be a far cry from what I had known before or during the Army. I wasn't much for academics in high school, and the Army certainly was not a bastion of higher learning! Nonetheless, I had always been naturally inquisitive, and Army life was the very definition of discipline. So, despite a soft scholastic background, I felt prepared for what awaited me.

Unlike today, summer courses were a rarity in 1946. They would become popular in these postwar years to accommodate the huge influx of GIs, who sought to learn marketable skills to qualify for good jobs in what was sure to be a booming economy. The Government quickly passed the GI Bill, which entitled all servicemen to free college tuition. Employers were encouraged to hire returning servicemen. Few had to be reminded; the mighty efforts American soldiers had displayed in war, when harnessed to the world's most intact and most modern industry, would surely bring unprecedented prosperity. But first, these men needed training for the peacetime world they had helped create.

Long Island University had established an innovative program that offered two six-week summer semesters, with each course designed to cover the material of the usual three-to-four-month terms. The prospect of this intense program whetted my desire to get a career in gear. I was impelled to choose LIU–but I knew its curriculum would be rough for me, accustomed as I was to studying only under the pressure of impending exams.

LIU, despite its more suburban appellation, was actually located in the boro of Brooklyn (which, technically, is on Long Island) near the downtown area, on Pearl Street and Flatbush Avenue. Getting there would be a job in itself from Flatbush, my part of the boro. The daily commute consisted of a long subway ride, including a couple of transfers, and then a fairly long walk, through a neighborhood that was not very picturesque.

I quickly deduced the stark reality of my workload, that each day would be a war without guns or truce. Every new student was required to take a science course. Unless one was premed or predental, the student had no say in the first course. Given the lack of control over my studies, I opted to include two mandatory courses in my first semester: chemistry, which I had never studied in high school, and a business course.

At the time, deep in my heart, baseball aside, I probably

desired to be a doctor. I wanted to help people, to make a good salary, to comfortably raise a family and make my parents proud of me. Subconsciously I may also have wanted the prestige that comes with it, kind of like a medal of honor, or playing in the World Series every week of one's career. But I still lacked sufficient faith in my abilities—and the thought of the required years of grueling study had given me pause. Little did I know, some months later, having made a decision, the true breadth of what I was in for!

My father's best friend, Dr. Danoff, lived two houses away. As you may recall, he was a dentist, and his acquaintance would prove momentous in my young life. I had been a patient of his since I was a kid; every session with him seemed endless. Not that my teeth were so bad, or that he wasn't a good dentist, but he was just so damn meticulous, translated as s-l-o-w! But he was very proficient; years later, his work in my mouth was admired by several other dentists. And, believe me, when a dentist has something good to say about a colleague's work, it's nothing short of a miracle.

Dr. Danoff tried desperately to persuade his two sons, both of them younger than me, to study dentistry. Neither did. He must have deemed me a surrogate son, because that is where his attention fell. He used every angle of persuasion: the direct lure, reverse psychology, constant bulletins about the wonderful profession. It was your own business. Your own schedule. Rates. Location. Clientele. It was a noble calling, to be the captain of your fate and reaper of the rewards.

I resisted him manfully. "I could never stand the thought of putting my fingers in someone else's mouth," I had remarked. And I meant every word of it.

Lacking confidence in my intellectual abilities, I briefly toyed with the idea of majoring in physical education. And I hoped that, by having a solid college baseball career, I could be signed as a "bonus baby" by a major league club. Athletes of the time were signed while still in college and allowed to complete their studies before joining the team. Unfortunately, the physical education courses I was keen on wouldn't be available to me until my junior year—two school years away!

So I eventually took the road to New York University dental school not by design but by default.

On the first day of classes at LIU—an exceptionally warm day in May—I went to the BMT subway platform at Avenue U and East 15th Street full of expectation. But no train arrived. I waited and waited, with a growing throng of people headed to work. Finally, we learned that a power outage had shut down the BMT lines. I never got to school that first day. It was not an auspicious beginning.

New York City in the post-war years seemed like a paragon of style, of publicly respectful fashion and decorum. Most men wore jackets and ties, women dresses, and the bustle of people going about their business lacked the tormented rush that seems to be the present norm. And the cars on the streets!— each company had its own unique design and appearance. Robust elegance. Sleek virility. Swept hoods, chrome fenders, deep fins. They may not have been environmentally friendly, but they had irreplaceable style. I wish the cars of the 21st century would go retro, because there was nothing like a Cadillac 62 or a Chevrolet Fleetline.

On the second day I made sure to leave early. This time I reached my destination. I discovered that most of the students in chemistry class were premeds, and what is more, that they had freely, confidently chosen the subject instead of having it mandated for them. I was already intimidated, and I hadn't yet cracked a book! They had learned about "valences" on the previous day of class, which of course I had missed. I didn't even know what the word meant. As the professor lectured about pluses and minuses in relation to the various elements, I became thoroughly confused. Some guy named Panic grabbed me by my collar. Without the emergency tutoring and gracious help soon offered by some classmates, I might never have completed that course!

The weeks flew by, but I hardly noticed; I was so busy time

ceased to have any meaning for me. With my load of chemistry lab work, school ran six days a week. Moreover, I hit the books from the moment I reached home, not stopping, except for a dinner break, until one or two in the morning. I was often so tired by the evening, both because of the hard day at school and the standing-room-only subway ride, that after dinner I went straight to bed. I set the alarm for the middle of the night so I could rise and study until it was time to leave for classes again. This routine occasionally conjured unpleasant flashbacks to 3:00 a.m. KP! "'Round her neck she wore a yellow ribbon . . .'"

The chemistry and business classes were packed, with each student trying to absorb every morsel of knowledge. Although the class was considered "co-ed," the class was virtually all male, with many ex-GIs. The competition was keen. I teamed up with a few premed students and did a huge amount of studying with them in the home of Jerry, a student who lived in Brownsville, a nearby neighborhood. This was sometimes fun, with crash quizzes and friendly arguments and brainstorms. Just as often, if the material was dry, it was nothing but a chore.

Frog dissections were required in biology class. We'd pluck these large slippery amphibians out of formocresol much the way one collects pickles from a barrel, with tongs. (Except that pickles are awash in brine and taste great.) The frogs were stone dead, of course, and the acrid, toxic formocresol wasn't something to play with or get into your eyes. Then we'd trek off to Jerry's house, with the smelly cadavers in a big Mason jar, and lay out the monstrous *Rana catesbeiana* on his mother's dining room table. Each of us would choose a different anatomical structure to dissect: muscles, nerves, arteries, etc. Once the operation was completed, we would quiz each other on our findings, deep into the night. In the morning, Jerry and I would wash up and go off to school together, satisfied or even smug in our knowledge of frog innards.

I finished both summer sessions in very good shape, receiving a B in Chemistry I and an A in Chemistry II. I received two

As in biology. But the two business courses were a joke; I earned an A for both semesters. My later excursions into the arena (or swamp) of business–raising money, investing my own, dealing with patent lawyers, listening to high-rolling bulls–were sometimes inadvertent and frequently disastrous, and thus may be proof that these courses were worthless, at least as they were taught at the time. Nothing teaches like experience. Short of that, a would-be entrepreneur at least needs meaningful, practical academics with a large dose of caveat emptors about protecting one's innovations and investments, and about judging potential partners. Many of us–me included–walked out of school and sooner or later, fell right into a common trap of free enterprise: the business venture that was too good to be true! Because it usually is! Untrained to spot the red-flag clues, reluctant to speak up, one might not be the wiser until it was too late.

Jerry and other friends urged me to switch my major from physical education to premed. Because of the new faith I had in my abilities–and that they had in mine–and because I had grown impatient for a lucrative profession, I soon agreed. Even so, I still planned to play baseball for the university as a premed student, in hopes of obtaining "bonus baby" status. It is difficult to let go of one's dreams; I had so long envisioned playing professional baseball that it was part of my identity and virtually second nature to me.

There were, however, several huge problems with those dreams. In the first place, I needed to spend every single free moment studying just to stay afloat in the academic ocean. I had no time for practice or exercise. Without both, my skills could not be maintained, certainly not at a high competitive level. Secondly, to my utter disappointment and disbelief, LIU had no baseball team. No team! I had assumed they would have a baseball program! Didn't everybody? Notwithstanding the administration's declaration that a team would be established in a year or two, my hopes of bonus baby status were shattered. Fortunately, I had very little time to mope over it; I

had very little time for anything except study. The only baseball I could get was occasional play with the Betsy Head Cardinals. I gained more important lessons about human nature in
these first college months. The Army had been an intensive
physical drama, a world of men and routines and duties. School
was a more universal experience, with leave to explore, within
limits. Academia, by definition, encourages thought and creative solutions. The Army, conversely, discourages free thinking. One is a robot, a part of a huge machine. The service had
been my first major experience away from home and, by extension, in life. The traits I had brought with me, some of them
commendable–a good work ethic and enthusiasm for physical
exertion–and some not, like an inclination to misjudge a situation, were enhanced. Without a broader frame of life-refer-
ence, I held several misperceptions about motives and character. For instance, I was so naive about some fellow students that
I judged their intelligence by the way they looked. If they looked
intelligent (however that manifests in physical or behavioral
qualities), I assumed that they had more gray matter than I;
they were smarter and I was inferior. That was boneheaded
thinking, of course. But with my first solid marks came an increase in self-esteem and empowerment. I began to notice
that some of those I first assumed to be geniuses had dropped
out or been dismissed from the university because of failing
grades. However, I continued to study long and hard. Nothing
about education came easy to me. And I was tired of being left
behind, of missing opportunities, of being trapped in KP with
no exit.

The nights of studying dragged on and on. My desire to
complete college evolved into an obsession. Moreover, I wanted
not only to complete my studies, but to finish with grades high
enough for acceptance at a good medical school. I also made a
decision to complete the premed program in less than four
years–less than three, if possible. At all of
20, I was in a rush to make up for some of the time I had
"lost" in the Army. I was especially impatient because I knew

that medical school requires four years to complete, and after that, even more years of internship and residency.

This meant that ten years of work lay ahead of me. That seemed like an eternity. This would be like hauling a one-ton load uphill; the sooner I crested the top the better. Somehow, despite doubts about my direction, I may have set some kind of record for gaining the one hundred and twenty-eight credits required for graduation. I entered LIU on May 10, 1946 and graduated August 28, 1948: two years, three and a half months. And I missed summa cum laude only because of a "D" in advanced French and a few Bs among the As. I'd taken as many as twenty credits each semester, carried three sciences simultaneously, attending classes six days a week. Whew! No wonder I was tired. But this whirlwind and comprehensive education did not necessarily make me wiser. Not knowing any better–and taking little time to find out–I had applied to medical schools at the end of my first college year. Predictably, they responded that I was applying much too soon and should not reapply until my junior year. I didn't hesitate to inform the schools that I was interested now because my academic progress was such that I had planned to be in my junior year in less than ten months. I was sincere, and on schedule, but perhaps they nonetheless concluded I was a foolish and flaky guy.

Finally, my credits were nearly complete. I decided to send my transcripts to only three medical schools: Harvard, Yale, and Princeton. I was shooting very high, although not very accurately; Princeton didn't even have a medical school, but I hadn't taken the trouble to learn that either. I received warm letters from them saying that because of the tremendous influx of applications, students from their respective states would be given priority. In short, I was not accepted.

But Dr. Danoff's persistent talk about dentistry–what amounted to friendly brainwashing–must have had some effect because I had also applied, although very reluctantly, to a single dental school. I assumed I would not be accepted, and if the truth be told, I had no real desire to go. That one school was the New York University College of Dentistry.

The school scheduled me for an interview. I arrived on that June 1948 morning to find five or six applicants ahead of me. Each exited their interviews wearing broad smiles. Those of us still waiting inquired about their experience: what questions were they asked and how did they reply? Everyone said their time in the batter's box had been a piece of cake. Nothing more difficult than "Why do you want to be a dentist?" and "What are your hobbies?" Well, that seemed odd. Or at least, inadequate for the largest and presumably most prestigious school of its kind in the New York area.

My turn came. I entered a room with a very long table, at which sat six or seven solemn men who scrutinized me as I sidled in. One came forward to introduce himself. When I thrust out my hand for a shake he did not reciprocate, leaving my friendly appendage dangling in mid-air. I was hit by a nervous wave. I wanted their approval, but just as much I wanted to know ASAP where my life was headed. They could tell me.

Before I even sat down, one of the interviewers tossed a question which caught me completely off guard. It was kind of like parachuting; the scene went topsy turvy. "Can conductivity be measured?" he demanded. I was dumbstruck. I could not answer the question, largely because it was out of context and outside my expectations.

"You mean to tell me you don't know?" he mocked. "What's the formula for conductivity?" he asked. "I don't remember." My mind struggled to retrieve the information from the summer of my junior studies, when I had crammed a year of physics into twelve weeks. But I simply couldn't remember the formula. What if he was trying to trick me? I would be in more trouble if I guessed wrong. So I asked, somewhat firmly, "Why don't you question me in organic chemistry or biology, where I got straight A's? I just can't remember the formula for conductivity."

They showed some compassion. One of the examiners patted me on the back. "Don't take it too seriously," he said. "We just wanted to see how you would react under pressure."

And that was that. No more questions on physics or organic chemistry or biology, or even why I wanted to become a dentist. Which was just as well, because I didn't want to become a dentist.

I was escorted to the door by one of the examiners who told me, "You'll be hearing from us." I left in total bewilderment. Here I was, a young man, and had been obliged to put my life in the hands of people who were older, who could make decisions for me, determine where I would go and how quickly. They had been granted much control—perhaps too much—over where I went to school, what I learned, whether or not I played baseball, what hours I kept. I was hustled out the door from a brief and strange conversation with men whose names I didn't even know, who would now judge whether I was worthy to study for admittance to their profession, who might make a value judgment based on my name, clothes, self-expression, the look on my face. It was all unnerving. Perhaps the Army hadn't been so bad after all.

# Six

## THE COLLEGE OF DENTISTRY AT NEW YORK

## UNIVERSITY

One day in late August a letter arrived from the New York University College of Dentistry. Congratulating me on my acceptance. Was I elated? Never! Scared out of my wits was more accurate. I felt fear, insecurity, reluctance–even a dash of horror–when I received the notice. Where was I going and how would I get there?

The College of Dentistry sat in unlovely Manhattan splendor on East 23rd Street between Second and Third Avenues. The Third Avenue El kept rows of buildings in perpetual shadow, and supplied plenty of noise. The neighborhood was depressing, the surrounding real estate dilapidated and run-down. It was an alien world, hardly conducive to higher learning. A queasy feeling washed through me when I entered the "campus" to make last-minute arrangements and to get my load of books, a collection that seemed substantial enough to serve as the foundation to a building to replace the one in which I was standing. A peculiar odor wafted about, a charac-teristic medicinal smell, one we all recognize and seek to avoid: zinc oxide and hydrogen sulfide, this last one the equivalent of rotten eggs. Hydrogen sulfide, commonly used in quantitative analysis, was a reactive agent that let one measure how much of a given element resided in compounds.

The drab, antiseptic atmosphere in the worn-out walk-up was especially discouraging to me, since I still had a strong desire to play baseball in the summer sunshine. Hell, in cold pouring rain if it came to that!

I was on the cusp of very difficult years of relentless work, a restrictive learning environment and constant pressure to perform. I began my studies with great reluctance–if I had divined what lay ahead, I would have quit–and squirmed whenever I contemplated the moment I would have to insert my fingers into a stranger's mouth. The thought of it actually nauseated me. Paradoxically, however, I also believed I was well suited to be a physician, although this would mean that I would have to examine gall bladders, colons, boils, wounds! The human mind, sometimes averse to the innocuous and indifferent to the grotesque, can be a strange mechanism.

More frightening was the thought that I might not be able to persevere through four years and graduate. Even if the task is odious and the burden great, I'm no quitter. Which in one sense may not be a great advantage, since great perseverance can remove the option of cutting one's losses.

But I had a more immediate fear: the day when I would have to look at a cadaver–and, worse, dissect it. Anatomy and histology were the first two sciences in the curriculum. A professor by the name of Dr. Butcher (I kid you not!) ran the anatomy course. On the first day of anatomy lab, we were presented with rows of dead bodies on narrow marble slabs. Thank God they were covered with sheets. But the smell! A combination of formaldehyde and death itself, a pungent odor that, more than piercing your central nervous system and eliciting several unpleasant physical reactions, gets in your skin and clothes. It takes permanent residence in your nose and leaves the room with you and on you. Some students gagged; others passed out and had to be removed.

The first dissection we performed was on the upper back of a cadaver. In truth, it wasn't as bad as I had feared; anticipation is the major battle, not the act itself. In time, we got used to the tasks and the conditions and took them much more lightly. For some of us, human anatomy became almost an obsession. We wanted to know it all–not just to pass the course, but because we realized that we would need some of this knowledge in our careers.

It was trully fascinating. In a few short weeks many grew so accustomed to the grisly work that they would eat lunch right over the cadavers! It saved time, and in a strange way, though we never acknowledged it, it was a celebration of life over death. We were learning valuable skills because some of these people had donated their bodies. (Most, though, were "John Does" or drunkards found dead on the streets with no known next of kin.) But to an outside observer, our behavior would no doubt have seemed callous and macabre!

At lunch time on one such day, as we munched over the corpse, I said to my three partners, "If you look hard enough each and every day of your life you will see a horse's ass."

Only a few minutes later, one of my compatriots went to the sixth-floor window of the anatomy lab overlooking East 26th Street and 1st Avenue. He started screaming and urging us to rush to the window. We did so, and I saw something I never saw again: a wooden ambulance–pulled by two live horses! So, in one way or another, I was a soothsayer!

The courses in the first two years were virtually identical to those of medical school. All the basic biological sciences were required: human anatomy, physiology, biochemistry, histology, pathology, internal medicine, microbiology, and much more. We were expected to master them all, even though most of them were incidental to the practice of dentistry. But that was custom and that was the law; we were vying to become doctors of dental medicine but were expected to study as if future brain surgeons.

These first two years were rougher than necessary. The instructors took delight in teaching by intimidation, denigration or humiliation. This was uncomfortably like the Army; having seen such tactics before it is one reason why I survived these rigors. They repelled me, of course, but I would never forget KP. The professors maintained their depersonalized, sometimes inhumane regime my entire four years. And I have never really forgiven the instructors for it. We were subjected to constant surprise examinations. The prospect made life nearly unbearable. We had to memorize our work each and every day for fear of yet another exam ambush. There was no breathing space, no time to reflect on what we had learned. In contrast, NYU medical students were required to take only one exam—their final–per semester in each subject. If they did badly they could take the exam again! What a life . . . Needless to say, the med students were far less tense than their dentistry counterparts. Moreover, they enjoyed more free time during their first two years, for which I deeply envied them. Even if our academics were grueling, with just a little slack we could have fared much better and been less stressed.

It was bad enough having to always be on edge in anticipation of a surprise exam, but the way in which the instructors rebuked anyone who failed a quiz could induce ulcers or a seizure. A case in point was anatomy class. The one hundred and fifty students were divided up, four to a cadaver. While the teams labored at their corpses, Dr. Butcher (a/k/a Dr. Death) and his entourage slowly made the rounds, looking in on each quartet. Sometimes he would make a few remarks and then move on, only to come back in ten minutes and tap someone on the shoulder. That tap was all too often the end of someone's career. The student was to follow Dr. Butcher back to his office, usually to be told, in as demeaning a manner as possible, that he had flunked. Picture one hundred and fifty students nervously concentrating on dissections of, say, a lung or the spinal cord while awaiting that tap on the shoulder. It seemed to us that those torturous lab sessions would never end.

One of the students in our group was a young man a few years my senior; "Herman" seemed like a bright, decent guy. He was always soliciting our opinions about what questions might be asked during the many "practical examinations." We freely shared our predictions, and gave him the correct answers to boot. But we began to notice that when we asked Herman for information, he grew mysteriously, maddeningly silent. Either he didn't know—in which case he hadn't done his homework and was freeloading the answers off us—or he was selfish with his knowledge. Neither, of course, was acceptable.

Before every practical exam, the anatomy instructors would use pins to designate various morphology—the adrenal gland, the renal artery, and so on. And sometimes they might remove an organ and place it in another area of the body cavity, concealing it with arteries, nerves, veins, etc. to camouflage the organ before demanding that we identify it.

On one such occasion, after we had entered the abdomen of our "stiff," I panicked. There were so many pins protruding from the body that I became confused, unable to determine what organ or structure a particular pin was supposed to indicate. Desperate, I turned to Herman and asked him for help, quick, before Dr. Butcher came over to us. Herman seemed to suddenly develop a "hearing problem." I asked him again, louder this time. He ignored me, again, so I reached across the slab, grabbed his head, and shoved it down into the open belly. He came up looking as if he had just been underwater in the Okefenokee Swamp, his glasses and face smeared with fatty substances from the gut tissue. He immediately answered my question! Just then, before he had a chance to clean up the mess, Dr. Butcher strode to our work area, threw Herman a puzzled look and said, "You must either like this kind of work very much or you must sure be near-sighted."

The tension we were all under sometimes caused irrational behavior. The constant fear of failing exams and not graduating placed a terrific strain on me, which elicited physical symptoms. I developed unbearable stomach cramps which would last for weeks; they were so severe that my father insisted that he take me to our family doctor. When he couldn't specify the condition to our satisfaction, I went to a specialist in internal medicine. The undramatic diagnosis turned out to be a nervous stomach. I was relieved to discover that I didn't have ulcers, but I was still gnawed by a terrible empty and painful feeling which even a good meal couldn't alleviate. This misery persisted almost until graduation.

There were never enough hours in the evening for me to study because of my peculiar methods. Somehow it was psychologically impossible for me to read textbooks and highlight the most important sentences, the way most other students did and still do. I was a slow reader, and long assignments in fat medical tomes were daunting and discouraging. To get around what amounted to a reading block, I devised a laborious but ultimately quite effective system. I rewrote each book I read—but in my own simplified language, by condensing and paraphrasing each pertinent piece of information, then writing it down. It was not only my strategy, but my technique, that was peculiar. I would edit out any verbiage I deemed unnecessary. And I would write the central, condensed text in as tiny a script as possible. As a result, each page of my notes covered five to fifteen pages of text. This tedious process consumed days on end. Once completed, however, the core of study was a mere forty or fifty handwritten pages: the equivalent of an entire book. Perhaps the Freudians would find something anal in this, expressing itself as a need for control, but this method, whether psychological trickery or simple efficiency, always worked well for me. With my keen memory I was almost able to recite the distilled text word for word. I could even relate almost the exact line on which a piece of information was to be found.

Not surprisingly, there were times when my mind was so saturated that it couldn't accept another particle of knowledge. I dreaded that state. One incident brought home—literally—how tense I had become. It may have been a symptom of stress-induced depression. About one o'clock on a weekday morning, totally unable to concentrate, I spontaneously flung one of my heavy books across the bed. It caromed off the tropical fish tank, sloshing the water and terrifying the helpless fish. I stormed out of the house and my poor father, awakened by my stomping footsteps, followed me and implored me to tell him what was wrong. I swore that I was going to quit school; I couldn't take the pressure any longer. I had a duplicate set of keys to his '44 Dodge, so I jumped in and started driving. Fast. I finally stopped, at Nathan's–the original Nathan's in Coney Island, which was always open until the wee hours of the morning. I stuffed my gut with three or four hot dogs, dripping with mustard and sauerkraut, then indulged in a hamburger, hot corn, and the greatest French fried potatoes in the world. Eating may soothe the ravaged soul; or, the way to a man's heart is through his stomach. Either way, I felt a little better! When I returned home, my Dad was waiting for me despite the fact that he had to be at work in a few hours.

He gave me further encouragement and strength. When I first entered dental school we had our doubts that I would make it, but he played a tremendous role in my eventual success. I didn't realized the depth of his influence for almost forty years, when I could better grasp his insight and wisdom. All I knew then was that he sacrificed a great deal of his time and energy, prodding me to concentrate, quizzing me informally, and generally pushing me on, higher. He was my inspiration: I wanted to show him how much I knew, and he was always there to buck me up on my days of dismay.

Somehow I got through anatomy and histology and all the required, burdensome coursework during the first two years. Nonetheless, my trepidation at having to one day place my fingers in someone's mouth had not entirely subsided. This remained true even though I'd already worked on human cadavers, dissected cats, dogs, fish, bull frogs, and even performed surgery on live dogs that were under general anesthesia. So how bad could someone's mouth be?

Toward the end of our second year we learned dental anatomy and were introduced to a panoply of dental methods. We were required to know how to carve a duplicate of each tooth in the upper and lower jaw. Because each tooth has its own distinct features, to restore a badly decayed or broken tooth one must know its anatomy to the millimeter. We learned root canal therapy, which involves the proper removal of nerves that are abscessed or dying or nonvital. These can all cause tremendous pain, swelling, cysts, loosening of the teeth and other adverse symptoms. The lack of preventive procedure will later require a more radical solution. If not attended to in time by excising the abscess from the root, the tooth often has to be pulled. And the primary goal is to save, not remove.

We learned about periodontal surgery–the treatment of the soft gum tissue surrounding the teeth–and how to keep the gingival sulcus clean by removing tartar, calcium deposits, and plaque. And we learned a little about orthodontia: how to move or adjust badly aligned teeth and bring them into the correct position. This improved the patient's appearance and, structurally speaking, reduced or eliminated destructive stress on the jaw.

Crown and bridge work was very important; we had to learn how to precisely drill down teeth into small, tapered shapes–"pegs," as the patients generally described them–so that a normal and cosmetically acceptable crown could be fitted and cemented over them.

We studied operative dentistry, too, which taught us how to drill out the decay inside a tooth and prepare the hole in a way that the filling would lock into it. We also had to learn how to make dentures–"plates"–for people who had no teeth left, and partial removable dentures for those who had some teeth but were missing quite a number of others. Our training in oral surgery, however, was inadequate. I believe the only "hands on" training we had was in removing a half-dozen teeth from hapless patients.

It was at about this time that I fully realized that people who had lost their natural teeth were in a very bad way. From the start, I saw that dentures seemed to be unwieldy contraptions. They weren't convenient or sterile, not completely reliable, and their appearance attractive. They looked like what they were: false teeth. Their basic shape and function had not changed since the days of George Washington, who had received some of the most advanced dental engineering then available.

I remember vividly–what dentist doesn't?–my very first patient in the operative clinic. She was a young girl of about fifteen. With all my prior apprehensions, I had no trouble placing my fingers into her mouth. I found a large cavity in the back portion of her upper left molar. For the first time I worked indirectly by using a mouth mirror, and had great difficulty in seeing what I was doing. I could only stumble along. To make it worse, the topical anesthesia was poor. Just as I completed the preparation of the tooth, the frightened young lady leapt from the chair and dashed from the clinic in tears. She did not return. Just great! I'd ended up driving my first patient from the office weeping. Thank God, however, things got much better after this unhappy experience.

During the latter part of my dental education, we spent six hours each day in various clinics working on patients who had opted to have their dentistry done through the university so as to save the fees they would normally pay a private dentist. Anyone who resorted to a clinic could expect a time-consuming process because students did not proceed at the customary speed. And, in addition to the hours at the clinic, we also spent two hours each day attending lectures.

To qualify for graduation, each student by his or her senior year was required to accumulate two thousand clinic points. Three points might be awarded for completing a complex amalgam filling; twenty-five points for an elaborate three-unit gold fixed bridge, and so on. Additionally, these two-thousand-points had to be distributed over all the dental disciplines. Each

department had its own work standards and point requirements.

This was the time when I started to excel. I was competing
against myself, something I had always done in sports, my passion before dentistry. My ambidexterity (bats righty, throws
lefty) made me a whiz in the clinics. I began setting performance records. By the end of my first year in the clinic, in
effect my junior year, I had completed close to two thousand
seven hundred points—more than almost any graduating senior. I never felt or wanted to be in competition with my peers.
I was probably driven by lingering insecurity—even though, at
the time, I had boundless endurance and great optimism in
my abilities and in my future.

Unfortunately, many resented my achievements. I heard
remarks like: "Linkow, why don't you slow down? You're ruin-
ing it for the rest of our class!" Believing them to be joking, I
joked back and went my way. But they were indeed serious, as
I later learned, as was the jealousy—and eventually, animosity—
many felt toward me. And even if I had discerned that they
were serious, I may have proceeded in the same way. Should I
have held myself back because they were less compelled or
less capable?

When I first entered dental school, I had two central feelings: I was scared to death, and I believed that everyone there
was honest and decent. I had been raised to think that no one
wanted to hurt another person. I guess I had always been fortunate; because I had good friends, was lucky enough to be a
gifted athlete, and often had an active romance, I was near-
blind to less pleasant emotions like envy, jealousy and hostility.
I finally became more realistic, though not until the end of my
senior year. Though I had a few very close friends, the majority
of my fellow students chose to distrust me.

Another explanation for the anger I incurred lies in the
personalities of my fellow classmates. With the possible exception of myself, virtually every student had a life-long dream to
become a dentist. Because of the academic pressures, there

was little chance for them to socialize. Nor did many of them had much life experience to reinforce their studies. I don't recall any military veterans. Nor many athletes. My rigorous youth had been spent on ballfields, and later, in boot camp. They may have perceived me to be something different–and because they couldn't quantify, manipulate, or compete with me, they instead chose to be resentful.

Having already acquired enough clinic credits to graduate before my senior year ended, I had the luxury of sitting in on post-graduate lectures between my regular classes. I became active in the crown and bridge department. I made several full bridges, and also performed restoration work on patients who were missing some teeth but had enough remaining to support a full-arch fixed bridge. They would then possess a complete set of teeth and could dispense with cumbersome, archaic dentures, which I was coming to despise. In this variety of applications, I found bridgework to be among the most fascinating.

The pressure was constant during my dental school years, and I was very prudent with my precious free time. What did I do with it? Baseball mostly, and an occasional girl–what else? I played ball with one or two teams on the weekends and kept my male ego oiled by pursuing paramours. One in particular captured my interest in the clinic during my junior year. I espied her in a dental chair where she underwent an examination. She had an exquisite figure, and I thought her to be a splendid-looking girl. Unfortunately, it wasn't my dental chair she was sitting in. But every time I glanced at her she cast me suggestive, encouraging looks. When she was through I asked for her phone number. To my delight, she gave it to me.

She lived in the Bronx, to which I had to take a train from deepest Brooklyn, clear at the other end of the city. When I first visited her home, she had taken to bed sick with the flu. But she admitted me even so. She was quite a sight in her silky nightgown, with lovely breasts and smooth, shapely legs. It was a Saturday afternoon and we were alone after her mother left the house shortly after my arrival to help her father in the family store. I started kissing her. "Please don't do that," she said. "I don't want you to catch anything." I reluctantly relented, but a diagnosis of diphtheria would not have dampened my ardor.

I continued to see her. One Saturday afternoon she met me in Manhattan and I took her to my West Side fraternity house. In fact, it wasn't much of a house, only two rooms, one a bit larger than an average living room, and another, a cubicle which had a cot in it should any of the brothers need a nap. We tangoed into that small room moments after entering the house. Of course I had no intention of using the cot for rest or sleep.

Around noon, as we were about to leave, the front door burst open. A group of my classmates came in. My heart thumped. We gulped for air. I was unsure whether we should brazenly walk into the front room or sweat it out in our cubicle. I chose to wait. They left shortly afterwards, never knowing who was beyond the door nor what had transpired.

Dental school itself was far from recreational. I received no special treatment and got only grudging respect from most of the instructors. They were frustrated dentists who lacked enough patients for a full-time practice. With no power in the real world, they took out their frustrations on the students, ready-made victims in this insular ward. At times it resembled a scene from a Victorian novel: the headmasters could taunt and abuse with no fear of authorities or consequences. Constructive criticism of the curriculum was not allowed; indeed, it was often treated as a personal attack. Should anyone dare to exercise their freedom of speech and protest the conditions, they were chastised, degraded, or worse, thrown out.

No one questioned the necessity for hard and demanding study. Dentistry is a complex profession with many skills to be mastered. But there is a substantial difference between rigorous intellectual challenge and academic slavery. After a student had invested great time and effort he or she was not inclined to throw it away by protesting. So most simply endured it, which only perpetuated a system badly in need of repair.

In fact, to the shame of this system, during my four years in NYU there were at least four students from various classes who took their own lives. Coincidence? Not likely. This is a damning indictment of professional education gone haywire. About ten years after I had graduated–an entire decade in which the College's masters continued to trap themselves and the students in a horrible rut–I learned that a class, which had been either brave or simply fed-up, went on strike to protest their treatment. They claimed an abuse of their rights and demanded, as one of their conditions for returning, that certain incompetent, browbeating instructors be fired. Their twin complaints–disrespect and poor teaching–were quite familiar to me. I understand that afterwards things started improving. Treatment of the students became more humane and the prison atmosphere that prevailed while I was there gradually lessened. Three cheers for the striking students!

My years in the College of Dentistry were not grim every moment of the day, of course. And during the summers, well, they were not grim at all. All the frustrations–social, psychological, sexual, even financial–that I endured between September and May suddenly dissolved. Near the end of my second year, I applied for a job as athletic director at an exclusive hotel, Lake Tarleton, in Pike, New Hampshire, near White Mountain National Forest. The man in charge of hiring, Mr. Gross, was also the head physical education teacher at Alexander Hamilton High School in Brooklyn, where I was interviewed for the position–so near to pursue a job far away. Mr. Gross, impressed with me, offered me the spot. It paid $250 for the season–not a lot of money by American standards but not bad, either, in 1950. My daytime job was to supervise athletic activities, including baseball. At night, however, the position would take on a different cast. I was expected to entertain the girls who had been neglected by the young male guests. A good host is naturally attentive to everyone's conviviality. But I wasn't allowed to flirt with these girls/women, much less have an affair with any of them. This was not a burdensome task–indeed, it would likely be a pleasant one–so I gladly accepted the job.

Several days later Mr. Gross called me on the phone. He inquired if I knew how to play tennis. "Sure," I replied. How well did I play? I replied honestly that I probably could hold my own against most recreational players. He then told me that there had been a change in the summer plans at Lake Tarleton. The "tennis pro," none other than Pancho Gonzales, who had won the U.S. National singles title in 1948 and 1949 (and was a world champion during the late 1950s) had been signed as their tennis pro, but at the last moment bowed out. "I can't take over his position," I asserted. "I don't play *that* well. I'd rather be the athletic director." But, Gross said, it was either the tennis pro spot or nothing. He told me not to worry about my skill level because I would chiefly be teaching women, who he said were less athletic than men and thus not as likely to criticize their mentor. And I would make much more than the $250 I had been promised as athletic director. Well, this was quite fortuitous; I would get more than two for less than the effort of one!

As it happened, it was even better than that. Lake Tarleton was one of the most beautiful resorts I have ever visited. The food, the ambience, the good times and my happy indulgences with lovely women made that summer the finest in my young life.

Within a few days of starting my sinecure I was booked solid, sometimes for nearly eight straight hours. I often missed lunch, but was thrilled to discover that so many lovely, single young women wanted tennis lessons. That golden season heralded scenes from "A Thousand and One Arabian Nights."

The magnificent mountain setting and the casual atmosphere were conducive to romance. About a quarter of a mile out into the lake sat a tree-covered islet, a speck of land surrounded by a moat, just out of easy reach. On cool, humid early mornings it was sometimes thinly veiled in mist, like Avalon, home of mystical forces. Twice or so I skipped lunch and, seeing that the way was clear, would row an agreeable girl to a spot on the far side, beyond sight of the hotel.

I'm sure that the average psychiatrist would probably declare that lusting after many women is an expression of insecurity, a fear of intimacy with or commitment to one person. And I can see why they feel that way. I have treated dozens of psychiatrists and can say with great candor that many are themselves bundles of neuroses. Despite claims to the contrary, I suspect that those I met do not know much about elemental and quite natural physical joy. That, or they were afraid to learn, lest it disrupt their dearly held concepts of passion and the psyche. I wanted to make love to women simply because flesh on flesh with a receptive woman is one of life's great sensations. If myth and legend harbors a kernel of truth, Venus and Eros were healthfully sexual, the goddess and god of love, not deranged like Bonnie and Clyde, and I was just doing my best to find out more about them.

I returned to Brooklyn in late August with a smile on my face and well over $1,300 in my pocket–much more than I would have made as athletic director. I had charged $5 for each half-hour lesson, and $25 for a series of six. That, and all the pleasure I had experienced–was like getting paid twice for a ten-week vacation!

# Seven

## PASSING THE TEST

The summer had passed much too quickly, proving the dictum that time flies when you're having fun. Even before I departed Lake Tarleton many girls I had met were sending me letters. Fond correspondence; love letters or close to it. At home I dated several who were New York City natives, but most of them faded from my life as the pressures of dental school quickly mounted once again.

About halfway through my third year, when classes brought us into the same orbit, my gaze was arrested by a senior dental student. "Linda" seemed to be the most popular person in school, and for obvious reasons: she was a beauty that could easily have passed for a chorus girl or a Rockette. She was model-pretty, blonde, proudly possessing a sexy, sensuous look and a body that defined "voluptuous." I couldn't get near her, though. For some of the same reasons she caught my eye, many of the older instructors and associate professors were always at her side.

Then one fine day I did get close enough to have a brief exchange with her. I couldn't waste the opportunity and was very direct. "I really have been admiring you from a distance and would like very much to date you," I said. "Could I have your telephone number?"

Linda thanked me for the compliment, but quickly added, "I have never dated anyone from the school because I don't think it's a good policy." My pride was hurt a bit, but I said something to her I had never said to any other girl when I had been spurned. "If I ask you again another day, do you think you might possibly change your mind?" Her answer, or maybe the way she said it, gave me hope. "Maybe," she said, with a grin that hinted there was meaning (or mischief) between the word.

I was persistent. Learning that she lived in the Bronx (another one), I called and asked Linda out. To my delight—perhaps she admired my tenacity—she accepted. When I arrived at her house she introduced me to her parents. Evidently they both liked me. At least that's what Linda told me on our *second* date.

Linda swore to me that during her four years at school she had never before dated anyone else there. There's a first time for everything. Our affair quickly grew passionate. With our relentless studies, we were seldom free during the weekday evenings. We made up for it on the weekends, however.

I was a year behind Linda, completing my junior year and surpassing the 2,000 point requirement the summer she graduated. I figured this to be my last summer of fancy-free living, so I accepted an offer to spend the season as a lifeguard at Green Mansions, a resort in Warrensburg, New York. It was another idyllic scene, although it couldn't compare to Lake Tarleton. But Green Mansions did have that familiar and matchless advantage: many more young women than young men. Many of them were schoolteachers, free to indulge themselves during the summer break. It was another time of "free picking" for me.

I was partnered with another lifeguard. Len, my namesake, was a pleasant, well-built, handsome young guy. We shared a small bungalow with two other fellows—the tennis pro and the master of ceremonies for the nightly shows. Len and I became friendly, and we joked a lot with each other and with the guests, earning a reputation not unlike Martin and Lewis, the two reigning cut ups of the era.

The summer season began and we were fully attuned to the bevy of available women around us. But like the would-be lover in the famous 1936 Bunny Berigan ballad, "I Can't Get Started With You," Len really just couldn't get started. He was good-looking, but I guess at heart he was shy. Len soon lost confidence in himself, or was simply unable to overcome the fear of rejection, an aura that may have preceded him. We had a lot of fun reliving my experiences. A great summer for me, a bummer for him. Perhaps he learned a few pointers and went on to greater success. This must sound like bragging–and yes, I guess it is!

I returned in late August of 1951 and resumed seeing Linda, who'd been corresponding with me for most of the summer. She and her parents had rented a small bungalow in Rockaway Beach, so I went there to visit her. The moment I saw her on the beach in her bikini–the skin-baring rage since their introduction in 1947, I became excited all over again. She looked even more shapely than before. Our romance continued into the fall of that year. But, as is the case with lovers who can make no great commitment to each other, and are far from certain sure they want to, the affair eventually faded out.

\* \* \*

One Sunday night toward the end of my senior year at dental college–I was 26 years old–my friend Harvey convinced me to accompany him to a dance at the Jewish Center in Forest Hills, Queens. It was likely to be a lively crowd that contained lovely, available women. But after about an hour I saw no one appealing and was ready to leave. Harvey and I were just departing when I noticed a lovely young woman descending the stairs next to a smiling fellow. I stared. Raven-haired, elegant, with luminous skin and a dazzling smile, she was truly one of the most beautiful women I had ever seen. Compelled to meet her, despite the other man, I persuaded Harvey to act as my second and introduce us. He had a knack for interceding like that. The man, I was happy to learn, was the woman's brother.

Rosita Niego lived with her parents and brothers in the fanciest apartment building in Forest Hills. This was quite a contrast to my tiny house in the Flatbush section of Brooklyn. Her father, a Spanish Jew with a thick, hypnotic accent and a very distinguished appearance, owned a lingerie shop on Madison Avenue. Rosita's physical attractiveness virtually blinded me; I couldn't see beyond it. But I was young and in spite of all my experience with women–pleasures of the flesh, not insight of the heart–I was soon to discover that I had a great deal to learn.

*     *     *

I had more breathing room in my senior year. Seniors were required to have two thousand dental points to graduate, and I had compiled more than enough a full year early. Many students, though, had trouble reaching the quota. In fact, the most attained by some was sixteen hundred and fifty points, requiring them to work through two summers. A few even had to repeat their senior year of dental school. Moreover, before anyone was licensed to practice, we had to pass a New York State Board examination consisting of questions based on all the sciences we had studied in our first two years. And we were expected to perform a variety of dental procedures on both live patients and mannequins.

The date of graduation approached; most of us were elated. But as adept as I had become at clinical work, I was scared stiff to review all my past studies for the New York State Board license exam. The weather was unbearably hot in July of 1952 while I crammed for the exams. Temperatures soared over

100 degrees for several consecutive days. There were no air-conditioned comforts. The stifling heat inside our house drove me to sleep outside in the alley most nights. Bad enough to fight for the rigorous test; I had to fight nature as well. In the end, my determination at the fore, I felt prepared.

The day of the infamous gold-foil clinical examination nearly ruined me. A 100-degree heat wave was peaking. This compounded my misery, for the gold foil procedure was among the most difficult in dentistry. I have never grasped why students were tested on this procedure. It was an anachronism and very rarely performed after graduation.

Each of us tried to recruit several patients for this exam to be certain that if one did not show there was still a patient or two available as back up. I had secured two patients–but neither one appeared. Their absence, probably due to the heat, was understandable, but that didn't help me. Fearing that failure was lurking around the bend, I panicked! I ran around, perspiring, begging the other students to "give" me one of their patients. But they were nervous and reluctant because if work on their first patient became too difficult they wanted a second one at their disposal. What is more, some still held a grudge that I had easily surpassed the point spread. Now I could be taken down a peg or two. When the exam began at one o'clock I had no patient. I kept hunting. No luck. One-thirty. No patient. Two o'clock. Still no patient. I was desperate. The exam concluded at four and if I didn't find a patient soon I would fail completely. Finally, close to two-thirty, I prevailed upon another student to give me his patient. I thanked him as profusely as I was sweating and went to work.

The patient was a young man of about fifteen. (This was the second time I had gotten an adolescent at a threshold moment.) I don't know who was more nervous, him or me. I frantically started drilling a cavity preparation that would be undercut enough so that when I finished tightly plugging the tiny pieces of gold foil, bit by bit, into his tooth, the Board instructor would not be able to extract the material. If he did it meant immediate failure. And maybe worse, humiliation, given the scores I had racked up in lab work. This was D-Day, the supreme test!

Suppressing my anxiety I plugged in the tiny shreds of gold foil, one by one, while rivulets of my sweat dripped on the poor patient. I thought I was making good progress when I noticed that the material was loose and moving around inside the cavity. I had just ripped it out and was starting to insert new gold foil material when I heard the dreaded voice of Dr. Sussman, our weasel instructor.

"Where is Linkow working?" Sussman wanted to know.

He saw me and his gaze fixated my sweat. I mentioned my late start and borrowed patient, but he ignored my entreaties. Touching my soaked uniform he said, "Linkow, you wouldn't want a dentist to ever work on you the way you are working on this kid, would you? Go down to the basement and change your uniform."

Racing the merciless clock, I ran down six flights of stairs, hurriedly changed into another gown, and rushed back up. These two almost breathless dashes, of course, produced the same amount of perspiration as before. But, bless his heart, my patient was still there when I returned. So I poked and plugged, carefully but quickly. I glanced at the clock and saw that the hour hand had already passed four. Nearly everyone had completed their work an hour earlier and departed. I needed more time. More luck: one of the State Board examiners was decent enough to give me another few minutes. Finally, having stretched my allotted time, I finished the operation to my satisfaction and called him over. He tried to pull it out. Thank God, it held in place. I had passed by the skin of my teeth–or of my patient's.

A few minutes later I chased Sussman down and, grabbing him by his shirt, screamed that after graduation I might well blow his head off! That no good, frustrated failure of a dentist and a human being had been envious and spiteful toward me since I first stepped in the clinic. I wasn't going to take it any

more! To have worked so hard to come this far only to be un-
done by this cretin had pushed my emotions into the red zone!

About six weeks later, in late August, in cooler weather
and a calmer perspective, a letter came to my home in Brooklyn: I had passed the New York State Boards. I had become a
dentist.

# Eight

## STARTING OUT

By the time of the heat wave, the Gold Foil Affair, and my graduation from dental school, Rosita and I had been going steady for several months. She was alluring, feminine, graceful, shapely. Rosita, to my mind, had many of the physical and personal qualities that a man likes in a woman, even if he can't (or won't) quite describe them. They're ineffable, but he knows them when he sees them. And I thought I did. A curvaceous body, a beautiful face and the scent of a garden in perfume will go a long way to camouflage less delightful qualities, especially for a man not greatly inclined to look beyond them. It was part of my plan to welcome my adult career and begin a family, in one fell swoop. I was heady, giddy, seriously glad to have met my female match. I never stopped to soul-search for the kind of love I knew we were sure to need. And I discovered, far too late, that I needed a more practical view of matters.

We became engaged shortly before my graduation in the summer of 1952. Rosita attended the graduation ceremonies. Something about her bothered me, like the vague omen of a headache, or a puzzling conversation among your friends that you overhear and are not quite sure if it concerns you. A wide-brimmed hat, more suitable for Rosalind Russell on a shopping spree at Bergdorf's, hid Rosita's face. Her bearing was more haughty than happy. She seemed to feel out of place, or irritated. I didn't understand it, so I forgot about it. Almost a year later, we wed. A well-known rabbi administered the wedding vows in his study at Temple Emanu-El in Manhattan. It was a quiet wedding, just for members of the immediate families. Because we kept it small, I was able to use the $10,000 gift from her father to better equip my practice and give us a start on our married life. I had never looked for such generosity from him or from anyone else, but he had deflected my uncertainty about accepting by assurances that he could easily afford it.

Even before we wed my new in-laws struck me as a curious family. Although Rosita's father and his four brothers lived in the same Queens area, several years had elapsed without any of them even speaking to one another. It had something to do with a business affair. Money can solve problems, to be sure, but can create even worse ones. Especially in families, which are the most intimate and potentially the most painful partnerships of all. Apart from her father's substantial check, the wedding gifts from Rosita's side of the family amounted to a single aluminum picture frame from one of the uncles. And it was an ugly frame at that! My family–by far the poorer party to the union–gave gifts that totaled at least two thousand dollars, a sum that must have seemed princely to them.

When the ceremony was over we boarded a plane for our honeymoon in Miami at the renowned Saxony Hotel. The weather and locale was beautiful, the perfect setting for passion. But the honeymoon was not. From the very beginning we quarreled over matters big and small. Consequently, from the beginning our intimacy was poor. I was dismayed to be on the horns of a growing dilemma. So we already had three strikes against us. Mismatched temperaments, and little in common.

I was an Army veteran and now a professional dentist after over six years of study hell–experience that I knew counted for on a scale of maturity–but I humbly attribute these initial problems to youth and nervousness. Even though Rosita and I came from two very different worlds I was convinced that our union would work out. How naive! A frank admission of my true feelings–if I had been in touch with them–before the marriage would have spared my new bride and I the agonies to come.

Starting a dental practice is not easy now, and it was no easier in 1952. Finding a location, a place to hang the shingle, can be difficult for a twenty-six year old who has never run a business. Where should I go? How should I begin?

Opening an office in Manhattan would have been wonderful, but I could be certain of spending my first few years in the struggle to find patients in a very competitive arena. And anyone starting in Manhattan needed a great deal of money–money to obtain and equip the practice, to pay higher rents and to live on while waiting for patient referrals and a cash flow. I certainly didn't have that kind of dough. Either I would have to find a lucrative location elsewhere, or form a partnership with another dentist who was nearing retirement. One way or another, I needed to start building a business immediately.

One day, shortly before the wedding, while I was walking through Forest Hills on my way to see Rosita, I stopped to chat with an Italian worker who was putting the finishing touches on a building. I mentioned that I was looking for a good neighborhood to open a practice. Forest Hills, he told me, was not the place; there are too many dentists here already. But he expertly advised me to scout a number of new buildings that were almost ready for occupancy in the upcoming area of Kew Gardens Hills. I did just that. It was a middle-class and lower-middle-class section, home to many young married couples with small children, assuring a constant supply of patients.

I brought my dad over to negotiate with the renting agent, an attorney named Jules Weinstein (who would later become a patient of mine). Shortly thereafter I had an office, which is to say, raw space. To conform it to my specifications I needed an architect. I hired one and told him what I wanted: two operating rooms with space for expansion. Weeks became months before the plumbing, painting, wallpapering and decorating were completed. Then I needed dental equipment, which I covered with the ten thousand dollar wedding gift from Rosita's father, and an additional ten thousand from my father, which I vowed to repay. I had no idea how he had gotten such a sum together; but I'm sure that it was hard-won. (Within two years, I'm proud to say, I had repaid all the money my father had laid out for me, including what he'd given to buy an engagement ring for Rosita. It made Rosita very angry because I did not give any money back to her father.)

I placed orders for the office equipment one by one, top priorities first, thereby stretching out the money. While I waited to complete outfitting my base of operations, I began extern work in the oral surgery department of Manhattan's Lenox Hill Hospital under the direction of Dr. Squire Dunn, a famous surgeon who specialized in cleft palates and hare lips. A wealthy resident of Connecticut, he even had his own plane which he regularly flew to La Guardia Airport, connecting there with a limousine which took him to Lenox Hill. Although he was a rather demanding taskmaster, he was fair, and sufficiently impressed with my abilities to take me on as the first dental extern Lenox Hill had ever had.

As an extern rather than an intern, I was free to leave the hospital every afternoon to work in my office. I assured Dr. Dunn that I was a fast worker and could handle the hospital cases between nine in the morning and early in the afternoon. Thus satisfied, he allowed me to arrange my own schedule.

Among my many memorable patients was a plump black woman who during my first week came into the hospital clinic with an impacted molar. It needed to be removed. I was all alone and had never done this procedure. What if I tried and something went wrong? Even though she was in pain, I played it safe. I went to the head nurse and asked her to reschedule the patient for another day, when one of the residents would be present. Didn't they know I was just out of dental school?

That night, when I got home I grew annoyed at myself for not knowing how to help this woman. So I read about it at great length in my oral surgery texts. The next day I told the nurse to please contact the poor lady, as I wanted to do it after all. When she arrived and I got down to the task, I saw that it was quite simple. I removed the impaction in only twenty-seven minutes. On my own! I likened it to hitting one's first big league home run! Flushed with first victory, I was now certain that I could conquer the world of dentistry.

I learned a great deal at Lenox Hill, and Dr. Dunn enjoyed having me assist him. I wanted to master everything. When I expressed an interest in orthodontics, Dr. Dunn immediately placed me under the tutelage of the heads of the orthodontic department, the Feldman brothers. I gained a great deal of knowledge and practical experience.

At just that time, all my new equipment was finally in place. Shiny Ritter dental machines and drills, rich with chrome and high-tech alloys, were set beside lustrous S.S. White leather chairs. I was the proud owner of the beautiful craftsmanship and furnishings that were also implements of medical technology and the tools of a lucrative profession. The first day of my all-service practice had finally arrived. I remember–how could I not?–my very first patient. Mrs. Teplitsky lived directly across the street from the office. I had seen her many times on the stairs leading to her tiny front garden apartment, or squeezed into a folding chair on the sidewalk, from which she would espy me rushing about, a man with a mission. She was remarkably kind and generous, and quite obese. Like a jolly patron saint, Mrs. Teplitsky looked after me, referring patients and expressing concern for my welfare. She did everything but make me chicken soup! And it wasn't as though she had nothing else to do. She had two children and a husband of her own.

My practice grew in leaps and bounds. New patients came

in for check-ups every day. In fact, business became so good that I hired a woman who lived in one of the adjacent buildings to track all my appointments. Mary had a son confined to a wheelchair with polio and she really needed the money. She was a diligent worker with a warm heart and helped me prosper in those early months.

When my year at Lenox Hill Hospital came to an end I was presented with a special certificate for my externship in oral surgery, something I didn't expect. I continued to maintain an affiliation with Lenox Hill for several more years, where I learned more about orthodontics while assisting one day a week in the oral surgery department, as well as assisting Dr. Dunn in cleft palates and hare lips, which was his specialty.

I began a grueling but challenging schedule: 8:30 in the morning to 9:00 at night on my own patients, five days a week, and over eight hours on Saturdays, too. In addition, at least three nights a week I worked until nearly midnight on friends who needed dental care but couldn't afford to pay for it. Within three years I was seeing eighty to ninety patients a day. I often took a three-hour midday break to visit the gym, a half hour drive away. I would return at about three in the afternoon and work mainly on school children until six, when I'd turn my attention back to the adult patients. Finally, there were my friends. Even if they offered to pay I declined. Perhaps I wanted to be liked more than I wanted to be affluent. This was likely the result of yet another complex rooted in my childhood!

As I spent more time and much energy building my practice, sad to say I was failing as a husband. Rosita and I fought constantly, mostly because of how seldom I was home. I know that now, but I didn't realize it then. Or I denied the gravity of the situation. Nor did I fathom just how blind Rosita was to the rigors of building a business. After all, her own family's prosperity grew from the efforts of entrepreneurs, not a fixed corporate salary earned on more normal hours. Worse, she was high-strung with a very short fuse–that ignited whenever I made the slightest misstep, or didn't agree with her, or just carried on as I had been without appearing to heed her demands, much less express contrition. I told myself that Rosita knew where I was headed when she married me, surely she must know that no one who craves true success works a mere eight hours a day and dawdles on the weekend. Rosita evidently wanted all the rewards–without making the sacrifices! So here I was, in debt, newly married, trying to build a practice, to make a life, always anxious about where my next patient would come from, and all the while trying to keep a disgruntled wife happy. Even today, with all my experience, it would be no easy task. At age twenty-six I found it impossible.

Nonetheless, in matters of love I was still an idealist. I believed that it would grow, conquer all, and last a lifetime. I also still believed that most people were honest and meant well. I was confident that two people in wedlock should do everything in their power to make their union work, even when it was not going well, when the fairy tale had faded. So I persevered, hoping, perhaps foolishly, that our relationship would improve. But I overlooked Rule # 1: a newlywed's belief in love is a castle of sand if true ardor is absent.

During those first years, we occupied a three-room apartment in Forest Hills consisting of a large living room, a small raised dining area, a kitchen, and an adequate bedroom. As a bonus, we had a terrace overlooking Queens Boulevard. The rent was ninety-eight dollars a month. Though it seemed exorbitant, I could easily afford it. We were comfortable, and we should have been happy.

A few months after we had wed Rosita became pregnant. She carried to term with no difficulties. Robin Cindy was born on December 7, 1953, a wee, beautiful, five-pound, two-ounce daughter. When I first gazed at her through the maternity ward window in Doctors Hospital, I knew she would resemble her mother: dark eyes, dark hair, pouty lips. This was fine; her mother was a beautiful woman. It was rapture to me, a dream come true, a claim to a piece of Nirvana. I could scarcely believe my eyes. Such innocence! And me, a proud father! Now

I was confident this would get my marriage back on the road to bliss.

I loved babies instinctively. Whenever I saw one in a stroller, I stopped to chat. They of course didn't understand me, not in so many words, but smiled as if they did; maybe in their pure state they know more than we assume. They are an image of ourselves, the way we once were, an adult under construction before the weight of the world begins to impose itself and disenchant the spirit. Babies usually took to me, too— and now I had one of my own. The love I felt for that darling was beyond words.

Sadly, the marriage didn't improve much with the arrival of Robin Cindy. But neither was it further strained. The decline had been arrested. Rosita had another responsibility, another focus for her attention besides herself. Two years and four months later, April 21, 1956, my second daughter, Sheree Lynn, was born, at 6 pounds 4 ounces. She, too, was a jewel to her doting father. When she was tiny, I showered her with kisses and nibbled her fingers and toes. This father to two sparkling little lovelies felt like a king! They came to be the most important aspect of my life. All my work and hope was for them. The present augurs the future in the form of a child, and I wanted theirs to be one of boundless promise.

With offspring in the playpens, we quickly outgrew our Forest Hills apartment. We needed a real home, but it took time and effort to find a suitable candidate. Finally, Rosita and I got excited over a property in Woodmere Park, on the south shore of Long Island. It belonged to an older couple who were retiring to Florida. The features were ideal and the price was right. After much deliberation, I signed the papers. And was glad I did. The home was beautiful. The rooms were spacious and well laid out, and its grounds so ample that soon after we moved there in August of 1957 I acquired an interest in gardening.

The moment I came home from the office I would go to my daughters' room to gaze at them as they slept. (I sensed

that Rosita was jealous, even resentful of my devotion. Her reaction to my normal, happy fatherhood was an omen of dark
and troubled behavior.) When Robin and Sheree were awake
and I was home I taught them how to catch and throw baseballs—of course I did!—and to swing a bat and perform calisthenics. Playing with them was my very favorite leisure time.
When they were old enough I took them to the amusement
parks at Far Rockaway and Coney Island to ride the Cyclone
and the merry-go-round. And to the Bronx Zoo. And I brought
them to the ballfield on the weekends to watch me play. At
such tender ages, they didn't know what the game was—sometimes they even fell asleep in the sunshine—but just having them
nearby was a delight. In my eyes, I was hitting 1000 as a father.

Despite this joy, the whole time I worried about getting my
next patient. Old insecurities were bobbing to the surface. I
craved to assure myself that given sufficient ambition, prosperity was certain. I wanted guarantees. Of course, there are none,
no matter who you are, but sheer hard work, I felt, could buy
off the darkness, or the devil himself. I confided my modest
goals to my father-in-law: if only I could meet my bank notes,
pay my rent, and put two hundred and fifty dollars in the bank
at the end of my first year of practice, I would consider myself
lucky. Of course I accomplished this goal, and exceeded it by
several thousand dollars. I now think I was afraid to want too
much, to let my fervent hopes and grand plans race ahead of
workaday reality. To ask for a little and get a lot somehow seems
the instinctive psychological choice because then the gratification is multiplied.

Notwithstanding my busy and demanding practice, my passion for baseball still burned. And I really enjoyed children. So
I formed a young team to coach. It wasn't hard to find players—
I had many athletic thirteen—and fourteen-year old patients
who enthused at the idea. Coaching a team, I felt, would be
great for me, and it was. I would get exercise while teaching
kids the nuances of the great game. It would be terrific for
them, too; they would be coached by someone with an inti-

mate knowledge of the sport and could teach them a great deal. I provided bats, balls, uniforms, and the team name: The Senators, taken from a team I had played on as a youngster. I was reliving my youth. No, not living in the past, but marveling at the many simple, elemental joys I had experienced on the diamond when I was the age of my crew.

Baseball is a nine-man game, but at times I had over twenty-five on the roster. This was deliberate on my part; I wanted the players to have to hustle all the time in order to remain a starter. Everyone knew that as soon as he got lazy or lagged behind, there was another eager beaver in the wings. It gave them a real competitive edge. As a result, we won most of the games.

I had terrific fun, too. I would bat for an hour at a time (monopolizing the batter's box, a cynic might say), smacking the ball all over the field for the practice of the first team. Meanwhile, the non-starters and hopefuls would run the bases. Everyone worked hard and we enjoyed it, although secretly I was the most enthralled of all. The first year we won the Kiwanis League championship; I bought them trophies. The second year my guys were the Police Athletic League champions. I bought them all trophies. The third year they won the Queens Alliance League championship. Once again, trophies all around!

But between the office and my family, life had become too frantic. There was no free time at all. I had no choice but to resign as coach at the end of the third year, the summer of 1956 (when the late, great Mickey Mantle won the Triple Crown and the Yankees beat the Dodgers in the Series). The team chipped in and bought me a huge three-foot trophy with the legend: "To Doc, our friend, advisor and coach." It marked the end of some great times. And perhaps began to close a window on my youth. No longer would I mingle with young fellows who reminded me of days at Camp Ta-Ri-Go and Madison High, or later, of trying out before the grand likes of Carl Hubbell and Mel Ott.

Nevertheless, sports, or at least the idea of them, was an

addiction for me. I couldn't completely give them up. Perhaps I was selfish. Or unwilling to completely face my responsibilities. Or arrogant; with a wife, two children, a new home, a growing business and, of course, the bills to match all of the above, there was never enough time simply for me. I joined a softball team that played evenings in a Flushing schoolyard, and played for five seasons. The keen competition kept me on my toes. It also helped to keep me sane during the difficult months preceding the inevitable break-up of my marriage.

Rosita and I were drifting far apart. We could not communicate, and when we did talk, it usually collapsed into shouting and recriminations. Our sexual appetite for one another virtually disappeared. I devoted most of my time to my daughters and to my practice, but not to my marriage. Frustrated, not coping and refusing to waste the best years of my manhood to a marriage without love or true pleasure, I started seeking comfort from the soft words and open arms of other women. After a few cautious years, it became a way of life. These relationships, however, lasted only for short periods, when the reality of my actions would come home to me.

Rosita and I both consulted marriage counselors–separately. My psychologist asked about my Dad. "Your father must have been a very domineering man," he remarked. I considered this presumptuous, or an insult. "Absolutely not," I countered. "He was the warmest, most understanding man I have ever known!" I was blinded by my respect for him, unwilling to acknowledge this insight, perhaps fearful of the implication that my parents, my upbringing, and by extension, me, were not as I wanted to believe. My father was indeed a domineering man, a trait I didn't fully realize until over thirty years later when my sweet mother passed away. He had repressed some emotions and denied some realities–traits I now saw in myself. He could not negotiate some of life's frustrating complications, and made it difficult for anyone in our house to do so either. But my affection and loyalty had kept me from admitting, even to myself, that my father had any faults at all.

I think now that perhaps my failings as a husband stemmed, in part anyway, from my relationship with him, and my obsessive desire to please him. His streak of negativism made me feel as though nothing I did was ever quite good enough. I did not understand how this had influenced me until I was about fifty years old, and had in many ways become like him as a man, a father and a husband. I never doubted I had my Dad's love and devotion, but also was never quite sure of my worthiness in his eyes. He was never fully satisfied with anything; neither was I. As a result, I was always trying to prove myself. To find a better situation. Another woman. Another patient. From the moment the Army cut me loose, I started racing the clock. I never slowed down. Was I running away from something? Or just highly ambitious? Just whose approval was I seeking?

My patients, for one. My fees were probably the lowest around. I charged three dollars a filling and thirty-five dollars for a veneer crown; if a patient needed more than three or four teeth repaired he would usually try to bargain with me to lower my fee even further. Too often I agreed. As P.T. Barnum said, "There's a sucker born every minute."

If someone presented with a completely broken-down tooth, I would try to build it up with cosmetic acrylic to save that patient the cost of a full crown. Sometimes it would require placing four or five fillings in a single tooth. This was not cost-efficient for me, and ultimately bad for the patient. Wisely, I stopped feeling sorry for them when one suddenly appeared in my crowded waiting room and loudly declared that a filling had fallen out, and what was I going to do about it? Soon after I no longer struggled to rebuild teeth. I capped them–like everyone else–and for a lot more money.

By this point I still hadn't entirely given up on my marriage. On the contrary, I kept trying to bring the entire family closer together by having Rosita's parents to our home on weekends for home-cooked meals. When they didn't come to us, we went to them. We also spent many weekends visiting my mother and dad on Avenue T. I couldn't shake my belief that families were supposed to be close and loving. And if they weren't, as ours wasn't, I was somehow to blame.

There was another obstacle to family harmony: my sister, Enid. Five years my junior, she had never gotten along with Rosita. The tensions between them made everyone uneasy. They clashed in minor and major chords, creating a dissonant symphony nearly every time they met, sometimes before even a word had been spoken. The chemistry, similar to that between Rosita and myself, was almost toxic. The strain grew worse in 1955 after Enid married another dentist named Roy. What a disaster! After their ten-year union ended, the bastard abandoned Enid and their two children, a boy and a girl, to marry his nurse. He never saw the children again. Troubled marriage or not, it is hard to imagine, and impossible to forgive behavior so low! The stress rippled right down to me because it made my parents so unhappy. Which meant I had to do more to hold the family together, which included not quarreling with Rosita.

It still angers me when I recall how my dad and I ran all over on behalf of that punk seeking the perfect location for his practice. Adding insult to injury, my dad–domineering or not, his heart was pure gold–actually paid for his office. But my brother-in-law never showed an ounce of humility or gratitude. Whenever Dad asked how he was doing, Roy would give a variation on a predictable reply: "Don't worry, I'm not doing as well as your son." He even accused me of purposely giving him wrong information on an orthodontics case that I suspect he had royally botched. In his mind, I was somehow to blame for his probable incompetence.

I missed many of the little things that are so important in a marriage–a hug or a simply warm smile when I came through the door each night, however late it might be. I know Rosita had needs and desires of her own, but it wasn't like I was out gambling or bar-hopping. In the first years, Rosita knew that when I wasn't home, I was at the office. It was simple algebra–not here, there. But the normal tokens of wedded love were absent and that vacuum kept me awake on many nights. I was troubled by a desire for something I could not define. I knew that Rosita needed a life of her own, an existence not so reliant on me. If I wasn't making the time-consuming effort to build a lucrative practice, how else would I pay the endless bills? There were children to clothe and feed, debts and a mortgage to pay! There was money to be made in dentistry and I wanted my share. I wasn't greedy, but I knew that hard work could generate a small fortune and a sizable nest egg for early retirement if I so chose. I also realized my desire to make up for the risky but potentially rewarding baseball road I had not taken. Living well, they say, is the best revenge.

I was obsessed that it all could have been very different. What if Rosita had given the love and understanding I yearned for? What if I'd been able to pour my heart out to her? (And she to me. Ideally, husband and wife are kindred spirits; someone with a listening heart finds their equal in an empathetic soul.) What about a wife as a true partner in union? Could true love make hard work more fulfilling; would it ease frustration? Could it chase away nagging inadequacy? I had no way of knowing. However, during those years her younger brother, Eddie and I became very close friends. We were like brothers. In fact there was a time when I taught him some of the skills for being a dental technician and hired him.

That spring, in our fifth year of marriage, disaster struck like a cold flood. Rosita had been seeing a psychiatrist. Evidently she was extremely depressed. Running in the seemingly vicious circle of a busy practice and an unhappy marriage, I was blind to many distress signals. Maybe I was afraid to see them. Late one Saturday afternoon while I was home with Robin and Sheree I received a phone call from her doctor imploring me to immediately go to Suffern, New York. There, he said, Rosita had driven herself and taken refuge in a motel. She was deep in despair.

Anguish washed over me like a wave. I was devastated, terrified to the core of my soul, guilt-ridden as never before. I ran to my neighbors and asked them to watch the children. I called my best friend Harvey, briefly explained my plight, and asked him to drive up with me. I thought we might need two cars because Rosita's doctor said that she was refusing to see me and it would certainly be necessary to bring her to a hospital. This was an agonized cry for help or attention. Who else but me would come to her side?

The sojourn to Suffern took two of the longest hours of my life. On arriving I went straight to the registration desk and asked for Rosita's room.

Peeking out the window of her self-imposed cage, she refused to do so until I left. Upset as I was, I had no choice and receded to the background. She was indeed very distraught. My guilt and helpless panic became unbearable. Here I was in a strange place with a wife who seemed to be a mental shambles, and who refused to talk to me. What were the options? I called a friend of mine, Dr. Clement Weinstein, whom I thought of as a genius. Luckily he was at home and advised me to take Rosita to the psychiatric department at Hillcrest General in Jamaica, Queens.

It took several agonizing hours to persuade Rosita to abandon the motel room for the trek. Even then she agreed to go only if she traveled in Harvey's car. It was already the middle of the night. We didn't arrive at Hillcrest until almost dawn. By then Harvey and I were both utterly exhausted. He, especially, seemed in a stress-daze; he had listened to her intermittent rear-seat tirades. We finally brought Rosita into Hillcrest General. Just when we thought we'd found a place for her, a doctor informed us that we'd made a mistake; the rest home didn't provide beds for "this sort of thing." Whatever that "thing" was. I attempted to reason with him, and even though he saw my desperation, I made no headway. Infuriated, I again called my brilliant doctor friend–whose suggestion it had been to come here in the first place–and apprised him of the situation. The alternative was a private hospital, he said, and mentioned a few candidates. About two hours later–it was now about noon on that unforgettable Sunday–we arrived at South Oaks in Amityville, Long Island.

I gently escorted Rosita into a doctor's office and resigned myself to the torturous wait for his initial diagnosis. After what seemed an interminable span he called me in. Hearing of her deep melancholy, I broke down in uncontrollable sobs. "Don't blame yourself, son," he said, to comfort me. I didn't know if he was merely being kind or sincerely empathetic. "She will be all right. She needs rest here for several weeks." At that moment it was hard to believe. When I left her she was cursing me with a fierce vitriol that shocked even me. What made it worse was that I felt I deserved it; I punished myself over and over again during the few weeks she was hospitalized. I visited her two or three times each week. It was a relief to get out of the house because I was certain the walls were closing in on me. At the office, I managed to perform, with intermittent attacks of anxiety. At least I had found a lovely housekeeper to care for our home and two little girls.

What with my crazed office routine, then coming home to devote every spare minute to Robin and Sheree, and visiting my wife at South Oaks, my life was more hectic than ever.

After my third visit Rosita started to show improvement and even expressed some affection. I was elated. I vowed to the doctor that if my wife stayed as loving as she now seemed, I could be happy for the rest of my life. But his response made my heart sink. "Unfortunately, she won't remain this way," he said. "After her last treatment it will only be a matter of time before she reverts to her real and troubled self. The same things that bothered her before will start to bother her again. How she reacts to them the second time around depends on many factors."

Once or twice I brought the children with me, telling Robin and Sheree that Mommy was resting at this "hotel" and that she would soon be home to take care of them again. It's easy to pass fairy tales–or loving lies, which was what they really were–to sweet innocent little girls. But the truth was unfathomable, even to me, and would certainly have confused children. They needed protection from the errors of their guardians; why lay on them the sins of the father? My love for them had always been deep and abiding, but now that it was all tangled up with feelings of guilt, it became even more extravagant.

A few months later, Rosita returned home. Despite the doctor's pessimism, I maintained hope for a renewed marriage. Still a romantic, I never dreamed of a divorce. No one in either of my parents' family had ever taken that drastic step. It was unthinkable. I looked to the marriage–this marriage–as an anchor for my life. But, inevitably, I sensed that our relationship was headed for the shoals. For one thing, there was no support system. Rosita's own family had been of little help in this crisis. And she had no friends. The situation was pathetic. My wife was now scarred by mental illness, and her marriage to me exacerbated her inner turmoil. Cruelest of ironies, I was also her only good hope for recovery. Moreover, how could Rosita ever reclaim, or discover, a sense of self when our community was so barren and artificial? We had few real friends in the neighborhood.

Like it or not, succeeding in the high end of the dental profession was driven by social contacts. Attendance at many community parties or country club galas was *de rigueur*. Whether or not it sounds dyspeptic, the truth is I didn't like most of the people I met at them. The husbands, it seemed, either worked for their fathers or their fathers-in-law: nepotism run amok. They sounded so cocksure and smug in their arcane financial analyses, or the certainty of their sales commissions or legal cases, but I thought that many of these characters lacked the backbone to work for themselves. They seemed to be shallow people, and the men, who naturally gravitated to one another, were worse than the women in their costly fixations with golf, liquor, fine cars and other luxuries they had made few true sacrifices to obtain. I was one of the few self-made individuals in the neighborhood, and every so often I felt lightly stung by the subtle barbs of their resentment.

Custom called for each host to outdo the last. This was one-upmanship at its finest. Or, more accurately, its most ludicrous. These people would really put on the dog, often hiring a ten-piece orchestra and striptease artists. They would stage the most outrageously catered dinners. Their clothes were more appropriate for Mardi Gras. Many wives were frustrated because their husbands paid so little attention to them; their lives were B'nai Brith or Kiwanis or the department store. I didn't want to appear to descend to their superficial level of pleasure when there was so much unacknowledged pain and frustration in their lives. I knew too well what that meant.

At about this time I met frustration at my office, like hitting the wall of my ambition in slow motion. Many patients would visit only for minor procedures like fillings, little bridges and implants. For major full-mouth rehabilitation they would seek a dental specialist–and not just any specialist, but a Manhattan specialist, because it was assumed they were the best. This was nothing but snobbism, a surrender to a mystique that didn't exist. It drove me crazy to hear such nonsense.

I had expanded my office to include two more operating rooms and a private office, a staff of a secretary and two dental assistants, as well as my own lab technicians, two very talented hard-working guys named Bob Bosworth and Andino. They toiled day and night to keep pace with me. I worked in part to compensate for my marital heartbreak. I wasn't so much escaping as tacitly admitting the futility of seeking a happy solution, or one that simply would last to everyone's satisfaction. But, just as vital, I was unwilling to settle into a small practice. I was determined to pursue the level of recognition that my skills could attain, and the rewards commensurate with them. And I knew my skills to be very high. If my family life was a shambles, I would triumph in my profession.

Sue Cotrin was a student at a nearby college who was earning a degree in education with the goal of becoming a school teacher. She started working for me part-time after school. Sue was far from the most beautiful girl (thick glasses made her look homely), but she was soft-spoken, understanding and compassionate, and had a great, happy, personality and a magnificent figure. In my eyes she was stunning. I knew I could fall in love with her. But because I was fifteen years older, and because she had a steady boyfriend, I didn't have the courage to make a real pass at her. We flirted, harmlessly by most measures. I was inhibited because for better or worse, I was still married.

Ironically, it wasn't until after Sue had gotten married that our affair began in earnest. One evening about nine o'clock I left her in the office to get my car just prior to my homeward trek. She beckoned me to come back for a moment. As I did, pleasantly puzzled, she shut the lights and kissed me. Sensually. Erotically. I was baffled. What had inspired this giddy boldness? I couldn't resist. Months of frustration and turmoil had found an outlet. I made love to Sue that night and for several nights afterwards. On graduating from college she began a job teaching first grade students in a school on Long Island.

We cared a great deal for each other—so much so that she admitted a willingness to divorce her husband if I would leave Rosita. But I couldn't summon the courage to do that, even though our marriage had withered a long time ago. Eventually, Sue's husband, received a good offer to move to another state. She asked me for advice, indicating that she would agree to whatever I said. I loved her, but I could not yet face the harsh reality of a divorce, its final implications of failures, the certainty of Rosita's contempt, and the fate of the children, even though I now knew it was all almost inevitable. I advised Sue to go and start a wonderful new life for herself and her husband. We saw each other once or twice afterwards when she visited her family. But then there was no more contact.

More months elapsed. As the doctor had predicted, Rosita's sweetness evaporated. Her harsh sarcasm and aggression reappeared; her passion and understanding were gone, seemingly for good. Eventually it became unbearable. She asked for a divorce. I told her father that once I left his daughter I wasn't coming back. I felt justified because it was she, after all, who wanted me out of the house. And I had to assume that, despite Rosita's illness, she made this decision with full awareness of the consequences. Then again, perhaps she knew exactly what she was doing.

Our marriage came to an end seven years after it began. Rosita shrewdly chose her lawyer, one of the biggest divorce attorneys of his time. I had overdosed on a drug called Naivete and retained no lawyer at all. My feelings of guilt and inadequacy had blinded me to financial realities and the moral relativism of the situation. Whatever Rosita asked for she received. I foolishly convinced myself that she would soon remarry–that even with her persona she would attract a suitor–and raised no objections to her lawyer's demands. So now, *over forty years* later, Rosita is still single, and I'm still hobbled by alimony payments.

I moved to a studio apartment in Jamaica just off Hillside Avenue in Queens. I was alone and lonely. I couldn't get over the divorce, or at least the terrible guilt of disrupting the lives of my two young daughters. Perhaps, too, I felt I was deserting them. Or fearful that something would happen to them if I wasn't around. Thoughts like this kept me in a prolonged state of depression. Then, alas, something did happen.

Shortly after our divorce, Robin, by now seven years old, rapped her knee against a table. It became badly swollen. An orthopedic surgeon recommended her leg be placed in a plaster cast for several weeks. At the same time she developed a uveitis (inflammation of the iris) in one of her eyes. This was symptomatic of a much different, potentially more serious problem. Several weeks later Rosita took her to a doctor, who was also the president of the American Rheumatoid Arthritis Association. He said that the orthopedic surgeon's diagnosis and the subsequent treatment was wrong. Robin had contracted rheumatoid arthritis. It can be induced by a traumatic shock or a profound disappointment.

When the cast was removed from Robin's leg it had atrophied to half the diameter of the other. I was extremely distressed. One of parents' primary objectives is to protect their children from harm or serious illness. In this I believed myself to have failed.

For several months, even with the collapse of my marriage, I had been planning to open a second office at 30 Central Park South in Manhattan so that I too could be considered a "full mouth rehabilitation specialist." In fact, the building owner had agreed to move his office from the fifth floor (which had a spectacular view) to the first floor so that I could assume tenancy. I had my heart set on that space. But I realized that for now I had a much bigger and more important obligation to aid in Robin's rehabilitation. I stopped working entirely on Wednesdays and Fridays so that I could be present while she underwent therapy. Several exercises were prescribed. In one, while lying down she was to raise her leg slowly as many times as possible and tighten her calf muscle. When we first began, poor Robin couldn't lift the leg. But I persisted, spending hours on hours with her four days a week, coaxing, encouraging, challenging and pushing. The young have a miraculous power to heal; Robin's leg soon redeveloped and again became symmetrical with the other.

Looking back, Robin grew up to be a terrific athlete and a beautiful girl. She went to sleepaway camp nearly every summer until she was fifteen. Apparently she had inherited some of my abilities because she won the all-around athlete award year after year. But, as I was still haunted by her bout with rheumatoid arthritis, I put all my love into her. And in retrospect I feel depressed over my so-called love for her. Of course, I loved her—but much too much, or in ways that did not succeed in getting the best from her. Sometimes that means being a mentor armed with a whip and stern words, not a soft-hearted father with a gentle touch. From her early childhood I thought she could do no wrong, and treated her accordingly. I thus failed to instill and teach her discipline and to properly weigh her relationships and the consequences of actions.

Robin played a game with me and I fell for it, always taking her side against her mother, Rosita, when she came crying or complaining to me about the basic requirements for living as a family, such as it was. The obligations that every parent has the right to expect. Chores. Homework. Cooperation. She expected others around her to do the tasks she should have been doing. I never gave Robin important lessons otherwise, and thus she never taught her own three beautiful children discipline. She had to be the chambermaid, chauffeur, cook, and so on. This deficit in my attention to my daughter was passed on: Robin lost control over the children, and without a firmly guiding hand they lost most of their respect for her. Fortunately, with time and the good reasoning of all, those conditions righted themselves. I conclude that one should *never* ever stop disciplining one's children. Loving them very often means being tough!

In addition to her obvious beauty, my younger daughter Sheree was also strong and charming, as a child and later as an adult. She too won several athletic awards in consecutive years; one summer she even received the highest distinction of the all-around camper award. I was very proud of my daughters. They were the result, the embodiment of all the hope and love of a marriage otherwise fated to misery. I often wonder if I would have had such lovely children had I not married Rosita. What combination of spirit and genes and environment contributed by any mother and father unites or blends to create particular people? Is it all mere destiny, or a mysterious, undefinable essence that makes us, anyone, who they are? I recall a quote from one of my favorite authors and thinkers. Kahlil Gibran wrote in *The Prophet*, "Your children are not your children. They are the sons and daughters of Life's longing for itself. They came through you but not from you. And though they are with you they belong not to you."

I still recall driving through a terrible blinding blizzard in February of 1959 to get to Woodmere for Robin's leg treatments. I had the roads, what I could see of them, completely to myself. I endured a traveler's nightmare, driving through a horrific white out for two hours to go twelve miles. When at last I arrived, I discovered that Bernie, one of my freeloading acquaintances, whom I had once considered a friend, was also present. He had just delivered some liquor, apparently at Rosita's request. Why else would someone go out in this weather? She had a talent for strong-arming what she considered her opposition, and even better at indignation if she was denied. I disapproved of the purchase, if it even was a purchase; by my alimony payments I was actually buying the bottles. And there were far better things to do with the money than indulge my ex-wife.

Lunch was nearly ready. Rosita asked *Bernie* if he'd like to join her and the children. Pointedly neglecting to ask me. I was left to sit, miserable and alone, in the living room of what had once been my house (or, in a sense, still was, the mortgage being in my name) while I waited for my daughters to eat. Rosita maintained, loudly and for my benefit, a running commentary about her qualities as a wonderful, sweet person and devoted mother. As much as I sometimes wanted to go back to Woodmere for the children's sake, I knew I could never again endure that kind of treatment.

# Nine

## NEW BEGINNINGS

Less than three months after I started my practice I performed my first implant. It seems to me now a milestone day. It was like many other sessions–a patient presented with a problem, and I pondered the options. But this time, I had more of them in my arsenal. Rather, I had a new one which superseded most others. But at the time it certainly didn't feel like the start of a new era in dentistry. The patient's name was Sam Cohen. He had a hectoring wife who not only kept him in line, but who also scared the wits out of me!

How did I come to implants? Like many momentous developments, it began quite casually. In my case, I overheard a chat in an elevator. One evening I was heading to a party on the Upper East Side's posh Sutton Place. I waited for and shared the elevator with two dentists who were avidly discussing an operation they had just seen. They described the incising and reflecting of a patient's gum tissues to expose the underlying bone. Once this was done, an impression of the bone was taken and a horseshoe-shaped casting of a special inert metal–vitalium–was made to fit a model of the bone. Finally, the casting was placed over the patient's bone and the soft tissues sutured over it. A set of teeth could then be made that was totally supported by the implants alone. It didn't rest on the gums like a removable denture so it would seem to the patient very much like natural teeth.

Eureka! What a great idea, I thought! Sensational! I realized that this was a revolutionary concept; I knew in a flash of inspiration that I could do it. I could scarcely wait to try it on one of my patients. I did my first unilateral (on one side) mandibular subperiosteal (under the gum and atop the bone) implant within two months. Sam Cohen was the recipient. It seemed simple. The task did not seem to entail any difficulties. I knew that this was the direction I wanted to take. In the back of my mind I had been seeking an alternative method of replacing teeth, one that eliminated those grotesque dentures.

I was certain that the concept and application of dentures was obsolete. Although in more primitive forms, they had been in use since the Middle Ages and I wanted to banish them just as modern society outlawed medieval torture devices. Dentures *were* a kind of medieval torture device. Most of my patients referred to them as "pocket teeth"–because they wore them in their pockets as much as in their mouths. Some of the patients also called them "gum coverers," a practical term for their main and ludicrous function. Years later, a dentist said, "Dentures are dentists' ultimate failure. I've never really seen a good denture." I concurred with this in spirit from the start and began a crusade to liberate denture wearers from bondage.

Sam's implant functioned for seven years, just like a fixed set of teeth rather than a partial removable denture. He was delighted with it, and if not for his overbearing wife (who was certain she knew more about dentistry than I did), I could have easily replaced that implant with an improved design.

Through intuition, trial and error, I was pioneering the field of implants from the fateful moment I overheard that fateful conversation in the elevator.

I learned that implants had been attempted in ancient Egypt and in the Inca cultures of Peru. Some years later, while lecturing in Lima, I visited a museum exhibiting a skull which had twenty-eight quartz implants embedded in its jaws. The concept was primitive but essentially correct. The Peabody Museum at Harvard has a skull with a few triangular-shaped implants made from sea shell material to replace missing lower incisor teeth. Implants, however, though centuries old, had long since been supplanted by dentures. This, I suppose, is progress by regression; implants had been the best idea all along. Nonetheless, despite the prejudice, implantology continued to move ahead, in fits and starts.

Modern implantology didn't really take root until the late 1940's and early 1950's, about the time I discovered it. There were, however, some very notable forerunners. One of the most important was Dr. Gustav Dahl, a Swedish dentist, who developed the first mandibular subperiosteal implant in 1938. Another trailblazer was Dr. Alvin Strock, from Boston. The same year that Dahl made his breakthrough, Strock established his place in dental history by inserting screws into dogs and later, into humans. Dr. M. Formiggini, from Italy, refined his own type of implant–wire bent upon itself–and in 1941 he placed many of them in patients. Doctors Aaron Gershoff and Norman Goldberg visited Dr. Dahl in the late 1940s, obtained his impeccable advice, and afterward began to perform subperiosteal implants in the United States. They were followed by Isaiah Lew, Roy Bodine, Nicholas Berman, Norman Cranin, Sam Weber, Paul Mentag, myself and many others, as time went on and the procedures proved viable.

In those days when a patient came to my office and merely mentioned the word "implant," I found that the best strategy was a fast one. If I didn't quickly sit them down–on that very day–and undertake the initial surgery, which entailed opening the gum tissues and taking a direct bone impression, the patient too often vanished. Invariably, in the interim s/he would speak to an ill-informed friend or consult some conventional, bush-league dentist. One of these know-it-alls would make self-satisfied remarks such as, "Don't go to Linkow, those implants don't work, you can get a terrible infection from them, it's experimental work and shouldn't be allowed," etc., etc. As doctors, ideally they were urged to maintain an open mind about new procedures. The ultimate aim is the benefit of the patient, not the profit of the caregiver. In a perfect world, a medicine man remains abreast of new techniques and is willing to investigate them. Instead, there was an insidious mindset, in dental society, and thus in patients, that "only the tried and true had virtue." Like so many other walks of life and professions, if someone slides into a rut devoid of imagination, curiosity and a desire to expand one's talents, the results are what I consider the eighth and ninth deadly sin: prejudice and ignorance. Among dentists, these conditions were often on wide display. In the early years of implantology the average dentist was likely to have mistaken an implant for a small skate key or another device far removed from its sole, true purpose. Such was the resistance, or denial, that even well into the 1980s there were many dentists who would have made the same error.

I began to feel like a gladiator stepping into the lion's den nearly every day I went to work. One would think, given the forming resistance, that I was a disciple of Frankenstein, performing horrific surgery for my own twisted gratification. I worried about the influence of my enemies–dentists who were quick to tell their patients that implants were ineffective or even capable of causing cancer. This allegation is absurd; I know of no scientific paper published anywhere in the world that contended that any type of cancer or tumor was ever caused by an implant. If anything, cancer can develop from a poorly fitting denture because it constantly rubs and irritates the underlying tissue. Despite the challenges, I remained undaunted. In fact, I made implants an ever larger portion of my practice. News of my expertise and success began to spread. In 1953 "Dental Digest Magazine" published my first article about implants. Six months later I was invited to lecture to the Central Queens Dental Society. Not yet twenty-eight years old, I was petrified. Waiting to be introduced, I sat at a table with several older dentists. One of the statesmen, Dr. Edward Kaufman, was then a professor of fixed prosthodontics at the NYU College of Dentistry. (More recently, in the 1980s, its dean would embark on a project bearing my name.) Kaufman sensed my anxiety and spoke reassuringly, encouraging me to relax because I knew more about implants than anyone in the room. His kind words did nothing, however, to calm the cramps in my stomach. (It was a déjà vu of my bar mitzvah–an irony that somehow eluded me just then.) In spite of my nervousness the lecture was a success–at least until I wrapped up and took my seat. Some of the older, traditional dentists felt duty bound to be harsh critics. This couldn't work, I was a dreamer, and so on. (What they really meant was that implants posed a threat to the status quo.) But I survived their skepticism. It even helped me, because I began to develop insight into the mindset of the establishment I was challenging.

That lecture initiated a perpetual series of talks and seminars on implants, a mountain I continue to climb. Over the years my implant crusade very possibly made me a most controversial figure in the field of dentistry. What I accomplished has been deemed equivalent to the achievements of such exceptional–and controversial–men as Galileo, Copernicus, Einstein, Fleming, List, Schweitzer and Salk in their fields. I'm certainly not comparing my work to the sublime theories of planetary motion or physics, or the cure of disease. But on a *relative* scale–devising new theories and techniques to solve old or vexing problems–I was helping to initiate an untried but perfectly viable field of endeavor. Furthermore, by providing an alternative to typical dental practices I was helping to eliminate singular and at times excruciating human pain. Who has ever had a headsplitting toothache, or endured a root canal, and enjoyed it? Implantology would relieve the agony of those unfortunate dental cripples who were doubly cursed: painful floating dentures, and deceitful dentists who convinced them no other treatments were available.

In retrospect, however, I realized that my best work was

done too soon. I was introducing the breakthrough blade implant to a hostile environment. I was like the firebrand who comes to town with an utterly new religious view, the well-armored academic more than willing to argue that the old means and methods of a powerful school of thought are effectively obsolete. History often shows us the reaction these kinds of figures received. Otherwise decent and sensible people got their backs up, as if someone was attacking their family, trying to steal their estate or challenge their integrity My goal, however, was always very simple and direct and no cause for such alarm: make all work the best it can be.

\*    \*    \*

I had a brief experience in the winter of 1957-58 that serves well as a metaphor for my life at the time, and certainly the one to come. I sought challenges, taking on tasks or learning techniques which at the outset were new to me, perhaps even intimidating. I mastered many of them, some sooner, others later. But this one I disdained from the first few seconds and never again attempted.

It had been a long, rigorous winter season of snow and cutting cold. I was invited by several pals to go skiing at Bear Mountain, a famous spot in what is now (and maybe then) Palisades State Park along the Hudson River south of West Point. It was a rural area, not yet touched by suburbia or heavy traffic heading into or out of New York City. This was to be a real getaway jaunt. I had never skied before, never even put on skis. How difficult could it be? The lure of adventure was irresistible. I figured to pick up this skill like I had everything else. Ski poles, slalom technique, telemark turns–what the hell were those?

The moment my downhill run began I was in over my head.

I hadn't noticed that the top of the hill was all ice. Rather, the snow underneath had been pelted by rain, which subsequently froze to become a small-scale glacier.

None the wiser, I pushed off. Acceleration was immediate. Fine. But how do I slow down? Having no experience to draw upon, my mind was a blank. Well, not completely. There was something like prayer. And panic. The pine woods to my left and right seemed solid, blurred green walls. I could chart no course, had no strategy, knew nothing but the fervent desire to stay upright until I got to the bottom of the hill. By Rocky Mountain or Swiss Alp standards, this was a modest slope. To my eyes, however, it was a steep incline, and the valley appeared to be beyond Cleveland. I never thought of stopping my run-away self with a controlled fall. At what seemed like a meteor speed, there wasn't much time to think. Instinctively I bent my knees and dropped into my center of gravity. The ski poles were useless in my hands. I began to drift sideways on the course and was slowly tilting out of balance. Just in time two women appeared in my sights, watching me, assuming I would turn away from them. I didn't. In a wobbly reflexive instant, and scaring me almost as much as them, I used their shoulders as leverage to right myself and turn slightly back toward the cen-ter of the course. Ahh. Down I came, straight on, a bat out of frozen hell, into and through a parting sea of ski wizards await-ing the T-bar lifts that would hoist them to the top of the course where they would schuss like the masters they no doubt were. I had broken every rule of ski slope etiquette. Better that than my neck!

My new hobby ended the instant I slammed into the snow-covered haystack. I sheepishly removed the skis as if they were a dangerous foreign growth or a gun in the hand of a myopic fool. I spent the rest of the day giving thanks I hadn't gotten hurt or injured someone else.

\* \* \*

About two years after my divorce from Rosita I was ready to give marriage another try. Jean was a patient. Not surprisingly, it was her physical appearance that first struck me. Jean was not cover girl pretty, but she had silky skin and a lovely figure which she alluringly displayed. Moreover, I discovered that she was warm and good-natured. In those miserable months after my separation from Rosita I sought an understanding woman with compassion and a capacity for love. Jean gave me all that and more. Then I learned that she was married, with a daughter, and despaired of an intimate relationship. However, she confided that though her husband was a nice fellow, for all practical purposes their marriage had been over for a long time.

I asked her to work for me, and she agreed without hesitation. She proved extremely capable and versatile, doubling as secretary and researcher, and became indispensable to me. She voluntarily spent many extra hours and long nights typing the drafts of my journal articles and the manuscripts of my first three books. She was so dedicated that she even cleaned the office when no one else was available. I grew very impressed with her. Rather, enamored. She was good to her daughter Shelly, and it led me to think she might be the same for Robin and Sheree, at least on the weekends when they would stay with me.

I introduced Jean to my father–but I quickly and sadly saw that he wasn't pleased. I sensed a low level of tension. He hadn't liked Rosita when he first met her, either. This was not a good sign. He was never less than polite to Jean, but she easily detected the coldness in his voice. I could understand, in retrospect, his reaction to Rosita. Jean, perhaps, was another matter. I kept my own counsel. I felt my worst mistakes or relationships were behind me and, by logical extension, that Jean and I would be a wonderful match.

We were married one afternoon in a civil ceremony at City Hall in Jamaica, Queens that cost all of two dollars. We didn't even go on a honeymoon. So anxious to work in partnership, we went right back to the office.

Jean and I purchased a home in Cedarhurst, less than two miles from where my children lived with Rosita. I was certain that in this new home and marriage, life would improve dramatically. A good plan, or wishful thinking? I had the entire scenario figured out. Robin and Sheree would sleep over each weekend; of course they would get along marvelously with Shelley. Jean would keep them all occupied on Saturday while I worked, and when I got home everyone would jump for joy.

This fantasy faded to a shadow in very little time.

Shelley, age nine, was a year older than Robin. She was tall for her age, had very badly aligned teeth that needed braces, and because of this she struck people as gawky. And Shelley was far from an athlete, indeed a bit clumsy. I didn't hold it against her; she was a child. Children need and deserve the chance to grow into their potential without adult pressure or criticism. Rushing the process runs a risk sure to make someone unhappy. Shelley was just that: self-conscious, extremely sensitive and easily upset. Robin and Sheree, on the other hand, were blossoming into gorgeous girls: they had fine teeth, were outgoing, mischievous and, to my great delight, excellent athletes.

This didn't bode well for harmony between our two bonding families.

Understandably, Jean was very protective of Shelley, who would begin to cry at a mere glance of my daughters or myself. To complicate matters further, Rosita was trying to twist my daughters' minds against Jean and Shelley. Jean, according to Rosita, was for any number of reasons unfit to be their guardian, if only part time and if only by marriage. One of the prime reasons I had tied the knot for the second time was to create the semblance of a genuine home for Robin and Sheree. I knew that, even though the divorce settlement entrusted them to their mother, she could not and would not provide the supportive atmosphere they yearned for. The long shadows now cast upon my most heartfelt desires slowly led to considerable friction. And to great confusion for Robin and Sheree. It was bad enough that Rosita defamed Jean and I; but she was using the children to further her own agenda. This, naturally, was nothing but the behavior of a deeply insecure soul with a curious need to obtain solace by discreetly dispatching venom.

The sight that often greeted me when I came home late Saturday afternoon was nothing like the happy domestic tableau I had imagined. Too often Robin and Sheree were sulking at one end of the house while Jean and Shelley huddled at the other. Walking in the door I would be immediately besieged with complaints. My house was a war zone, and I was cast in the role of peacemaker. Of course, I had no choice but to listen Solomon-like to each side and devise an acceptable solution. I felt like an accordion being pulled and squeezed from both directions; if I stuck up for one side, I would be despised by the other. It was horrible. I wanted to be a family man, not a referee.

If Jean was to be believed, my daughters were always at fault, but Shelley was an angel. The stress opened up a yawning need for material goods so that everyone stayed content. Jean became a champion spender of my income. Money was not in rapid or full enough supply. This irritation was compounded by my aching need to spend more time with my daughters, who were gone five days a week, and living daily with a child who was not my own. Despite my best thoughts, I saw Shelley as an impediment, and I came to dislike the girl. Naturally, reflexively, I grew somewhat biased. I simply couldn't help it. The situation was aggravated because Shelley and not my daughters always seemed to emerge smelling like a rose. My resentment spread like a slow rash.

But time, as it so often does, had an ameliorative effect. To jump ahead nearly ten years, Shelley bloomed into a lovely young lady–with straight teeth–and went on to attend college in Connecticut. My daughters also flourished. After Robin's graduation from high school, she followed in her "father's" footsteps and studied dental hygiene at Armstrong State College in Savannah, Georgia. Afterwards she worked as my hygienist and proved to be a thorough, devoted and talented assistant. I regret that she didn't pursue the study of medicine because she would have made a wonderful doctor. Unfortunately, the daunting studies necessary for such a path push aside all but the most dedicated students.

Sheree graduated from the same private high school as her sister and entered Boston University with a place in their first class for cardio-pulmonary therapists. After graduation she found work with a cardiologist, which wasn't easy since cardiopulmonary medicine was a new discipline at the time and not many jobs existed for those with degrees in it. All this is to say that, despite the disappointments of their young lives, they grew into flourishing and accomplished young women.

Over years, my domain continued to expand. I purchased a small practice in the Squibb Building in Manhattan from twin brothers who were moving to California. Within two years I outgrew my office in Queens and finally moved to the thirteenth floor of 30 Central Park South—the office of my dreams! Even at the prospect of this my father remained skeptical. He voiced his concern over the expense and the potential for failure in my move to Manhattan. Why was I being brash? Why abandon Queens when I was doing so well there? he bemoaned. There was no way that I could get him to understand.

In one sense, my career couldn't be going any better. More patients were requesting me to perform implants. Many of my articles about the new procedures were appearing in professional journals in this country and abroad. But in another sense, I was waging an uphill battle. As I have begun to relate, politics, not accomplishment, was a prime force in the various dental societies, especially the First District Dental Society in Manhattan (of which I was a member). It, arguably, had the nastiest politics of them all. The sundry committees were comprised of oral surgeons, periodontists, orthodontists, et al. who, rather than convene to share knowledge and advance an increasingly technical profession, attended meetings chiefly to socialize with other dentists and obtain prized referrals. Some members were merely journeyman, others failures in their practices who eased their frustrations by vying for power and control of the professional lives of their more successful colleagues. How did they manage to get on these committees? In truth it was rather simple. It was the Clique of the Month Club, a sycophant's delight. The hobnobbing of the wanna-be rich and famous. Most successful, progressive professionals had no time for this because their patients, practices and own expertise were a top priority.

Nonetheless, the patron brokers installed their choices for the prestigious lectureships and important teaching positions. Their cronies received the papal nod, so to speak, the stamp of approval with a tacit agreement for status quo quid pro quo. Breaking ranks earned demotion to the black list, where an offender had a snowball's chance in an oven. In time, with my skeptical bent, a resolve to push the technical limits, and a decision to not suffer fools gladly, I made the black list, and every other list, too. I didn't fully abide by a cardinal rule of large organizations in a competitive society: "to get along, go along." I was considered outspoken, abrasive and aggressive. Worst of all, for them, my clinical results supported me, so I had grown popular as well. Moreover, opinions on implantology from the early 1950s outset had been hostile, and would remain so until about 1980. That's more than a quarter-century of self-induced blindness. Many other medical breakthroughs had been embraced virtually overnight. The new system, likened to a huge, powerful warship moving full-speed ahead through storm-tossed enemy waters, needed a long time to maneuver in evasion of many torpedoes. The powers that be were ill-prepared, both clinically and theoretically, to realize that the age of implantology had arrived. Many colleagues saw me as an invading force. But in my view, I was their relief from themselves, their own worst enemy, and a boon for their patients, too.

I taught merely once under the auspices of the First District Dental Society: a one-day course on dental implants in 1963. The day prior I called the registrar's office to inquire how many people would be attending. I was sure the place would be packed. I was flummoxed when the secretary, having set down the phone to check the records, returned to divulge with some embarrassment that not a single dentist had signed up.

After a long pause of bitter disappointment, I asked what was the minimum number of dentists required for the course to be given. Five, she replied, and then it was the instructor's decision to proceed or not. Well, I wasn't that proud; I would settle for the minimum. Determined not to be defeated, I contacted a couple of older, trustworthy dentists I knew and asked them to bring some of their junior colleagues. I mustered up the necessary quorum, and even went so far as to spring for the $250 ($50 per man) to the Dental Society's continuing education program so that I could give the course.

Giving matters the full scope of irony, two of the attending dentists had been designated by the First District Dental Committee to give subsequent lectures and seminars on implants because they already held positions of political power. They learned from me and went on to inform everyone else what I already knew better than any of them! Many times, they encountered difficulties with their cases—more often than I'm sure they'd like to admit—they would call on me for assistance. Nonetheless, being politically favored, they continued to give the courses even though they had little proficiency in the subject matter!

Frustration was gnawing at me. How could I convince, or even fight, a herd of envious fools? But should I have been surprised? Too often the fools constitute the majority, and the majority rules. Politics has never advanced science or technology or done much for its various proponents; on the contrary, corporate, social and governmental politics has probably done more to retard than inspire progress. It certainly retarded mine!

# Ten

## THE CLIMB BEGINS

In 1962, a decade after I graduated from NYU's College of Dentistry, I was asked by the school to participate in an evening lecture with Professor Louis Blatterfine, who had headed the department of removable prostheses at NYU for many years. I had been invited for no other technical purpose than to speak about my implant interventions. But this wasn't Dr. Blatterfine's assumption. Perhaps because Blatterfine had grown crotchety with age, he believed that my true intentions were more sinister, that I was really there to criticize removable bridges, his specialty. He was the first speaker, and the moment he opened his mouth he spoke in a defensive, strident tone. Without so much as glancing in my direction he asserted that I intended to denigrate the more conventional kinds of dental techniques which for decades had been the profession's core stock in trade.

Had my true aim been to disparage removable bridges, I could not have done a finer job than Dr. Blatterfine himself. He was as biased and subtle as a demagogue, displaying many symptoms of the insecure who fear, without great foundation, that they are about to be made extinct by an indiscriminate new weapon. As I knew then, and have said many times since,

I was not out to take away or detract, but to add and share. This point was overlooked, or ignored, in the addled ranks of the vested interests who perceived me as a threat.

By the time I replaced Blatterfine at the lectern, he had already buried his own arguments in the eyes of many dentists in attendance. Knowing that less is sometimes more, and deducing that Blatterfine had already promoted implants by default, I merely described and illustrated my techniques with many color slides, and then sat down. This created something of an uproar. Many of the attendants voiced their dismay with Dr. Blatterfine, stating that they couldn't understand why my work had never been shown before. It was clear why: he and his cohorts had quashed it. In effect, the audience had backed him against the wall, barraging him with questions about removable bridges versus fixed bridges supported by implants. Unable to redress several of these queries, he at last lost his cool and stormed out of the room in full retreat. Trying my best not to gloat over Blatterfine's disgraceful behavior I remained to take questions from the dentists who chose to stay.

I asked myself: What was happening? Was there a change in the offing? Could it be that segments of the dental profession were finally becoming interested in implantology? It was much too soon to know.

In the meantime, life on the domestic front was again worsening. Saturday afternoons had become more painful to endure. I too often would find some grim family drama being played out. Either Jean and Shelly, or Robin and Sheree would be in a snit. Apparently it was impossible for everyone to be happy at the same time. I tried, but I was helpless to change the setting or the characters in the script of this predicament. Nor was there any change in Rosita's modus operandi. She continued to manipulate our daughters so that they sometimes turned up at my house with chips on their shoulders, looking for trouble.

Rosita would send them over with holes in the soles of their shoes and wearing torn, dirty coats, especially on snowy winter days. In retrospect, this reflected on her much more than me; after all, I provided plenty of money in child support. If anything, a case could be made that she was depriving the children of necessities simply to hurt me. Forcing our daughters to act out the roles of needy waifs when they were anything but made me angry–but it also worked on my guilt, which of course was the desired effect. Jean and I would immediately go out and buy them new shoes, coats, hats, and anything else we felt they might need. In that respect my second wife was very generous; however, whatever my girls received, she made sure that Shelley received just as much.

The cycle grew more and more tangled. As a way to deal with my guilt I put ever-increasing time and energy into my practice. It helped me to forget, or deny, and lent a sense of being in control. One undesired effect of these longer hours was the generation of more money, which Jean appropriated and spent, which then required working longer hours to stay ahead of the curve. The dilemma sent me to and from the frying pan of marital dissatisfaction and the professional fire. When I wearied of the battles at home I could always enter combat with the backbiters among my peers to whom, despite my instincts, I looked for recognition. Every day seemed to be a cauldron of controversy with hardly a hope of escape.

The struggle began first thing in the morning, at 6:30 a.m., as I wound my way through Long Island traffic jams–gaining infamy as one of the world's longest parking lots–into Queens. This was merely a prelude to the ordeal between Queens and Manhattan. Then every evening, I would do it again in reverse flow. This tedious circuit, a one-scene-two-act-four-times-a-week drama, only compounded the frustrations at home in Cedarhurst and in the office.

I was also just plain sucker-bait. I had a tendency to empathize with those I believed had less than I did, or had been wronged, harmed or disappointed. That is, until I ended up in a similar state of mind through those I had tried to help.

Sometimes the results were comical. They certainly seem that way now.

There was a dentist I called Old Man Weiss. At one time he was what his peers considered a highly qualified professional in gnathology, the science of occlusion, or biting. But he had absolutely no personality. Stern, humorless, neurotic, all up-tight business, on a one-to-ten scale of charisma I would rate Weiss a zero! But I knew that deep down he was a nice man. He meant well, although he was certainly one of the more stubborn people I have ever encountered.

In the early 1970s, I briefly let Dr. Weiss "rent" a room in my office suite. It was a one-way exchange. Weiss paid no money; he simply needed a place to practice. He was in dire straits: his wife of forty-plus years had walked out on him and one of his two daughters had taken her own life. I did not inquire into the circumstances, and did not care to. By Weiss's own heed-less behavior it was clear what one possible cause of his travail had been. But dentistry was supposed to be a brotherhood. I was able to offer some minor help, so I did.

It soon seemed that lending him an office was not enough. He also wanted several of my patients to work on. I was reluc-tant because his cold personality and obstinate demeanor would make it difficult for any patient to trust him. This was a delicate issue. I certainly couldn't afford to lose any patients!

One day, I received a visit from a long-time patient, Cantor Moish Gamshoff. Twenty years earlier I had done a full lower subperiosteal implant on him. He was now in the office to have his upper denture realigned so it would fit tighter over his upper gums. He was a superb cantor and a fine fellow–but a hypochondriac to beat the band. He would drop by my office on any pretext, in the same way he would pay a visit to his physician, always for some trivial, overblown difficulty. As was his wont, he would arrive without an appointment. I allowed it without protest because he had been the cantor at both my daughters' weddings.

I decided to perform a procedure called a vestibular extension. Simply put, I would separate the soft tissue covering the underlying bone in his upper jaw and raise the tissue up, then attach it at a higher level between his cheeks and his gums. In this manner I would create a larger and deeper area of gum which in turn would allow for more surface contact with the denture he was wearing.

The cantor's denture, however, would have to remain immovable for at least two to three weeks to allow the newly attached tissue I had sutured higher in his vestibular areas to heal properly without sliding down to its original position. I had developed a rather straightforward surgical procedure: I would first reline the denture with an acrylic mix and extend it around its periphery to reach the new and higher tissue. But I just couldn't do this for at least another hour; a patient who had made an appointment had been prepped for surgery and was now ready and waiting. The cantor, bless his heart, wanted the work done immediately. He actually expected me to put him first. This I would not do.

Then Dr. Weiss chimed in. He said he had a method to lock the denture in place. Cantor Gamshoff and his wife, after a few uncertain moments, and deducing I was committed to proceed with my prepared patient, expressed their willingness to let Old Man Weiss perform the work. I certainly wasn't going to stand in the Cantor's way, but I must have given him some pause when I said, "Okay, now remember: you asked for this, not me. Good luck."

I returned to my scheduled patient and forgot about Cantor Weiss—but not for long. A short time later a scream wafted into my room. It sounded border-line comic, but then I realized that the source was Cantor Gamshoff! This was serious!

His wife burst in on me, unnerving my patient, who was under a strong but local anesthetic. Mrs. Gamshoff was frantic. Hurry! she said, I must come at once to aid her husband. But I, deep in my patient's gum line, was helpless to follow her. When I finally got Mrs. Gamshoff to calm down this is what she related:

The cantor wore a toupee, a significant detail in light of Old Man Weiss's method. He had proceeded to mix a very large bowl of Plaster of Paris. I imagined Weiss at this–like a doddering East Village bread baker convinced he is concocting the finest Sorbonne pastry. Before the Cantor could stop him Weiss began to impersonally trowel the white-gray sludge over his wig and head. Gamshoff protested vehemently, asserting that he was obliged to teach Hebrew every day and couldn't possibly appear in front of his pupils looking so ridiculous.

Old Man Weiss berated him to sit still and blithely proceeded. That was when the cantor screamed and his wife hastened to fetch me. Undeterred by this commotion, Weiss calmly assured the cantor to sit still. He would be back in fifteen minutes. Asked where he was going, Weiss replied: to purchase some screws from the hardware store! And then he was gone.

I finished my immediate task and excused myself from my befuddled lady patient. Like a world-weary cop in a domestic spat, I sauntered onto the scene of the attempted crime. Mrs. Gamshoff implored me to remove the plaster from her husband's head. By now the quick-setting plaster was becoming as hard as a football helmet; it was already rigidly affixed to the poor cantor's head. He was a Jewish Crash Corrigan! It was difficult but I tried valiantly to keep a straight face. "Well, are you finally satisfied?" I asked. "Do you want me to take over?" They shouted in unison, "Yes!" I sent one of my assistants to find a surgical mallet.

With a few deft blows on the top of the cantor's form-fitting "crown" I cracked the plaster and it cascaded to the floor.

After the cantor cleaned his wig–vanity comes first–I carried out my original plan. I drove in four pins, horizontally, through the cheek side of his upper denture, into the bone, and through the palatal other side. I snipped the excess ends of the pins so they would be flush with the denture, and then I locked them in, using a quick cold-cured acrylic resin powder and liquid to blend with the pink portion of the denture. In other words, I nailed his denture to the bone and sealed the entry points. When the tissue healed, I would remove the nails. This simple task took less than ten minutes!

Old Man Weiss finally returned from the hardware store–nearly half an hour after he had left–with the screws. What he had intended to do was insert two of the screws into each side of the plaster "helmet" near the ears, and an additional two into the cheek sides of the denture, and then wire all screws together and have the wire extend over the top of the helmet to the screws on the opposite side, thus fixing the denture around the top of his head to prevent it from falling out. This "technique" was wildly impractical and would have been a real disaster. The conspicuous absence of the Plaster of Paris notwithstanding, I let Weiss proceed as if nothing had happened.

Weiss stuck his hand in the cantor's mouth to remove the upper plate, to further his "screwy" project. He panicked–it wouldn't come out!

Then I told him what I'd done. Clearly dejected, Weiss faded away–for the remainder of the day. The next day he was back. In fact, he hung on for weeks. I didn't have the heart to disinvite him, but tried to make clear my disapproval by other means. Finally perceiving I had little faith in his old-world methods, and that I would give him little help simply because I could not, Weiss drifted away.

\*    \*    \*

My first book, *Full Arch Fixed Oral Reconstruction—Simplified*, had been published in 1960 by Springer Publishing Company, exclusively for the professional dentist. Though only one chapter was devoted to implants, it helped expand my reputation. Two years later I was invited to lecture to the Miami Dental Society on subperiosteal implants. These implants rested directly over the bone, and were shaped according to a previous direct bone impression usually taken three weeks prior to its insertion. In Miami I met for the first time the famous French implantologist, Dr. Raphael Chercheve. He was lecturing on his screw implant, a method designed for insertion directly into the bone instead of resting atop it. Fascinated by this technique, I immediately introduced myself and asked him to send me his implant kit. Within a few months I was using his implant techniques and inserting his implants directly into the jaws of my patients.

The following November, after some communication, Chercheve invited me to lecture at his annual seminar, at Lariboisiere Hospital in Paris. Not only did I go but I assisted him with his surgical interventions, broadcast over closed-circuit television, for an audience of four hundred people!

But I soon began to realize, after inserting several hundred of his implants into my patients, that Chercheve's design had flaws. In 1963 I developed my own vent-plant screw implant. For the first time in the history of implantology, a device was available to allow bone, rather than fibrous connective tissue, to grow through a large opening at its apex. It was also the first "self-tapping" screw implant ever developed. Previously, all screw implants had required an initial trephining, or drilling, into the bone with a special tap. My implant, by contrast, tapped its own way into the bone. Chercheve designed his threads to resemble a double helix, similar to the spiral-ladder model of a DNA molecule. Its openings made the threads very fragile; many would break when screwing them in. The spaces between the double helix configuration did not allow for the regeneration of bone, only of fibrous connective tissue. My implant had a V-shaped vertical notch down and inside the threads which allowed the implants to self-tap its way into the bone. As it penetrated and crushed the bone, the chips went down through the V notches and deposited into a large apical vent, which was large enough to allow bone regeneration up through its interstices. Nor were my implants cast as Chercheve's, in vitalium, a cobalt-chrome molybdium metal, which because it was so brittle, often broke. I instead had them tooled from pure titanium, what has proved to be the most versatile, the strongest, and the most inert metal of them all.

(The superpowers sought titanium for weaponry, including the hulls of deep-diving submarines and the nose cones of space ships, so I suppose the material was cutting-edge.)

A year later, in 1964, while assisting Chercheve during a procedure at his yearly seminar, I saw an opportunity to prove my device. Chercheve was experiencing some difficulty inserting his implant. I implored him to let me try my vent-plant and he agreed. Several moments later I had easily screwed it into position. It wasn't just that the implant worked, but that it had worked in such a difficult situation, and in front of three hundred or more dentists from all over the world. To say that I was elated is an understatement!

Chercheve recalled this moment in a letter he wrote to me twenty-six years later, and I cherish this correspondence as much as any I ever received.

*     *     *

Several years later I published two more books–*Theories and Techniques of Oral Implantology–Volumes I and II* (in 1970, C.V. Mosby Company of St. Louis, Missouri). Out of respect for Dr. Chercheve and our earlier collaboration, I named him co-author, although he had nothing to do with writing the books.

Chercheve had one major rival in the profession: a fellow Frenchman named Jacques Scialom, developer of the so-called "needle implants." Like Chercheve, he had acquired his own following and his own implant society. He was a constant thorn in Chercheve's side, and vice-versa. I had met Scialom a year or two after my first meeting with Chercheve, and discovered that I liked what Scialom had created, too. Using Scialom's implants as a guide, I developed a technique for circumventing the low flaring upper sinuses that appeared in many X-rays of my patients. Via Scialom's needles (or, pins), I devised a posterior abutment in the upper jaw; before, it had been nearly impossible to use any type of vertical screw implant. The needles were used in threes, with each needle driven into a different spot and angled obliquely in a different direction into the maxillary–upper– bone. But their ultimate destination was the same: the outer cortical layer of the jaw. I then joined the protruding ends of the pins together with cold-cured acrylic to form a tripod. After the acrylic hardened, the core was prepared in much the same manner that a tooth would be prepared for a crown. These tripods were the missing link I had been seeking to create the posterior abutment support in the upper jaw. It was this support that made it possible to reconstruct a patient's mouth with a full-arch fixed prosthesis instead of a removable one.

Chercheve and Scialom were 18 to 22 years my senior. They had introduced their systems to dentistry a few years before I presented my own implant methods. The evolution of Linkow came as a result of the examples set by my illustrious predecessors, who provided the keys for my improvements.

As I had with Chercheve's screws I placed hundreds of Scialom's needle implants in my patients' mouths. But then, to my dismay, I found that in time, many of them would loosen. What made the problem so confusing was that even though they were loose, it was very seldom that radiolucencies–indications of bone destruction–would show on the X-rays. It was something more fundamental, in the design or implant method, not its effect on or in the jaw.

In 1969, I undertook some innovative work using cinefluorradiography–X-ray movies that reveal the implants while mouths were in motion. Patients were given bread to chew and water to drink, and while they did so their jaw movements were recorded. Cinefluorradiography provided the dentist a privileged vantage point; the patient's flesh became virtually transparent, affording an unimpeded view of the skull and teeth. Using this technique I could see the maxilla and mandible with all the implants and any remaining teeth. It was like watching the head of a living skeleton! When the film was projected on a screen, the tiniest movement of any implant could easily be observed. I observed that nearly all the Scialom pins or "needles" moved.

It was time for a permanent solution to this discouraging development. I rented a tiny recording studio in which to tape voice-overs for the cinefluoroscopic films. The space was not air conditioned and the session spanned a stifling hot summer day, from 11 a.m. to 3:00 a.m. the next morning. When finished, in great discomfort, I had documented the observable drawbacks to Scialom pins. An evolution was due in implantology, a movement for new tools, new materials, new methods and a new mindset for their application.

My own devices had some drawbacks as well. The radiographs showed that many of the screw implants I had used, including my self-tapping vent-plant, could also loosen. At that time, dentists using implantology techniques were drilling or screwing the implants directly through the gum tissues and into the bone. This had several distinct disadvantages. For one, the tissue–especially covering the upper jaw, or maxillary bone–was much thicker than the underlying bone, which was frequently knife-edged from lack of teeth, which in turn caused the bone to resorb, or shrink. The thickened tissues camouflaged the thinner, underlying bone. Implants placed directly into these gum tissues and through to the bone often ended up coming out–because the bone was simply too narrow and too shallow to lock on to the implant systems. It was impractical to emplace a long screw with a relatively wide diameter into narrow, shallow bone that had less depth or width than the screw. In many cases, it was obviously impossible. It is accepted dental wisdom that the capacity of any screw to be retained by the bone relies on several factors. First, the period of retention is directly proportional to how much of the screw–length and diameter–actually rests in the bone. A second factor is the ratio of difference between the screw's outer and inner thread dimensions. Finally, it depends on whether the screw is vented or solid. A vented screw will eventually afford more retention as bone grows through the openings. But that still left the problem of where one inserted the implants if there was no bone to receive them.

When I started incising the gum tissues and peeling them back to inspect my implants I realized that virtually everything we had been doing in implantology, with devices anchored to the bone by screws was, at best, incorrect. I was forced to conclude that without a totally different concept and design, implantology would limit the subperiosteal–or on-the-bone implants–for the lower jaw only. Wrestling with this seemingly intractable dilemma I was inspired to create a new device: a horizontally designed blade-vent implant.

I had seen direct proof of how much the bone would resorb. A reliable and totally new implement was needed to penetrate the shallow and obliquely flaring bony ridges that often were all that remained beneath oversized gum tissues. The new implant would have large openings to allow passive bone regeneration that would reverse the resorption and secure the implants to the jaw. The new bladevent implant was to be horizontally designed and very thin, no more than 0.2mm to 1.5mm thick, with vents or openings through its body and a narrow neck on its shoulder or top portion which supported a post. The neck could be easily bent to parallel the posts with each other or with other teeth, and its body bent to fit into a curved channel. The new implant would also require flexibility to follow the curvature of those very thin ridges, and need a neck portion that also could be bent so that the posts on opposite sides of the obliquely flaring bony ridges could be made parallel with each other. Only then would it be practical for a fixed prosthesis to be constructed that would easily fit over the implants and might stay in place for years, or even decades.

Dentistry could then expand its traditional methods with the option to insert implants from the horizontal dimension as well as the vertical one.

A new era in implantology had begun.

# Eleven

## MAKING MY OWN PATH

One day, not long after I met Jacques Scialom in France, he wrote to me and proposed a private meeting when he was next in New York. I eagerly agreed, honored to be invited to meet such a luminary in my profession. Arriving a few months later, he called to suggest business and lunch at his suite in the Plaza Hotel, on Fifth Avenue and Central Park South. This fine new phase in my career, I imagined, would begin just a brief walk from my office. I usually refrained from a lunch break but of course I made an exception. Scialom had taken over a sumptuous suite, further evidence (if I needed it) as to how well he was doing and how big a name he then was in implantology.

I brought along thirty-two full-mouth x-rays, which included my newly designed horizontal blade implants, assuming that he'd be interested in examining them as solid evidence of my work. I was proud of these accomplishments and wanted to share my expertise. I also wanted to signal my ambition and, in a friendly manner, announce the position I was staking out. After all, Scialom had requested me to join him. Why should I shrink from a golden opportunity to promote one of the first breakthroughs in my career? Entering his huge suite I found him entertaining a colleague named Jean Marc Juillet (another enemy of Chercheve and a firm discipline of Scialom). Scialom was enthroned in a large, oak-frame chair, smoking a cigar that appeared longer and thicker than the diameter of his head. He evidently fancied himself a tycoon and had acquired all the trappings.

In the ensuing conversation he casually revealed the reason for his visit to the States. "I tried to swamp the United States with my needle implants and even formed the Pin Implant Society of America and made Jean Marc Juillet the president," he began. "Unfortunately, it never got off the ground. I finally realized that in order to make this society a success, and sell a whole lot of my implants, I would have to select a president who is very well known. You are that man. If you accept, I will give you twenty per cent of every needle implant that is sold in the United States."

For a number of reasons I was uncomfortable, and quickly changed the subject.

Would he be kind enough, I respectfully asked, to look at my x-rays? But Scialom declined to so much as glance at a single one. He had only one goal—luring me or intimidating me into acquiescence in his scheme. "I know what they are," he said impatiently of my x-rays, "and I promise you that if you accept the presidency of the Implant Society and allow me to keep *your* implant a secret in Europe for the time being, I will give you my word that I will announce it to my society members after a year's time is up."

I was infuriated at these terms. Scialom's offer, if I agreed to accept it, was likely to make me wealthy. But it amounted to hush money. A payoff. I would work in his shadow, as hard as ever, knowing full well from empirical and clinical evidence that his implants weren't nearly as effective as my own. He so much as admitted it by his impolitic refusal to let me share my results with him. Scialom wasn't confidently superior; quite the contrary. He was afraid, but the kind that generated haughty deception, not wary dialogue. He didn't want to learn or improve but merely to heed the baser motives of control and profit.

I departed in anger and returned to my office. When my frenzy subsided it occurred to me that I had made an enemy of one of the most important, and powerful, dentists in the world.

But I had other things on my mind besides worrying over the future threat Scialom might present. For the most part, from the beginning the universities in the United States had no interest in me; nor were they, as large, inflexible institutions, ready for what I could show them. But I did get a break—from Dr. Mac Lieb, who was the founder of the privately owned Institute for Graduate Dentists on West 67th Street. Dr. Lieb provided the inspiration for this unique organization that kept it going for more than thirty years. He was intrigued by my work and pleased with my enthusiastic teaching. In 1967 he had invited me to give a post-graduate course on implants. I went on to a rewarding relationship there, teaching the course an average of four times annually for the next five years. Through this and similar venues, I gained the momentum that otherwise may have been missing. Here, in audiences of objective, open-minded peers, the evolving field of implantology was recognized for the innovation that it was.

Because of space limitations, the Institute could accept only fifty students/ doctors at a time. Most often, however, we moved one of the rolling walls to accommodate sixty-five instead of fifty. They were clamoring to take the course despite its demanding agenda. It began at 9:00 a.m. and lasted until 7:00 or 8:00 p.m., interrupted only by lunch and one or two brief coffee breaks. I would talk tirelessly for hours as I showed the thousands of slides which represented all the knowledge I had amassed from my implant cases. (In those days I took the photos myself with some inexpensive camera gear that had been configured for oral photography. Later on, much more sophisticated cameras were used. In recent years the pictures have been taken by my surgical assistants.) I demonstrated my techniques using real mandibles (lower jaws), which were imported from India and easily available at the time. The attendants also learned how to screw the holes for inserting the vent-plants and to make channels to tap in the horizontally affixed blade-vent implants.

I showed films of my surgical interventions, and operated on patients while the students watched on closed circuit TV. On the last day of the course, I would usher in up to twenty of my patients, all bearing their X-rays. They had already received implants, some of them years ago, and were willing to be examined and questioned by the students.

Implantology was truly on its way—and so was I.

Dentists from all over the world started to visit my office to learn more about the implants and procedures. My doors were always open for both the believers and the skeptics. In most cases, I was able to convert the doubters. Truth be told, altruism and the spirit of scientific inquiry was often not a primary reason. The implant market was still relatively untapped and I, among the first prospectors in this mine, knew many of the secrets that would open a more lucrative vein in the dental world's motherlode.

I could not anticipate, however, just how true this was to become. The Italian connection enabled a great acceleration of my work. One fateful day in the winter of 1970 I received a phone call from Dr. Giorgio Gnalducci of Milan. He, or rather his assistant, as Gnalducci spoke poor English, requested a visit. An interpreter translated our conversation. He was a dentist, an implantologist of repute, and wished to discuss some important matters with me. Gnalducci sounded intriguing and I was pleased to make an appointment with him, whether or not he spoke English. Just prior to Gnalducci's call, I had been visited by Dr. Antonio Morro Greco, native of Naples. Through him I was later to make contacts with many leaders of the Italian dental societies. Morro Greco was a very fine and honest man who took to me at once and soon became a close friend. I had been immediately struck by his uncanny resemblance to

Tyrone Power, the Hollywood star of the 1940s and 1950s. Like I had always imagined Power, one of my idols when I was a youngster at the Saturday matinee, Antonio was urbane, dignified, gently assertive. During his stay, Antonio had accompanied me to Hartford, Connecticut, where I gave a two-day course to the Connecticut Dental Society. He saw the full scope of my presentation and the technical methods it defined.

Dr. Gnalducci had arrived in New York the morning after I returned from Connecticut and called me to confirm our appointment. A burly bear of a man walked in soon thereafter. He was my height but much wider, and between his swarthy, broad, puggish face and deep, bristly voice he seemed to me the perfect embodiment of a Mafia capo. Or, for that matter, the Don of a family. Appearances can certainly be deceiving. Giorgio had the soul of a saint. In the coming years he was to become my brother-in-arms and together we set out to conquer, or at least tame, a large part of the dental empire all on our own.

Our meeting, in my office on Central Park South, got off to a dramatic start. Gnalducci wasted no time. His first act, after an honorable introduction, was to stand at my desk and throw down, like a gauntlet, an 8 x 10 photograph of an X-ray of a Scialom tripod implant. The mere sight of a Scialom device unleashed my agitation. I angrily threw the photo back at Gnalducci, to his momentary surprise. His attempt at intimidation was obviously a flop. Perhaps he expected me to be a pushover, obsequious to someone of such renown as Scialom or of such bearing as himself. I can state that anyone who underestimates me or condescends to me is quickly brought up to speed or shown the door. This was such a time. Given my glaring, uncompromising response, Gnalducci quickly re-evaluated his strategy, deducing that I had much faith in my own work. My bravado screamed out: I don't need and don't want to serve a master! Be a colleague or get lost!

Despite this inauspicious beginning, we talked for a while. I formulated a plan to show Gnalducci my work evidenced in the extensive slide collection I kept in my Queens office. I invited Gnalducci to visit me there the next day. He, being a reasonable and open-minded fellow, accepted.

The following morning I took Gnalducci to my private office in the rear of my suite, confident that he would have the courtesy to give my work a fair critique. I sat him at a projector and indicated the stacks of trays, ready and waiting, containing thousands of slides in all, most showing various versions and applications of my new blade-vent implants. Then I returned to work.

Every hour or two I would peek into the back room to see how he was getting along. Each time I would observe him peering intently at a slide, often with his mouth agape. I knew he was seeing a whole new dimension. If his idea of great progress in dentistry was Scialom pins, then he was now taking a crash course at the next level. At the end of the day I went into the room and silently stood by as he completed the last tray of slides, awaiting his response. This mountain of a man rose from his chair, threw his large arms around me in a genuinely friendly hug and kissed me Italian-style, man-to-man, on both cheeks.

He then confessed his true mission. As if it was a surprise. No matter that he spoke very broken English, he could make himself understood well enough. Since Jacques Scialom had not prevailed upon me to head his American-based implant society, Scialom's *wife* had appealed to Gnalducci on her husband's behalf. She told him that if he could convince me to accept the presidency of the Pin Implant Society of America, he would receive a twenty per cent cut of all needle implant sales in northern Italy. The attempted bribes formed a thicket of temptation. If only the method itself justified them.

Giorgio confessed that as of this moment he was no longer an adherent of the Scialom method. He was now a disciple of my own techniques. Moreover, he said he was prepared to sponsor me in Italy. To be my agent. Little did I know at the time, but I would sorely need one. Like Bogie says to Claude Rains at the end of *Casablanca*, this was the beginning of a very beautiful friendship. I have never met a more honest, decent, but dare I say it, shrewd man.

That same summer, before I got to Italy, I lectured at an annual convention in a hot, overcrowded room in Paris. There I met Hans Grafelmann, a German dentist from Bremen. At the end of my lecture so many attendees clamored to ask questions that Grafelmann took charge and urged those with inquiries to write them out and pin them to the wall. In short order, the wall was covered with sheets of paper. It took hours to answer all of them, with the help of my newfound friend as interpreter. This meeting with Hans Grafelmann, too, marked the beginning of a long and fruitful relationship though, alas, one that ended in a quite different and less memorable way than the one I enjoyed with Giorgio Gnalducci.

The blade-vent implant became the most talked-about topic in dentistry. As a result I, its inventor, became more controversial than ever. This was only the beginning. Now, I was bent not only on developing a new system, but a system of systems, each one applicable to a different problem, or group of problems. After all, no two people or their mouths are alike. Why should the remedies for what ails them not be subject to variations?

For years I have widened bone with the insertion of my blade implants, especially in thin ridges which can only seat a blade since other implant types are much larger than the bone dimension. The channel drilled into the bone must be carefully and skillfully created so that it is narrower than the wedge-shaped blade implant; as the implant is tapped in, the bone is gently spread. If the bone is not traumatized nor permanently damaged, it will grow to fill inside the channel and penetrate the vents of the blade. As a result, the ridge is enlarged first mechanically and then physiologically. Some dentists, like Hilt Tatum, have performed the same procedure with root-form implants.

All this progress, however, came against a tide of great struggle. By no means was this struggle for recognition unique to me. On the contrary, it's a struggle known to all innovators, great and small. It was the fate of Pasteur, Fleming, and innumerable others. And the battle is certainly not confined to scientists and doctors. Broadway greats like Cole Porter experienced it; his first Broadway show, for example, lasted only one night. The battle is daunting, but to be an innovator one must first be a survivor. Whatever the creation—a vaccine, a new song-style or painting aesthetic or a new medical device—the goal is resistance-free exposure to get the concept known and accepted. Better devices, methods, and so forth, by themselves do not automatically create a market. The recipient must be coaxed with a binding agent of trust, proper timing, persistence—and a quality product.

Naturally, I suffered from doubt. It was true that with success I might become world-renowned. But if my theories proved to be inadequate I wouldn't just be subjecting myself to ridicule. I could very well earn opprobrium or worse, lose my license.

# Twelve

## TO THE MOON

Italians, I've always believed, have been more receptive to implants than Americans because they are more spirited, more determined to follow through and cast out half-measures. The men, especially, could not abide the idea of daily life with a removable slab in their mouths. As a group, Italian dental patients were ready for a pure, natural and lasting solution. Word spread that I could provide it.

In the early fall of 1969 when, at age 42, I made my first expedition to Italy I had every reason to expect a warm welcome. However, I had overlooked one actor in the scenario of triumph I had envisioned on foreign shores: my old antagonist Jacques Scialom.

Nor had I been prepared for the imbroglio that erupted in Reggio Emilia, the small city where I had conducted my first seminars and implantations. There was the small tempest over the illegal videotaping of my lectures, instigated by my somewhat duplicitous host, Dr. Bertolini. Then I had to contend with the controversy stirred by the publicity I received in the *Oggi* article, which falsely credited me with fitting astronaut Neil Armstrong with an implant.

In spite of the setbacks I'd experienced in Reggio Emilia

(relatively minor ones given the enthusiasm with which my work was greeted by the Italian dental and medical professions), I had no cause to be anything but optimistic about the reception I was likely to receive in Rome, my next destination.

There, under the auspices of Dr. Giorgio Gnalducci and Mr. Raoul Beraha, owner of a large dental supply business, I launched a three-day series of seminars and demonstrations in the grand ballroom of the Cavallieri Hilton. The audience of nearly 400 was ardent and eager to embrace the doctrine of implantology I had brought from America. And then on the final day, just as I was prepared to start my last surgical procedure, my attention was drawn to a knot of commotion in the back of the ballroom. There, in the portal of the large wooden doors leading to and from the ballroom, the men within were pushing out against an unknown group attempting to push in. It was like a medieval mob storming a castle. Gnalducci and several other men came forward, advising me not to worry. That's when you start to worry, when uneasy men tell you there is nothing to worry about. I was hustled from the podium before the battlements broke. Later I learned that the *polizia* sought to arrest me for performing illegal surgery. They had been tipped off by Dr. Tambura de Bello, the leading pin implant dentist in Italy. He had once been a close friend of Dr. Gnalducci, but that was certainly no longer the case–not after Giorgio had broken from my old nemesis, the pinman Dr. Jacques Scialom, and threw in with me. I was being made to pay–and pay dearly–for spurning Scialom and his offer to head the implant society in the United States. I was spirited by taxi to the railroad station and put on a train to Zurich. My clothing and slides arrived at my hotel the next day with one of Gnalducci's friends. Had I not fled the premises just then, I would no doubt have been arrested and charged.

I quickly learned of the other, hidden, and probably more lucrative half of the business; hence, the underhanded methods to protect the gold. Scialom's influence in Italy ran far deeper than I had realized. In fact, as a result of his dynamic self-promotion, he was considered a technical genius and a god. Many Italian disciples did a brisk business in sales of Scialom implants to Italian dentists, and he reaped considerable profits. In exchange for a huge sum, up to $25,000, his disciples were allowed to affix a brass sign on their outer doors: Pin Implant Center of Rome . . . Milano . . . Pavia . . . Padova, as proclamation of quality and a peculiar form of brand loyalty. It was like a Coca Cola distributorship or a McDonald's franchise! Indeed, the absence of such a plaque was considered a signal of inadequacy. And, in any form, Italian men could never let that term be applied to them.

Because of their association with Scialom, this clique of Italian dentists was entitled to certain privileges. For instance, the lords of implantology, often Tambura de Bello himself, would visit local offices to perform surgery, conferring prestige on the practitioners. The "Pin Implant Center" dentist would first prepare the patient for the surgery—for a fee, of course—and then the "elite" guest dentist would descend to do the implants (for a fee), leaving the "Pin Implant Center" dentist to continue with the restorative work that was needed (for a further fee).

Not only was I a threat to Scialom in the United States, who had told me months before how he intended to "invade" the American market with his pins, but now my own blade implants loomed in Europe, troubling those elite Italian dentists making fabulous incomes on Scialom's inferior method, going office to office, charging exorbitant sums of money to perform the pin-implant operations on other dentists' patients.

After my ignominious flight from Italy, I had a greater appreciation for the opposition I could expect from Scialom. But I was resolved to return. And next time, I vowed, no one–certainly not Scialom–was going to send me packing.

Nonetheless, I remained apprehensive. Even after my return to American shores I was nervous that either the Italian authorities would pursue me across the Atlantic for my offense against the state and Scialom's allies, or that the equally skeptical dental establishment of America would strip me of my license for daring to challenge their orthodoxy. But, as it turned out, my fears proved groundless. My American license was never threatened nor did I ever face any difficulties from the Italian government. At no time, on many return visits to Italy, was I ever detained or questioned at customs. Perhaps the scare given me in Rome could be likened to the animal kingdom: the dominant male, used to having his way in every respect, is challenged by a strong newcomer to the territory and resorts to bags of tricks or brute strength to retain his rank. I have seen these same shrewd and strutting tactics, in various guises, for decades. If this theory holds any water, then it is an illusion that humans have a clear cut and virtuous advantage over nature. Some among us, anyway, may be fundamentally motivated by the very forces we believe we're smart enough to rise above. Why slave away in school, and afterwards, to learn an expanding bundle of complex techniques and technologies if some prime ingredients to success remain heartless deception, character assassination and the cunning manipulation of the law? I take a dim view of anyone who abuses qualities like fortitude and fair competition to get ahead, or to knock others down. And that, for the record, is one key to my professional philosophy. Work hard, lead well, follow honestly–or stay out of my way.

The virtue of perseverance paid dividends. I soon realized that far from being anathema in Italy I was considered by many dentists there to be a great influence. For my early turmoil there, the country later proved indispensable for my climb to the top. By networking the Italian connection, within a few years invitations to lecture and perform demonstration surgery began to pour in from all over the world. Eventually my techniques gained so much influence abroad that they could no longer be credibly ignored at home. It didn't help the image of the American dental societies that an expatriate could go abroad, amiably interact with seminar crowds whose primary language he does not speak, but be understood quite well and showered with acclaim. The word spread. More than twenty American dental universities invited me to play an integral part in their continuing education programs. Linkow the Nomad Implantologist was really getting in high gear.

My trajectory was humorously encapsulated by this vignette.

One evening, in 1969, I was in a Chicago hotel to give a lecture. I was idly standing in front of the auditorium door about a half hour before the scheduled start time.

A young, handsome fellow was the first to arrive. Through such earnest fellows do new ideas and methods take root. As he did he stopped to curiously inquire of me "Do you know anything about this guy who is speaking tonight? I hope I'm not going to waste my time."

"I really never met him," I slyly replied, "but I heard he is one kind of a sensation."

During the next thirty minutes the place grew packed. At last, when I was introduced as the speaker, I glanced to the gentleman auditor and clearly saw the embarrassment on his face. His name, I later learned, was Gerry Reed.

I laid my information and ideas on quite heavily, and well, and wowed the house. After the presentation, Gerry approached me. One might describe his demeanor as sheepish, self-effacing or plain old red-faced. I followed his several apologies with a hearty laugh. He had integrity and a good sense of humor, and I invited Gerry to my Manhattan office to spend a week studying my work. In fact, he took to the system so well that he wound up staying for five weeks. Over the years we became close friends, and Gerry became a top implantologist.

From 1970 to 1976, I toured the national lecture circuit about forty weekends a year. I was a guest to the universities of Maryland, Alabama, Mississippi, Oregon, Indiana, Detroit, and Boston; Albert Einstein in New York, Emory in Atlanta, Ohio State, Buffalo, Washington in St. Louis, Tufts in Boston, Louisiana State, Loyola, Temple, Louisville, Missouri, Tennessee, UCLA, the Medical School of South Carolina, and the School

of Dentistry and Medical School of Virginia. The courses I conducted usually lasted for a minimum of eight to ten hours each
day for three days. They were physically and mentally taxing. I
was obliged to be on my feet the whole time; like a caged lion,
I paced back and forth on the podium, an electrical pointer in
one hand, a remote control for the slide projector in the other.
It was all difficult, but at the same time often gratifying and
fulfilling.

In 1970, my large two-volume treatise, *Theories and Techniques of Oral Implantology*, appeared. I expected a great
groundswell of appreciation from the readership for which it
was intended–but I was in for a disappointment. In retrospect,
publication came nearly twenty years too soon; the profession
was not yet ready for such seemingly radical procedures as I
was propounding.

As an anonymous pundit or author once said, "Every conventional procedure was once considered radical." I was frustrated by this aphorism. Even so, I didn't despair; I was certain
the time had come. No matter that much of the dental profession played deaf and blind (but could not convincingly act
dumb) to the benefits of implantology. I would let nothing
stop me from creating my own devices, nor improving them.
This included my often grueling schedule of pilgrimages to
dental schools and research centers, shedding new light on
old practices and encouraging practitioners to adopt state-of-
the-art methods instead.

I covered great distances on my trekathons. For instance,
every September I would catch the "Red Eye" from Los Angeles on Sunday at midnight after giving my regular weekend
course at UCLA. Landing at Kennedy at 6:00 a.m. I would immediately take a cab into Manhattan. By 8:00 a.m. I would be
in my office, ready for a full day of surgery.

My regular trips took me to universities in Europe, the
Middle and Far East. Leaving for Italy, for instance, on a Thurs-
day night, EST, I arrived at my destination early on Friday morning, local time. I lectured at the finest schools in the great

cities of Italy–Milano, Bari, Pisa, Pavia, Padova, Bologna and George Eastman University in Rome and Torino. A welcoming committee of professors from the host university would be waiting to drive me to my hotel. Concluding my course on Sunday at noon, I would catch the last plane for the U.S., arriving back in New York virtually at the hour I left Europe (having gained six hours). I would get several hours of restless sleep before arising the next morning to go back to work. I often endured intensely disorienting jet lag; my biological clock badly needed to be synchronized. Sometimes I could even make the adjustment before the next expedition. I tried to avoid looking in a mirror: haggard in appearance and sleep deprived, I appeared a little like a fatigued soldier forced to endure an all night march to the battlefront. There was no way I could long avoid the tremendous toll of such an agenda.

Lavish stories about me and my techniques appeared in popular magazines, accompanied by photo spreads of my implants. Most of these articles appeared in *Two Thousand, El Tiempo, Readers Digest* and other publications I cannot recall, and many newspapers, too. I even made a reappearance in *Oggi.* Some things, though, never changed: not a single reporter from any Italian magazine or newspaper ever interviewed me. The material was gathered from second hand sources, or simply invented. By now I was accustomed to these "journalistic" methods and largely untroubled by the exaggerations and fabrications.

Giorgio Gnalducci was my personal public relations firm. By the same token, he benefited from his association with me. Between 1970 and 1975 I would fly into Milano at six-week intervals to perform implant operations in his office. When I would arrive at Gnalducci's office early on a Friday morning, the three large waiting rooms in his spacious and well-appointed offices were already packed with patients. Patients for me. On those seemingly endless weekends, I felt almost as popular in Italy as Frank Sinatra.

My very first weekend in Gnalducci's office I performed

twenty surgical interventions on patients who each paid him—
up front—six thousand dollars. A grand total of $120,000in one
weekend! Incredible! I could imagine him yelling at his patients: "Do you think Professor Linkow would fly all the way
across the Atlantic Ocean, as busy as he is, just to do a little
surgery in my officeand not be paid in advance?" He somehow
convinced the patients that the money was going directly to
me. From these advance fees I received a total of $12,500—
eventually raised to $15,000–which more than satisfied me.
Besides, it wasn't so much the money I traveled to Milano to
receive, but recognition. The patients who departed
Gnalducci's office, pleased with my work, enhanced my reputation by word of mouth (pun intended) more than the out-
landish articles in *Oggi* could have.

Gnalducci was totally different than me in his business practice. My main motivators were a form of medical altruism and
a need to share my knowledge. Giorgio, however, emphasized
money-making. He liked money because he most enjoyed life
by possessing everything he saw and desired. He owned four
magnificent condominiums. One was a duplex apartment at
Super Crans, a site nestled high in the snowy Alps on the border of Italy and Switzerland. I first saw the building on a November evening after a drive from Milano. Perched on a rugged crag, its large, bright white curved facade beehived with
tiny windows somewhat resembled a jet airliner or a space-
craft. Few lights were on within; the aerie, covered with a veil
of snow, appeared deserted, ghostly and intensely romantic.

It was a hideaway for very rich and famous people, all of
whom paid considerable cash on the line for a key and plenty
of discretion. But if one hung about long enough, there were
some beautiful people indeed, many from the jet set, including the radiant French actress, Catherine Deneuve.

The next morning, looking out from the tiny terrace adjacent to my bedroom, I was to astonished to find myself in the
clouds, unable to see the hill below me, the valley or other
mountains. It was a very Olympian perspective, above the cit-

ies, almost off the earth, isolated on a lonely, breathtaking pin-nacle. He also owned magnificent apartments in Milano, Pisa and Monaco.

Gnalducci put a proposition to me. "Len darling," he be-gan, "I give you my Rolls Royce and you drive it to this place which you will eventually buy from me for three hundred and thirty-five thousand dollars because my heart cannot take these high altitudes and my doctor told me not to come here any-more. You will rest for twenty-five days and then drive down the mountains to Milano and work in my office for five days and then repeat the trip up the mountain again and rest for another twenty-five days and repeat the trip down to Milano again. For this I give you a salary of two hundred and fifty thou-sand dollars a year."

He meant every word of it. Just picture: Giorgio Gnalducci, big, heavy-set, rough-looking, weighing well over two hundred and fifty pounds–but most of it heart–begging me to do this. If I had been without other business commitments or such devo-tion to my children, I would have accepted without hesitation.

Giorgio also owned a magnificent set of offices in a huge condominium he had purchased with cash. And he boasted a collection of exotic, expensive automobiles, although he rarely kept the same one for very long. Among them were a 450 Mercedes Benz and a 730 BMW. He gave the BMW to his Rus-sian girlfriend (whom he'd met in Russia where he performed surgery on some Kremlin big shots and brought to Milan, even-tually inviting her to move in with him). He also had a Porsche, with zebra seat covers, which he gave to his older son, Marco. He even bought himself an American Jeep.

During my first visits to Milano in 1970 either he or his wife, Titi, would be waiting for me at the airport in his Rolls. In a few months another, larger Rolls appeared. A few months later that luxury auto was gone, replaced by a Bentley. One day I asked him why he was constantly changing cars. "It's those damn Communist kids," he replied. I asked him what he meant, and he said that protesters vandalized the Rolls, crushing in the roof by bouncing on it and setting a fire underneath it. "So," he said, "I got rid of it."

"So why," I asked, puzzled "did you get a Bentley? The same thing will happen."

But that was Giorgio. A wealthy man-child. He acquired what he wanted when he wanted it. And Giorgio could most often afford the indulgence.

I had many unforgettable times with Giorgio. Not to mention fattening. Long, sumptuous feasts at the finest Milano restaurants will do that. Immediately on returning to the States I would do penance: six weeks of a rigorous diet. It was the only way I could go back to Milan in good conscience. Giorgio seemed to know every fine eatery in town. And wherever we went it was usually with an entourage of Italian dentists eager to meet me; what would otherwise be a quiet dinner for two or three people often became a crowded banquet. Nor was it enough for Giorgio to simply sit at a table and be served. He would go into the kitchens of these famous ristorantes and tell the chef what to prepare for his special American guest. Then, in a kind of ritual, the chef and his staff would parade out and place in front of me a roast that appeared to be half a cow, or a sumptuous and hugely portioned pasta dish. Whether I was hungry or less so, it was impossible to finish, but impolite not to. The grandeur of this presentation often caused a considerable stir among the other patrons who would stare and whisper, trying to figure out what celebrity warranted such privileges. These feasts usually went on for several hours. They were events in themselves!

Giorgio's sweetheart nature matched his size. One afternoon, while we were at lunch, I casually mentioned that it was February 25, which happened to be my birthday. Without a pause, he took a large diamond ring off one of his thick fingers and insisted that I take it as a gift. A cynic might say, well, he owed it to you, considering all the money he was making from your efforts. But our two relationships–business and friendship–were separate and distinct. The ring was not a casual token, but a genuine expression from one kindred spirit to another. I still have Giorgio's ring, and I treasure it with all my heart.

Of course, most of my weekends in Italy were consumed by work. Usually there wasn't time for much else. The first time I gave a course at the University of Pisa in May of 1971 I stressed to Giorgio that I didn't want to leave town before seeing its most famous site–the Leaning Tower. On the final day of the course I reminded him not to let any of the dentists pump me for further information until dinner. Then they could ask all the questions they wanted. I figured that, once dinner and the questions were out of the way, I would still have enough time to take a look at the tower. Little did I know!

To Italians dinner is nearly a sacred rite. Under almost no circumstances are they willing to postpone it. For all I know, it may be against the law. The usual dinner starts between eight and nine o'clock and runs for about three hours. That night, dinner took *six* hours–three to eat, and three more for a question-and-answer session. We didn't arrive at the Leaning Tower until 3:00 a.m. There was no moon in the dark, overcast sky. I was, of course, irritated and very disappointed. I work to capture and enjoy these grand moments, and it somehow seems cruel to be denied them, as they happen too seldom.

For all the seeming vitality of this bon vivant, Giorgio was not a well man. Perhaps his illness actually heightened his embrace of life. All the time I knew him, he was on dialysis. Both of his kidneys had failed from chronic poor health and too many indulgences of wine and feasts on the beau monde track. He had a dialysis machine on his yacht, another in his office, and yet another in his home in Milano. Each machine cost thirty-five-thousand dollars. The veins in his forearm, where the needles were relentlessly inserted, had ballooned to many times their normal size. Treatments were required every other day, for four and a half hours. As I performed surgery, he would be in another room having his blood cleansed, after which he would come out raring to go, heart and soul primed for the next project, as if nothing had happened. And at no time did I ever hear him complain about his health. He accepted his lot in life, and enjoyed it to the fullest.

Giorgio's energy and enthusiasm–all that immense drive–occasionally caused some problems. I got into a dispute with the Board at the University of Milano because of all the self-congratulatory media publicity Giorgio had generated for himself. The university eventually refused to allow him on its premises. In 1973 he was even denied access to the Linkow Seminar at the university, which Giorgio had always attended in the past. I protested to Professor Oscar Hoffer, who was in charge, that unless Giorgio were allowed to assist me, I would refuse to continue the series. I was diplomatic and calm, but forceful enough. My ultimatum apparently struck a nerve. Giorgio was allowed to remain throughout my lectures. After all, his audacity was to be credited for the repute in which implantology–and my contribution to the field–was held throughout the country. Despite indications that my loyalty to Gnalducci had cost me a measure of credibility, I was determined to act out of gratitude for the good fortune his faith had bestowed on me, as well as for Gnalducci's own considerable and well-deserved technical reputation.

Indeed, his skill and imagination were so substantial that he once performed a most extraordinary implant operation. I doubt there have been few that could compare. The patient for the insertion of two blade-vents was Jumbo–an aging 500-pound male circus lion.

First, Giorgio called on Siemens, a German conglomerate with a dental equipment division (probably the biggest such company in Europe, if not the world) to supply him with the necessary tools. And big-cat jaws require custom tools. He commissioned the fabrication of two oversize blade implants to replace the feline's massive two-inch cuspids, the terrifying fangs that in the wild puncture and tear its prey, which had fallen out.

Jumbo was housed alone in a large cage. Before the operation could begin, the beast of course needed to be sedated. This was no easy matter; it was, indeed, nearly an operation in itself. For perhaps fifteen minutes, five people stood around the cage shooting darts full of anesthetic at the animal from a special air rifle–to no effect whatsoever! Jumbo was not hit with enough force for the syringe to penetrate his thick hide. The darts would simply glance off; this enraged Jumbo, as he was used to a certain amount of respect, or at least indifference, from his human handlers. The lion would rush at the bars of the cage, snarling with great menace at the invaders, then opening its portal-like jaws to emit a slow, rumbling explosion from its bottomless throat. And this was a "tame" lion; imagine the fury of a wild animal! The darts that did succeed in striking their mark didn't seem to work. But finally, one made optimum penetration and Jumbo tumbled over into a deep sleep. He was hauled up onto a low table, splayed out and prepared for surgery.

Only at that point did Giorgio, his assistants, and the rest of the crowd–over two dozen people, including reporters from various publications, and a film crew that had come to capture the event–venture into the cage. The group did not go in too fast, in case quick escape was imperative. But they could not long delay, either, lest the anesthesia wear off and the huge beast spring to its paws out of sheer irritation! I watched it later on videotape, and everyone clearly knew this was a unique and dramatic scene.

Well aware that, besides Jumbo, he was the center of attention, Giorgio showed no hesitation. He sliced into the animal's ample gum line and reflected the tissues to expose the underlying bone. As much like a carpenter as a dentist, he drilled into the lion's huge lower jaw which, even absent the formidable cuspids, was a potent weapon. Giorgio asked for the specially prepared blades, rapped them into place with a hammer, secured the pre-fab cuspids and carefully cemented them over the blades. The entire procedure took about forty minutes.

Dentists are precision craftsmen and often need to work at very close range with the subject, eyes near the fingers. But I noticed that as Giorgio was drilling into the jawbone his head was quite far from his hands. I assumed that he was–quite understandably–acting from fear. When I asked him later, though, he said Jumbo's breath was so bad he couldn't bring his nose any closer!

The publicity that this remarkable operation brought him–like a cover story in the Italian weekly, *Oggi*–enraged his University detractors. Smart human doctors don't waste time on stupid animals, I suppose was the rationale. But Giorgio was really something, and if he wasn't the best implantologist I've ever taught or been associated with, he surely was the most convincing.

\* \* \*

I was often on the go, short on time and long on responsibilities, and as a result I became short-tempered and irascible without being quite aware of it, especially with my staff. I was a tough taskmaster. Irritable over what I perceived as low patient turnover, subpar office management and the like, I coined the rather demeaning phrase "Beauty fades, but dumb is forever." I asked one of my patients–an artist–to make fifteen small paintings of girls, each with a different shade of hair and in a nurse's uniform, with this phrase made conspicuous. I then had them placed in every room of the office, including the restroom. I could never not bear to see a mistake repeated. I reminded my surgical assistants that I would rather them break a piece of equipment worth a thousand dollars than repeat a single error. It was a question of professional pride, integrity and reputation—qualities that, to my mind, are no less important than clinical skill.

I was always thinking ahead and expected my staff to do so as well. I didn't want patients waiting in the reception room when they could be brought directly to one of the operatives and prepped so I could go from one room to the other. I thrived on assembly-line efficiency. In this way, I often found a way to have a few personal moments with my patients, particularly those queasy at the prospect of open mouth surgery. They needed reassurance, and if I had the time I could give it to them! Despite my idiosyncrasies and a no-nonsense ethic, I really did try to treat them fairly and squarely, my short fuse notwithstanding. I truly loved almost everyone of them, and I know for sure that they loved me, and do to this day.

I was fast learning that fame was a double-edged sword. The good edge: my reputation through the world of dentistry had risen to where the name of Linkow was synonymous with implantology. The bad edge: my need to constantly drive myself to do more was slowly getting the best of me, and my health was beginning to suffer.

# Thirteen

## CLIMBING HIGHER

My career trajectory continued upward, but my domestic life was a growing shambles. A second marriage was crumbling, and one of the reasons was identical to that of the first. Time. Rather, the lack of it. With every effort I made to further the acceptance of my techniques, the level of resistance, particularly stateside, would be raised to match. If I liken this to an athletic competition, it was almost as if I was required to tie or set a world record every time on the field. I felt this to be unnecessary–though at times I resented it–but was forced into the game so that my work wouldn't be swallowed up or appropriated by others. Thus I was challenged to an ongoing series of one-upmanship. The stakes, on a personal scale, were huge: global recognition. In a sense, perhaps this was the world championship that in my younger years I never came close to pursuing on the ball field. Who knows, really, how, or if, the mind sublimates one foregone opportunity and overlays it with another that comes later on? In any case, difficult as it was, the professional commitments took me away from home quite frequently. This caused friction with Jean, which gave me a reason to go away, which caused more friction . . .

Several times in my life I was accorded astonishing recognition. In 1972, on one of my frequent visits to Milano I was invited by Carlo Sirtori, a renowned professor at the Carlo Erba Foundation, to give the first of what became a semi-yearly lecture series in the foundation's magnificent headquarters. The main hall was extraordinary, what I believe was Baroque-era architecture and artwork. The vaulted, gilded ceiling was painted in a sequence of radiant frescoes. Ornate chairs, upholstered in embroidered cushions, had been set out for the large audience. This was a site more befitting heads of state and coronations. For all I knew, in the past had hosted such a function.

Professor Sirtori was a brilliant medical research doctor who specialized in cancer. He was one of the elite who had earned the privilege to nominate candidates for the Nobel Prize. Just after I had completed the vibrant and rewarding weekend seminar, he called me to the podium along with Gnalducci and began making a speech in Italian. I presumed it concerned me, or else why would I be standing there? Not speaking Italian–except a few standard phrases, like "you're a beautiful woman" or "what is the weather report?"–I had no idea what Sirtori was saying.

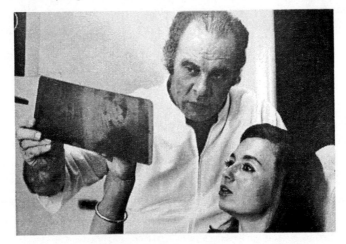

*My dear friend, Giorgio Gnalducci, looking over an x-ray with one of his attractive patients.*

*One of the biggest moments of my life, just after Professor Carlo Sirtori announced he was going to recommend me for the Nobel Prize. Left to right: Hans Grafelmann, of Bremen, Germany; Professor Carlo Sirtori of the Carlo Erba Foundation and medical research doctor in cancer; Giorgio Gnalducci, Milano, Italy; Jack Wimmer, Park Research, New York, N.Y.; and Antonio Moro Greco, Naples, Italy. I am placing my signature in Professor Sirtori's special book with signatures like Albert Schweitzer, Christian Barnard, Michael DeBakey, Denton Cooley, and Sir Alexander Fleming.*

(Indeed, I had few skills in the language of any of the nations I visited. German, Japanese, Italian: my knowledge of implantology was far wider than my glossology. First, there was seldom time to learn. Language is best studied in a versatile, casual social atmosphere. But I did little socializing outside of the seminars. And many of my international colleagues frequently knew sufficient English. Those who did not, when visiting the U.S. for seminars, obtained translations through the provided headsets. Similarly, every audience member was supplied with a headset for my lectures in Europe or Japan. My

English became German, Italian, French, and whatever language was spoken by the remaining majority of the attendants,
be it Spanish, Greek, Portuguese or Japanese.)

From time to time the audience burst into applause. Once
they rose to give a standing ovation. What was the Professor
declaring to cause such a stir? I turned to Giorgio and asked
him to translate. He was wearing the broadest smile I had ever
seen on his face. Then he astounded me. "Professor Sirtori,"
he said, "has just informed the audience that he is going to
recommend you for the Nobel Prize for Medicine."

The Nobel Prize! I couldn't control my emotions. I started
to cry and had to turn away from the audience. Italians, being
such a sensitive people, were so moved that their applause
only grew louder. Someone snapped a photo of that unforgettable moment. It still hangs in my conference room.

I was especially heartened to also have my dear friend Jack
Wimmer as a witness. He was so touched that he cried along
with me. A concentration camp survivor, Jack was an exceptional man for whom the American dream came true. Early in
his career he established himself as a technical pioneer in
implantology, and became the owner of Park Dental Laborato-
ries on East 34th Street in Manhattan, one of the most distinguished labs in the country. Before Jack sold it in 1977, Park
Dental had fabricated the subperiosteal implants I used. Their
work was precisely tooled to specification, made from the finest materials and always delivered on time. In short, the best.
Jack's innovation and integrity had been very influential in
advancing the science of implantology and gaining its acceptance by the dental community. We became very close friends.
The two of us were often on the road together, in the States or
abroad, spreading the gospel. So here we were, in Milan, as I
basked in the applause and considered the prospect of a nomination for one of the most distinguished awards in the world.

I considered that my work on the cardinals of Milano had
played a part in the discussion of a nomination. During my
surgical visits they, quite elegant in their red robes, would come

for the implants. I was honored to perform as their chosen specialist, and never charged for the service.

I did not get the Nobel Prize or a nomination that year, nor did I ever think I had a real chance, given the nature of the competition and the nominees who won, absolutely brilliant people like Gerald M. Edelman and Rodney R. Porter. The gesture, however, was fabulous. It's truly the thought that counts. I was further honored by Professor Sirtori when he requested that I sign a special book he kept for the signatures of great men in medicine, titans like Dr. Albert Schweitzer, Sir Alexander Fleming, Dr. Christian Bernard and Dr. Michael DeBakey. Giorgio and Jack stood by as I proudly added my signature to those of my legendary contemporaries and predecessors.

In these months and years I was showered with honors. The mayor of Milano received me at a special commemoration. I was officially knighted as a Knight of Malta; I, a Jew joining a centuries-old circle that is traditionally Christian, and Catholic. Nor was I overlooked by the Roman Catholic church; I have a magnificent citation from Pope Paul, a very prestigious memento, honoring me for being a father of implantology, and for my gratis care of many cardinals. Additionally, several world-renowned Italian universities wanted to bestow citations upon me for having taught the highest caliber implantology to their alumni.

Another of my biggest thrills also caught me completely unawares. Professor Hoffer, also of the University of Milano, was not just a knowledgeable teacher, but a very accomplished musician and conductor as well. He invited me to an evening concert he was conducting at La Scala, the magnificent, world-famous opera house. The occasion certainly promised to be pleasant in itself. But then he announced to the full house that the concert was being played in my honor! There I sat, front and center, applauded by the audience. I was dazzled and elated as the Professor lead a 21-piece philharmonic orchestra to the majestic works of Beethoven and Bach!

I was scheduled to leave the next day for Rome, there to give a course to yet another implant society. But Hoffer expressed his disapproval, saying that my appearance there would result in what he called "self-serving publicity" for the doctor who was the president of the Roman society. Hoffer stressed that this group was not from academia, nor were they premier dentists. He implored me to cancel the course. I didn't know if I was being caught in the eddy of a feud between rival factions, or if there was truly a serious professional or ethical reason behind Hoffer's request. Ordinarily I frowned on such changes at the last minute, especially without sufficient information on which to base a decision, and I always stood by my professional commitments. But I felt that my alliance and friendship with Professor Hoffer, the president of the Italian implant society, was more important than any agreement I had with the group in Rome. Nonetheless I must have been quite embarrassed because I had someone else call the president of the Rome society and inform him that I had decided not to go.

The following evening, right after Hoffer's concert, I took a train to Zurich, accompanied by two American colleagues, Drs. Charles Babbush and Charles Weiss, to visit my good friend, the great implantologist Dr. Alfred Feigel. When we checked in to the Schweitzerhof, a Zurich hotel, my colleagues wandered off and left me in the bar near the lobby. I was there less than half an hour, and had just begun to relax with a soda (I seldom drink liquor) when I heard a man at the lobby desk ask for Dr. Linkow. I turned to espy who was seeking me and to my consternation saw the president of the Roman society! I recognized him from a visit he had once made to my New York office. I deduced that someone in Milano must have told him of my Zurich destination. Luckily, he hadn't yet seen me. I felt too ashamed to meet him so, turning to the lovely woman bartender, I assured her, in English that I hoped she understood, that I wasn't a criminal on the lam, and pleaded with her to help me hide. Just don't ask me any questions, I said. I would explain everything later.

The idea of being in on a conspiracy (however odd to her) must have appealed to her because she smiled and led me through a door into a dining room. The room, now closed for the night and empty, was dark and quiet. I waited there for at least an hour before I chanced going to my room. But soon after I returned, the phone rang. I took the precaution of responding in a disguised voice (perhaps not too convincingly), and a good thing, too–the calling party was the president of the Roman society. I politely insisted that he had the wrong number. "But he's registered in your room," he insisted. I mumbled something and hung up the phone, then immediately summoned my compatriots Babbush and Weiss. No sooner had I explained the situation to them then there was a knock on the door. They agreed to intercede, to play hardball and bring a quick end to this embarrassing episode. They entered the hall to tell the disgruntled president that I had decided not to present a lecture to his society because I believed that it would hurt my image throughout Italy. They justified my decision by asserting that there were reasons to suspect that the Roman society was not serious and that it wanted to exploit my name to garner publicity.

You can imagine the president's response. They argued for several hours, in the hall right outside my room. I stayed out of sight. To show my face now would be a tacit admission of discomfort and guilt. The Society president, thus prevented from meeting me, left the next day. I truly regretted not being able to deliver the lecture, but I was baffled by these high-pressure political maneuvers. On balance I had only broken a professional engagement for a seminar which would only have covered material already well-known–hardly a reason to tail me to another country for an explanation! The talk, I had correctly deduced, would have been more important to the reputation of the president than to the advance of implantology. It may have been his top priority, but not mine. I needed a break in the agenda. Nor did it surprise me that I was never invited to another Rome Society lecture. I had to admit that, in those years, despite many travels to these shores, my ignorance of Italian dental and cultural intrigues remained virtually complete.

But I figured I still owed the attractive barmaid an explanation. She was sufficiently interested in my tale to invite me for lunch the next day. At least there was one positive result from such a ludicrous contretemps!

That night I left Zurich by train. I gazed out the window as the train hurtled through the Alpine countryside. The night was exceptionally clear and the sky so flush with stars that it almost equaled dawn. I put aside my earthly cares; my mind began to wander effortlessly, inspired by the view. How had this universe, deep and complex beyond all imaginings, ever come into existence? Was the so-called "big bang" theory right—that in a mere micro-instant of time an infinite density of raw elements exploded into existence from nothing? It seemed to me that the answer must be: Never! The universe is too magnificent. It was overwhelming to imagine such harmony and order, from an individual atom to a string of vast galaxies, emerging from a single cosmic explosion fifteen billion years ago. Before it, absolutely Nothing. The Ultimate Void. How can human science possibly explain the phenomena that is the very origin of all existence? No, I reasoned, the universe must have emerged from something much bigger. There had to be a creator—call it God if you will—a Being so all-powerful and far too mysterious for the human mind to ever be capable of comprehending Him. We are simply not equipped to do so, no matter our thoughts or aspirations otherwise. Still, this infinite force, all-loving, all-knowing, must be the source, not some theoretical super-nuclear event. The Big Bang seems inconceivable, particularly if it is the human brain that conceptualized it in the first place.

I used to believe that of the many billions of stars in the universe, many millions surely had planets revolving around them, and many of them had come to shelter life, regardless of the variety that life took. Unless those other heavenly bodies contained living creatures, I thought, why would there be so many of them? A plausible explanation occurred to me. My feeling–my personal theory–is that God created the universe with the goal of absolute perfection. He intended all or most of the planets to be inhabited with Life. Perhaps intelligent life of the human variety was a primary goal. But after observing what happened with the two first sentient people, those we call Adam and Eve, who quickly surrendered to physical temptation and the search for forbidden knowledge, He changed His mind and ensured that the other planets remained uninhabitable.

People talk today about becoming spiritually involved, and say that until people have risen to an enlightened level they will have to suffer. I'm talking as a Jew, but hardly a religious one. I believe in God but I seldom attend synagogues, except on the high holy days of Rosh Hashana and Yom Kippur. I have no clear idea whether I could ever become a truly spiritual being. For though I consider myself an honest, decent and charitable person, I do suffer from a weakness for women and assume that this susceptibility, this penchant for lust, would result in my being blackballed from the spiritual world. It always occurred to me, however, that if there was some ultimate test of spirituality and one passed it, then travel to wherever one wanted would be easy. Soar to any of those magnificent heavenly bodies that decorate our skies every night! Perhaps that's why they've been put there: waiting to receive our souls. For surely a soul, that indefinable essence within us but apart from our physical selves, has no concern whether the atmosphere on a given planet is hospitable to human habitation or not.

Curiously enough, my late-night departures from Milano have often been memorable, even if they didn't all inspire such metaphysical speculations. I remember one very funny moment while boarding the midnight train to Paris. Just as I was about to get on the escalator ascending from the main street level floor of the station to the train platforms I ran right into a dear friend of mine, Dr. Leonard Copen. It's a small world, indeed. He too, was a dentist. Recovering from a recent nervous breakdown, he was touring Europe to regain his balance. Although he was a good dentist, I always thought he should have been a professional songwriter. He would have made a great one. I would spend hours listening to him perform his songs at the piano in my home and at parties, mostly ballads about love and tenderness. His melodies had a quality of genius to them.

Both of us were burdened by hulking luggage (I required three large valises for my slides alone) and because it was midnight there were no red caps available to help us. We began up the escalator together. I was positioned ahead of him with all my baggage in front of me. But upon nearing the top of the escalator I couldn't lift the five bags off quickly enough; inexorably they started backing up into, then behind and past me. Before I could stop them, they tumbled into poor Len Copen. Picture a short, heavy-set man suddenly staggering with my heavy bags, plus several of his own. He struggled to keep his balance against the bags that continued to bear down on him, pulled by gravity, pushed by the escalator. I was fighting the forward momentum of the machine and frantically attempting to retrieve the bags. Just as I did so and flung the bag back upward behind me, two more bags would crawl down past me and press up against Len's legs. Our struggle was in vain. Laurel and Hardy would have emulated us! Laughing heartily, we both wound up back on the street level where we'd started. We recovered and started up again, but this time had the good sense to take only a few bags at a time, though this required several trips.

Len spent the night with me in my sleeper, which was equipped with bunk beds. I volunteered to take the top rack, reasoning that in the event of an accident, I sure as hell didn't want Len Copen to fall off the bed on top of me!

*   *   *

These and other journeys occurred at the time that Jean, my second wife, and I had agreed to separate. It had been a long time coming. My discontent at being trapped in a lifestyle I had not willingly chosen had eaten through the ties that bind. My divorce; my daughters not living with me but rather in the care of their domineering mother; endless money pressures; and the equally endless competition in my profession–contributed to the tension of a teetering marriage. Perhaps Jean was envious of the success that she, with all due credit, had indeed helped me to further create. After our wedding we hadn't embarked on a honeymoon but simply returned to the office and made my practice our lives. In the early stages, she seldom complained. Perhaps she came to see this as her unrequited devotion. Later on, concluding that the situation would not improve to her expectations, it was heavily on her mind. Then again, perhaps it was no longer a question of mind. Inside her, where she lived, where women live, was a hot house of feelings, and it had grown to a temperature that was helping to stifle our marriage. She was seething. A volcano may be active even if it is not exploding, and every moment I was home I expected an eruption. And I often experienced one. There were episodes so out of control that it was apparent we could not continue down this dead-end road. There were scalding fights about issues so minor we could not even recall them the next day. Fighting for the sake of fighting, I suppose. Essentially, they were not clashes about minor domestic disputes like household chores or the credit card bill, but about power and control.

The pressure and tension built to such a level that on occasion I packed all my bags in preparation for clearing out. Jean strategically waited while I put the luggage and myself in the car, then stood by the garage door switch and depressed it so the door would not rise. This was either very spiteful behavior or a message that she did not really want me to leave. Eventually, I would give up and go back inside. I could not, or would not, just smash through the garage door with the car. It had crossed my mind; but despite my angry impulses, I am neither violent nor destructive. Nor would I act undignified. There was already a serious shortage of dignity in our house.

One afternoon I attempted to make a hurried exit. The garage door was already open. The button would not engage to close it. Perhaps from overuse, or from the angry stabs of Jean's finger. Escape beckoned. But she defiantly threw herself behind my car so that if I backed out I would have to run her over.

Was it me–my personal chemistry, habits, behavior–or the mixture between us? Did Jean sense I was not totally committed? Was she jealous? Had she come to dislike me or the state of our marriage merely because to do so gave her a sense of substance and power? Perhaps, simply, we were not meant to be happy together, and it had taken us fifteen years to realize that fact. Familiarity, it is said with some wisdom, breeds contempt. There were no new dimensions for us to explore and our union stagnated. I guess timing is everything, or damn near everything in life. Perhaps, if the children had been older when we wed we wouldn't have the complications which in hindsight were an essential factor in our break up. Jean truly loved me–but I guess I was not man enough to accept the fact that Shelly and not Robin and Sheree lived with me, and that my wife was the jealous type.

At last, I left for good, on the high holy day, Yom Kippur. I had always spent that day in synagogue, from the time I was eleven years of age. The home front had to have been really miserable for me to move on that sacred day. Today, Jean and I are good friends and we speak every few months. But, except for one brief visit she made to my office about ten years after our split, we have not met since that awful day. Jean does occasionally call to ask how I am faring, and often expresses regret over how our marriage ended. I, too, call her. We long ago reached an understanding and have let that guide what remains of our relationship. I still hold her deep in my heart.

1973: two marriages down the drain. This was not definitely quite the opposite of what I thought life would be.

But there was sunshine behind the clouds.

One very busy afternoon in the office, about a year before my divorce from Jean, one of my marvelous technicians introduced me to a young lady who had just arrived from Poland to visit her aunt. Wiesia Pollack came to the office in a miniskirt and boots because in 1973 that was the style. She had a lovely face, an exquisite figure and a soft, glowing personality. I thought that she defined beauty. For me, it was love at first sight.

That very evening, I was scheduled to leave for a lecture in Houston. I quickly asked her–on impulse, without thinking, such was my craving!–if she would go with me. Wiesia's answer, naturally, was no.

Several weeks later she again visited my office. I offered to drive her home to Brooklyn, to her aunt's house, that evening. At first she declined, but a friend of mine, Abe Leverant, who was also Polish and in one of my chairs at the time, had built up my image for her. Finally, she said yes. I drove her home. The hard rain falling was rather romantic. She gave me a small kiss on my forehead and exited the car. I was in love. Or I was lonely and really needed someone. In my mind, they had become synonymous.

I saw Wiesia on many occasions after that drive home. After about a year, when my divorce from Jean became final, I rented an apartment in Forest Hills. It was very deliberate; Wiesia lived in the same building. Eventually, we moved in together. Then, we became engaged.

And while we lived in Forest Hills I risked my life for her.

Someone had innocently mentioned, perhaps at a social gathering, that she was lucky to have met a world-renowned, well-to-do dentist. Then, in a bizarre and unknown way, a group of Hispanic thugs seeking a lucrative scam got this information. These low-lifes boldly telephoned me several times. At first I, with no experience at all in such matters, thought it was an obnoxious prank–but then they threatened they would harm my fiancée if I did not meet with them and give them what they wanted. I realized they meant business.

A date was arranged. Details passed. I approached the Lincoln that was parked in front of our Forest Hills apartment building. A well-dressed, handsome Hispanic fellow, about forty years old, was in the driver's seat. I could have beaten the hell out of him because he was smaller than me. And I was very angry, almost blind with rage, which lent even more of an edge. However, the man spoke very softly and with what seemed to be reason and compassion. The first thing he said was, "You look like a really nice person. I am going to try to get those gorillas off your back but I can't promise you." This disarmed me. I naively believed the tale. I thanked him very much, and even gave him two hundred dollars. At first he refused but at my insistence he accepted. I left the car feeling confident that this episode was over.

I received no more telephone calls for several weeks. Then they started again. When my secretaries delivered the messages to me, I told them to say I was too busy. The issue would go away if I simply ignored it.

One Saturday afternoon, while I was doing some extra work in my office, Wiesia telephoned. Hysterically crying that she was being held captive in her apartment. Two bastards from the gang had wormed past the doorman with the ruse of a flower delivery. They used the same ploy to get into Wiesia's apartment: the flowers, one of them said, were from me. She told me if I did not speak to them they were going to harm her. I told her to put them on. I said little but listened to a rough Hispanic voice telling me to expect another phone call during the week to arrange a meeting. Do not contact the police or I would be very sorry. By getting into Wiesia's apartment, they had proved their resolve and potential danger.

That evening Wiesia and I talked it over. I insisted on calling the precinct. In fact, we went to the detective unit that very night. It was a tense meeting. These rat bastards were setting me up for extortion, I said, and threatening my fiancé and future wife, so I did not mince words about what I expected the cops to do. They asked if I would be willing to wear a wire for the meeting. The detectives would be nearby, within eyesight. I absolutely agreed because I was developing an urge to kill.

As I had been told, the phone call came that week. I was to meet them at 7:00 p.m. that Wednesday. They had a plan, but so did I. Wednesday afternoon I left the office and drove directly to the precinct. The detectives rigged me with a radio microphone and a recorder, taping the wires to my chest, waist and back. I went to Wiesia's apartment for dinner, then left, stressing that she was to admit no one for any reason. It was January, in the middle of a ferocious cold spell which had dragged the temperature to zero. I was pacing up and down 108th Street in Forest Hills, freezing to my bones. My nervousness must have had an influence, but I was also responding to the cold and, keyed up, not frightened in the least. But perhaps a bit crazy. The police were prone on the floor of a TV repair truck nearby; as I walked past, one of them popped his head up so I would know where they were. I was wired so they could hear me, but I did not have a receiver for their voices.

My contact never showed. After I returned to my apartment, frozen but still pumped with adrenaline, one of the officers phoned me to say I had walked right by my contact several times but never knew it. He did not show himself, probably to be certain I had no associates in this cat-and-mouse game.

The next day one of the scoundrels phoned–yelling and screaming that I contacted the police. I of course totally and coolly denied it. This was a psych-war, a battle of nerves, and I found myself equal to the task. A bit to my surprise and much to my relief, he believed me. We arranged another meeting for the next evening. A taxi would pick me up at my apartment and drive me to a declared destination. But I was in no mood to be bossed. I knew it was vital to be clear-headed and assertive, so I bluntly said there was no way would I get into a cab driven by a complete stranger–but I would run alongside it. The extortionists were baffled but apparently felt, having come this far, that they had little choice but to agree.

I was wired up once again. The deep freeze continued. The cab came. When the driver emerged to open the door for me I yelled at him that I had no intention of sitting in his cab; I was going to run alongside. He looked at me as if I were deranged. His expression was sincere, and so I knew he was probably innocent of the scheme. He had simply been told by phone to find a fare in front of the Birchwood Towers apartment on Yellowstone Boulevard.

I ran with the slow-moving cab for about six windswept, deserted Arctic blocks before it turned down a side street opposite a public school. The driver told me that this was where he had been told to take me, and then departed. The street was pitch black on this moonless, sinister night. Nobody came. I did see some man in his underwear, stretching and peering through the window of his third-story apartment. I silently cursed him, for a moment thinking he was my tormentor.

After about a half hour, the police officers–in a different truck this time–retrieved me. As they related the reason for their caution, all of a sudden I saw the Lincoln Continental man on whom I had wasted $200. Telling the cops to stop the truck, I jumped out and gave chase, determined to pound the bastard into the frozen dirt. Seeing me, or more accurately, my fearsome mug, the mark panicked and began to flee. I caught up, tackled him on the concrete and we tumbled into some bushes on Yellowstone Boulevard. I was about to exact my own justice when the cops jumped in and separated us, or rather, saved the man from a serious beating. They told me to go home and stay away from the precinct for at least an hour. When I arrived home Wiesia and my daughters, Robin and Sheree, were waiting in the lobby. I told them the tale and they jumped for joy.

Wiesia and I returned to the stationhouse. In the next room I heard the officers smashing the juice out of that pig. Finally, they called us in to identify him: he looked like hell after his "interrogation." Still, he put on an act when I appeared, urging me to tell the police that he was my friend and had tried to help me. It remained a mystery exactly how I had been tagged for the scheme, and by whom.

I was required to appear before a grand jury to get him indicted. He was found guilty. His cohorts were acquitted because it was their first offense. In about four weeks one of the officers called me to say, just as I had predicted, that the guy was out on the streets again. I minced no words about that development. The legal system was as lax as these criminals were corrupt, I bellowed. But the officer told me not to feel so bad; now the guy had a record, and the next time he pulled such a stunt the sentence would be a great deal heavier. This was cold comfort while Wiesia and I waited for whatever revenge the gangsters might take. Mercifully, It never came.

# Fourteen

## WAR WITH LITTLE PEACE

Throughout the 1960s and 1970s I may have spent as much time on planes as any member of the "jet set." But unlike that high society crowd, I worked when I was en route, often so absorbed in writing that I was oblivious to long flights. These extended journeys presented a golden opportunity to accomplish what I couldn't in New York. And once I was safely on the ground I certainly had more to do than write or even socialize.

I seldom enjoyed the traveling itself, but the destinations, what I saw of them, were splendid. I'm sorry to say that European cities have qualities their American counterparts cannot match. They are immaculate, and radiate a peace and contentment that is often absent in my native land. The history in every metropolis and village is as resonant as the stones of the huge cathedrals are old. Energy emanates from street corners, buildings, cafes. In cities like Milano and Frankfurt, ages long past are still with us, to be conjured up by anyone who cares to recall what life may have been like in the centuries of monarchs and empires. All this repeatedly drew me on enthralling pilgrimages to Europe, especially to Italy and Germany.

The Germans came to admire and even love my dental techniques, and I began to travel there more frequently. In

1969 the German Society of Dental Implantology–Deutsche Gesellschaft fur Zahnarztliche Implantologie (DGZI)–was founded and made my friend Hans Grafelmann their president. At the society's first meeting, in 1969, in Bremen, I had been elected the honorary president, a lifetime post. DGZI sponsored twenty-one consecutive years of Linkow Seminars before they ended in 1989. (Hans would lose his position as president in 1989 when it became clear he had more interest in business and money than in DGZI and the progress of implantoloy.) He took it upon himself to heavily commercialize my implants, compounding the slight by sharing none of the proceeds with me, and essentially choosing the pursuit of maximum profits over a priceless friendship. At their inception, the number of attendees was small mainly because so little was known about implantology, and what was known wasn't especially believed. But in the ensuing years, on the heels of global renown, the audience greatly expanded, from forty or less to a norm of between three and five hundred.

Hans orchestrated these seminars with the finest taste. He saw to it that they ran smoothly, and helped to assure that the guests enjoyed magnificent meals and special trips to various nightclubs at the day's end. Saturday night balls were a regular feature; they were like something out of Scheherezade, or at least was a modern spin on Old World Europe. The ladies wore designer gowns, the men tuxedos; I was the only one dressed like a New York City business bum until I finally grew wise enough to bring my own tux.

A number of rituals were featured on these Saturday night galas, many of which centered around me. For Hans, it wasn't enough of an honor to adorn the stage with a huge sign proclaiming "First Linkow Seminar," or "Tenth Linkow Seminar," or whatever. That was the least of it. Just before the dessert carts crammed with sumptuous Viennese delicacies were rolled out, a trumpet blast or a siren or a drum roll would silence the soirée. When everyone was rapt the waiters would file into the room in formation, pushing an oversized cart that bore a huge and accurately rendered ice sculpture of one of my blade implants. They would be followed by other waiters who bore smaller versions of the form, all carved in ice, to place on the tables. Then came the dessert wagons, laden with the most delicious treats imaginable. On one occasion the ceremony was accompanied by a display of lit candles, sparklers and small firecrackers.

*Myself, Dr. Gustav Dahl, of Stockholm, Sweden, and Hans Grafelmann, in celebration during one of the Linkow Seminars held in my cities in Germany.*

Inevitably speeches were made, mostly about me and my work, and I was always summoned to deliver the keynote address. I tried to say something new, inject some humor, show everyone that it was not just business we were doing, but forming friendships that I hoped would transcend the work.

Sunday marked the final day of the seminar. When it ended there was a question-and-answer session which could last for two hours. The awarding of certificates of attendance was always the finale of the agenda. Many participants would gather around me afterwards, shaking my hand and expressing their gratitude for my contributions to dentistry. This was the kind of treatment more often accorded a sports or a film star.

In 1970, while conducting a seminar in Frankfurt, I formed one of my closest friendships–but in a rather unexpected way. Although accustomed to obtaining volunteers from the audiences who would allow me to demonstrate my techniques, I was nonetheless surprised when Dr. Alfie Fiegel, an elderly man, made an offer. He had long been one of Switzerland's most distinguished dentists, and I was a bit taken aback. But when I examined his mouth, he became the patient and I the boss, but not happily so. He was suffering from severe, irreversible periodontal problems. In an unusual one-act drama staged for several hundred colleagues, I extracted many of his teeth, which had become loose in both jaws, and then inserted blade implants right through the cribriform (sockets) and into the interseptal bone between. Without these implants his only option was removable dentures, which to my mind was and is hardly any option at all. From that day, Alfie and I were best friends. Notably, soon after that procedure in Frankfurt he formed the Swiss Academy of Implantology. In 1995–twenty-five years later–Alfie still retained most of those implants.

*Dr. Alfie Feigel of Zurich, Switzerland, a very dear friend of mine and an excellent implantologist.*

Naturally the women were an added inducement for my many happy returns to Germany. In all my travels I have never met women so beautiful, so sensuous, endearing, and understanding as the German frauleins. One day, not long after the seminars had first been instituted, Hans Grafelmann brought two beautiful friends of his to hear me lecture. They were aware of my reputation and eager to meet me. Hans let me know that the choice was mine. Both of them were gorgeous, but one of them seemed strongly attracted to me. So Loren was the one.

I was staying at the Park Bremen Hotel, at the edge of the city. Of all my hotel suites, this was the first time that I could say I had slept in a palatial bedroom. It was the size of a five-room apartment, and not a five-room Manhattan apartment either. For those of you unfamiliar with average Manhattan apartments, it would take three standard five-room apartments in Manhattan to equal the size of one five-room home elsewhere in America. My Park Bremen room, fit for a king, must have spanned forty by fifty feet. The bathroom was a veritable grotto, and the ceiling extraordinary, soaring fourteen or fifteen feet and bordered by ornately carved molding. It was an architect's dream.

The gigantic windows reached nearly to the ceiling and provided a panoramic view of a vast and manicured deep green lawn. Hundreds of poplar trees flanked the grass; standing in rows as straight as lines of soldiers, they extended to a horizon perspective where the rows seemed nearly to converge. At the end of that huge expanse stood an antiquated carousel, out of commission for many years, the remnant of a bygone amusement park. Yet the proud, pretty wooden horses remained intact, and one could imagine that they were still moving to music that had ceased long ago.

After dinner I took Loren to my room, certain that she would be equally impressed. It lent a remarkable sense of freedom to be so splendidly accommodated. Our night together was passionate and blissful. I woke from a deep sleep to see her sitting beside me, gazing into my tired eyes. I felt very close to her. Our relationship didn't end when I left Germany. On the contrary, it grew stronger. We corresponded frequently and saw each other whenever I returned to Germany to conduct a seminar. She exclaimed many times that she was in love with me. This long-distance affair endured for four years, ending when she married a man from her own country who, of course, was a more dependable presence.

Was it a crime to seek out and love such beautiful people? Green mountains, fields of flowers and flitting butterflies, shimmering snowfields, the sun, the stars, the moon—one can admire all things in nature. Why not beautiful women, too, in a similar way, with great admiration and curiosity, but without shame? To touch, to make love to and be in love with—is this amoral, a sign of a Lothario, or simply of someone genuinely smitten by a lovely face, figure and persona? It grew clear that I was ever seeking that perfect woman: shapely, voluptuous, pretty, sensuous, intelligent and spirited. To find all this in one woman, and then sensitivity and patience, too, was perhaps too much to expect. Even though millions of such women could easily be on this planet, life is short and just once around, so the chance of falling truly in love with one such gal is a search seldom favored by the odds. Some are "lucky in love." At one period of my life I thought I found my true soul mate. Time sometimes heals everything—sometimes it doesn't.

I could identify with those lab experiments where mice are placed in the maze. The creatures rush from corner to corner, wall to wall, in a bid to find a pellet of food or escape from their prison. And all the while some scientist is watching, taking notes on behavioral conditioning, memory, intelligence, and so on.

Why did I have such inclinations? My dear mother, as I knew her, was a very shy woman. Although I know she loved me very much she seldom articulated her true feelings for me, rarely expressed grand emotion. We had pleasantly co-existed, each accepting the other without judgment or the need for approval. But I always felt the need to prove myself to my father. I knew he loved me, too, but if Mother was reserved, Father was repressed. Much later in life I realized why he couldn't tolerate imperfection or sickness. The reasons were key to his psyche. Although he always showed concern, he would be annoyed at any display of what he considered weakness. I deduced these to be symptoms of fear, and consciously or not I made an effort to live differently. In my adulthood this emerged as a decision to live robustly, and largely without the traits of shyness I had retained until entering the Army.

I believe that a driven person has many loves and a passion to live life large. Few so blessed—and maybe cursed—feel genuinely fulfilled with their counterpart or their present situation. Compromise becomes the rule. In success, the money, and the opportunity to be at least sharing center stage with one's foremost colleagues, whets the appetite for conquests in other venues. I have seen it over and over with my associates in implant societies throughout the world, especially in American academies. I recognize the signs: many married members have mistresses. Willie Nelson's song, "To All the Girls I Loved Before," illustrates the dilemma and sure brings back memories for me and many friends.

Needless to say, none of these liaisons helped my marriage to Wiesia. I loved her very much, but our relationship lacked vital intimacies of communication. She claimed to want to devote herself to me, which was wonderful. This implied a degree of flexibility, that she knew what my life entailed and was willing to adapt to the demands of an ever shifting landscape. Cancelled flights; a last-minute substitute destination or itinerary; a quickly arranged speaking engagement in another city; overlong office hours; weekends spent compiling notes for books and articles. Wiesia did not easily deal with this everevolving, stop-and-go, slow-motion and frantic orbit. Whenever a sudden schedule change altered our agenda, she became confused, angry or irrational, which turned me off. I was not the villain; the clock was! Would it be better if I had wasted

time in an alcoholic stupor, or toured golf courses a hundred
times a year? If, for example, we had dinner plans and a colleague arrived unexpectedly in town, I sometimes would want
him to join us. But almost invariably Wiesia would object. She
had a problem with spontaneity. That, or a need to be in control, or the center of attention. Even when I devoted time exclusively to her, if at the last moment I changed a reservation
at one restaurant in preference for another, she'd become
upset. "When you make plans you shouldn't have to change
them," she would protest. I'm sure that her years growing up
in Warsaw influenced this rigidity; Poland, a Communist country, seemed to have created in her such an addiction to con-
formity that she found it threatening to loosen up. This trait,
indeed, was a psychological red flag that, as with Rosita and
Jean, I had again misunderstood or ignored.

Wiesia really was a wonderful person, kind and loyal, but
seemed unwilling to overcome self-imposed limits to her per-
ception and imagination. She was not the "go-getter" type and
I think may have harbored hopes she could get me to adopt to
a more easygoing lifestyle. Impossible.

That said, she was a loving and tender companion who cared
about my interests and frustrations. I never had any doubts
that she tried to console me as best she knew how. Wiesia loved
me for my accomplishments, for my boldness and honesty. But
we were friends who, perhaps out of fear of loneliness, had
gotten married. I wanted and very much needed a soul mate.
As it was, again our marriage didn't provide it.

All the familiar symptoms of marital disintegration were there.
At home I was a baffled and annoyed husband, but abroad I was a
different man. There, I had a sense of freedom, not obligation.
In a successful marriage, it should be the other way around. Naturally I was eager for my trips to Italy and Germany. I seized every
opportunity to lecture and perform surgery, accepting engagements at Frankfurt, Munich, Bremen, Hamburg, Travermunde
and Dusseldorf. But mostly I stayed in Frankfurt and Munich,
where the majority of my seminars were held.

Although I was known at universities across the U.S. and internationally, I continued to meet heated professional opposition at home, especially in New York City. This had endured for nearly two decades. The main "establishment" die hards were a group of what I call "politician dentists." They had the free time to convene at dental society meetings strictly to network with other dentists so as to guarantee a steady stream of referrals. The goal is to perpetuate an "old boy" network so that only certain influential dentists will have patients referred to them. What is worse, many patients then endure lengthy or unnecessary, expensive and perhaps even counterproductive procedures. Thus, against all evident logic, the cycle feeds itself. The players in this chess game include dentists practicing under a variety of aliases: periodontists, prosthodontists, endodontists and exodontists, who were better known by the fancy (if silly) title, "maxillofacial surgeons." Now I call them "born-again implantologists."

You have gathered what I think of American dentists as a result of my encounters with their status quo mind-set. I direct my remarks to those politically minded dentists who for almost half a century have spoken for "the powers that be" in the First District Dental Society of Manhattan. (The very title makes it sound like a hierarchy, which to my mind puts in charge many of those who don't deserve to be in charge.) The Society remained intransigent towards me, even through the transfer of power from one generation of politicians to the next. On a par with lawyers, many of them are–pardon my candor–paranoid, egomaniacal, small-minded, greedy, nasty and envious. And they suffer from acute tunnel vision. Or perhaps worse, they lack any vision at all.

For example, in over forty years of practice, I obtained exactly and only two patients as a result of referrals from all my former School of Dentistry classmates. Nor was I ever invited to lecture at their monthly meetings. I was judged too controversial. Judged–of course, they loathe being judged in return–and treated as if I were a voodoo dentist. Ironically, though I was unwelcome, many of my former students, now successful in their own right, were eagerly invited to address their blessed conferences. Of course, to this day, whenever I meet these people in buildings, on the street, at this function or that, they pay a plethora of compliments. They respect my creation of, and leadership in, implant surgery. But no sooner did I turn my back than their attitude, it grew clear over the years, underwent a pronounced change. Am I paranoid? Or expressing resentment at the slings and arrows of unacknowledged mentoring? No; I am firmly but objectively identifying a disagreeable aspect of human nature where the self-righteous so often prevail over the strong-willed who know better. The latter are constrained by good taste and the overriding need for professional cooperation from speaking their minds. In other words, they have the good grace to turn the other cheek. But I have disdained such diplomacy, believing that such behavior is an affront to Mother Nature; twisting the law of survival of the fittest with cheap talk and deceptive tactics, and smiling about it, insults those who play by the rules and are content to do so. In the animal world, say, on the Serengeti Plains of Kenya, those creatures unable to keep pace with the herd or adapt to changes are left to perish. The law has a brutal simplicity: stay together and thrive, or fall out and be eaten. But ill-equipped humans survive, and even prosper, in their professions despite, and sometimes due to, a cunning refusal to compete fairly, notwithstanding codes of ethics—those natural and appropriate edicts of honest minds—that everyone has sworn to uphold in order to get a license. They realize, consciously or not, that they are insufficiently equipped to contribute to and win big in a business of astute and dedicated souls based on merit, so they resort to subversion to have their way.

I grew aware of this attitude during my fourth year in dental school, when I incurred the displeasure of my peers for collecting the clinical points required for graduation long before they did. Nor was it just the students; some of the instructors also felt threatened by me. Perhaps they felt I was upsetting some holy order of nature, or trying to rewrite or append its Darwinian precepts. If the strong simply survive, than the invincible will conquer all. But if they could have read my mind, ignored their insecurity, or been more incisive about my motivation, they would have seen that my hard work was nothing but overcompensation, a hedge against inadequacy or failure.

What particularly galls me is the accusation that I am an anachronism, that what I have to say is old-hat and easily heard elsewhere. What of my techniques have these dentists been striving to apply? They take a fourteen-hour weekend course in implantology–learning methods that I pioneered over years of trial, error, research and expense–then perform a few implant operations. Suddenly they're experts and my contribution is dismissed. It would be too much to expect credit that my innovations enable them to greatly improve their salaries prior to learning implantology. But should I be surprised? Dentists seldom say anything good about another, whether it is of manner or of methods. And I would bet that most dentists would agree with me, although they of course would deny any denigration of colleagues. Perhaps you can appreciate why I am a failed idealist, a cynic. We are doctors. Our prime directive is to help people. Not to form cliques to protect our own interests at the expense of truth and camaraderie, progress and innovation.

The sad truth is that nearly all malpractice suits in dentistry are instigated by another dentist. A patient's present dentist, by decrying the quality of work done by the previous dentist, and by commiserating about the pain that has been or will be caused by said work, will provoke a suit of this former dentist and then offer to testify–for a fee–on the patient's behalf if the case comes to trial. Personally, I believe that many patients who sue would not do so on their own volition. In large part, these lawsuits were inspired (if that is the word) by envious dentists who opposed implantology because they presumed it would deprive them of business.

My rivals become ecstatic the moment they have discovered any patient of mine who was having trouble. I can imagine their thoughts: "Here's a chance to nail Linkow." And I was far from the only victim. Other implantologists were also the target of unscrupulous lawsuits. Implantology itself was on trial. It seems to me that suits are like rolling dice. There doesn't seem to be any merit, much less justice, to many of the allegations and claims. They are laden with absurd assertions supported by bogus reasoning and flimsy proof. Lured by the buck, goaded by a lawyer, a plaintiff will assert just about anything and believe it to be gospel.

To be sure, not all well-meaning doctors avoid doing harm. Some fail to rise to the medical challenge; others are in over their heads. Even the best physicians, in all fields, make mistakes. Some of them even turn out to be tragic. But the last time I checked, doctors are human, like the rest of the population. A medical degree does not confer infallibility. Given the hundreds of thousands treated each day, the great majority of diagnostic or remedy errors are minor, and honest, and a far cry from the gross incompetence so many suits proclaim with such conviction. And I have observed that they increase in relative proportion to one's notoriety.

The greater my fame, the more my enemies, and the more I was beset by threats of suits and malicious rumors. My success, perversely enough, was in part gauged by how many people wanted a piece of my hide.

But in my view, my detractors were only weasels angling to make an extra buck on some hapless patient. My original dental work might have been excellent, but over time, for reasons somewhat beyond my control and/or responsibility a small percentage–10%–of the implants began to fail. Surely the dentist cannot be held accountable for the wear and tear that naturally occurs, or for the poor hygienic habits of the patient, or for those whose initial substandard condition posed a higher level of risk! What is more, implants aren't a TV or a car. There is no one-year or 50,000 mile warranty. Yet my critics–who often were members of the species that disdained Linkow and implantology in general–would wave every report of a patient's dissatisfaction, every half-baked research finding, as if it were Holy Writ. And the courts would rely upon them, largely because The Bench had scant criteria, other than the farce of a time-consuming trial, to measure such claims against my solid casework. It is disgraceful that our judicial system elevates these 'second opinion' characters into experts when nine times out of ten they are really the ones who lack technical knowledge and clinical expertise. The percentage of their ineptitude would seem to match the ratio of my success!

In the late 1980s and early 1990s a number of my colleagues asked me to be their expert witness in a lawsuit that had been filed against them. I have always been ready to do so, because it is my own work that is also being adjudicated. The plaintiff's expert witness is most often a dentist whose main, or only, qualification to be a witness (a well-paid witness, I might add, commanding hundreds of dollars per court appearance, negotiated and eventually paid, usually by the deep-pockets insurance company) is a weekend course to learn only how to perform a screw implant. Blade or subperiosteal implants are levels above what they grasp; if they had made the effort to learn, they would see the ingenuity of these systems and perhaps stop selling their profession short, and out. Then again, they would forfeit those sweet appearance fees for which, treated like celebrities, they are the center of attention around whom a tribunal sits awaiting his sagacious bombast.

It is exasperating to occasionally hear one of my patients describe a critic, whom they usually believe is some fine young fellow. They'll assure me that he was an 'implant expert,' notwithstanding that he only recently graduated from dental school, and that the techniques, tools and methodologies of implants are not mastered overnight. To hear about these "experts" from my patients is aggravating enough. But then they candidly admit that another amiable young dentist advised them not to consult me, contending that I had been sued so often that I couldn't possibly be competent. Sure, I have been

sued, but these suits contest a minimal percentage of the thousands of implants I have successfuly completed. Such nonsense
is not only appalling, it is near libelous. If many of the dolts
propounding this ran into me on the street they wouldn't know
me from a hole in the pavement. After all, my "reputation
proceeds me," and for small minds that is enough. But then
this shouldn't amaze me, either: from early in their careers
these dentists learn how to build themselves up by putting a
colleague down. It is a technique common to many professions, but especially that of dentistry, which I sardonically call
"the profession of brotherly love."

Other fields of medical practice and care are light years
ahead of dentists in ethics and mutual support. I do not believe that there exists a health profession with principles and
morals as disgraced as those defined by the dentists' "Code of
Ethics." Even in our prestigious American Academy of Implant
Dentistry are individuals who continue to support plaintiffs in
lawsuits against colleagues who are fellow members. This is scan-
dalous! It's all about money and ego. Not the work! How can a
professional system function when some component members
are falsely accusing fellows of negligence and/or incompetence?

I should, however, emphasize that there are a large number of ethical dentists, members of the American Dental Association, who are men and women of integrity and never get
involved in these nasty games. I am proud to know many of
them and respect and appreciate their work. More than that,
I am delighted to have many of them as friends and acquaintances.

The dentists I hold in high regard are, alas, outnumbered
by those propagating a cancer in dental societies by playing
the political card. Pretending to be advocates of our profession, they volunteer to oversee committees that make judg-
ments about many issues–like choosing whom to invite to address society meetings. The set of criteria is like a broken and
rusty machine. The ethical corruption that these politically

connected dentists encourage and engage in is no different in its cause or effect than that which has proven the undoing of much of our country's legal profession, or have besmirched our government.

What happens when a particularly dynamic individual comes along? If he hails from another state–meaning that he is a threat to no one's local business or profits–all well and good. He often is invited to deliver a lecture. It serves the host, too, suggesting he (or they) had cast far and wide in an objective search for new blood and fresh ideas. But if he lives in the town where the society has established a monopoly, he is less than welcome. The power brokers perceive him as an antagonist, as someone who is conspiring to steal their patients. It would be somewhat different if these princes actually made significant contributions to dentistry; that would be the price for advancing the profession as a whole. I would be glad to help pay for it. But instead they discriminate against deserving, innovative members of their profession so they can retain power. Thus nothing changes: year after year these same fellows have stepped up to the podium to deliver the same lectures that essentially amount to recycled paper. Out of politeness, or to retain their place in the pecking order, or in a collective fog of illusion, everyone pretends that they're hearing something new.

Though many will declaim me for making these statements, in their hearts many know that they are true.

It wasn't only my adversaries who induced misery by urging patients to press me with incessant litigation. Some of my patients also sued me on their own, disappointed that they hadn't gotten as many years from their implants as they had hoped. But instead of returning to me, where they would have had a ninety per cent chance of success from a second intervention, they instead relied on the advice of envious dentists who were eager to take all the implants out and substitute them for dentures. Once they had the patients in their confidence, or under their spell, they would encourage them to "sue Linkow."

Despite my share of suits I've only had to appear in court several times, and on two of those occasions I testified on behalf of another dentist. The other suits were settled before trial. But I still have a recurrent nightmare: I am served a summons and complaint commencing the Suit From Hell. For my antagonists such a document-weapon was easy to devise; for me it was like a shadow of terror. Each time I climbed a little higher on the ladder, the hands grasping to pull me down seemed stronger and more numerous.

And who were the individuals who made up the panels of arbiters, to whom the Society gave the power to judge dental work? Dear reader, you can guess: the politician dentists. In their archaic views, implants simply did not work. End of story. They held to the obsolete notion that if a tooth was loose then the only solution was to pull it; if it could be justified, pull all of them and make a denture. Then charge the patient a fat fee and wait until they returned with problems.

It was like being in two eras just plane hours apart: the Pleistocene Age in New York City, where a dinosaur hierarchy still ruled, and the Space Age in Europe, where dentists were eager for the high-tech knowledge I could, and gladly did, give them.

One day, while I was en route from Japan and my fifth seminar at the Linkow Academy of Implant Dentistry of Japan, I discovered words of consolation that have since greatly inspired me. I had been seething about the New York scene when I leafed through a Buddhist text that someone had given me as a present during my stay in Japan. I discovered the following passages:

"Endurance is one of the most difficult disciplines but it is to him who endures that the final victory comes."

"A scripture that is not read with sincerity soon becomes covered with dust; a house that is not fixed when it needs repairing becomes filthy; so an idle man soon becomes defiled. But the defilement to be most dreaded is the defilement of ignorance. A man cannot hope to purify either his body or mind until ignorance is removed."

The "political dentists" reviled me because not only was I successful–as they perceived it, at their expense–but because I had the fortitude to create a new discipline. Instead of learning this new discipline, they fought it. Their slogan might as well have been: "No lectures, no patients, and no credit for Linkow."

I've also found something Theodore Roosevelt wrote to be especially pertinent.

"It is not the critic who counts, not the man who points out how strong the man is who is actually in the arena, whose face is marred by dust and sweat and blood, who strives valiantly, who errs, and comes short again, because there is no effort without error and shortcoming, but who does actually strive to do deeds, who knows the great enthusiasm, the great devotion, who spends himself in a worthy cause, who at best knows in the end the triumph of high achievement, and who at the worst, if he fails, at least fails while daring greatly, so that his place shall never be with those cold and timid souls who know neither victory nor defeat."

However reassuring these words were, I still couldn't erase the pain and anger that these frustrations brought to my heart. Every time an attorney appeared in my office I excoriated him. Attorneys, I felt, were like gangsters. If this particular group of insurance/ malpractice attorneys were honest, then why would they eagerly represent the people who were obviously initiating suit for their own gain, and not for a higher ethical or legal crusade? What, to make the world safe for dentistry? Why else but for money would they be so concerned about protecting racketeers instead of guarding the rights of honest victims by denying the merits of these lawsuits? Their responses to my brutal candor were flimsy and equivocal. What is worse, they evinced absolutely no compassion for the distraught victims. Their excuse was a variation on the theme: "Every person is entitled to a fair trial."

So be it.

In 1971 I allowed myself to be "sweet talked" into signing over my blade implant patents to a company that was planning to go public. The market was ripe for an aggressive company with an innovative and high quality product line, and this one had been specifically set up as a sales enterprise. Against the advice of many friends—especially my dear friend Jack Wimmer, an excellent businessman who had proved his acumen with the very lucrative sale of his own superlative dental laboratory and dental supply business—I consented to and signed a contract. It called for me, the inventor, to receive a $7,000 a year. But the man who formed the company, Chad Witty, who was ostensibly responsible for raising venture capital of several hundred thousand dollars, immediately granted himself *$60,000* and an unlimited expense account. And he saw to it that this account was indeed unlimited. My patents; his annuity. The company was given rights to manufacture any invention I might design in the future. Loyal, diligent and foolish to the last, I innovated widely and made major improvements to my existing implants. But despite what I believed were ironclad guarantees that my work would be produced, this company failed to manufacture them! They simply refused to do it. We effectively had no collaboration. I was simply a brain to be periodically picked for the enrichment of others, and paid a pittance in the bargain.

Apparently, Witty, the president, had evidently and secretly decided that unless the patents were in *his* name he would block their production. In retrospect, I now believe that the entire scheme was to wait while I did the work, for nominal money, and then somehow appropriate the designs, claiming the patent rights and of course collecting the royalties, all under the grateful aegis of the company Board. If he brought them money, they were only too glad to look the other way. I was too naive to understand this until much later. But I should have known; the signs were there. Witty was a dentist himself and apparently admired my expertise. We had been classmates at New York University School of Dentistry. Since he found it difficult to understand the advantages of my new designs, he chose to remain with a family of blade implants where his name appeared with mine on one of the patents. Taking advantage of his expense account, he would ensconce himself in a lavish hotel suite, declaring that nothing less would do because he required the proper setting to display and sell the implants in the evenings once my seminars, which to him were virtual promotion fests, had concluded. He often would travel to the cities where I was giving a seminar. Succumbing to his hunger for acknowledgement and accepting his sales rationale, I arranged for him to lecture for an hour during my two—or three-day seminars. Since the sponsoring institutions only paid my fees and expenses, he naturally billed the company for his time and travel. Talk about the best of all worlds! Exploiting knowledge he had little experience with, and making money on a product he didn't invent. I was extremely angry with him those many years ago.

(In fairness, I qualify my candor with this: in ensuing years he developed into an excellent implantologist, quite wise in the range of techniques and technologies.)

My only excuse, and admittedly a poor one, is that I was blinded by business ignorance. Since my early university days, I had spent the greatest portion of my time in massive, rote learning or in development, surgery and seminars, not mulling over investment opportunities or tax shelters. It was a language I did not speak well, nor did I find it interesting enough to learn. A further incentive was an unfounded fear that should I be forced into a do-or-die confrontation with the "powers that be," my work in someone else's name was safer and less stressful. Last but not least I wanted to be respected, and desired to advance the dental profession as a whole, and gain wider recognition for my underappreciated specialty. Not necessarily in that order. In any case, I was gullible to Witty's blandishments and grandiose talk. He was a consummate seducer.

This clarity in my outlook took years to achieve. At first, I

didn't understand what was happening. I had been "snowed."
After several years of increasingly impatient waiting, I concluded I had been stymied in America. Mate. But not check.
After getting no firm commitment from Dr. Witty as to the
status of my work, I saw that my only alternative was to find a
manufacturer abroad to make my new designs. In this, I sought
the indispensable help of Giorgio Gnalducci. As always he came
through. Consequently, I ended up using only Italian-made
implants, whether in my surgical procedures or for seminar
demonstrations. And frankly, they were as good or better than
any American fabrications could have been. Meanwhile, Dr.
Witty's company continued to hold my domestic patents for
the original devices. Of course, Dr. W and the other company
executives were furious and threatened to sue me, their cash
cow, if I didn't stop using the Italian implants and, according
to him, rightfully so. But at no point, despite my explicit contract, did they ever actually commit to manufacture my Italian
devices in the U.S.! This was arrogant self-interest, writ large
and obscenely. What is more, as I said, the Italian implants were
improvements over the older American models and I was not
about to practice with any devices that were less than what I
considered state-of-the-art. Dr. Witty & Co. had been given
the chance for a lucrative and mutually beneficial partnership.
They ignored me. So I returned the favor.

I resigned as chairman of the board at about the end of
the company's first year and surrendered a company credit
card authorized for up to $10,000 a year. I was motivated at
least in part by fears that the stockholders would sue me because so little money had been made. Meantime, Dr. W continued to draw an $80,000-a-year salary for a job that required
him to be in the office only three days a week! But even so he
wasn't content. He would spend the next fifteen years filing
suits against AAID and dental companies for various grievances,
real and imagined. And of course, he sued me. Suing people
became another vocation for him. Through non-stop legal fees
(buying his power), promotional expenses (buying his friends),

his penchant for indulgence (buying illusion), and general poor management (buying time)–all of which can fall under the general heading of incompetence–he drained the company and caused it to sink into ever greater debt. Somehow Dr. W hoodwinked the stockholders when they complained. Too bad and how sad he failed to use these talents to turn the company into a dynamo. After I resigned he brought in a gaggle of his friends as board of directors, none of whom appeared to give a damn how the company would stay afloat. They even authorized a subsidy for all the frivolous litigation, and any other expenses that Dr. Witty could concoct.

Years after the company's inception I became fully aware of Dr. W's duplicity; during lawsuit proceedings the court judge informed me of the facts. While it had been my contractual understanding that the patents were registered in my name alone, Witty had contrived to put one of them, which he did help to design, in the names of himself and his wife as well as my own. Not coincidentally, this particular patent, my third blade patent, was the very one he was more than happy to manufacture and sell! He declined, however, to manufacture my newer, improved devises, reasoning, with some justification, that he would be unlikely to pull off the same duplicity again without being discovered. In retrospect, this chicanery appears perfectly obvious, but it caught me completely by surprise. It took me eleven years to fully shake off Dr. W's shrewd influence.

Here is the sequence of my blade patents:

Patent No. 3,465,441—filed March 20, 1968—patented Sept. 9, 1969

Patent No. 3,660,899—filed Sept. 16, 1970—patented May 9, 1972

Patent No. 4,024,638 – filed Feb. 24, 1969, patented May 24, 1977

Patent No. 3,729,825—with Dr. W—filed Aug. 2, 1971—patented May 1, 1973

Patent No. 3,849,888—filed Oct. 19, 1973—patented Nov. 26,
   1974

So you can see I had filed and/or been granted three previous blade implant patents before my fourth with Dr. W.

In hindsight, a sense that many have improved as they get
older–if they pay attention–Dr. W and I have buried the hatchet.
Not in each other, but in the block of time. For all our misun-
derstandings there is one great credit I must give to Dr. Witty.
He has remained loyal to the implant and has been a force in
keeping the various systems propounded by me and others at
the forefront of dental technology. Of course, this is part self-
interest, but in his case at least it also demonstrates a particular
acuity lost on others who admittedly seem to be more scrupu-
lous in their business practices but have also made it a sport to
oppose me. And so, on occasion, Dr. W and I speak and even
meet socially, somehow enjoying each other's company. After
all, some Union and Confederate generals, on opposite sides
in the Civil War, were known to have afterward hoisted a few
glasses to each other's bravery and skill.

However, as I look back at our early relationship I must say
that much I mentioned in the preceding paragraphs was
prompted by my anger and frustration. Perhaps things were
not as bad as they seemed at the time. Indeed, we now meet
for dinner at least every month. I guess Chad had a great deal
of anger toward me also.

My bad luck with patents–which have been proven to be of
great benefit to people–stands in marked contrast to those of
Dr. P.I. Bränemark. Now there is a lucky man. Dr. Bränemark
is a Swedish orthopedic doctor whose main contribution to
implantology was the development of a submergible two-piece
screw. Bränemark coined the multimillion dollar term
"osseointegration." This meant that by first burying the screw
for three to six months before attaching the abutment, bone

would grow against the screw, locking it in place. In principle this was not wrong. But many of the screws and implants designed for immediate function–which were also osseointegrated–worked just as well as those that had been buried before being made functional, i.e., have teeth attached to them. The Swedish screw is supposed to have been invented in the 1980's but, in fact, it is an old device developed by Dr. Bränemark two years after I developed my early vent-plant screw implants in 1963. And its design has not varied since that year, 1965. In 1975 Bränemark published a tiny book about the work he had done between 1965 and 1975, but there was no disguising the fact from trained and knowing eyes that his results were far from excellent. And once the Swedish screw was actually lodged inside someone's mouth, the cosmetic effect was the worst ever, as was seen in the photos published in his own book. Entitled "Osseonintegrated implants in the treatment of the edentulous jaw: experience from a 10-year period" (Bränemark P.L. et al. Scand. J. Plast. Reconstr. Surg., (16) 1-1B2, 1977, it shows the poor cosmetics and the various "confusing" charts on success and failure.

Bränemark, however, had two things going for him. First of all, Sweden has a nationalized health care system. The government foots the bill for patients. Secondly, he had the backing of the powerful Nobel Pharma Company, its parent organization being an armaments company founded by Alfred Nobel, the inventor of dynamite, who put up the money for the prizes that bear his name. With its extraordinary resources, Nobel Pharma is able to dominate much of the manufacture and sale of dental implants throughout the world, and is also one of the world's largest medical equipment and supply houses, period.

The government paid for Bränemark's periodic follow-up examinations, supplying him with a large backlog of cases from which to draw data. He used these data to publish the first real study describing his conclusions. But it was cluttered with many different charts. The results were obscured, perhaps deliberately, and few American doctors realized just how poor they were. My staff broke out all the statistics and combined the profusion of charts into just four. And the poor results were quickly obvious. Although I published a paper that exposed the Bränemark system's failings, few people ever read it. Clearly the dental profession was being "Branewashed" by the aggressive and deceptive Nobel Pharma people.

Nobel Pharma spends multimillions annually on marketing. In the case of the screw, their first step was a survey to assess the situation of oral surgeons. It must have soon become clear to them that many oral surgeons were financially strapped, in large part because they had missed Linkow's early boat to implant heaven, and even almost twenty years later, remained ignorant about the methods and procedures of the specialty. They were behind the curve because most of them had refused to take the same course with general-practitioner dentists. (There is a self-evident maxim–which many tend to ignore–that says if you think you know everything, you cannot learn anything new. To which I add that sooner or later there is a harsh lesson for snobbery.) Also, as more and more of the general practitioners took postgraduate courses, they were extracting their patients' teeth–doing apicoectomies and alveolectomies–instead of sending them to oral surgeons (exodontists) to do the extractions for them. This quite negatively impacted the income of oral-surgeons. And this group, naturally, became an inviting target for Bränemark marketers.

Nobel Pharma devised a strategy: permit only the oral surgeons to take the Bränemark course, and let them be the only ones to use the implants. This effectively established a monopoly among oral surgeons. It also ensured that the beneficiaries of that monopoly would battle any attempt to weaken what amounted to a cartel. Not all oral surgeons jumped at the bait, but many did and were hooked. Bränemark became their guru and master. With religious fervor they grasped the lifeline that had been thrown to them.

The first claim made by the Bränemark partisans in these Swedish screw classes was that many blade implants failed. They then showed how these failing implants could be replaced by the Swedish screw. The syllogism imparted to these neophytes was unmistakable: that where blade implants failed, Swedish screws would succeed, and thus that blade implants were inferior to screws. The dentists who attended these classes had no frame of comparison to temper this black-and-white view. They overlooked that, in medicine as in life, there are few absolutes. Absolutes, however, are handy as marketing tools. As in: ours works; his is junk. So the oral surgeons preached the concept of the Swedish screw as if it were a revival. It was, for them. Nobel Pharma paid for newspaper and TV advertising, extolling the design of the screws and hawking them to thousands of people who didn't know any better, especially senior citizens living in retirement villages who prevailed upon their dentists to use them. Ironically, I myself introduced the very first self-tapping screw type implant, which I named the ventplant.

As you might expect, it is very difficult to fight such tactics backed by a copious flow of money. Nobel Pharma has since supplied many universities throughout the world with their Swedish screw, gratis or at a fraction of its typical cost, assuring that the university's faculty will use its product in classes. How do you contend against a Goliath who will deceive to sell his wares? I often wondered if my slingshot would last long enough.

But all in all, Bränemark's book was written honestly, often explaining and illustrating that in numerous instances it would take as many as three surgical procedures after the first two failures before success was to occur. However, the confusion of his success rates as shown in his charts were not so much a factor of the remaining implants themselves but the retainment of the prostheses. In other words, if six screw implants were used to support a fixed bridge or removable "snap on" overdenture and three of them failed but the prostheses still remained functional, he claimed 100% success, when actually only 50% of the implants remained.

# Fifteen

## TRAVELS AND TRAVAILS

I shall never forget an episode that occurred in Giorgio Gnalducci's Milano office. The tiny lady I diagnosed, then in her fifties, had been fitted with Scialom needle implants perhaps two years before. In the previous two months they had become very loose and continually painful, and had to be removed. As they were poorly affixed I could do so very quickly, preparatory to fitting her with more appropriate implants. But the session did not go the way I had planned.

To recap: Scialom, the Frenchman who invented the pin or "needle" implants, together with Tambura de Bello, the Italian implantologist who set up "needle" franchises throughout dental offices in Italy, had informed the police that I was illegally performing "blade" surgery at the Cavalieri Hilton Hotel in Rome. Their action was another concerted and devious attempt to corner the Italian market for their own, now-primitive implants, and do so by preventing the introduction of my more sophisticated devices and techniques.

I started the surgery to remove the Scialom pin implants from this little signora. I opened her mouth; she screamed. I probed her teeth; she screamed loudly, loudest. Giorgio sympathetically stroked her head. "I am so sorry for you, you poor lady," he said, "but soon Dr. Linkow will remove all of those terrible, terrible implants."

And he made sure he said it clearly, because the entire operation was being recorded on closed-circuit television.

I stopped, reluctant to continue the extraction because of her unceasing shrieks. When I requested more anesthesia for her, Giorgio responded immediately with several injections. He urged me to not rush, but go very slowly.

When a procedure is painful, there are two methods of work. One is to proceed gently and gradually, to avoid causing a big shock of pain. The pain of course persists for a longer interval, but there is less at any one time. The other method is to get the procedure over with quickly, if possible; while the pain will be greater, it is mercifully short-lived. The chosen method depends upon many factors, but the essential one is the patient's temperament. Giorgio advised the slow method, and I concurred. She was his patient, after all, and I had only seen her briefly. Perhaps he thought that if I pulled everything out with one hard jerk it would be too great a jolt.

But the injections of local anesthetics seemed to have no effect on the poor lady's pain. She continued to howl. And, of course, the cameras dispassionately recorded the entire scene. Deeply embarrassed and frustrated by her great discomfort, I finished at last.

I expressed my vexation as Giorgio and I headed for his home that evening. Unable to contain himself, he erupted in peals of devious laughter. The entire performance, he said, was a set-up to tarnish the image of Scialom and de Bello. The injections he'd given the little lady had contained only water! They were a placebo! I was furious! Giorgio had caused the woman needless pain. I regretted not having quickly concluded the procedure. Even as I vented much anger at him Giorgio continued to convulse with cackles.

By the next day we were friends again. A compadre like Giorgio, a dear and good man in so many ways, can also have grievous faults. He had done a terrible thing, in my opinion, by breaking several ethical rules of medicine. Even though we were helping the woman, what we had done amounted to torture for personal benefit. But Giorgio was still my friend because his generosity far outweighed any callousness or self-interest.

\* \* \*

In the summer of 1975 my agenda and my patience hit overload. There was a break in the on-going series of round-the-world seminars. For the time being, there was little to do. I was compelled to take a rest. Where better to turn than my paisan, Giorgio? He certainly wasn't a man to let anything stand in the way of fun. So I spent the only two-week vacation I've taken since I became a dentist in his company. He and his Russian girlfriend invited Wiesia, my younger daughter Sheree and I to join them on a cruise off Ibiza and the coast of Spain aboard Giorgio's magnificent 78-foot yacht. Naturally, we were treated to gourmet meals, prepared on board by his two cooks. One day, basking in the endless Iberian sunshine, we gazed astern. There cruised a boat that was even larger than Giorgio's, proudly flying a Swiss flag that flapped in the crisp, dry breeze. What a look crossed our captain's mug when he came up from below. Giorgio, who had always regarded himself as king of the sea, now had to eat humble pie; his position had been usurped by an interloper! He was so stung by the perceived humiliation at the sight of the craft that it ruined his day and nearly scuttled his vacation.

Combining my fondness for boats with my ability to mismanage business affairs was a recipe for calamity. During the time I was married to Jean we had owned a condominium in St. Thomas, in the U.S. Virgin Islands. We would often spend weekends there in the winter. Sometimes I would return to New York and the office by Monday, leaving Jean and her sister there to spend a few more days in the sun. One night, shortly after I'd gotten back to New York, I was awoken from a deep sleep by the ringing phone. It was Jean, all excited. "Lenny," she said, "you must buy this thirty-nine foot yawl I saw–and you can get a great bargain. It recently sailed from England across the Atlantic Ocean and it's now here in St. Thomas. I met two lovely young boys who are both sea captains–I know, they showed me their licenses. They want to live on the boat and take passengers on daily cruises to visit the islands nearby. They'll have lunch prepared on the boat and guess what? They say they'll weave straw hats for the passengers. And what's more, you can get a tremendous tax deduction and a write-off."

I fell for this lunacy. I should have known better: on the very first cruise with its new "sailors," the boat capsized somewhere between St. Thomas and St. Kitt. I hired Bart, a fellow I had played several sets of tennis with and who owned a boat basin, to find them. Bart in turn had to hire a small plane to fly over the accident site. Once this had been accomplished, the boat was towed to the nearest island, repaired, and then returned to St. Thomas by Bart, who sold the boat for me at a forty percent loss. And if it weren't for my tennis friend the loss would have been greater still. The two so-called captains were never seen or heard from again. About a year later several island newspapers carried a story about my ex-yawl–on which I had never so much as set one foot. It had been seized somewhere in the Caribbean with several million dollars' worth of cocaine on board. What luck, I thought. At least I wasn't still the owner; it was one thing to lose several thousand dollars on a bad business deal, but at least I had avoided the Drug Enforcement Agency's most-wanted list.

These relatively minor misfortunes were offset by the considerable success I had met in the publishing world. Though I had written innumerable articles on implantology for various dental journals, my true achievement was the two massive volumes of *Theories and Techniques of Oral Implantology* (C.V. Mosby Co., St. Louis, Mo., 1970). This visionary work anticipated techniques years, even decades, ahead of their common acceptance. And, of course, it upset the tidy notions of many dentists, who felt compelled to resist the concepts I endeavored to share and had slaved to lay out in text and picture. The first print run of five thousand books sold out, but the publisher was unwilling to finance another edition because the books were expensive to produce and took too long to sell. They were also well ahead of their time; the market had not yet evolved for them. In the end, it's all about cash flow, not about improving medical procedure or public health.

The human head is the ultimate marvel of known biological engineering. Neurosurgeons and plastic surgeons, ophthalmologists and dental surgeons and other specialties spend decades discovering its wonders. There are twenty-two bones and eleven ligaments surrounding the–literal–jewel in the crown of the human brain. The mouth, especially, is a splendid multi-function device, but most of us take eating, tasting, talking and breathing for granted. The teeth, for example, are thirty-two separate but integrated units that are vital to eating, talking and appearance. Only when one or more of these functions grows difficult or painful does a patient become keenly aware of the jaws and teeth. The teeth are intended to be permanent, but in many people, quite clearly, they do not remain so, and sometimes for much less than half of their lives. Genes and hygiene play more or less equal roles. When failure comes, I am one of those they turn to for help.

I offer the mini-essay, "Changes in Surgical Direction According to the Underlying Bony Topography."

Bone always resorbs at the expense of the buccal and labial bone [cheek and lip side], resorbing obliquely from the horizontal plane. The channels for blade insertions therefore must always be directed obliquely off the horizontal plane nearer to the palatal side [tongue side] of the maxillary crest and away from the labial and buccal side. In this manner the labial and buccal surfaces are preserved rather than resorbed if the implants were placed nearer to that surface. Also, the necks of the implants, whether blades, screws or subperiosteal implants, must emanate from the palatal side of the crest (lingual side of the crest in mandible) because those are the only areas attached to gingival or at least keratinized tissue.

New techniques were inspiration for further writing about procedures the dental community could practice. In 1977 I showed how a blade implant could gently separate and lift up the sinus membrane from the bone beneath without perforating the sinus. Then Hilt Tatum developed the lateral approach technique. The sinus membrane is raised by first carefully cutting a small rectangular area of bone on the cheek side of the sinus, then pushing the bottom portion of the rectangle upward so the rectangle becomes the top wall, while simultaneously separating the thin sinus membrane from the bone that surrounds it. Synthetic bone and freeze-dried bone are pushed into the area below, in front of, and in back of the membrane. The bone mixture is also added on the cheek side of the membrane as the membrane itself is raised. This creates an area of bone below the newly raised sinus deep enough to enable the insertion of endosseous screws, cylinders, or blades. I published the news about the technique in my 1990 three-volume book, *Implant Dentistry Today: A Multidisiplinary Approach.* I consider these the bibles of implantology. Dr. Hilt Tatum did a massive amount of research for this procedure. Other dentists, including Manuel Chanavez, Bob James, Dennis Smiler, Carl Misch and Jon Wagner also made a significant contribution.

GoreTex, the synthetic wonder material (commonly used in outdoor clothing, but having many other applications), was used to grow more bone over a failing implant or over an implant that wasn't buried deeply enough. It also was used for covering a site where, due to thin bone, the wider implant was perforated through it, allowing more bone to freely grow lateral to it. GoreTex does not shrink, it is not incorporated into the bone, and it doesn't decay. A thin sheet, emplaced over the bony lesions, provided protection from any epithelial or fibrous tissue invagination which would prevent bone growth.

Several years later, however, I realized that in most cases the GoreTex-based procedures did not work well. The lateral sinus lift techniques, however, have remained quite effective.

My two new volumes, *Maxillary Implants: A Dynamic Approach to Oral Implantology* was followed in 1982 by its companion *Mandibular Implants: A Dynamic Approach to Oral Implantology* (both by Glarus Pub. Co., North Haven, Connecticut). They contained between them thirty-five hundred pictures and line drawings. The text was so tightly written that I don't believe there was a single sentence which could have been deleted. Later I wrote two more books–*Dental Implants Can Make Your Life Wonderful Aqain* (Speller Brothers Pub. Co., New York, NY, 1983) and *Without Dentures* (Frederick Fell Pub., Inc., Hollywood, Fla., 1987)–for the general public.

The joy I derived from these accomplishments, however, was not shared by my wives. Maybe I'm only imagining that they weren't interested, or perhaps my expectations for their enthusiasm were unrealistic. But it seemed they primarily desired the gratification and security of a full-time husband, not a partner challenging the tenets of his chosen field, of pursuing his life's work with rare passion. My first wife, Rosita, who was already long gone during the 1970s, my most progressive and demanding years, certainly had no professional dynamic, nor much knowledge of her husband's aspirations, and had little or no desire to learn. I had served two purposes: to provide her with a life of luxury, and to assuage her ego. Jean, however, was from the beginning fully aware of the goals Leonard Linkow, DDS had set out to attain. Her complaints, therefore, rang hollow. She had worked for me so to my mind she entered the marriage fully aware of my schedule, hours, works in progress, and the demands of running a business on the cutting edge. I indeed wished for a respite, a window to relax for a month or more. No one wanted it more than me. Doctors and other professionals routinely got away from the battlefront for some R&R. But in the 1970s and 1980s I was the general, the troops, the supply depot, the sharpshooter, the reconnaissance and the staging area in a long campaign. Without me the offensive was sorely strained. In the face of the opposition, leisure time was tantamount to dropping my guard or, worse, waving the white flag. Why be the swimmer who brags he intends to swim the Atlantic, trains for years, invests his total energy, reputation and soul, enters the water, traverses half the distance, then claims he has grown fatigued–and turns around and goes back whence he came? My philosophy: go all the way or stay out of the game. There was no bullpen or half-time for Leonard Linkow. No surrender or retreat. Always forward, even if it is just an inch at a time. Such is a workaholic's credo.

My wives had every opportunity to develop lives of their own. Sure, I led an existence quite apart from theirs. It was another world, of foreign cities and galas, of intellectual rigors and technical commitment. By definition, this was a world that I alone–of our marriage partnership, that is–could comfortably inhabit. Unfortunately, there was little room for common, trivial domestic needs: to dine out mid-week, bring home some ice cream, take the car for an oil change. Jean and Wiesia expected such attention to detail, but my mind was often elsewhere and I made no apologies for it. The money I made, the respect of my international colleagues, the excitement I generated by my passionate promotion of implantology, was not bestowed on a part-timer, a dilettante or an opportunist. I was in this for the long haul, as a way of life in itself, not as a means to support a lifestyle nor as a daily hiatus from a marital agenda. I was hunting triumph–complete and unconditional victory over the forces of time and opinion–and simply not equipped to resign my seven-seas battleship commission for a harbor-bound sloop.

What was happening to me? As if watching another person in a surreal, intimate drama, I saw myself giving up friends, my wife and colleagues. I became a recluse as I plunged ever-deeper into work to devise new designs for implants and armamentarium, to improve surgical techniques and procedures.

I didn't know what a vacation was. Although I traveled the world over for my lecturing commitments, I almost never toured the places I visited. I was never able to spend an extra day in any location to simply enjoy myself. I needed the income from the next engagement to pay off my never-ceasing debts for equipment, research, prototypes, travel, business expenses. Then there was the alimony and child support I was obligated to pay. In 1975 I had seventeen patents–by 1994 that number had grown to thirty-three–but my ineptitude at business had seen to it that I earned virtually no income from any of them. They should have made me millions!

# Sixteen

## BESET AND BELEAGUERED

I had founded the Institute for Endosseous Implants with several other colleagues in the late 1960s. I chose Dr. Isaiah Lew, some years senior to myself and a great implant pioneer, as the first president. Every couple of weeks the two of us would gather together audiences of interested dentists at Polyclinic Hospital (formerly French Hospital) in downtown Manhattan. Dr. Lew and I would preside over candid debates that grappled with alternative techniques and procedures. These informal conventions were valuable forums for dialogue with an assembly of peers. It was a form of exercise, a method of rejuvenating the field. The recent scene has changed, and not for the better; when implantologists congregate the arguments tend to revolve around politics or money. The meetings are usually of little benefit to those who would come simply to learn. Many of the lecturers are on the payroll of the multi-million dollar marketing companies who have one two-part goal in mind: selling their exclusive systems to a paying audience by making their wares appear to be the greatest of all possible implantology evolutions.

After developing my first titanium vent-plant screw-type implant in 1963, I naturally assumed it made sense to discuss it

*One of the great implant pioneers, Dr. Isaiah Lew, myself and my lifetime friend, Dr. Bruce Fishel.*

at one of the meetings. Believing myself among an august, like-minded assembly, I told them I was certain that the bone itself–and not just fibrous connective tissue–would grow through the vents. To my surprise and dismay, the group took this for an absurd declaration. The meeting nearly devolved into a fracas. How could bone grow inside a foreign body? my fellow dentists demanded. What they failed to recognize was that the implant was inorganic; the body would accept it. If it were organic, such as a reimplanted tooth, or a lung or a kidney from a donor, the immune system, programmed with a rigid genetic code unique to the recipient's body, would form antibodies to attack it and antigens to expel it as an intruder. But this wasn't the case with my metal vent implants. One need only look to the staples and pins of orthopedics for corroboration.

The people who disagreed with me, though mistaken in

their underlying assumptions, at least were being honest. About a year later, however, another controversy erupted wherein the motives of its instigators were far more questionable. I began to glean from some of my patients that various colleagues were spreading malicious rumors about implants. These patients would in some way come to an oral surgeon, a periodontist or some other dental specialist–at a party, or through a referral if they had tooth pain or suffered an implant failure and I was out of town. On examination they were often told that through implants they could contract cancer or a virulent infection, suffer irreversible bone loss, and so on. My patients were naturally frightened by such a prognosis. Although I successfully countered the decisions of a few, I was compelled to remove many successfully functioning vent-plants. But I did so with total bone blocks. Then I sent the bone blocks, containing the implants, to histopathologists such as Dr. Robinson from the NYU College of Dentistry and Dr. Greene at Buffalo University, and later and most exclusively to Dr. Carl Donath at the University of Hamburg, one of the finest in the world. The specimens were parsed into hundreds of ultra-thin slices which were examined under high-powered microscopes. They could observe exactly what kind of tissue had been growing against the implants. There would be no hiding the facts should the dire predictions prove correct.

The conclusion: the tissue was healthy. There was never any danger of cancer, infection or bone loss. I subsequently published the results of the histopathologists' findings in one of my books and in several articles. The irrefutable conclusion: bone did in fact grow through the vents. Not occasionally. Always, if the implant was functioning successfully. Because I expressly designed it to be so. When I reminded my sanctimonious colleagues in our periodic gatherings that my objective investigation had thoroughly vindicated my practices, they acted astonished that I would even raise the issue. Their irksome response was usually something like, "Well sure, so what? We all knew that."

Michel de Montaigne, the great 16th century French essayist, observed that when a discovery is made it is untrue. Twenty years later it is true but unimportant. Forty years later it is true, it is important . . . but, I added, we have something better now anyway so why make a fuss about it?

I earlier called dentistry the "profession of brotherly love." I was being sardonic, of course. Now, I no longer use this phrase even in disdain, for no love is lost among dentists. I've rarely heard one dentist say a kind word about another. It's true that the competition and rivalry, sometimes bitter, between such giants as Salk and Sabin, Cooley and DeBakey, and Pasteur and Lister is legendary, but on a dramatic and ethical level their tales are seldom a match for the disputes among dentists. I don't know what it is about the human mouth. When it comes to envy, I believe that among all medical professionals dentists come out "numero uno."

*Very early in my career, my Dad, who was an ultra-conservative man, was only worried that the "powers that be" would send me to prison for the "experimental work" I had been doing.*

One item of strange behavior I discovered about the profession is that it apparently is not even necessary to have an acquaintance with a dentist in order for another dentist–or many dentists in one sweep–to feel threatened. Here's a case in point. I had just completed an all-day seminar at the Rochester Dental Society. During the lunch break their president asked if I would consent to an interview with a newspaper reporter. My guard lowered and antennae retracted, and delighted to be written about rather than doing the writing, in the spirit of generosity I accepted the request. And courted disaster. The young woman rookie reporter, when later writing her piece, made several large and amateurish mistakes. (I try to be indifferent if someone is naive or incompetent–as long as I am excluded from the consequences.) What is more, she evidently found implantology by itself to be too dull. She believed, or had been taught, that good journalism equaled conflict, and thus was compelled to spike her work with controversy. This being a subject free of murder and espionage, she had to do *something* to spike the punch. So what if the interviewee might rue the outcome? It would not be her problem. She wouldn't even know about it! As ever, I trusted the process and was blind to the dark alleys. Deferring to the power of the press, I proceeded to be mugged.

One question she had asked was, "Are implants more difficult to do than removable dentures?" It was a direct, forthright question, and easy enough to answer. I told her the simple truth: for a number of reasons–which I briefly explained–the answer was yes. But the article was quite at odds with what I had in fact asserted. Dr. Linkow said "implants are much more difficult and more skill is required than in making a removable denture, where very little skill is required."

The commotion this "quote" created is hard to overstate. The distortion spread like a virus. Prosthodontists (specialists in removable dentures) in Rochester regarded this statement as a concession of my defeat, of my unworthiness, in that I had to denigrate others to redeem myself. Tufts University in Boston, where the continuing-education courses I directed each year were packed, canceled a forthcoming date, stating that they could no longer invite me because I was too "hot" for them. University officials remained unmoved even after I swore that the quotes were a fabrication, and I offered to sue the newspaper. I surmised that my colleagues/rivals in the establishment had been waiting for me to make a mistake, or even merely appear to make one. This contrived newspaper article, summum bogus journalism, was their cue. They offered it as proof positive that since I held many of my colleagues, or at least their skills, in low esteem, they were justified in so holding me.

But I wasn't too hot for everyone. Indeed, because of the momentum of implantology, I was so overwhelmed by lecture commitments that I was obliged to send my friend, Dr. Paul Glassman, out to cover some of the engagements for me. A very articulate fellow, Paul loved to deliver lectures using my slides. There was only one problem: after he had given lectures dozens of times on my behalf, and become very familiar with the material, he began to act as if it were his own work he was talking about. I overlooked it because he really was a fine friend, dedicated and brilliant. Unfortunately, in 1979 he was forced to end his practice abruptly on account of a tragic auto accident. Nonetheless, he has remained involved in dentistry, lecturing to various implant clinics and societies.

Paul wasn't the only dentist to assume a proprietary interest in my work. One time, in the late 1960's, I lent some of my slides to Sidney Freed, another colleague who needed assistance in a table clinic he was set to direct. Sid, bless his heart, began to talk of my work in a possessive fashion. What made the experience quite irksome was that I sat in the audience, in plain sight. Even after I caught his eye–projecting my displeasure as if a telepath–he went right on, unblinking and unfazed. I was flabbergasted. When Sid was through I marched over and candidly asserted that he was presumptuous and self-serving. Rather than explain, however, he acted like he was the offended party. Sid turned his back and left me standing there, feeling like a fool. So much for collaboration. One odd measure of success, I suppose, is the envy and posturing it arouses in others.

While these were isolated incidents in my career I believe they help to reflect a larger problem. In sum, implantology has often attracted the wrong type of dentists: those seeking a quick buck, who may be willing to ignore the learning curve or to pretend they don't need it. After these fellows perform a few implant procedures, they're convinced of their expertise and rush out to give lectures, using them as a promotion to attract patients through referrals. These novices often have to mislead about their experience, knowing they will only be perceived as experts if they have substantial "credentials." As such, they put their own prosperity ahead of the patient's welfare, unaware or indifferent that if they make a mistake it may well cost them later in a malpractice action or in lost referrals. I guess it's the nature of this beast to think that he can walk on water! Or that he is entitled to stretch the rules of professional comportment to carve out a niche for himself in the face of plentiful competition. Again, it is the struggle to survive. Too often, however, such behavior denigrates the profession and, almost like guilt by association, makes all veteran and reputable dentists look like louts. Imagine if a second-rate major league baseball player proudly set out to badmouth and undercut his distinguished competitors. The Players Association would censure him and threaten to grand-slam a bat across his backside! Then the libel lawyers would pounce and he would *really* be in trouble!

All this infighting was a drain. Dentists thought themselves to be a fraternal community, but the constant sniping amounted to civil war. I expended many resources to wage battles to win any peace. When I was a young man and did something eccentric, unexpected, or plain foolish, my Dad would joke, "My son fell off a hammock when he was an infant and must have landed on his head to act in this manner." So for years I must have displayed symptoms of falling from a hammock.

I ask questions which of course I cannot answer, or might not even if I could. If had I settled for the predictable comfort of marriage, would I have given up my research, my quest for breakthroughs in implant surgery techniques, and my consuming need to prove their validity to disclaimers? Perhaps, if I had the right woman to occupy the void filled instead by my work, I wouldn't have had the burning desire to carry out my rigorous and often frustrating mission. Instead, I may have retreated to her consolation, found a way to be content, and paid much less attention to my self-proclaimed objectives. Truth be told, I was restlessly seeking something else–a greater sense of self-worth, perhaps even after a measure of fame and fortune. Or perhaps I was Don Quixote, on a long, benevolent crusade against unreasonable and hypocritical forces that squelch the truth so that their own agendas may prevail. This was an aspect of life which, you have gathered, I found almost intolerable. If I could not have, or find, or keep, permanent, true love, than I would gratify myself in other ways.

On family matters, all the love that was missing between myself and my wives I directed into my two girls. I was happy when Robin and Sheree were happy. I loved to hear their innocent laughter. I played with them on weekends until they were exhausted. Then, filled with their love, I could cope with another week in the office or in another city or country or an airplane between them.

The course of a pioneer is not a straightforward drive to a goal. There are detours. Philosophically speaking, I have believed that the journey and its lessons–hard they may be– and not the destination or the desired reward, is a core value of life. It may even be a blessing and, moreso, life's sole or central purpose. But knowing this, and matching that knowledge to one's daily living routine can be a woefully confusing enterprise. As Mark Twain said, "Life would be infinitely happier if we could only be born at the age of eighty and gradually approach eighteen." So as my renown grew, and my reputation—good and bad—expanded accordingly, I was obliged to continually accept life's disenchantments, like being misquoted in the media and earning the opprobrium of some cynical peers, or being snubbed because my innovations had shown the limits of others. I tried to take a brighter view of a bigger picture. One obvious conclusion is that I have been places, met people and done things that very few are ever privileged to enjoy.

One of my adventures, in Katowice, Poland is truly a standout. Invited there in 1979 by Drs. Marion and Jolla Manka, two native Polish dentists who had married and moved to Germany, I was to perform some rather unusual surgery: inserting implants into twenty-six dogs. Taking advantage of a hiatus in my lecture and surgery schedule, I committed several days of my help to a worthy experiment that Marion and Jolla were performing. As it turned out, those several days were barely sufficient for the task at hand.

It is hard to imagine a more depressing enterprise, in part because there is scarcely a more depressing place than Katowice (pronounced Kat-o-VEET-sa), located in southern Poland in the coal-mining region of Silesia. Part of my view may indicate my state of mind at the time, but Katowice isn't a city to visit for an uplift in spirits. The vaunted paradise of socialism was not in evidence here. Everything about Katowice was tainted, often in gray. The snow was the color of smoke before it even reached the ground. The local mines, the mainstay of Katowice's economy—such as it was—and the power plants spewed ash into the sky day and night. The people looked miserable and for good reason. They didn't have enough to eat, and it showed. There simply wasn't enough nutritious, varied food available. Subjected to this plight by their government, which had been foisted on them with an empty pledge of universal salvation, their vibrancy was obviously diminished. There was scant joy, and no local culture to speak of. They were nice people, but trying to survive in a bankrupt and forbidding Communist system appeared to have cheated them of the best things in life, and they knew it.

I did not go there because the dogs had any problems with their teeth. Not at all; that is a task for a veterinarian. The canine surgery would yield insight into human dental conditions by initiating a similar situation in animals. All the molars and six front teeth had been removed from the dogs about six months prior to my visit. All types of implants were to be emplaced and at a later date removed with bone blocks for histological sections. In this way, the bones would be fully healed before the insertion of the implants. All the canine teeth were left because, as a dog's largest and most powerful teeth, they were deeply embedded and almost impossible to extract without harming or killing the animal. The pathology and hematology departments at the University of Katowice were to do the follow-up work after my visit.

I inserted somewhere between one hundred and one hundred twenty implants into the dogs—many of them monstrous, seemingly lion-sized, with massive heads. Befitting this, they had huge jaws; the span between their canines and molars in some of them was as much as five inches. Unbelievable!

On the first day, my Polish assistants and I worked from 7:00 a.m. to 1:00 a.m. the next morning. But at the end of that eighteen hours we only had twelve implanted dogs to show for our effort. There was only one surgical set-up and the drills were moved slowly, using an old-fashioned foot pedal. After every thirty seconds we would have to stop and fill up the water unit to keep the drills cool. All the halts, taken together, slowed me down for hours.

I hadn't anticipated just how difficult it would be to reflect the gums and expose the bone in these beasts. On the second day—which began at 7:00 a.m. and didn't end until 2:30 the next morning—I completed procedures on ten more dogs. By this point I had to delegate the dissection of the tissues to another dentist because of severe pain in the fingers of both hands. Nonetheless, I returned on the third day, starting at noon. We finally finished at 6:30 p.m. and celebrated as if we'd just been released from prison, jumping for joy, hugging each other and kissing. This had been a marathon. I was totally exhausted.

I will always remember Katowice. The doctors and others who assisted me devoted three solid days and nights, and part of their blood and souls as well, to complete this taxing task. My Polish colleagues, the Mankas, contributed a tremendous amount of work to this study, and both of them were enormously helpful. I also have heartfelt thanks for a lovely young German dental assistant named Susan, who, in addition to administering the routine tasks of a dental office, also had cleaned up after each large dog–the back end as well as the front. And I thank the veterinarian, Adam, and the lady technician, whose name I believe was Mariona, who poured up to fifty-two models of the dogs' jaws before the implants were inserted, and another fifty-two afterwards. And I acknowledge the quiet photographer, who stood almost as long as we did, shooting countless stills and operating the video camera. And the kindness, the cordiality, and hospitality that my then brother-in-law Tomac and his wife Barbara extended was heartfelt and splendid.

Strangely, I felt sad for the dogs. During the surgery I sensed a kinship toward each of them, a reaction I had not expected. One day soon all the animals would be sacrificed for the jaw dissections necessary to obtain the bone blocks that would further the study. There was no feasible alternative for these creatures.

I could hardly wait to leave this dismal city. From Katowice I went right to a lecture at the University of Warsaw. Soon thereafter I went to Frankfurt, Germany. Always the nomad, I was performing surgery, speaking, researching, seeking an oasis of fulfillment, and building a bastion of accomplishment no one could besiege.

But I was paying the price. Although I didn't realize it at the time, I was developing chronic high blood pressure. Now in my forties, I was still eating like a young animal and never bothered to look at a menu. "Just bring me the biggest steak you have," I would order the waiter. "Smother it with onions, and bring plenty of French fried potatoes." I was an ardent meat eater. After the ample main course, I swallowed the richest desserts in seconds and no matter how many I consumed, I could never get enough of them.

In an early symptom that my system was approaching overload, my fingers were becoming severely arthritic, swollen and deformed. After a time I couldn't bend a single finger more than twenty degrees, and only with intense pain. I could not button my shirt in the morning. While I worked I was too often consuming painkillers—Codeine and Tylenol, anti-inflammatories and emperin compounds. Though this behavior was not entirely legal, I was never in danger of addiction. And I knew it was either take the medication or stop working, as it was impossible to perform any delicate task in such agony. I obtained a hot paraffin heating chamber in which to bury my fingers. The burning wax would surround my fingers, improving the circulation and granting some relief. But this nightly therapy was time-consuming, and itself very painful. It was a necessary evil; except for opting out of surgery for some weeks to let the joints recover, there was little else I could do.

Finally in the summer of 1978 I sought relief in a spa in Czechoslovakia famous for its treatment for various ailments. My schedule gave me a brief hiatus between lectures in Hamburg and Brussels. I arrived alone on a Sunday at Piestany (in what is now the Slovak Republic) north of Bratislava. All the clinics were closed, so I chose to stroll the lovely grounds. Wandering about, quite relaxed, I discovered an immaculate meadow and garden about a half mile from my hotel where many of the spa guests had gathered with visiting family members. It was a peaceful scene, serene in a very Continental, old world way. Always a nature lover, with a keen interest in horticulture, I was delighted to have found this spot. One of the pastimes I most missed was maintaining a garden, as I had in my first home in Woodmere, with Rosita, where there had been ample room for flowers and vegetables. I felt the load of my cares fall away, cast off by the higher power of peace of mind. Flanking the Piestany meadow were fully mature paw-paw trees, bearing enormous leaves, a brownish purple flower, and a yellow fruit shaped like a zucchini with an aroma similar to a banana. I had never seen so many in one place before. It had recently rained and the moisture brought forth a lovely scent from the varieties of budding flowers and from the earth itself. Gazing in wonder, I stepped back to get a wider view. At that moment my arthritis pain completely disappeared.

Alas, this was no miracle cure. Because the agony in my hands had been replaced by that of torn left ankle ligaments. I had stumbled into a hole in the ground. I dropped like I had been shot. In addition to the great pain, what flashed through my mind was humiliation. I, a grown man, innocently standing among people in a local park, had suddenly collapsed to a muddy patch of dirt as if having imbibed one vodka too many. Dozens of people in the vicinity stared at me. I suspected they were thinking much less than kindly of this stranger. That is why no one came to my assistance. I attempted, with near-futility, to arise from my prostration. My tan summer suit was soaked and stained, and worse, my dignity was wrecked, a loss signaled by the fearful dismay that surely had taken up residency on my face. I began the slow, excruciating hobble back to my living quarters. A nurse attended to me. Now my trouble had been compounded. Ultimately, a local doctor put my ankle in a cast, and for my stay I limped about with a foot and shin encased in plaster and a cane to support me.

I didn't remain at the spa long enough to obtain any beneficial results for the arthritis. While I had half-suspected that no renewal would be achieved, I still hoped for a little alleviation. In any case the spa was relaxing, a bay of calm from the ocean of storms. In the evenings I would sit in the park beneath the trees and listen to a magnificent symphony orchestra. I was all alone, but in spite of my arthritis, my pathetic ankle and my presence in a Communist country, I had found a great amount of peace and contentment.

* * *

I always received a warm welcome in Japan. I made my first trip to that emerging giant in 1971 at the invitation of Nihon University, which was presenting my first Linkow Seminar, and at the request of noted dentist Dr. Yana Yanagisawa, whom I had impressed by constantly improving the implants he and his colleagues were enthusiastically using. Yanigasawa respected my determination not to rest on my laurels. In his view, the improvements were the natural result of performing a great many surgical interventions and adjusting course toward a better system. He believed that I was much better qualified to teach implantology than the majority of others in the field. Yana became another close friend of mine.

One evening he invited me to join him, his wife, two friends of his–Professor Niikuni, who was the dean of Nihon University, and Professor Sarenji–and other faculty members to a traditional *seisan,* a formal Japanese dinner, at his home. To my surprise, on entering I was confronted by a greatly enlarged photograph of myself on the wall. It had been taken while I was lecturing as one of my implant slides could be seen in the background. "Yana," I said, "it isn't necessary for you to have hung up my picture for the evening."

"Oh, no," he replied with a smile, "I have had it here for nearly a year, since I took it when you were lecturing in San Francisco last year. Before we do an implant surgical procedure, we bow down in front of your picture asking for your help so that the case will go on successfully."

I was humbled, but also elated. The Japanese invest great belief in their shrines, revering as they do, among other matters, the pure spirit of life within everyone, and the uncanny abilities and talents we each possess, which gives us a duty to enhance them and share our insight. They invoked me to help bring out their best efforts. The place they accorded me in their thoughts and efforts was an extraordinary–and another completely unexpected–honor I have never forgotten.

After dinner, Yana offered to entertain me at his home, but some of the other Japanese dentists attending my course were eager to show me the town. They urged me accept their invitation. The first item on their agenda was to provide me with a Japanese woman. (They were indeed honorably generous to their guests.) Driving me through the crowded streets of downtown Tokyo, without comment, the car would stop and a few of my companions would clamber out. As I watched in some bewilderment they would reconnoiter certain apartment houses obviously familiar to them. Eventually I was told their purpose. And they were dogged in their search. Finally they found a Geisha who they thought I would like, and placed her in the back seat with me and another Japanese dentist. She was rather attractive, but was no more fluent in English than I was in Japanese. We sat in awkward silence all the way to our destination, a luxury apartment building. We removed our shoes and my escorts led us up a stairway to a small living room. We were invited to make ourselves comfortable, which was exactly what we did.

After the Geisha poured me warm sake, she guided me into an adjoining room–a gigantic bedroom dominated by a huge round bed with a violet cover. The ceiling was covered with mirrors. As a result, somehow our interaction was both less and more of a mystery. When our session was complete we went downstairs, where the Japanese dentists awaited with inquisitive eyes. We returned to the car, prepared to take her home. But instead she pleaded to be invited to a large reception that evening to be given in my honor. She would help serve the refreshments with the other Geisha girls who would be present. She smiled with delight when I agreed.

Over the years, I was invited to Japan by other implant societies, and had the opportunity to spend more evenings being scrubbed by beautiful Japanese girls. I certainly enjoyed those evenings, and I respected the generous tradition they represented.

In time I began lecturing to another group of Japanese dentists who eventually named their society the Linkow Academy of Implant Dentistry of Japan. The Academy, located in Nara, lies on the main island of Honshu, east of Osaka in the shadow of a beautiful mountain range. Nearby, to the east, is a large park sprinkled with Shinto shrines and Buddhist temples. I was told that as many as two thousand wild deer roamed freely through the city and are fed by its attentive citizens. It would seem that Japan is wiser in the ways of nature, willing to coexist with what they have displaced rather than destroy it.

*Myself with Bue Inada from Nara, Japan, about 1974. He referred to me as "Dad."*

Dr. Bue Inada, an excellent implantologist, now the president of the society, was such a dedicated follower of mine that he called me his dad and himself my son–not only in private, but in the presence of society members, too. I suppose I made him terribly nervous; whenever near me, he carried a towel to wipe away his perspiration. Under my close guidance, Dr. Inada became an even more skilled implantologist. And he truly grew into a son to me. Or a father. Whichever he prefers, since it was a give and take, deeply sharing relationship. I had come to love him and his wife, Tamami, very much. Nonetheless, in ensuing years, as often happens in important friendships, several strong disagreements over the proper conduct of the seminars led to a rift in our relationship. What is more, in recent years Japan's economy and society have been deeply shaken by a downturn. Many Japanese are dejected to see their self—and—national image obscured by troubles. This has affected all aspects of business. And yet, in my visits there to AAID conferences during the late 1990s, Dr. Inada always has dinner with me and presents me with an expensive gift. We honor each other despite our differences.

Each year the members–forty when it started, now over seventy–turned out for their annual meeting, all identically dressed in a uniform they chose: a royal blue sports jacket with the society's emblem and logo beneath the left lapel, white shirts, solid red ties, powder-blue trousers, white shoes and socks. Uniformity and cohesive group activity is a Japanese trait, indeed, one of the very foundations of their society. The overt expression of individuality, at least the kind readily familiar to Westerners, is discouraged.

The Japanese, I sincerely believe, are the most "put together" people in the world. They are supremely efficient and diligent, follow instructions precisely, and are very attentive. Many of them, I would say, show signs of a sixth sense. They proved this to me several times beyond a doubt. They could read the moment my thoughts changed, or interpret my body language through faint signals. And always, courtesy. I'm speaking from a fair amount of experience, having made over a dozen visits to Japan. For example, once when walking to lunch through the famous Ginza I was absently flicking a cuticle on

*Dr. Shumen Otobe, myself and my daughter Robin, in Tokyo, Japan, 1973.*

my left thumb. Before I knew it one of the group members ran into and out of a pharmacy, having bought a Band-Aid for the minor irritant.

More than cherished friends, they have developed a commendable proficiency for implantology equal to any place in the world.

I would like to cite Dr. Yanigasawa, who had been an important researcher in implantology and a friend, too. Yana died of cancer in 1978 at the age of 65. Dr. Yamane has his own implant society and is called the 'Linkow of Japan.' Nor shall I omit Drs. Otobe or Kojima, both of whom became prolific implantologists and dear friends. Dr. Otobe, an inveterate smoker, died of cancer in 1995. Not even doctors are immune to disease.

Denmark also evokes fond memories, not the least because it was home to Dr. Ole Kroogsgaard Jensen, a dear friend, whom I consider one of the best students I ever had. Dr. Jensen hails from Copenhagen, and was once destined to become a highly skilled implantologist. But though he had great talent he was much too honest for a small, relatively conservative country like Denmark. He allowed himself to be quoted in some popular magazines which publicized his work in implantology. This was considered self-aggrandizing by that global nemesis, the Dental Establishment. Talk about a monster with many heads! To make it worse, Jensen bragged about the high fees he received. This did not sit well with the academic professors in Denmark, who in 1978 were just beginning to learn about implantology. His irrepressible Nordic nature and incisive candor ultimately was part of his undoing.

One evening he attended a lecture given by two Danish professors of dentistry from the university who showed slides depicting two cases where blade implants they had inserted had failed to take: two failures among thousands of successes documented around the world. The professors held up these examples to their students as proof that blade implants don't work and should be avoided. (They had just begun their adherence to the system of the Bränemark Screw, so in their masquerade as clinical analysts they were de facto company spokesman too!)

Ole immediately challenged the professors. The reason the implants had failed, he said, was because their procedure had been totally wrong. Why should the concept be faulted if its execution was poor? (Indeed . . .) A cardinal rule is that one does not ever directly contradict a European professor, especially in front of an audience, and particularly if they are his own countrymen. Ole knew that, by their imperious standards, this was an affront, but he relished the opportunity to fly in the face of custom. These academicians are treated like the gods even though it had become quite obvious to me that if one could extract all the best clinical and technical knowledge of European professors regarding implants at that time, it would not fill a cup.

That incident led to Ole's downfall. About a year later two of his own subperiosteal implants in two patients failed. The case studies were obtained by the university with which the

*With Dr. Ole Kroosgaard Jensen, from Copenhagen, Denmark, who became a very dear friend of mine.*

two self-satisfied professors were affiliated. Now Ole was in for it. When two lawsuits were subsequently filed against him there was scarcely any doubt that the professors were responsible for instigating them. These men, in effect attempting to destroy a man's career, had gone from vindictive to vicious. Ole's lawyers informed me that I was to be one of the expert witnesses. Prior to the trial I examined all of Ole's X-rays and clinical work sheets that had been mailed to me, and was satisfied that the work had been done exceptionally well. The two patients, however, had been poor surgical risks to begin with. Sometimes it may be worth trying an implant on such risks, but only with the provision and the understanding that there is a significant chance of failure. Ole's confidence in his abilities was justifiably high, but in these cases he had been a bit too earnest.

The flight to Copenhagen was one of the worst for me, truly a nightmare. We encountered a tremendous thunderstorm at the European coast. The big airliner was knocked around in the turbulence as if it were a glider. I thought the flight would never end, or else end disastrously. Finally, with God's help and blessings, we touched down. I dragged myself off the plane, onto the tarmac and into the torrential rain. Ole was waiting to drive me to his apartment, where he lived with his wife and three lovely children. I felt I had come to help save a friend's career, and to spread the gospel of implants, and to do so forcefully. A challenge had been set down. I was in my element.

Three judges presided over Ole's cases, without a jury. I spent two full days on the stand. When my testimony had concluded I was sure the two lawsuits would be dismissed. Furthermore, his detractor, the oral-surgery professor, who had been warned by the judges that he must either attend or face a warrant for his arrest, had failed to appear. He didn't have the courage to face me in court because after just one meeting with me he had enough sense to know that I would cut him to ribbons. By exposing his meager knowledge of implantology, I would have ruined his reputation as a professor. This was obviously the exact opposite of what he intended, so he declined the risk. I am perpetually amazed at how such people are so highly regarded as specialists when in fact they don't know much more than most general practitioner dentists.

Anyway, the absent professor was busy on another mission, his back-up plan. He visited the tax bureau in Copenhagen and leveled allegations against Ole that seemed sufficiently credible. The authorities were led to suspect he must be cheating on his taxes. The Danish penalty for refusing to pay one's fair share of taxes is not unlike the U.S.: if convicted of a serious breach, the reward is prison. Ole heard from the bureau, alright, and realized that drastic action was necessary if he was to come away with anything. So he contrived to divorce his wife and give her all his money, an action that is legal in Denmark. Their stratagem: when everything had been resolved they would remarry.

But there were two obstacles. First, the judges decided not to use any testimony of the expert witnesses, primarily myself and Gustav Dahl, relying instead only on the testimony of the plaintiff patients. Without the support of expert testimony, Ole's case fell apart. He was found guilty. But the second obstacle proved worse than the first. Indeed, it was a disaster. By accident, Ole's wife opened a letter addressed to him. It was a love letter from another woman, one of my own dental assistants, a girl from the Philippines, with whom Ole must have been having an affair.

The result: no remarriage and no money back. Ole eventually lost his office and his practice in Copenhagen, too. His wife was an orthodontist who had shared the office and practice with him. In her fury she decided to take it all, and the court agreed with her. Ole spent several months in jail because he couldn't come up with all the money he owed his government.

My friend Ole, now a beaten man, potentially one of the greatest implantologists in the world, settled into practice in a small town far from Copenhagen. He was no longer allowed to practice implantology. He pulls out teeth and makes dentures for patients who will never know the wonderful liberation of implants had Ole been allowed to do the work. What a terrible, depressing shame.

Many years later, I learned that Dr. Ole Jensen took his own life. It shocked me very deeply. To this day I think of the mental anguish he must have endured over the end of the best years of his career.

Incidents like these–failed marriages, business disputes, friends ruined by quirks of fate–always put me in a contemplative mood. What is the nature of these storms that toss people about, even those with money and fame, like toy boats? We take ourselves seriously, a state of mind that often seems inappropriate, but it also seems that if we are to stay in the hunt for success it is almost a requirement. So many contradictions. But what about times of my life when such reflections did not matter?

In the springtime each year, I would reminisce about my youth, the summers in Camp Ta-Ri-Go, in Fleischmann's, New York. In the first week of each July, I would drive up with my wife of the time to those beautiful mountains to revisit the ghosts and scenes of earlier days. I would visit Pacey Salzman, the camp's owner, and Lou Wilder, who did the maintenance. Pacey was an inspiration. He poured his heart and soul into each camper and counselor. He was a stocky, powerful man, six feet tall and about two hundred and fifty pounds (not unlike Giorgio Gnalducci). In his younger days he'd been a wrestler.

I enjoyed going to the big social hall, to gaze on the plaques from summers gone by hanging on those rustic wooden walls–plaques announcing the results of the yearly "color wars," plaques commemorating the medal and trophy winners for athletic events, and those listing the "all-around athletes" and "all-around campers." My name appeared on many of those awards, as a permanent reminder of past glory.

One season, God was not kind to Pacey. He had a horrific accident. Pacey went to the refrigerator in Lou Wilder's maintenance shop and thirstily poured a drink from what he thought was a can of orange juice. But it didn't contain juice: it was rat poison, which Lou used around camp. Immediately Pacey knew something was terribly wrong. He felt himself becoming paralyzed, and then lapsed into a coma. What a tragedy! It was a miracle that he even survived. Several months later, when I was allowed to visit him in the hospital, Pacey cried on seeing me. He was half the size that I remembered, and totally paralyzed in both legs. He had a modest amount of sensation in his arms and fingers. Part of his therapy was to squeeze a small rubber ball. It was very depressing to see such vitality and strength reduced to a shadow. A year or two later Pacey sold the camp and moved to Miami Beach. Several years afterwards I made it a point to visit him. He was sitting in a wheelchair by the swimming pool. Pacey had gained much of his weight back, could move his arms and fingers, but remained paralyzed from the waist down. He had taken up a hobby in oil painting in which he was busily engaged while I shared the morning with him. His work reminded me of the American modernist James Whistler, most notable for "Whistler's Mother."

It was the last time I saw Pacey. He died several years later. I was very sorrowful, in part because it signaled the ever-dwindling connections I had to my youth, when just about everything was beautiful and nearly pain-free.

I still returned for visits, summer after summer, to walk through the fading echoes of my past. First I would gaze at the plaques in the social hall, then walk by one or two of the bunkhouses, and then proceed to the wonderful baseball field where I had felt so much at home. Of course, I had to scale the hill beyond deep left center field. From its summit opposite the diamond I could gaze down on the tennis courts. One time, on the cusp of summer, the courts were covered by hundreds of caterpillars, soon to transform into beautiful butterflies. I would hike the nature trail that led to the stream at the foot of a mountain. I was always alone there. No other crossed my path because the person Pacey had sold the camp to had gone broke after one or two seasons.

In 1982, I was stunned and saddened to see that the dreams of my boyhood had been laid to rest. I didn't even recognize the baseball diamond. Contractors hired by the developers had torn down everything except the social hall. The trees were cut to the ground, and instead of gently swarming butterflies there were only bulldozers. It had been my home away from home. It was no longer possible to go back there again.

# Seventeen

## DILEMMAS

My Manhattan office was considered by many to be the court of last appeal for those condemned as dental cripples and who weren't considered good implant candidates by other implantologists. Because I was constantly devising new methods for a variety of conditions, I often found it possible to help even the worst cases. The technical challenge and the medical results were very fulfilling. I was affronted, however, when a dentist with little experience or expertise declared to his patient that Linkow would do implants on anyone, that he himself was, of course, far more selective, and therefore a better investment.

My response: the true degree of selectivity is directly proportional to an individual's skills. The greater the expertise, the more that could be done to remedy all but a small minority of difficult cases. The novices and aspirants often disguise their limitations by quoting astronomical prices to the "difficult" patients–prices so outrageous that the patients couldn't possibly afford the service. Many such discouraged people found their way to my office, where I offered to perform the implants for a fee comparable to that of a routine procedure. I cringe at thoughts of those who were not daunted by the quotes they received from overpriced, underqualified dentists. Too often, I fear, they were victimized by mediocre work compounded by unsuitable designs.

My offices also served as open houses of learning, where over the years hundreds of professionals were welcomed to observe surgery on hundreds or thousands of patients. I was thrilled to have taught procedures to ranks of truly interested dentists, but I was sometimes saddened, too, by some of the reactions. Not a few of these dentists who had trained under me would later announce–as if claiming a badge of honor–"I do it differently than Linkow does." And they were right: they did do it differently in that their work was seldom as good. Preparation, precision, proper tools and compassion are all essential to a successful procedure. And that is defined as one that overjoys the patient and yields optimal long-term results.

By early 1982 I had already done more than 8,300 Linkow blade implants and subperiosteal implants. The techniques of implantology had come into their own. As a result of the seminars and the self-evident value of the systems, the methods were migrating around the world. Implantology was the subject of many newspaper and magazine articles, and my work was mentioned in a large portion of them. One patient of mine, Barry Farber, was a New York newspaper columnist and radio talk show host.

I first appeared on his program in the early 1970s. Barry was a candid, articulate, shoot-from-the-lip fellow, which is one reason I agreed to be a guest on his news-and-issues show. Barry's introduction stunned me; perhaps it was a bit melodramatic (Barry really went for the gusto when it came to grabbing an audience's attention) but it had elements of truth. His ability to find the drama in almost any circumstance was amazing.

"Either Dr. Linkow will end up in prison or he will go down in history as one of the great pioneers."

That was a hell of an introduction. But Barry, like his contemporary Howard Cosell, really told it like he saw it. If he thought you were a phony he would immediately express his thoughts on the air. At times it was a take-no-prisoners approach.

Barry became a patient of mine for a badly deteriorating condition. If there is one crucial thing that a radio personality needs, it's the resonant voice that a healthy mouth of lips, teeth and tongue can generate. Other dentists considered Barry too far gone, and by then he really needed help. He had a favorite expression, a kind of signature phrase to describe his dental condition.

"My mouth was a slum. I had so many cavities I talked with an echo and had to put my hand over my mouth like a Japanese geisha girl I was so embarrassed. If I smiled at a bureaucrat I would have gotten an immediate grant under the Federal Emergency Relief Act."

Around 1971 I removed a few of his teeth, replaced them with implants, gave him a great new appearance and restored his bite. He was thrilled and sung my praises on many of his radio shows.

Some years later, about 1986, a small swelling appeared on the right side of his palate. Nothing showed up on x-rays I took but it didn't look normal to me. I referred him to a specialist, who diagnosed an *ameloblastoma* or *ademantoma*. These are forms of bone cancer that stem from the time that Barry was a young boy and can remain dormant for an entire lifetime but sometimes appear later in life. It was agreed by all parties that it had nothing to do with my implants.

Barry decided to get another opinion from two medical doctors from a small hospital in Manhattan which I don't want to name. They called me one day, explaining the urgent need to operate on Barry. This would require extensive surgery and would involve a good portion of his palate and face which would totally ruin his career.

I knew from my little experience regarding *ameloblastomas* that although they move in the mandible (lower jaw) they progress much more slowly in the maxilla (upper jaw). I told them that I did not believe it had to be done as drastically as they claimed. They responded that I would be responsible for his death if I prohibited him from having this radical surgery.

To shorten this story, Barry found another surgeon who totally disagreed with these doctors and said it could easily be removed without a radical procedure.

However, I first had to remove the implants so that this surgeon could gain access to the areas for his treatment. All went extremely well. About six months after the surgery I once more operated on Barry, giving him a full maxillary subperiosteal (on top of the bone) implant which he was still enjoying in 2002.

Barry wrote a column in August 1980. "If I were a nation instead of a person, everything would come to a halt at noon tomorrow and there'd be free champagne, firecrackers and dancing in Parliament Square to honor my dentist, Dr. Leonard Linkow of New York. His picture would cover every building and the finest engravers in the land would be excused from the rally so they could hurry up and figure out how to best put Dr. Linkow's face on a postage stamp. And we'd change the name from Parliament Square to Implant Square in honor of the technique Dr. Linkow has done so much to pioneer."

Of course, all this was whimsy; after all, I hadn't affected or changed the course of history. Well, just dental history. Barry Farber called me the "Michelangelo of the Mouth."

\* \* \*

My third marriage was sliding into deeper trouble. Wiesia and I were feuding, and often would fight until the wee hours. If I did something wrong I was quick to apologize, anxious to have it behind me before bedtime. For Wiesia, however, perceived misbehavior was to be roundly scorned. She was loath to accept an apology; it wasn't sufficient. An argument could not be resolved until she had dredged up every point and detail of its cause, and extracting a promise that it wouldn't occur again. I poorly tolerated these frequent battles. She was persistent, I have to grant her that. When I was infuriated enough to leave our bed and take refuge in an adjoining room, locking the door behind me, she would pursue, jimmying the door open with a screwdriver, screaming all the while. I was under siege in my own home, living an interpersonal nightmare, a recurrent, unpredictable storm of indignity. A marriage from hell. Another one. I had again stumbled into, or had contributed to, a tense and torturous partnership. Our arguments worsened over time, until they almost ceased to be disagreements but high-volume grudge matches.

In addition to a wretched domestic situation worse, I discovered, purely by accident, that a secretary had been busy stealing large amounts of cash from the office. Worse still, she had been running her own business from there.

My personal trust factor of friends and associates was at times foolishly generous. And so with the secretary. Since I was often traveling, out of the loop, the opportunities to abuse that trust were abundant. This person, who had been hired as my helpmate in a this enterprise, had decided to help only herself instead. She had written several hundred prescriptions, often for as many as sixty capsules of Percodan at a time, and signed my name to them, collecting a hefty fee for the "service." Percodan is a very effective painkiller, but it is also a "controlled substance," a potentially addictive and dangerous drug. Whenever I write such prescriptions, it is never for more than twelve capsules or tablets at a time. By enabling this drug to be indiscriminately dispensed, she was placing me, ultimately the responsible party, seriously at risk.

One Saturday, on my way into the office to fetch some paperwork, the building doorman proffered a small paper bag. "Doctor," he said, "what should I do with this?" The bag was from a pharmacy and bore the name of one of my patients. But I had not prescribed anything recently for that person. In any case, it seemed odd that it was in the doorman's possession. This was not the regular practice of my office. "Someone" had told him that the patient would come by to retrieve the bag. Thus far no one had appeared.

By such careless slips do criminals get tangled in their own web.

I opened the bag and saw that it contained a large, full vial of Percodans, about sixty. My name was on the label as the prescribing doctor, but I knew that this wasn't so. The poor doorman! He had no idea what to make of Dr. Linkow's instant transition to an apoplectic, raging bull. I raced from the building to the pharmacy and demanded to know why they were dispensing narcotics in such a sloppy manner. I was inclined to assume that this was some lazy oversight. But the pharmacist showed me a prescription form, which while not in my handwriting, had my name on it. I quickly began to grasp the scenario.

Returning to my office building I recognized a patient parked curbside: the fellow in whose name the bag of pills had been left. He owed me a lot of money for work I had done some time back. He had continued to request painkillers. I angrily sent him packing. In the office I instantly traced the perpetrator of this fraud through the handwriting: my secretary. She was very shortly out of a job. The final straw: the attempted theft of $800 on a day I was in Philadelphia, at Temple University, where I held a professorship. While away, I of course was unable to preside. Such treachery by an employee, a welcome member of one's business family, is a very low form of human behavior.

The situation took yet another turn several days later when an investigator from the narcotics bureau visited my office. He returned to question me on many occasions over consecutive weeks. In his possession were over two hundred bogus prescriptions, each with at least sixty tablets, each in my name but in the ex-secretary's script. I was fortunate that the agent believed me when I pleaded ignorance of her actions. I could easily have lost my dental license.

By the mid-1970s there were thousands of implantologists throughout the world practicing my blade-implant procedures, and soon many of my other techniques: the pterygoid extension, tuber blade, multipurpose blade, ramus, and specially designed tripodial subperiosteal implant systems that I introduced in 1980. My blade-vent implants represented true medical progress and were a source of pride and satisfaction for me. I took comfort in knowing that every day, somewhere in the world, I was responsible for the relief of misery in people who suffered from various degrees of edentulism (no teeth). My courage and ability made it happen. All other things being equal, the full range of implantology may have been extinct by the early 1960's, leaving dentists only the alternative of the lower subperiosteal implant. I still remember the words on a poster given to me years ago: "Behold the turtle; he only makes progress when he sticks his neck out."

In the early 1990s I was invited to hear one of my dearest patients perform at the Merkin Concert Hall, West 67th Street near Columbus Avenue, on the occasion of his eightieth birthday. I went to the location on automatic pilot, not realizing where I was until I arrived there. Directly across the street was a small white two-story building, then smeared with graffiti, in which I had spent much time years ago. It was the former home of the Institute for Graduate Dentists, where I first began to add another chapter to dental history with three-day courses. Each course day was ten hour days, but the evenings were often the most memorable part. I was privileged to spend time with friends, especially Dr. Al Edelman, who assisted me at the Institute. We would stay up half the night with groups of keen students, answering hundreds of questions about implants. Their minds were like sponges, ready and eager to soak in all knowledge. It had been a wonderful time, even if my marriage was in turmoil.

The patient I'd come to see at Merkin Hall was none other than Cantor Gamshoff, the hapless plaster-helmet victim of Dr. Weiss, and one of the greatest tenors of his time. He wasn't much of a patient, but his voice was eloquent and polished, and his manner that of a king. After the concert I was thrilled that he and his wife invited me to join them for dinner. I was delighted that the subperiosteal implant that I had made for him over twenty-five years ago still successfully functioned.

Otto Preminger was a strong, steadfast man, very stern. He came to my office once accompanied by his dentist, Dr. Weinstein, a balding, diminutive man, perhaps 5'2", but attempting to bear the authority of someone two feet taller. His tactics were soon transparent, moreso in regard to the distinguished Mr. Preminger, the director of such notable films as *Laura, Anatomy of a Murder, Advise and Consent, Exodus* and *In Harm's Way*. He had worked and hobknobbed with some of the biggest stars in the film business, among them John Wayne, Kirk Douglas, William Holden, Frank Sinatra and Marilyn Monroe. Preminger, an actor himself, was a force of nature, in a patrician Austrian way; he got noticed and often got his way. Nonethless, he had a soft spot which he was not entirely successful in hiding behind a gruff exterior. And he was in some dental discomfort, which is more than enough to change the natural or chosen behavior of just about anyone. The director had been fitted with a removable denture that was now causing great dismay and discomfort. He properly sought an alternative.

Weinstein, Preminger's advisor in the matter of his teeth, was a shrewd man, compensating for his lack of dental skills by attempting to outmaneuver the competition. Credit must be given where it is due, however; Weinstein was the first to create the technique of bonding porcelain to metal. Much of his practice, though, was more to showcase his presumed talents than to make leaps of technical prowess. Weinstein had a team of dentists working for him. When one of the dentists would complete the session's work on a patient, Weinstein would enter the room, accompanied by a technician armed with a notepad. Weinstein would examine the patient as if on an aesthetic search, dictating to his attentive assistant about what should be done with this or that tooth. This would make the patient feel important, as if in meticulous and exacting hands. Weinstein and the assistant would exit, and the staffer would dispose of the note. This little theatre was intended to inure to the benefit of Weinstein, a controlling type who needed attention. And it was attention he got. Envy too; in the Fifties, Weinstein had one of the very few practices anywhere that grossed several million dollars in a year. He had at least twenty operatories in his large Manhattan office, and he catered to show business celebrities. Frank Sinatra, for one, had been sent Weinstein's way by his brother, who had renamed himself Weber and set up shop in Los Angeles as Weinstein's public relations and marketing officer. Unbelievable! In a similar fashion, Weinstein got hooked up with Preminger.

Implants were outside Weinstein's field of expertise, so they came to me. I looked in Preminger's mouth and peered at the x-rays. To me his case was a snap. No sweat all. I precisely explained what the procedure would entail. Without hesitation, Preminger wanted to get started. In a beat, I had become the leader of this duet. Just as quickly, Weinstein objected. "Oh, no, no. We've got to discuss this! You don't know Mr. Preminger. He's a very nervous man."

Preminger sat there, calm and collected. I suppose that working with Bob Mitchum or Paul Newman was a bit more taxing than what I proposed to fix his teeth.

"Well, he doesn't seem nervous to me," I dryly observed.

"Oh, no," Weinstein insisted, "he's nervous. You don't want him fainting on you."

Preminger now seemed ambivalent. He may have thought: is there something to these implants that Linkow hasn't told me? The implication: maybe I should further consult with Weinstein before deciding. Weinstein and his charge, one of Vienna's contribution to Hollywood, exited with a decision not to make a decision. For reasons known only to him, Weinstein had predetermined this outcome.

I was so aggravated at being deprived of the opportunity that I wrote Weinstein a letter. I asserted that Weinstein may have referred Mr. Preminger to me–why is a mystery since he refused to let the man have a procedure which he very obviously needed, and which was the only reason to have visited my office in the first place. You wanted to control him, and by extension, me, I declared. Moreover, you feared that if the implants were successful, which they would have been, and Mr. Preminger was relieved of his pain and misery, he would no longer require your lucrative services.

Weinstein responded with the claim that he had been planning to mention me at some length in a book he was writing, but now that I have been so rude it was out of the question. What is more, having transgressed, in his opinion, the normal bounds of customary courtesy, he would consider reporting me to the First District Dental Society. Well, the minimal credibility Weinstein had retained with me quickly evaporated. I am distinctly unimpressed with tattle tales. And threatening to report me to a group that was already my avowed enemy was like a cannibal complaining that the main dish was too salty.

And that is another thumbnail sketch of the dental world.

Alan Jay Lerner was a genius playwright, songwriter and screenwriter, half of the fabled duo of Lerner and (Frederick) Loewe. His stories and lyrics have graced such international theatrical hits as *Brigadoon, My Fair Lady, Camelot* and *On a Clear Day You Can See Forever* (all translated into successful films) and original films such as *Gigi* and *An American In Paris* (both earning him Academy Awards, in addition to a number of other nominations during his illustrious career). His brain was fertile, his heart chock full of humor and joy, but his teeth were a disaster. When Lerner would visit my office, his unhandsome face bearing heavy, thick glasses, he was often preoccupied, as if chasing the next inspiration. And when he had it, as if their own accord, his fingers would take to scrawling lyrics or ideas on an ever-present pad. He would write and write, even while leaning back in my chair, his eyes closed and mouth open to the proddings of my fingers and instruments. I have seldom seen anything like a man so obsessed, unwilling to let one creative moment slip away. He led a fearsome schedule, full of commitments in fiercely competitive show business, always raising money for new plays, producing the current plays or generating story ideas for future plays. He could not abide in long sessions, so we embarked on a series of implants for him, a few at a time.

His travels brought him to Boston for a road show of *Coco*. And right into conflict with his next appointment to cement the final full arch fixed bridge over his implants. We were in an important phase of the process, and Lerner insisted I come to Boston to perform the procedure there. He had rented a boat for the weekend, a large yacht, making an impressive tour of Boston harbor with a number of guests. I made the trip with an assistant technician and necessary mobile gear such as hand drills. Normally, in my office, the implants can be trimmed if the bridge doesn't fit precisely. Here, not only away from my office but afloat in a boat, my options were much more limited. I was praying hard that the full arch fixed prosthesis I had fashioned for Lerner would fit properly. Happily, it did. Lerner sallied forth into his social circles for an evening of entertainment. My assistant and I returned to Manhattan.

Not long afterwards, he received an honor at Kennedy Center in Washington for his cultural contributions. And not longer after that, in 1986, he died. So Lerner, unlike Preminger, still wears the Linkow hardware.

\*   \*   \*

Another valued colleague also passed on. Dr. Aaron Gershkoff, a pioneer implantologist from Providence, Rhode Island, was one of the few dentists I had ever truly admired. He contributed a great deal to implantology and though I was ten or twelve years his junior, we held each other in great esteem. Dr. Gershkoff and Dr. Goldberg were the first to visit

Gustav Dahl in Sweden, in 1948, where he learned about the subperiosteal implant that Dahl had invented in 1940. Gershkoff took the technique back to the U.S., and from there it evolved into the system, or range of systems, that Gershkoff, Goldberg, Lew, Cranin, Mentag, Weber, myself and others have utilized so successfully.

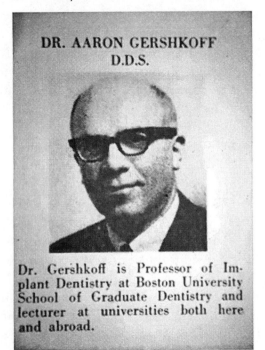

*Dr. Aaron Gershkoff was made Professor of Implant Dentistry at Boston University School of Graduate Dentistry in the late 1960s.*

In 1974 we were both named honorary presidents and invited to the first Australian Congress in Implantology in Sydney. But I was previously committed to conduct a seminar at a university in Rio de Janeiro and obliged to decline the Australian trip. But Dr. Gershkoff was going, and I provided him with a few of my surgical tapes to show. I flew down to Rio while he journeyed to far-off Sydney. After the congress he and his wife opted for a short vacation on an island resort near Australia.

LEONARD I. LINKOW

Dr. and Mrs. Gershkoff boarded a Pan Am flight back to the States. Less than two minutes after take-off, the plane suddenly lost power and plummeted into the ocean, killing everyone aboard. The dental profession, especially the world of implantology, had lost a truly great pioneer and an extraordinarily sensitive, humble human being. I miss him very much and I certainly could have used his wisdom all these years.

A year or two later I did travel to Sydney to give one of my Linkow Seminars at the University there. I left JFK Airport on Qantas, the Australian airline. The flight totaled nearly twenty hours, and I worked furiously at a chapter on implants for someone else's book virtually the entire time, including a brief layover in Hawaii. In Sydney I passed the manuscript to a professional typist. The typed copy came to one hundred and thirty-four pages. That was surely a substantial accomplishment for one brief journey. I had seldom looked out of the cabin windows at the continental U.S. or the huge blue Pacific below.

While I was in Sydney, a renowned implant patient, Jan Peerce, was singing in the magnificent opera house, an architectural wonder, on the harbor. It was a thrill to hear Jan's superb, sterling voice, even though, at that time, he was in his seventies. I took secret pleasure in knowing that I had played a part in extending his singing career for at least ten more years by eliminating his lower denture and installing a full set of implants that supported permanent teeth.

The clear night skies over Australia reveal unbelievable beauty. The southern hemisphere heavens are totally different than our northern-half firmament. The moon is tipped at a different angle; the "man in the moon" is leaning over. One can see the magnificent Southern Cross and other formations that offer an entirely fresh perspective on the place of our tiny Earth in the vast cosmos. The brightest stars one can see from anywhere on the planet are only visible below the equator, especially in the December sky. Oddly, too, given the gravitational orientation in the Southern Hemisphere, water runs counter-clockwise. It is not an illusion when the sink drains in the opposite direction of what a New Yorker is used to!

And of course, in Sydney, I thought about my lost friend, Aaron Gershkoff.

The American Academy of Implant Dentistry created the Aaron Gershkoff Memorial Award. I was the first dentist to receive that prestigious accolade, in 1974. I was delighted because it came from such a distinguished and supportive body of peers. The news that I would be the recipient had leaked out several weeks before the presentation, so I prepared a short speech. The next day I was scheduled to give a one-hour lecture During my delivery I projected slides of successfully completed implant cases, and the x-rays associated with them, on two large screens at the front of the hall.

## Oral Implantology—The Dilemma of Iqnorance

During the past two decades the utilization of posts, pins, or blades that are screwed, driven, or tapped directly into the osseous structures to act as artificial abutments for the support of fixed or removable bridges has become quite popular.

Implants of the endosseous type have been tried as early in history as the ancient Egyptians. The era of replacing teeth by the utilization of alloplastic materials is responsible for our present-day enthusiasm. Orthopedic surgeons have been implanting metallic stainless steel pins into the femurs of human beings at the rate of 700,000 per year. These pins are completely buried in the bone. In dentistry the intra-osseous implants have their occlusal shafts extending out of the bone and into the oral cavity. This protrusion and the lack of knowledge by the practitioners were responsible for the restraint of the early progress of implant dentistry. However, there is still a lot more that must be done and understood by even those who have been practicing implantology before it might someday be universally accepted as an everyday procedure.

For the next hour you will perhaps see well over a thousand or more slides of the countless thousands of completed cases that I have done. Most of the color slides have been taken on cases that have been in the mouths of these patients from one to fourteen years, with the blade implants, and up to twenty-three years with the subperiosteal implants. It is evident how so many of these cases have been functioning successfully in the mouths of these happy patients, many of whom were unable to be helped by the methods of our so-called conventional dentistry. So for the next hour or so let us go back in time.

It is difficult to believe that in this age of the atom and interplanetary voyages, men still accept the replacement of their lost teeth by large, cumbersome, removable prostheses, some of them unattractive and humiliating.

It has been said that history is the science of those things which do not repeat themselves. For medicine, it is the science of trials which are repeated until the day when they succeed.

The French philosopher, Pascal, one of the blazing lights like Einstein, once said, "The long series of men during the course of so many centuries should be considered as only one man, who always subsists, and who learns continually." I say, "If every twenty-five years, just one man from our profession would continue where his predecessors left off, implantology would eventually be a commonplace practice."

A pioneer, in any field of endeavor, especially in medicine or dentistry, spends most of his life as a controversial figure. It is not his choice to be considered in this light, especially during those struggling years of being condemned and considered an outcast by his fellow colleagues.

His belief in his work plus his undying energy that drives him onward to carry out his newer concepts enables him to bring forth to his profession after many hardships, trials, and errors, a completely new discipline that has possibilities of tremendous magnitude.

For some time now, investigators working in various areas of specialization have been developing their ideas and making small, but important, contributions to the field of implantology. Now comes a unifying concept that relates the data and a peak is reached. The concept is the endosseous implant.

The endosseous implant is the most exciting idea in modern dentistry. It is the herald of a new era that can benefit aesthetically, psychologically, and physically, most of the partially and many of the totally edentulous patients. The idea is to put into bone an implant designed to complement the natural forces operating in the health and welfare of the jaws. The implant is accepted by the tissues in which it has been set and is tightly bound there, providing a tenacious site to which a fixed or removable prosthesis may be attached. This gives the patient a prosthesis that is closer to the look and feel of natural teeth than any other artificial appliance to date. It is radically different in concept and totally exciting in its potential benefits.

The history of dentistry has also been plagued by the needlessly slow recognition and acceptance of a startlingly different idea. Despite ample proof that a new technique will immeasurably benefit a patient, there is a tendency to stick to traditional methods. This is understandably human.

To many operators, it seems preferable to repeat familiar techniques with predictable results than to experiment with the unfamiliar. However, this attitude should be honestly evaluated.

The ultimate goal in dentistry is maximum benefit to the patient, not the continuance of merely adequate methods for the convenience of an operator. Granted, the procedures involved in implantation are more radical than the now current procedures for providing removable dental prostheses. Granted also, the techniques require a great deal more clinical skill on the part of the operator than do current approaches. Yet the benefits to the patients are so much greater that the ethics of dentistry demand that the new techniques be carefully judged and evaluated in terms of their inherent merits.

*Pondering over hundreds of thousands of implant slides on film strip
using my specially designed "film strip" projector.*

Years, sometimes hundreds of years, are spent trying to
develop a technique that will solve a particular health problem. The early attempts usually fail, and for a variety of reasons. Sometimes the basic idea is not valid. Other times, the
idea is valid but the material or information necessary for its
success is not available. When success occurs, it is usually the
result of an inspired coordination of various factors.

An implantologist's attitudes toward morphology and prosthesis design differ from those of the dentist planning a conventional restoration. It is not a question of who is right or
wrong, but which information is used to develop their techniques.

The totally or partially edentulous patient presents his case.
The conventional prosthodontist selects a set of characteristic
soft tissue surface features and designs his restoration over

*With Dr. Raphael Chercheve from Paris, France and Lariboisiere Hospital.*

them. However, eliminating the alternatives does not produce The Only Solution; it is merely a convenient approach firmly established by long use. I have advocated another approach, which involves going directly into bone horizontally, based on frequently neglected observations in our field, and substantiated by clinical successes and histological evidence.

In continuing to help patients achieve the greatest measure of dental health, comfort, function, and appearance, the dental profession is constantly striving for improvement and better methods to accomplish these goals that both the patients and dentists desire.

For this reason, many dentists have expended their time and effort in "continuing education" to acquire skills they can bring to bear on the many problems of health, in order to resolve them for the benefit of their patients.

Many patients may not contemplate reaching the moon, but the vast majority of people certainly want to enjoy good health on earth.

Although we in dentistry have been uninvolved with the tremendous forward strides in the space program, our main objective is to serve mankind here on this planet: to help achieve, to the fullest, the goals of esthetics, comfort, and efficiency in the functions of speaking, eating, and smiling.

In an era where the observation "the only constant is change" has become trite, dentists hardly need to feel that they are mired in inertia. They should be running hard so that they can catch up to the momentum of medical advances.

I also wish to say that these colleagues who pursue this fascinating science of implantology should never forget their predecessors, and that merely making a slight change in a technique or design of an implant should not for a moment allow them to imagine that by substituting their name for that of the authentic author, they can improve a method already described for decades.

Let us as a profession give credit to those who so rightly deserve it.

To those great men of our profession who are presently practicing implantology, and to those who had previously paved the way through their unselfish work and their strong determination to continue despite the overwhelming skepticism from their colleagues' trying to constantly disprove the principles of implant dentistry, I dedicate this film.

Many new techniques in the fields of medicine and dentistry have been introduced to our modern world in the past several years. Until these techniques had been pioneered by men of vision, ambition, patience, courage, and the understanding of a great human need, thousands, perhaps millions, of people suffered and even succumbed to their individual maladies.

As an anonymous writer once said, "Every conventional approach was once a radical idea."

Implantology is the most controversial discipline in dentistry today. Its advocates claim that it can alter the course of restorative dentistry; its detractors criticize it as impractical and

*Left to right: Dr. Feliciano Salagaray, myself, Dr. Raphael Chercheve and Dr. Al Edelman in Madrid, Spain in 1970. Dr. Salagaray was one of the very early pioneers in the art and science of mandibular subperiostal implants. He was from Madrid. Dr. Edelman was a good friend of mine who helped me the day I was lecturing at the Institute for Graduate Dentists on 67$^{th}$ St.*

emphasize its failures. I, of course, am an advocate, but I must stress that I promote only a limited number of procedures suitable for specific situations. These procedures are based upon careful observations of tissue morphology and upon biomechanical principles applicable to both natural and artificial dentition. These procedures have also proven clinically successful in a significant number of situations.

Although dental implantology is not a new field, only recently has it provoked widespread interest. The major reason for this is the success of certain implant procedures. An added

*With Ronald Cullen, from London, England, 1970. For many years he was considered the top implantologist in England.*

factor is the recognition that technological advances, particularly in the development of light-weight materials tolerable to the human body, have resolved basic medical problems.

If there are successful implant designs and techniques, why does the controversy persist? Largely because implantologists have been isolated from the mainstream of dentistry, the profession has been unable to differentiate between practical implant designs and absurd ones. Due to its promise, implantology has attracted a flood of new experimentation that has obscured years of carefully refined concepts and techniques. The profession and the public are simultaneously presented with "advances" that will truly benefit the patient and contribute to the art of prosthodontics, together with so-called "advances" already explored and rejected in the Dark Ages of Implantology; just as in any other field of endeavor, those who are ignorant of its history are condemned to repeat it and its mistakes.

Another significant factor in the implant controversy is the large number of failures. Poorly conceived implant designs

*My dear friend, Dr. Antonio Moro Greco, from Naples, Italy, 1971.*
*He had an enormous implant practice in his city.*

cannot succeed, and they account for a significant proportion of the statistic. The most carefully designed implant will also fail if inserted incorrectly. Unpredictable circumstances, such as prolonged delays in laboratory procedures or faulty prosthodontics, also adversely affect stages of an implant intervention. The balance between success and failure tends to be precarious, even with good designs. A failure in implant insertion is usually detectable immediately, and the operator is aware of his mistake. Once the finished prosthesis is permanently affixed over correctly seated implants, a positive prognosis usually results.

Amid the confusion and often imperfect results, why persist? Thousands of former dental cripples who now enjoy successful implant-supported prostheses are grateful that we have. Hopefully as more practitioners become interested in implantology, their skill, energy, and intelligence will minimize errors and improve the overall prognosis.

Today failures can be reduced by critically evaluating current implant designs and discarding the impractical. Failures from inexperience will understandably persist as novice operators learn the skill, and should not be confused with failures from bad design. Clearly it is time for the critics to commit themselves to in-depth investigations of the various implant designs, implant histology, and the sophisticated prosthodontics required by implant insertion. Broad condemnations are neither fair nor adequate.

Implantology will probably always be limited to relatively few practitioners. It is cross-disciplinary, requiring a wide range of surgical and prosthodontic skills that are usually specializations in themselves. However, whether or not the practitioner wishes to become an implantologist himself, he should at least understand its principles and applications in order to expand his patient's prosthodontic alternatives.

The maxillary implantation story is dominated by the adverse influence of nondental anatomy. Sinus expansion sometimes hinders the use of the blade vent implant, which is most often highly successful elsewhere in the mouth, and makes it risky to position a subperiosteal implant's bar or strut over the fragile bone separating the sinus from the oral cavity. The pterygoid extension implant, followed by the tuber blades, from the moment of their inception, obviously contained the seeds of a solution. This implant's refinement into more practical, wider applications exemplifies the more rewarding aspects of implantology.

To those of you who find my implant concepts fresh material, I welcome you to the excitement and promise in dental implants. Although I have in many ways broken through the "titanium curtain," we still have much further to go, and many more battles to win, before our great field will become widely accepted throughout the world. Many dentists have never taken a course on the subject, but still continue to question the validity and results of implantology. Before preparing their patients for conventional dentures or removable partial prostheses, they should, I feel strongly, carefully inform their patients about alternative procedures, which should often include implants.

*With Dr. Sami Sandhause, 1973, Lausanne, Switzerland. He was one of the few geniuses I had known. He was the first to develop a non-metallic root form implant. Since then he has developed robots, which I have seen in his magnificent office, that drill into patients' jaws and are capable of inserting the implants. They are called Alpha, Beta and Gamma robots. The Gamma robots, believe it or not, are portable.*

It has been said that a prophet is never received in his own country. I have never confessed to be a prophet but I have said more than once: "Thank God for the followers." Because only through the thousands of followers who truly believe in one or two or three leaders can the field of implantology—or any particular discipline of medicine—be totally advanced and improved through their added contributions grounded on the original scientific principles of the honest leaders.

I am sure all of us are aware of the tremendous controversies that arise when new developments are announced. Implantology is not an exception. Pioneers are treated today as in years gone by: they are criticized for their failures, their many achievements are resisted and overlooked.

Inventors should be helped by peers to further improve

*With Dr. Stefano Tramonte, 1983, during the GISI meeting in Bologna, Italy. He was one of the very early implant pioneers who developed the "drive screw" implant and has inserted thousands of them into patients' mouths.*

their concepts. Professionals who continually undermine advancements owe it to their colleagues and themselves to at least be fully informed about the current state of the art before passing judgment. Implantation can enable many patients, even though totally edentulous, to again have fixed teeth. The technology is here now. Not informing a patient that he might be a candidate for fixed teeth is like not treating a person who is blind when techniques are available to restore sight.

When an idea is first conceived, it must go through many stages in the eyes of the profession before it can be finally and fully accepted. It first must go through the stage of discovery, then years of questioning by the inexperienced, then further experiments, then clinical studies, then re-evaluation by the profession, and eventual acceptance. Our hope is that now our peers will strive together for the true and unselfish advancements of implantology. This would result in more ben-

*With my very special friend and colleague, Dr. Giordano Muratori, from Bologna, Italy. Giordano was one of the most prolific and enterprising implant pioneers I know of. He was one of the most honest people I have ever known and I am very proud to have been a close friend of his.*

efit to mankind. Regarding my experiences in this, I must say that none of my roads were ever paved for me. But when an idea's time has come, it can stop an onrushing army.

On January 6, 1883, Kahlil Gibran wrote, "I cannot say much now about that which fills my heart and soul. I feel like a seeded field in midwinter, and I know that spring is coming. My brooks will run and the little life that sleeps in me will rise to the surface when called." Beautiful words from a man of great sensitivity, talent, and emotion. Let us, as dentists and humanitarians, become more sensitive, and tune ourselves into the requests of our patients, and enlighten ourselves as to the benefits of implantology.

Almost anything you do will be insignificant, but it is very important that you do it! Man's mind, stretching to a new idea, never goes back to its original dimension.

Many times, during my professional life, I have considered myself lucky to have so many colleagues who believe in me and carefully follow my teachings. However, too often, I have considered myself unlucky, because my work and philosophies have been subject to people's criticisms, whether they are familiar with implantology or not. Gibran also wrote: "There is a space between man's imagination and man's attainments that can only be traversed by his longing." I have lived by these words.

At a symposium at Harvard University, sponsored by a grant from the National Institute of Dental Research, forty-seven outstanding researchers and clinicians in implantology from throughout the country were invited to assess the benefit-risk ratio of several implant types. Blade implants were the only endosseous implants approved for use with appropriate guidelines. There is no other implant in the entire world that is used with more success or in such large numbers as the blade. I've always said, it is not the material but the design of an implant and how well it is used that is of cardinal importance for success.

To my skeptics: if I am wrong, then prove it to me, scientifically. But when I have been proven to be correct, won't you find it would have been disastrous for you if I had treated you in the same manner as most of you have treated me for the past twenty-five years? Instead, I invite you to join me and help contribute to this most needed and advanced field of dentistry.

The seeds of implantology have been sown. I can now only hope and pray that they've fallen on fertile ground.

*Cecilia, taking a picture of Giordano and I with a few very attractive young ladies looking on.*

*Dr. Ugo Pasquilini was the first to demonstrate the phenomenon of osseointegration of bone to implants.*

# Eighteen

## WORK AND WEARINESS

Writing this book has been a slow process. All of 1990 elapsed and I didn't have a chance to set down a single word for its pages. This is attributable to an overload of prior commitments. During that year I published my three-volume work, *Implant Dentistry Today: A Multidisciplinary Approach,* which included thirty-eight hundred color photographs and 750 black-and-white photos. I consider this the bible of implantology. Between writing, incessant travel, and running one of the largest and most demanding dental practices in the country, my time and energy shortage was no mystery.

Still, I enjoyed some wonderful days. I was always grateful when I saw how each patient reacted at the moment the provisional fixed prostheses were placed over the implants. The behavior was similar. The patient would first bite down experimentally, often tentatively, then progressively harder. Suddenly he or she would realize that, quite unlike dentures, the implanted teeth did not move. They would compare favorably to their natural teeth, a sensation many of them may have forgotten. Now, again, they could enjoy natural enunciation, smiling, eating, talking. Their faces would light up like a beacon. This transformation made me feel as good as they did.

I performed thousands of operations each year–replacing prostheses or effecting repairs–and put my heart and soul into each and every one. In addition to common procedures, I rehabilitated dentally crippled patients so that they could once again chew painlessly, smile broadly, talk normally, and rejoin society. I take great pleasure when I can relieve someone who, on an initial visit to my office, is holding a handkerchief to the mouth, will not smile and indeed will barely speak. This is not just a sign of discomfort, but of shame and suffering. Most presented with very few teeth, or none at all. This may be attributed to their own long-term neglect, or to poor prior dentistry which failed to arrest decay beneath improper fillings. The nerves there died and, remaining untreated with root canal therapy, eventually abscessed. Teeth were then extracted, replaced with dentures. My women patients, prior to implant procedures, often had handkerchiefs in hand to repeatedly hide what they felt to be unattractive "false teeth." What worried them most, indeed, terrified them, was the thought of some future admission to a hospital for surgery that would require removal of their dentures. Lying naked before strangers, about to be anesthetized and sliced, was not so unnerving as the loss of one's vanity.

Sometimes, of course, there is little or nothing to be done for a patient who has been previously mistreated by a dentist or an oral surgeon. Some of the worst cases involve paresthesia, characterized by a deadening of the nerves and a numbing of the lower lip and chin, or dysthesia, accompanied by great pain and burning of the lips, and dryness of the lips and mouth. This is one definition of total misery. Worse, these conditions may be irreversible. But most often, thankfully, most parasthesias eventually disappear on their own. Many of these patients appeared edentulous, but frequently I was able to at least insert some form of implants to support fixed teeth. Though some of these patients were never alleviated of their parasthesias, at least they could chew. After a triumph of corrective surgery I would yank off my face mask, often with the patient's blood splattered all over it and my forehead, a smile on my face. And on the patient's too. Once again, the misfortunes of poor advice and poor dentistry elsewhere, and the complex challenges of human anatomy and psychology, had been turned back at my door.

In December 1983 I received a letter from a patient, Harold Keppel, in which he exhorted me to found the Leonard I. Linkow Institute for Implantology. He stated: "You cannot escape your fate. God has chosen you as the moving light in this area, and there is *nothing* you can do about it . . . Your name should have been Abraham Linkow, because you are freeing the slaves who are in bondage to the dental contraptions, which have made these people prisoners for years, and who are now clamoring for the freedom that they justly deserve, and look up to you as their very Savior to free them from this antiquated dental anguish and misery."

National holidays, postage stamps, the recipient of coveted awards, feted guest, God's chosen one, Abraham Lincoln. I was thrilled at the suggestions, the praise, not to mention the comparisons. But I surely didn't feel so exalted.

In these years, when I gazed into a mirror I seldom liked what I saw: the man staring back at me had bags under his eyes, a pallid complexion, and hair that looked as if it had just come out of a washing machine. I was obviously subjecting myself to substantial stress in mind and body. I was helping people, but expending a significant portion of my vitality in the process. The good life was being sacrificed for surgery and lecturing, writing and globe-trotting. I found myself between the proverbial rock and its brother, the hard place. This was not an average professional highway; I could not just flip the signal, turn the wheel and glide over to a slower track. By slacking off I might relinquish some of the momentum I had gathered over these years. Now that I was growing older, the rhythm of travel and the lure of exotic places and new people (and vice versa) had lost much of its luster. The demands and obligations, however, remained the same. In all honesty to myself,

I recognized few options but to continue as I had. The summit of the mountain was still there above me, and I had to continue on.

When I reflected on my family and friends, it was clear that my obsession with implants was pushing them away. I once had crowds of friends, but now I was often alone. One of the reasons I lost Wiesia—at heart, a wonderful person—was the demonic compulsion that drove me night after night into the wee hours to prepare a group of slides for yet another lecture. Or compiling research. Or writing articles. Or dictating correspondence.

I began to lose sleep. Lack of time was always a factor; it added to the stress, or rather, helped to cause it. Soon I was getting no more than two to three hours of rest a night. It seemed that I needed just the bare minimum that would enable me to carry an enormous workload without impairing my clinical or surgical skills. It's something of a miracle that these skills didn't decline, given such a regimen. For this and my other capabilities—focus, determination, a head for details—I thank the great Lord in Heaven.

But, like a one-mast sailor trying to outrun a fast-moving storm, the consequences of my hectic life finally caught up to me.

I was in Hong Kong to give an implant seminar. I had nearly completed the morning program when I was seized by a fever. One moment I was my normal self, the next it was as if lightning had struck me. I began to shiver almost uncontrollably. That was bad enough, but then excruciating pain took root in my right eye. I had never experienced a sensation like it. I didn't even know there was agony quite this ruthless and focused, like the repeated plunge of an invisible ice pick. It was all I could do to close out the lecture. The moment the audience broke for lunch I rushed to my room and crawled into bed. I piled blanket upon blanket over me but continued to shiver. The house doctor responded immediately to my summons. And though I had never before in my life taken painkillers by injection I wasn't about to stand on ceremony now. I begged him for a shot of Demerol and to my relief, he obliged. In thirty minutes or so the pain subsided. Before the doctor left, he also gave me some pills to bring the fever down.

One of the more unusual symptoms he noted was that my right pupil had ballooned to three times the size of the left. He diagnosed the incident as the consequence of a viral infection, a one-time attack that wasn't likely to recur. Eventually, this proved to be a misdiagnosis, but it wasn't the doctor's fault. Few could have been accurate, such was the rarity of my true condition.

I was intensely stubborn and determined and naturally insisted on resuming the lecture once the lunch break ended. I lurched from bed to complete the task I had assigned myself.

For nearly a year it seemed that the Hong Kong hotel doctor had been right. I suffered no more attacks and the bizarre incident began to recede in memory. Then that comfort was shattered, along with part of my self-image as a still-vibrant professional man. The next attack was just as violent as the Hong Kong episode and lasted for nearly an hour. I thought it was the virus, lurking in my system, returning for a sequel. Three months later it happened again. The interludes of tranquility began to grow fewer and shorter; I was soon experiencing these attacks almost once a week! And it was always the right eye that was affected. It was like having your eyeball squeezed by a nutcracker. The pain would migrate quickly to my right temporal lobe, there to assault my brain tissue as if with repeated blows from a baseball bat wielded by Ruth or Williams. The pain was so intense that I didn't dare touch that part of my head. Even passing a light paintbrush over that area would produce agony and send a jolt to my right ear.

After consulting several neurologists and opthomologists, I finally had a name for my condition, if not a cure. What I was afflicted with, they said, were 'cluster headaches.' This condition is totally different from migraines, and the pain is greater by a multiple of magnitudes. If a migraine can be likened to a bad gash in a finger, a cluster headache is like having that finger lopped off without anesthesia.

The term "cluster headaches" implies that they come in bunches. From what I've learned, they often strike in certain seasons and can be dormant for up to three years. Unhappily, mine never seem to be long absent; on the contrary, they seem to have taken up permanent residence in my head. While I've taken a variety of drugs to squelch the pain, or at least diminish it, few of them prove effective. And some, might I add, are so strong that they should be enough to drop a horse. I've read nearly all I could find about this phenomenon. For those of you who might suffer from cluster headaches, or who know someone who does, here are a few tips.

Doctors have discovered that there are basically two types of cluster headaches–those like I experienced initially in Hong Kong, which occur rarely, and chronic cluster headaches, which I began to suffer later on. Only about two percent of sufferers are affected by chronic cluster headaches. It's just my fate to be in that small minority.

Doctors have found some unusual similarities among those traumatized by cluster headaches, not all of which they are capable of explaining. In 1972, Dr. Graham (whose first name I cannot recall) confirmed that most of the sufferers are big, muscular men typified by a rugged appearance and a lion-like physique. They commonly have square jaws, a cleft chin, and either light blue or green eyes. The clinical meaning or genetic association of these observations remains something of a mystery.

The cluster headache is believed to be a cyclical disorder that stems from imbalance in a person's biological clock. This theory emerged from findings that they occurred at roughly the same time of day during the cycle. Normally, the body's biological clock regulates enzyme activities, body temperature, hormone secretion, and other physiological behavior. In cluster headaches rictus the body seems to have difficulty coordinating and controlling these natural, circadian rhythms. The hypothalmus, the region in the brain which controls sleep and wakefulness, may be involved in the syndrome, initiating a central nervous system chemical discharge into the bloodstream. This causes the dilation of the blood vessels. But this dilation is considered to be the result, not the cause, of the trouble. Serotonin levels may be another factor. This brain chemical, along with histamine, regulates the biological clock and is connected anatomically to the eye. Histamine levels may also be involved since it is a vasoactive substance; it dilates the blood vessels and helps to regulate blood pressure. Researchers have discovered that by injecting a small amount of histamine into someone with a history of cluster headaches, that they are indeed able to trigger an occurrence. Consumption of alcohol during the period of vulnerability will have the same effect. Researchers have also reported that in about half the cases, patients are awakened by attacks in the middle of REM (rapid eye movement) sleep, the deepest sleep and most often associated with a dream state. But no one has yet offered a convincing explanation as to why this is so.

A surgical technique called radio frequency trigeminal rhizotomy has been developed to neutralize the pain. This sizable task requires the great precision of a neurosurgeon. A needle is placed in the trigeminal nerve near the brain to conduct microwave radio frequencies. Approximately seventy percent of the patients who undergo this operation have had positive results. Nonetheless, this surgery is recommended in rare cases, largely for chronic sufferers because it has the regrettable side-effect of numbing the facial muscles.

I have endured five to seven attacks a night, each one lasting between forty-five minutes and an hour and a half. At such times, of course, sleep is inconceivable. I've been awakened hundreds of times in the middle of the night by attacks which prompt a mad dash to the refrigerator for ice. Holding icebags over my right eye, temporal region and right ear, I've paced the living room like a manic tiger, screaming for surcease. For obvious reasons, this condition is also called the suicide headlock. I can easily understand why due to these attacks some men have taken their lives. Most of the time when they occur I drop to my knees and pray to God for freedom from this torture. I have tolerated these seizures through sheer will and the absolute refusal to suffer defeat. I manage to work and maintain a normal routine despite what is almost literally a sword of Damocles over my head.

In recent years, however, I have been temporarily helped with heavy doses of prednisone, taken for about two weeks, which seems to break the cycle. Also, mercifully, nearly all of my headaches occurred at night, always during the cycle of the body's recovery from fatigue, so their direct effect on work was limited. Caffergot depositories may be prescribed for the pain, because they constrict the blood vessels and thereby ease the pressure on the optic nerves. But as a consequence they can place excess pressure on the heart. Painkillers like Viocoden extra strength or Percoset or Percodan (oxycodone) seem to do no good at all. There is something of a partial solution, however. Sometimes, instead of an immediate and traumatic headache, an attack is signaled by slowly building pressure on the right eye; it "plays" with me and grants time to prepare. I have found that by standing on my head–a ludicrous position to be sure–while using a nosedropper filled with procaine topical anesthesia to wash my brain's spheno palatine ganglion has some effectiveness although it never lasts long enough. (The spheno-palatine ganglion is the "root" of the spheno-ganglion nerve. This largest of the cranial ganglia is deeply placed in the spheno-maxillary fossa, close to the spheno-palatine foramen. It is triangular or heart-shaped, of a reddish-gray color, and is situated just below the superior maxillary nerve as it crosses the fossa.) This is hardly a practical solution, but I will utilize whatever unharmful relief methods I can discover, and so would anyone else in this predicament.

I'm grateful that none of these attacks have ever occurred during the day while I was working on a patient. I ask myself: how can I continue to endure such torment? But throughout my life I've waged an uphill battle. Nothing ever came easily to me. I hold out hope that in this battle, too, I will eventually triumph. In any case, in many ways, for many years I've lived with stress. In a perverse way it has become my good friend because I'm so familiar with it.

There was a time, however, when I almost lost this life.

I always thought of myself as an athlete, and a good one. I got it into my head and heart that I should resume a training routine. Get in shape. Maintain virility and vibrancy. I assumed that, at the age of merely fifty, I could go out jogging once or twice a week–even though I had not jogged in years–and run five miles each time. Off I went to complete the distance every Saturday and Sunday, knowing very well as a doctor that this wasn't the proper way to proceed. In fact, whenever I was away on a lecture tour, whether to another state or another conti- nent, I had no opportunity to maintain such a senseless regi- men. During these periods I attempted these five-mile jogs only once or twice a *month*.

You can guess what happened. In late 1982, on a jog in Ft. Lee, New Jersey, a deep, great pain radiated through my chest like a hot, constrictive alarm. If nothing else, I was smart enough to stop and slowly walk home. But because it was my first en- counter with this kind of chest pain I pushed it out of my mind. I was, indeed, in witless denial. Perhaps, subconsciously, even self-destructive. Then, months later, just before a lecture, I was jogging in Las Vegas when it happened again. This time the pain was worse. Wiesia implored me to take a stress test at Columbia Presbyterian Hospital in New York City, and I finally agreed. I felt I had done reasonably well on the test, so I didn't hesitate to leave that same evening on a jet bound for Paris where I was to give one of my yearly Linkow Seminars. For my post-seminar plans I would fly to North Africa for a three-day vacation and then depart for Germany and a Linkow Seminar there.

I didn't take that long weekend in the Sahara. Out of the blue I heard from my attorney: I was to immediately return to

New York for a court appearance in my own behalf against Dr. Witty, who had filed suit against me because I had the temerity to try to make money from my own implants. (These implants were never sold–only Gnalducci and I used them and Gnalducci had been forcefully told that if he ever sold one blade I no longer would come to Italy to do surgery or lecture on his behalf.)

Dr. W initiated this law suit in the mistaken belief that I was selling these Italian-made blades and therefore not pushing his company's blades–the third patent, the one in with *his* name included with mine. It was high time to engage this lout, so I scrambled to make the plane connections. Missing one flight out of Marrakech, I hired a Mercedes to rush me across more than 100 miles of Morocco to catch another plane in Casablanca.

After eleven hours in the air I sleeplessly dashed straight to the courtroom. Cecilia, my office manager, awaited me in court. Worriedly she told me my skin was ghostwhite. I spent four long hours on the witness stand. My detailed testimony devastated Dr. W and his case. I was full of myself, secretly glad that he had underestimated me and delivered on a golden platter the opportunity to pummel him with his own blind arrogance. Without knowing the outcome of the trial–or of my stress test– I raced back to the airport so I could return to Paris and retrieve my valises full of slides. Then I would go on to Germany for the seminar. Jet lag, nervous tension, inflexible schedules, professional conflicts, naked compulsion, chronic ailments: I was dancing furiously to ominous music.

A telegram from my attorney awaited me at the hotel in Frankfurt. "Congratulations!" it said. "You won the case, and what's more you won back the patents you had assigned to the implant company." I was delighted to finally free myself from a man who had lived off my work and reputation for years. Actually, however, I was not completely free; Dr. W retained the right to sell certain blade implants, which he had originally called Linkow blades but then renamed to honor himself. I knew it would cost me another hundred thousand dollars to sue for patent infringement. And the company was in precarious condition; Dr. W was still draining the company of money it could instead use to reimburse the innocents who had been sweet-talked into buying shares.

No matter. There I was, rushing back and forth, continent-hopping.

I was deathly ill with angina: all three of my main coronary arteries were badly blocked, as I was sternly informed on returning to New York. My cardiologist insisted I take immediate action. "Check into the Cleveland Clinic. They have the most experience."

I continued to be a victim of self-delusion, of my own denial. I'm an athlete! I'm strong! Great will power! My rationalizing deafened me to my cardiologist's advice. I was my own worst enemy and had succumbed to the tunnel-vision mindset I disdained in others. Robin, my oldest daughter, was getting married in about six weeks. I didn't want to spoil the party and so I opted to wait. But the angina didn't. The attacks occurred more frequently, which prompted me to pop nitroglycerine tablets like candy.

Robin had her wedding, and then Wiesia and I headed for a week's vacation in Florida.

It could be that my delays weren't due to misplaced confidence in my fundamental good health. It could be that I was afraid that heart surgery would be my curtain. In any case, after the wedding I wanted to share a week with my wife before placing myself in the hands of the Cleveland Clinic.

My heart, however, would tolerate no further delays. Just a few days before New Year's Eve, 1982 I was rushed to North Ridge Hospital in Fort Lauderdale. A three-man team performed the emergency bypass without the senior cardiac surgeon, who was then on vacation. Just prior to the surgery I asked to meet the second man in charge. I liked this good fellow very much. I almost forced him to promise me that I would walk out of the hospital under my own power.

I recovered bleary consciousness in intensive care. It was

marvelous to see my two lovely and devoted daughters and my wife at my side, and to still be alive. But the pain in my chest was unbearable. Every hour I was turned from one side to the other to prevent fluids from filling my lungs. Shortly thereafter, to strengthen my lungs the nurses would have me blow into tubes. The stream of air was supposed to propel a couple of ping-pong balls up into a container. The harder one blew the higher they rose. But God, what a terribly difficult and painful task it was to get them to move at all! Even though the therapy was for my own good, I was glad when the nurses went away.

Eventually I became ambulatory, a walking stick of a man. I would wander through the lonely hospital halls at two and three o'clock every morning, sometimes in the throes of what could best be described as hallucinations. The same night nurse always seemed to be present. A woman in her sixties, her cap was different from the other nurses. The first night I told her to please free me from this Japanese prison boat. Perhaps for a few moments she thought I was actually making sense. On another night I grabbed her and said that a dentist was awaiting me at his office and that I'd promised to help him design his subperiosteal implant and that she must drive me there at once. Each time she would patiently calm me down and lead me back to bed.

One evening, when I was wired up with a multitude of medical appliances, I stepped out of bed to visit the toilet–and ripped all the connections from my chest. I remember looking down to see blood flowing down toward my belly. Then I must have passed out. The image and the moment cut directly to black and blankness.

Then I had a particularly vivid dream. It is certainly peculiar what the mind conjures up at times like these. The scene was surreal, like a Chagall or a Dali painting, certainly an identifiable image but far from easily explained. I was naked and shivering on a wooden bench at the back of a darkened church. I was terribly weak and could not move. Two figures approached slowly, both garbed in black gowns and hoods. As they came closer, a nearby telephone rang suddenly. Somehow–still in my dream–I was able to pick it up. It was my friend Dr. Feigel from Switzerland: "Lenny darling," he said, "please don't give up, don't let them take you from me. We all need you. The world needs you."

The next clear memory of the real world was of lying on my bed in a pool of blood with a team of nurses frantically working around me.

The miracle is this: the very next day I received a phone call from Dr. Feigel. He spoke the same words I had heard him say in the dream.

As the great playwright said, there is more on heaven and earth than is dreamt of in my philosophy. I never believed deeply in psychic bonds, but the proof here of a power and a connection beyond conscious power was irrefutable.

At last, about two weeks later, I was released from the hospital with a new lease on life. I spent the next weeks in our Pompano Beach apartment with Wiesia, Robin and Sheree. My strength slowly returned, and I joined the exercise program at North Ridge Hospital. My mother and father never knew the real reason I spent so much time there. Father would often ask why I left the office for such a long time. I told him I was doing what he always suggested that I do–take a long vacation in my Florida condominium. Perhaps my Dad had doubts but he never said a word. And he would have broken up had he known, so my silence on the matter was to protect them from my predicament.

It took three months to fully recover. When I walked back into my New York City office, tears welled up at seeing my staff for the first time since my brush with death.

They say that after bypass surgery, or many other kinds of trauma (and major surgery is, indeed, a form of trauma), people often feel very depressed and alone. This was true with me for a long time afterwards. I would walk in the busy Manhattan streets after a day's work with tears in my eyes and abiding sadness in my heart. My depression seemed to coat all of life in shades of gray, like the streets of Katowice. I searched for my old will to fight, to carry forth, but it was missing, perhaps for good. More than thirty years of combat with my rivals and with the forces of hypocrisy had at least for the moment proven to be enough.

I found myself staying home more and more, including Friday and Saturday nights that had once been important to me. Indeed, I had considered it vital to easing–or escaping– the go-go whirlwind of my profession. Now, my desire for fun had dissipated. I no longer went out to socialize. All those smiling, dressed-to-the-nines people pursuing pleasure on weekend evenings would only sadden me more. Was my numbness– like a huge shot of novocaine to my soul–driven by guilt at my failed marriages? Was I so battle-fatigued that there was no room for happiness? Perhaps my karma was to live this kind of life at last, assuming the role of a reclusive, far from the crowds, from the challenges and the accolades for successfully meeting them.

I felt more alone than ever, and not just because of Wiesia. Within these few years, both my parents had passed on. I keenly felt their loss. In 1985 my mother entered the hospital for a colonoscopy. I had serious misgivings about her doctor. To my mind his primary method of treatment was not compassion and prudence but the scalpel. Cut first, asks the tough questions next, and care last. I am certain that exactly the reverse is best. Sooner or later–if he had at that point not already done so–he would violate the Prime Directive of medical care: first, do no harm. And so he did. Her condition worsened, I surmise to the point where she knew the end was near. She was 84 years old. She asked the doctor to release her so she could go home to die in peace. But the sensitive fellow insisted that she remain in the hospital for further treatment. As if it was solely or even largely his decision. As if she would be offending him to withdraw from his care. I regret not intervening on my mother's behalf. All in all, I had faith in the power of medicine; I did nothing to counter the physician's advice. Perhaps because the doctor and I were medicine men, sort of a brotherhood, I didn't want to intrude on his province. Nor did my father. He tried to avoid the situation entirely, so much so that he resisted even going to visit my mother and his wife. I was enraged; I couldn't believe his behavior. I virtually had to drag him to the hospital. He was alone with my mother for perhaps half an hour while I waited down the hall. You know how hospitals are–sterile, vaguely alien, about as serene as a bus terminal. Not the best place to heal. Let alone die. I don't know what they discussed, but when Dad emerged from the room he clearly had been moved to tears. Nonetheless, it was the only time that he would visit. I guess I hated him then; insensitivity was not in his character, but I had no other explanation for his attitude. Later I realized that he simply couldn't accept my mother's illness and her impending death. It would mark the beginning of the end of his life, too. That would upset nearly anyone.

I asked the doctor if I should postpone a trip to Japan and a seminar at the Linkow Implant Society in Nara. I may have detected a scent of his wishful thinking–or was it merely his arrogance that she would not dare to die while in his care? Or was I passing on a signal that, as I did not want to cancel my journey, it was up to him? Truth be told, I was hoping he could keep her alive until I returned. During my last visit to her in the hospital Mother pleaded with me to take her home, to her familiar, comfortable home. I knew what she meant; a hospital is nothing but a warehouse. But I also knew my Dad wasn't up to the job. Perhaps she could have spent her last days with my sister instead of the stranger nurses on the floor.

The doctor assured me that my mother would be alive when I returned. I didn't take him to be a "famous last words" fellow. I hoped and prayed that Mother would be saved by remaining in the hospital, because I feared for her death if she came home.

During the first day of the Nara lecture, I received word

from Enid that my mother had died. I have never forgiven myself for being absent on May 4, 1985, nor for failing to press the doctor to heed her requests to be released for home where she could pass her last hours in a familiar, comfortable world, rather than the limbo warehouse of a hospital.

I adhered to the lecture schedule, but passing on the message to my Japanese colleagues, emphasizing that after I finished that day's course I must leave for home. Immediately, one of the audience members arose and spoke to the assembly in Japanese. He began to cry. Others followed. It was almost as if they had lost a member of their own family. No observation is true that says the Japanese people are cold and suppress their feelings, or have few of them at all, for people outside their culture. They insisted on taking me at once to the airport so that I could begin my journey without delay.

I will never forget my Mother's love for me nor mine for her. She was a regal, sensitive woman incapable of hurting anything or anyone. I was fortunate to be her son and to be guided by her warmth and wisdom. She was truly a lady.

My dear father, who turned 91 years old on August 7, 1988 (and who had enjoyed a full mouth of upper and lower blade-vent implants since 1983), was also a great source of happiness to me. He passed away shortly after that birthday, on January 18, 1989. It is irrational, maybe even selfish, to expect parents, or anyone you love, to live forever. Death is a part of life, a cycle that cannot be broken to spare one the sweet agony of loss, the end of a direct connection to bygone days—in my case a Brooklyn baseball childhood, summer days in an oxygen tent, Mother's review of my grammar school report cards, Dad waiting in his car at the subway station, dental school frustration. Sixty years of many rich and glowing memories are indispensable to a life well-lived.

I decided that it was time to repair my directional guidance problem. My career compass, in terms of compensation and personal pride and satisfaction, had been true. My personal compass, however, was not well aligned. For years I had

304 LEONARD I. LINKOW

been living two different lives–diligent and almost obsessive in the office, dashing and seductive on the town. Most probably my lust for women had been an excuse to forget for brief intervals just how I had lost my balance. The countless hours of study and preparation, of arguing, traveling, surgery, and lecturing left no time to think about the present moment, and near-future goals. I was neither here nor there, always in a hurry, always at work. Always searching for something I may already have possessed.

I am an essentially honest man: I pay my debts, tell my friends and family that I love them, speak my mind with firm diplomacy but also with a view to everyone's dignity. I admit to my mistakes, perhaps even confess them. My dalliances, however, were most difficult to acknowledge, to reveal. After my illness, when for the first time I had glimpsed my mortality and assessed all the years and people behind me, I felt vulnerable, emotionally exposed. The emperor had no clothes. It was frightening, but also rather liberating. Plausible denials could only give way to frank admissions. Now that I could no longer run ahead of a crisis, beyond fallout range, or behind it, engaging in damage control, news of my second, furtive life finally began to emerge. They were no longer mere rumors or suspicions. My darling daughter Robin, who always had the highest respect and admiration for me–and who herself had always upheld a very high moral standard–was overwhelmed. One reason may have been the shocking failure of her own marriage. She and her husband, Joe, whom I had once considered my son, had three unbelievably lovely children. I love all children; they are beautiful, boundless in their vitality, eager to be guided, curious beyond measure. And they are the future. Robin's three–Stephanie, Stevie, and Michael–were and remain pure joys. Smart, lovely, beaming.

Their father, Joe, however, picked up and left them all. Inexplicably, and despicably, he deserted his family. The challenges of providing for, of loving the four people who shared his name had apparently overloaded his woeful self-esteem.

The coward couldn't face the responsibility. In fact, he was not a well person. He had inherited $2 million from his father's estate, generated by several warehouses and a moving business for which Joe had once worked. One might think that a man with two million bucks would find ways to make the money grow: start his own business, invest wisely, spend with good taste and common sense. But Joe stopped working altogether. He sat around the house and got fat on the gourmet food he prepared. This in itself put a strain on the marriage. Moreover, other than procreating three children, he was unwilling or unable to perform sexually. Last but not least, Robin had little or nothing in common with her husband. In a few short years he had lost or exhausted much of that substantial inheritance, investing not one penny, but always selfishly spending. He purchased new suits by the closetful, and a penthouse in Fort Lee, New Jersey (not far from my home). There he shacked up with a bimbo who, according to my granddaughter Stephanie, had the habit of parading around half-naked.

Understandably, Robin was distraught at such crude behavior patterns in men. In my defense, despite my interpersonal and marital problems, I had not deserted anyone. But neither had I fully confronted my behavior. When Robin found out about one of my extramarital affairs she naturally lost a lot of respect for me. It's not easy for a daughter to discover that her father, a titan in her eyes, was—and is—only a flawed human being. My other daughter, darling Sheree, very seldom raised the issue of my other side. I guess—I can't do more—that she didn't like the revelation either, but she mostly kept it to herself. She and her husband, Nathan, had a precious daughter, Jennifer, in March 1993.

To truly love family and friends means one must be willing to genuinely take responsibility for personal failures which have adversely affected them.

# Nineteen

## TURNING POINTS AND DREAMS COME TRUE

Tribulations aside, the world was still my oyster. I was a cosmopolitan. An inventor. A doctor and technician. Known on four continents, I was invited to more events than ten people could attend. But of all the honors I have received, one of the most unusual, and among the most cherished, was to have a street named after me in 1986, in Germany.

Events like this are rare! In France, in 1869, during the reign of Louis Napoleon, a group of very influential people tried to have a street name changed to honor the great author Victor Hugo. They did not succeed. Hugo was still alive and well, a legend in his own time (and would not pass on until 1885). In Germany, sometimes a street, newly cut or re-paved, is named for someone who has died, if that individual enjoyed great popularity for his accomplishments, and was of German origin or had lived most of his life in Germany. Only once in the past century has a new street been named for a non-German who had never lived there: John F. Kennedy, and that was only after he was assassinated.

I owe the honor to Dr. Holger Burkel, a noted dentist who had attended one of my yearly Linkow Seminars in Munich in 1978. At every break Holger pressed me with questions, spoken in fairly good English, on how to learn more about implants. Holger was vibrant and vital, in his early forties. With his frizzy, tousled, thinning gray hair and glasses he resembled the stereotype of a professor. I could see in his enthusiasm that he was "hooked," probably for the rest of his career. I invited him to my New York office to watch my procedures. His faith in the system only grew.

Holger attended five annual seminars and then, at his sixth attendance, premiered a wonderful film on an implant case he had performed using my methods and designs. His admiration for me apparently was grand. I received a letter from him in which he announced that he and his wife had recently been blessed with a newborn son, who they had named Lenny. After me. I was greatly honored.

Four years later, Dr. Burkel sent me an even more unusual letter: "Dear Professor Linkow, I could never repay you in money for what you have done for my life, my ability to help restore so many previously unrestorable patients, and for what you did for my entire lifestyle, for me and my family. Before I met you I was merely a country dentist doing only ordinary things. Now I feel as though I have risen into an entirely new dimension in my profession. I am trying to have a street–the very same street where I practice–named after you. It may never happen but I will try very hard to make it so. Again let me thank you for changing my life."

I thought it was a very nice letter, certainly sincere and flattering, but otherwise I didn't think much about it. I knew only that his hometown was somewhere in the southwest of Germany. I really didn't consider the idea of having a street named after me there that big of a deal. This was shortsighted.

A year later, just before my nineteenth Linkow Seminar in Bremen, I was amazed to learn that Burkel had indeed been successful in his quest to have a street bear my name. I was met by Dr. Burkel's wife who drove me to Kappel-Graffenhausen (near Freiberg), Holger's home town on the Rhine. I arrived at Dr. Burkel's office and was amazed to find that it resembled a modern art museum; their huge house, attached to the office, was equally magnificent, a merging of Old and New European style. Acres of farmland surrounded the fairy tale setting. Taking up residence there were three horses, about a dozen sheep, a number of dogs, and two large, noisy and inquisitive ducks.

*Dr. Holger Burkel was the driving force to have a street name changed to Leonard-Linkow Strasse in Kappel-Graffenhausen, Germany (near Freiberg, 1988.)*

Two hours before the ceremony I was interviewed by two TV reporters and an interpreter in Dr. Burkel's living room. Their questions were hardly a surprise: Where did I get the initial idea for implants? Was there much resistance to it? What did I think of Dr. Burkel's work? What is the future for implantology? How old are you? The reporter blew this last question. When the story came out he'd added ten years to my age; that's no big deal when you're thirty, but when you're sixty and they call you seventy, you start counting how many days you have left!

The time for the ceremony arrived. Looking out the window I saw hundreds of people gathered on the street. To my amazement there was a *forty-nine-piece* orchestra, and its musicians in crisp, colorful uniform. The orchestra struck the opening notes of the fanfare almost at the dot of noon. Dr. Burkel led me outside to meet the townsfolk, some of whom would be using my name for the rest of their lives on every letter they wrote. Then came the speeches: Dr. Burkel's introduction was followed by the remarks of the mayor, a handsome and distinguished gentleman who praised me, although obviously he had never met me. I guess any friend of Burkel's was his friend, too! The entire time the interpreter was whispering translations into my ear. Then it was my turn to speak. Of course, I only knew English. But whatever the language, I became very emotional. I poured my heart out with an impassioned tale of my long struggle to promote implantology. The audience responded with eager applause and smiles on every face. Déjà vu once again, to my Bar Mitzvah. And what a place–Germany!– for a Jew to once again come full circle in his life.

After the ceremony we returned to Dr. Burkel's home for cocktails and hors d'oeuvres. I shook many, many hands, one of them belonging to a man who appeared close to eighty. I recognized him immediately–the patient who was the subject of Dr. Burkel's first implant movie. He seemed as happy as a lark. The party ended around six o'clock, when the celebration was relocated to the best restaurant in town, several miles away. But before we could leave, however, there was one ceremony still pending.

The orchestra reassembled to play first the American national anthem, followed by the German opus. I was guided to a spot beneath a street pole shrouded in a white cloth. As the last note faded into the evening the cloth was removed to great applause from the crowd. I gazed at that sign as if I were a young Red Sox fan, raising his head for a shy peek at Ted Williams. Leonard Linkow Strasse. Then, with a lump in my throat and joy in my heart, I walked to the car. There it was, like a moment in a dream. Come true.

All other things being equal, without the battles, there would be no moments like these. Fleeting but precious. Like diamonds washed downstream, dazzling you with reflected light before sinking away.

I was accompanied into the restaurant by my close friend Dr. Alfred Feigel, who had come from Zurich for the ceremony. A magnificent buffet awaited on tables bedecked with flowers. I chatted with the orchestra members, all forty-nine of them, a small army of musicians before they once again regaled us. There must have been about two hundred dinner guests, among them Barry Farber, the great New York City radio talk show host who had joined me on this trip and later gave an account of the event on one of his evening broadcasts. We didn't leave the restaurant until midnight. It had been quite a day!

\* \* \*

My sister Enid's husband, a dentist, left–rather, (like Joe) deserted–her and their children for another woman, never to see them again. At the time I was with Jean, my second wife. Shortly after Roy abandoned his family, we invited Enid and her son and daughter to our home one evening to renew acquaintances. Too many years had gone by since we all had sat down and talked with one another. We asked several friends of ours to join us, figuring that it would be easier to break the ice if it was not just a family affair.

My nephew, Richard, was eleven years of age, and niece, Susan, not quite ten. It was quickly apparent in their words and behavior that both kids had undergone what amounted to brainwashing by Enid, but especially by her now-estranged husband, the dentist. Richard and Susan were both certain

*1988 — with Barry Farber, the great New York City radio talk show host, who had joined me on this trip and later gave an account of this event on one of his evening broadcasts.*

that I was unscrupulous, untrustworthy, immoral. A monster. Such impressions could only have been put in their minds by two highly envious adults. The children were quite vocal about it, even though I was a virtual stranger to them. Finally I couldn't bear any longer to be so judged. I asked Richard to take a walk with me. I candidly, sincerely told him I was sorry for his father's desertion of them, and that from now on I would do my best to become a close friend of his.

His response was to spit directly in my face.

I was inclined to belt him—to his mind it would be proof that I was the bastard he thought me to be—but, having burned enough bridges, I controlled myself. Enid needed my support so it was important to make the new relationship work. But there are easier tasks than trying to overcome the disrespect of two kids who had been taught that their uncle was a wicked fool.

Several years elapsed. I saw Richard and Susan on numerous occasions when I drove my parents from Brooklyn to Enid's home in Syosset, Long Island. I maintained contact, and tried to keep an open mind towards them. But the children were always sarcastic to my parents and I. Okay, life goes on. During such a difficult visit in 1978 Richard mentioned that after he graduated from high school he planned to backpack through Europe. Sensing an opportunity for friendship, I casually told him I would be in Milan in July, giving a course at the university. If he happened to be in Italy then, we could meet at my hotel.

Strange as it seemed, or as telling, when the time came, after arranging the night before to join me for lunch, Richard actually did arrive at my hotel. He was very thin; he certainly had not been eating much. He was seeing Europe on the cheap. I felt good watching him fuel up on the typically wonderful Italian food, from the antipasto to the entrees to the desserts. I had to leave and get back to the university, but I invited him to share my room that evening. He was becoming very receptive. His maturity and my unconditional acceptance seemed to have broken the ice, or mended the fences.

That night, when I returned, I found Richard intently focused on writing in his diary. He let on that it was a memoir of his European trip. He had written a piece about me and offered to read it aloud. Although I sensed he was growing to like me, I said that I would rather not hear what he had composed. It seemed strangely intimate, I thought, and may make me uneasy. Richard tried several times to change my mind, but I stuck to my decision. So I never knew.

By now, my relationships with Richard and Susan have taken a one-hundred-eighty-degree turn. I'm proud of Richard. He has turned out to be a wonderful young man: brilliant, sensitive, caring. He graduated from the Albert Einstein School of Medicine and did an anesthesia residency program at U.C.L.A. He is a fine doctor, specializing in anesthesiology. He is now part of a group practice and is married to a beautiful girl named Pamela. I flew to California for their wedding. Their first child, Danielle Rose, was born in 1995. They later had a second child, a little boy named Brandon, as cute as can be.

Susan was always interested in environmental health and worked for several years in the field, spending nearly a year in Africa teaching people how to build stoves and lead healthier lives. It was commendably daring and courageous. She married a fellow named John, moved to Brooklyn and studied law at Fordham University. She eventually divorced her husband and moved to Albuquerque, New Mexico.

\*   \*   \*

I had boycotted the Israeli dental community between 1972 and 1980, opting not to lecture or teach there–though not for any political reasons. I had planned several years after my first seminar in Tel Aviv to return for surgical demonstrations there and in Haifa, but I was so exhausted from work and travel that I had to cancel. Fortunately, I called on Dr. Paul Glassman, a dear colleague, to go in my place. He was an excellent speaker and was often amenable to substituting for me. I paid for his airfare and hotel because in those days the Israelis didn't have the means to pay anyone a dime.

As it happened, the day he arrived in Israel I was ill and bed-bound. Paul phoned from the airport in Tel Aviv. In a very disappointed voice he said, "Len, they won't allow me to leave the airport to go to the lecture because they said it was Linkow, not Glassman, they invited." Sick or not, I got angry fast. My would-be hosts wanted my presence more for their prestige than the enhancement of dental practices. I told Paul to put the bastard he was dealing with on the phone. I blew up: "How dare you pull this nonsense! I'm sick and I could have canceled altogether but instead I tutored Dr. Glassman so Israeli dentists could learn the latest techniques!" They allowed Paul into the country, but because of this incident I declined their invitations for the next five or six years, after which they no longer extended them.

In 1980 an Israeli dentist, Dr. Sam Kaufman, approached me during a Linkow Seminar in Germany. His eyes were moist; he had been crying. "Professor Linkow," he said, "Why do you not come to our country, Israel, which is also your country, and teach us your life's work? We need you as our leader. You are the leader of the world."

He was impassioned and genuine and his words touched my heart. I had held an empty grudge for many years. It was time to atone. "Dr. Kaufman," I answered solemnly, "you arrange the seminar and you have my word of honor that I will be there." His sudden facial expression lifted twenty years from his apparent age.

And so once again I made plans to go. Just prior to my departure I was in the El Al lounge at JFK Airport when a familiar-looking man approached me. He asked if I would kindly courier an envelope to Israel. The moment I landed there, he said, I must mail it. He held open the envelope to show that there was nothing illegal inside, then sealed it. As we talked I realized we had once met at a house party given by one of my patients.

When I arrived in Israel a large entourage awaited me—several professors and their wives. And a beautiful, angelic-looking girl holding a sign: "Professor Linkow." As the doctors and their wives greeted me, I kept glancing at this enchantress and finally my gaze stayed on her. I was reluctant to make a pass at her, though, because these people thought I was married, even though I had already divorced Wiesia.

This beauty came over to me and asked in a few words of lovely dialect if I had the letter from New York. I was so enamored that it was only when she mentioned the man at Kennedy

Airport that I realized she wasn't with the others. I gave her the envelope and she turned gracefully to walk away. I called out, asking her name. Her response–so elegant and soft in manner–nearly took my breath away. She was moving out of earshot, so all I caught was Johanna Sarah something. I was too self-conscious to boldly request her phone number. That night I phoned New York to speak with the fellow who had given me the envelope. I begged him for her number. Oh, no, he said. That's my girl. I have been living alone now for fourteen years and if she will marry me she will be my bride.

In that brief encounter I pictured myself sharing the twilight of my youth with this vision. But I was a dreamer. At that point, my passion for women began to recede. The likeliness of such euphoria fades further away.

Just a few years later, one of my elderly female patients, who is very wealthy due to the estate she gained after the death of her husband, a former president of Sak's Fifth Avenue. She is often mentioned in newspaper columns that track the "elite" of New York City. Ironically, she knew very well the man who asked me to deliver his letter when I arrived in Israel. She told me that this Israeli woman was no good, a 'gold digger' only after my acquaintance's money–they had married and divorced and she took a lot of his assets. I could certainly empathize with his predicament.

\*    \*    \*

From the time I was knee-high, baseball had been my passion, fueling dreams of big league diamonds and grand slam glory. There are many roads we pass in our lifetimes; we must choose among them and make our travels as best we can. I did, in opting for LIU and NYU rather than making a bid for MLB (that is Major League Baseball). The dream of sport ceased to be a factor, but only by default, not consciously by design.

The sports path I had turned away from years before unexpectedly opened up again–only partially, of course, and by and large only symbolically. After a lecture in 1989, a colleague said: "Len, you've always spoken so passionately about your earlier days playing baseball. Why don't you go with me this coming February to Vero Beach, Florida? Just before the Los Angeles Dodgers report for spring training they have what they call the 'Million Dollar Dream Week.'"

What, I asked him, was a Million Dollar Dream Week? The Dodgers, he said, invited ninety frustrated would-have-been big league ball players to experience the same spring training rituals as the pros. The candidates form into six teams and play six games each. Former players (many of them Hall of Famers like Duke Snider, Harmon Killebrew, Don Drysdale, Ernie Banks, Bob Gibson, Lou Brock and Warren Spahn) would be coaches. Every participant had a final-game chance to play against a team of these legends. This privileged week didn't come merely for the asking—one had to apply—nor cheap, at $3,000 a man.

It sounded nothing less than grand to me. Nonetheless, I had reservations. Did I really want to take leave of my practice for an entire week? I had a business, with all its non-stop expenses, and most importantly, three ex-wives who had alimony agreements driven by the calendar and written in stone.

I carefully mulled over the opportunity. I decided—with a refreshing snap, a rare occurrence in my life—that I was only going to live once. I inquired of the Dodger office about the details, and made my reservation.

Realistically however, I hadn't played hard ball for at least thirty years. I felt I could still wield a bat with fair authority, but I also knew, from the softball I had played in my forties, that I no longer could throw with distance and power.

I wanted to take a mini-spring training of my own before Dream Week. But instead of practicing throwing or running, which was even more important, I went to an indoor batting cage and practiced my hitting. That, to me, was the heart of the game. I started in a slow-pitch cage where the balls came in at thirty miles an hour. I quickly noted that time had stood still; my timing was "right on." I met the balls solidly each time. After several no-baseball decades I hadn't lost my finesse or stroke. Within two weeks I had upgraded to a batting cage where the balls hurtled plate-ward at near major league speed, around eighty-five miles an hour. I was still doing very well.

The Million Dollar Dream Week arrived, as I did, in Vero Beach, on a chilly morning. After collecting my uniforms and gear, I proceeded to an introductory briefing. Soon thereafter, I and eighty-nine other ballplayers were rolling on the dew-covered grass performing stretches and calisthenics. I was the second oldest player there. Nearly everyone was in his early thirties; a few were in their forties, but only two of us were over sixty. However, my approach to the game signified a younger man. I believed I could compete with guys a quarter of a century younger–and that I was not vainly pursuing faded glory.

That very first afternoon, however, during one of the infield drills (I played first base), I stopped short and stretched too far before I threw to third base for an out. My right groin muscle was strained. It wasn't a good injury at all and did not bode well. I had violated a cardinal rule by insufficiently warming up and stretching; my muscles, tendons, and ligaments were cold and creaky, vulnerable to overextension.

The next morning, at bat in the first game of the day, I drilled a pitch down the left field line that caromed off the 332-foot fence on one bounce. It was sweet!: the swing, the thunking wallop of the ball on the sweet spot of the bat, its rapid flight, and the dismayed look on the pitcher's face as I propelled myself out of the box on my way to what I thought would be a double. I had forgotten that any sudden stretching movements could be dangerous. Indeed it was. By the third or fourth step I heard my left-thigh hamstring snap. I crashed to the dirt in agony. This had only happened to me one other time when, much younger, I had reached for a high ball in a tennis match to slam it down at my opponent. Then, too, I dropped like a toppling statue.

I was in tremendous pain. Dream Week baseball camp was

*A double down the left field line — but my hamstring snapped as I*
*ran towards first base. 1989, Dodger camp, St. Lucie, Florida.*

ruined. But I continued playing, despite the agony. After all, I
had paid for it. And no one complained. A young Japanese
man in his early thirties substituted as runner for me every
time I was at bat.

Nonetheless, I still hit well. I managed a .460 batting average, the second highest overall. Remember, I was the second-
oldest guy out there. It was ironic that the oldest fellow on the
field had the very highest average, over .500. Some guys are so
talented their skills only die when they do!

About the fourth day of that cool-weather week, we took
batting practice inside the cages. As I hit a terrible pain began
in the middle finger of my right hand. I thought it stung because of the cold and because I had hit a number of the pitches
with the thinner portion of the bat on or below the label rather
than the sweet spot above it. But even when I changed the
position of my hands and hit the ball solidly the pain persisted.

Indeed, it became even stronger. That evening, after dinner, I was shivering from the fatigue brought on by three injuries. I was so miserable that I went to my bunk and got under the covers.

I was very disappointed because each evening, immediately after dinner, two Hall of Fame players at the camp would step to the microphone and relive some important, even famous events in their careers. First hand accounts from the legends themselves! The dream of man and boy alike! My pain made socializing joyless and was so unbearable that I altogether missed the final two evenings of the week.

Finally, it was the climactic day and the final game. The Dream Week "championships." All the amateurs faced off against the Hall of Fame players. It was no contest; they really scalped us. The old timers could still hit the ball a country mile, and they racked up many home runs in their time at bat.

Then it was all over. Dream Week, that is, not the pain. It persisted throughout my homeward flight, a gnawing, leaden alarm that hammered at my brain as if something was eating my hand. That same night I was unable to sleep. My fat, swollen finger throbbed like blazes. Then it dawned on me that the discomfort was not from arthritis or from hitting the ball near the bat handle; I had a fractured finger. I had diagnosed myself a lot more poorly and slowly than any patient! Immediately I took a wide Emory board, placed it against the back of the finger and taped it tightly. In minutes the pain had subsided.

The next morning I used one of my X-ray machines to take several radiographs of the busted digit. Sure enough, there were not one but two vertical fractures. I had the finger placed in a plaster cast. For the next six weeks I was inserting implants with my patients prone to an accidental poke in the head or eye as I was prying in their mouths.

A self-evident word of advice for those who would join Hall of Fame players for a Million Dollar Week. Or anyone else tempted to pick up a rigorous sport idly set aside years before.

Practice running and throwing, or the equivalent, well before hand, and go a lot easier than I did. Stretch. Don't assume Father Time is the forgiving sort. Sometimes he takes no prisoners.

*   *   *

My accountant is in his 80s, but he looks like he's 120. He was married to the same woman for many years. They were both 69 years of age when she died. David was as lonely as could be. For five years he didn't socialize, he didn't date. Romance was, apparently, far from his mind. I guess that, after so many years with the same woman, he missed her, and had forgotten how to express interest in or draw the eyes of another flame. But, still, one has to live and enjoy it. Smile, though your heart is breaking.

Finally, someone introduced David to another lady. He fell in love. The wonderful woman did everything for him. But, in all candor, this tremendously nice fellow, though kind and caring (and a first-rate accountant) and tremendously happy to have another chance at love, is not an ideal of the handsome leading man.

He called me on the phone one night, somewhat comically distressed, lamenting that he could no longer perform his masculine duties with adequate rigor. "I don't know what to do with her sexually."

So he had gotten himself a pump, those bizarre gadgets with a big tube. The air pressure device stimulates the penis, coaxing an erection so that it and the man attached to it can perform their conjugal rites. But David didn't really know how to use the contraption. Perhaps he was too embarrassed to ask his partner for assistance. But we had been good friends for years. So what are friends for?

I immediately sensed an opportunity to be humorous, to help David come to terms with this typical late-life dilemma by getting us both to laugh at our common humanity. I wasn't married at the time, in between my marriages to Jean and Wiesia, and so I had dallied. David thought me to be a good source of advice.

"Gee, David," I intoned with put-on gravitas, "I've been thinking about that myself. I've got a new girl and I'm nervous and I have the same problem. Can you loan it to me so I can try it out? Then I'll tell you how to use it."

"Okay, okay," he said, as excited as an adolescent countryboy exploring a pond of frogs. He brought it over that night. The thing was about 15" long, more than big enough for the most freakishly endowed man.

The next night David called me. "What happened? Did that damn thing work?"

I had never even tried it on! The unit was more than a little ludicrous. But he, of course, didn't know that.

"Oh, David, I don't understand. I pumped it up. And I pumped it up. After a minute, there was no more room for my penis to expand."

Silence on the other end of the phone. To David the implication was mortifying. I'm sure I made him feel inadequate. But I couldn't much longer sustain my mirth, and I burst out laughing, not at him, but with him. I think that the humor enabled David to overcome his performance anxiety. I doubt he went on to win any comparisons to Casanova, but I'm sure he learned that, at our ages, some things in life are more important, and others less, than they once were.

*　*　*

Another great honor came to pass: the Linkow International Institute was established in Italy, my home away from home, land of my paisan Giorgio and other giants. I should have formed such an institute many years earlier, but for so long I was such a controversial figure that I had neglected a deed that would give it impetus: the formation of my own commercial company with the sole purpose of selling implants. A logical extension of this would have been in synergy with the company: my own institute. At the least, this would have irritated the academics who knew nothing about implants and have only recently learned about them, even though many are still restricting themselves to the screw forms. These know-it-alls, more proficient in criticizing than enhancing their technical expertise, would then have had an opportunity to meet me on my own ground. Instead, they chose to stick by their screw systems, even though some patients came to be dissatisfied with them, or the screws had simply failed. The Institute provided an opportunity for everyone in the field to freely compare my methods to the others vying for that special place, ultimately the one in the patient's mouth.

I owe the establishment of the International Institute to Dr. Francesco Mangini, a dentist from Bari, a seaport on the Adriatic Sea. Mangini, an excellent implantologist, is also a superb organizer. If the Institute was ever to be born and prosper, I needed someone with this combination of talents. Also, since anyone with a dental license can promote themselves as a specialist, I knew that the time was ripe to create this great learning Institute as a source of knowledge for dentists to learn implantology as I see it and as I have lived it. The Linkow Method. I had developed a multi-modal approach to implantology. A number of systems were now available for a variety of applications, not just screws and root forms, but an entire array of tools and devices useful in a wide range of cases.

This reservoir of implements meant that many more patients with a wider variety of cases could be successfully treated. Between 1982 and the early 1990s, the number of successfully completed Linkow implants had doubled, from 8,300 to 16,000 (and by 2002 exceeded 20,000).

In the spring of 1994, I was to be the recipient of another honor–in Romania, of all places! I was awarded an Honorary Ph.D. in a Doctor of Medical Science (DMSc) after previously being invited to give a three-day seminar, including live surgical demonstrations, to dental students at the University of

Bucharest. My books—*Mandibular Implants* and *Maxillary Implants: A Dynamic Approach to Oral Implantology*—had become influential in the Romanian implant field. Five professors had each taken a chapter or two from these books and spent close to one year studying the techniques. During this seminar they then expertly summarized what they had concluded. Afterwards, professors and course-takers alike said that they had never seen in any of the other standard anatomical or medical reference books they had read—Gray or Schaeffer among them—the morphology and anatomy as I had shown in my books. They had learned very much.

I was invited back in the spring of 1995 to lecture to the professors and listen to their thoughts on—and criticism of—my books. Then I was awarded a DMSc (Doctor of Medical Science). Throughout the session I was joined by the University dean, the rector of the country's entire university system, and General Augustine, the head of the army medical corps. It was the army, one of this otherwise poor nation's better financed institutions, that was to provide the funding for what was intended to be the largest implant center in Europe, and was to be named after me. However, corruption, that many-headed beast, once again reared its horrific head! General Augustine was an opportunist. The building, erected in my name and impressive at the time, had nearly been completed by October 1994. But the equipment, already paid for by the powers that be, never arrived. There was no such company! Someone surely was the undeserving recipient of a large sum of money!

But the most lasting and impressive accomplishment of my career—in terms of recognition—came not from dentists or academics abroad. It happened right at home in New York City.

\* \* \*

I graduated from New York University School of Dentistry in 1952. Three months after graduation I performed my first subperiosteal implant. The patient benefited from that work for seven years. But when the word spread that I was doing implants, the local profession was agitated. Other dentists judged me less than kindly, as if I were crazy. Before the universities came to accept me as a specialist worthy of guiding or shaping their dental program, I lectured at the Institute for Graduate Dentists on West 67th Street, for half a decade drawing dentists nationwide for the course four or five times a year. During these years this program helped to keep the school, a non-profit organization, out of the red. As implantology was more widely accepted many American universities invited me to give seminars. But one university continued to shun me–my own alma mater, the New York University School of Dentistry! Instead, at various times, the head of the School of Continuing Education would invite other dentists there to lecture on implantology. Ironically, many of these were dentists whom I had taught. It felt as though they were tossing daggers at me–while smiling. I began to loathe the school. As I have related, most of the profession from the 1950s through the early 1980s–four separate decades–simply was not ready for implant dentistry. I was "doing my thing" in a largely hostile environment.

Then there was a turning point. The International Association of Graduating Dental Students, who meet every two years in a different country, was scheduled to convene at the New York University Dental Center. The students nominate the dentists who have made significant contributions to the various specialties and then vote on the choices. I was the one they selected to lecture on implantology.

Thus I returned to my alma mater through the back door–because I had certainly not been invited by the faculty. The meeting was scheduled to be held in the Saklad Auditorium, named after Dr. Maurice Saklad, a fine teacher and leader in the university who had inspired very wealthy individuals to donate money for the auditorium.

The day of my lecture arrived. Several hundred students were in attendance from all over the world–Japan, the Philippines, Singapore, China, Germany, Sweden, Italy, Israel and many other countries. I was introduced by Dean Kaufman, whom I'd always admired. When I had been a student he was a professor in the crown and bridge department. He was an excellent dentist and a marvelous human being. I had a soft spot in my heart for him since he sat next to me the evening of my very first lecture to the Central Queens Dental Society, in 1954, when my career was in bloom. Dr. Kaufman had encouraged me before I began the lecture, telling me not to worry because I knew more about implants than everyone in the audience combined. Now here I was, nearly thirty years later, being introduced by that same man. Many aspects of my life had come full circle, and this was among the most prominent.

I spoke for seven hours. And they were demanding hours, packed with concepts not for the inattentive. I knew that minds were racing at the breadth and passion of my presentation, refined after countless hours of identical talks all over the world. And I made a special effort to be in top form. Afterwards I was surrounded by graduate students who, in addition to seeking more information about implants, were curious to know why academia was so reluctant to recommend their use. Many of these students were eager to visit my office during their one-week stay in New York. The next day, indeed the remainder of that week, my office was flooded with dentistry graduates from many countries seeking the secrets their schools had withheld.

On this same day, too, around noon, my secretary Edith entered to tell me that the Associate Dean of the NYU College of Dentistry was phoning. By intuition, almost as if by telepathy, I knew what he wanted. I had waited over thirty years for this call! And so, when I got on the line and Dr. William Greenfield, the Associate Dean, said, "How are you, Len?" I answered in a brusque voice. "Why are you calling?" I was not inclined to disguise my anger; after all, was I supposed to be grateful that I had been ignored since *The Honeymooners* was a hit TV show? My response caught Dr. Greenfield a little off guard, but he quickly recovered. Flattery works best. He had just returned from a sabbatical in Israel, he said, and every time implants were discussed there, my name was the first to be mentioned. As if, by some mystery, it was only last week that my reputation had made the rounds! Then Greenfield said, "Why do you want to teach implantology at Temple University, in Philadelphia, when you could do the same at your own alma mater?"

I burst out in stern candor. "Because at Temple they have always given me the red-carpet treatment, and allowed me to do almost anything I wished in the surgical clinic. I was never ever invited to give a single lecture at New York University– while students of mine have been invited time after time. So how can you ask such a question?"

"Things are changing now," he went on to say. "We realize you are number one in implantology, and we would like to have you with us."

"Why do you want me, when you have your other dentist advocating the Swedish system?"

Well, he said, don't worry about him–he won't stand in your way. Then he asked if I would be kind enough to meet with him and Dean Kaufman one day for lunch, to discuss this matter more thoroughly. No, I said, I haven't taken a lunch break in thirty years. My workload is demanding, and my patients come first. Then how about some night for dinner? he replied. I said to call me back next week and we might be able to make some arrangements. After we concluded our conversation, I said to myself that I must have blown the entire deal!

I felt like a woman who had gone faithfully steady with one guy for years, always hoping he would marry her. And you know what often happens with those frustrating, drawn-out affairs? Finally the man asks the woman to marry him and she says, pridefully, "Forget it, pal. I've had it with you."

That was what I felt about the New York University School of Dentistry. Not quite "forget it, pal," because in my heart I certainly wanted an association with my alma mater. But I had such a reservoir of frustration and anger that I'm surprised I did not offend them. Playing hard to get is an act of pride which, as Proverbs said, goeth before a fall. The NYU stewards continued to phone and I continued to put them off. One time I had the perfect reason, as I was ill in bed. Finally, on the sixth call, we set a date to meet at the dean's home. After a delightful dinner with the dean and his wife–when the Dean himself was now largely confined to bed from back pain–he explained that before his retirement he wanted to create the first endowed chair in implantology in the world. And he wanted to call it the Leonard I. Linkow Professorship in Implant Dentistry. He asked me if I knew anyone more deserving of it than me. My answer was a very brief. "No."

How much money does an endowed chair require? I asked. One million two hundred and fifty thousand dollars, he directly replied.

I was a bit taken aback. Was Greenfield making a pitch for funding? "I have no intention of buying a chair for myself," I said. "First, because I don't have that kind of money, and second, even if I did I wouldn't buy myself a department."

Greenfield laughed good-naturedly, diplomatically taking account of the many emotions he may have sensed in me.

"Don't worry about it," he said. "You have admirers from all over the dental world. They'll make contributions. It will all come to pass."

He was right. In a short time money and pledges amounted to almost $750,000–enough to establish the Linkow Institute of Implantology at New York University.

On February 22, 1991 the five-year struggle to open the Leonard I. Linkow Endowed Professorship in Implant Dentistry paid off. In his official announcement, Dean Kaufman called it an historic day for the New York University College of Dentistry. On this day, he said, "the foremost pioneer of implant surgery made possible the establishment of an endowment which will endure for the rest of our institutional future, the teaching and practicing of implant dentistry. Not only that, but this teaching and practice will henceforth be done in the name of Dr. Leonard I. Linkow. No other institution in the world can make that proud claim . . . "

Shortly after this occasion I was the subject–or you might say the object–of a magnificent roast in Chicago, to raise funds for the Linkow chair. Donations also came in from dental implant academies and individual practices all over the world. When, in 1992, the remainder of the money was fully pledged– in an amount actually exceeding what was required!–then the chair–and the department—became a reality. It was something I had only dreamed about. Dreams can come true, it can happen to you . . .

One sees on entering the implant clinic on the eighth floor of the NYU College of Dentistry on East 24th Street at 1st Avenue (only a few blocks from where I began my post-graduate education) a bronze plaque which declares:

"Dr. Leonard I. Linkow Professorship in Implant Dentistry: Established in tribute to an internationally respected pioneer in implant dentistry and beloved mentor to implant dentists the world over, Dr. Leonard I. Linkow, DDS: The world's first professorship in implant dentistry is made possible by the generosity and commitment of implant dentists across the globe to continuing research and clinical advances in implant dentistry: April 1991."

On the opposite wall is a huge color portrait of me.

An endowed chair means a department in implantology that remains forever. Even if the school should burn down and have to be rebuilt the chair remains, in perpetuity.

What an honor!

# Twenty

## OLD FRIENDSHIPS

In August of 1990 I received this letter from Raphael Chercheve. I corresponded with him many times in over a quarter of a century of collaboration and friendship, but this missive was especially fulfilling:

> Dear Lenny,
>
> I shall never forget the exceptional moments that we have spent together.
>
> The words I use are frozen but the impetus of our friendship is still wonderfully stimulating.
>
> We know sufficiently of the world to be able to distinguish truth from falsehood. This is why the authentic pleasure that we feel when we smile at each other or when we shake hands is truly exceptional.
>
> I must admit that for many years after you took over for me in Lariboisiere Hospital in Paris during my annual course in front of hundreds of students I became very jealous. Do you remember when my implant would not fit tightly into the maxilla of the woman patient and you successfully inserted your vent-plant after I finally gave way to your pestering?
>
> However, in time I realized that my own days of

glory were long and great and it was time for me to let
go. The years that followed proved to me that you,
Linkow, became the greatest implantologist in the
world. I'm proud that you still call me "mon pere."

You are very lucky and you must realize it. You have
recognition and this recognition is so strong that it
muzzles your enemies; whatever they try to do you are
and will remain the great Linkow.

The photograph I send you is in my eyes the sym-
bol of a great pride. It is your hand which is around my
back and I feel stronger from your presence.

On top of all what you have already done, the book
which we are going to publish brings a new prospect
and a new dimension to your work.

It will be a book full of life and this time with a real
collaboration of the two of us. . . .

With my love, yours, R. Chercheve

Writing this book has been like composing a long letter to
my friends, to strangers who might one day become my friends,
to my adversaries who are or will be neither, and to my family.
And there is that previously unexplored or often hidden or
unacknowledged side to friendship: brotherly respect and true
love.

I've previously mentioned Dr. "Alfie" Feigel from Zurich, a
fantastic dentist and brilliant surgeon. Alfie had been responsible for my lecturing at the prestigious University of Zurich, a
difficult feat for any outsider given the influence of Professor
Obergeiser, the head of the oral and maxillofacial surgery department. He was already world-famous because of his unique
and vital "sliding osteotomy procedure" which he taught to
thousands of oral surgeons worldwide. But he simply didn't
like a lot of people.

Alfie had become a disciple of my teachings and managed
to convince Professor Obergeiser to attend my 1970 lecture at

the Carlo Erba Institute in Milano. Alfie introduced us at the lunch break. And it was because of his influence that a year later I received an invitation from the University of Zurich to give a two-day seminar.

Except for one faux pas, everything went just fine at the University seminar in November of 1971. Even with the benefit of 20/20 hindsight, I would still have handled matters exactly the same. Alfie had told me previously that in recent years Professor Obergeiser had done some subperiosteal implants that by now had failed badly. These failures had persuaded the Professor that implantology as a whole wasn't feasible–of course assuming that his procedures had been perfect. And that the candidate had been ideal. To his mind the fault must lie in the methodology and not the execution. By this logic we would blame the car for the accident when a myopic or a inept driver had been at the wheel, or fault the teacher because the students were too lazy to do the homework. Given Obergeiser's poor results (on a limited number of cases) he fiercely opposed the techniques.

At lunchtime I was seated at the head table with Obergeiser to my right. Suddenly, in his stern Teutonic manner that broached no other view, he demanded silence. He stood to make what might have been a longer speech if I had not said what I said.

Obergeiser first looked at me, then surveyed the audience.

"I believe that the only viable implant that exists today are the blade implants of Linkow. But I definitely do not believe in subperiosteal implants." Turning back to me he said, "Do you agree with me, Linkow?" What was I supposed to say to that? And how? Knowing how tough he was–which seemed to account for why he had virtually no friends–I rose rather slowly. Dramatically. As if lifting the weight of the reply itself.

"I'm very pleased and excited that you accept my blade implants," I began. "But I must say that I do not agree with you regarding subperiosteal implants. These are excellent implants and can survive for many years, if they are done correctly."

Well, that was it! The blood rushed to Obergeiser's face.
He glared at me and turned away. He was so upset at what he
took to be an impertinent contradiction that he didn't finish
his speech. Nor in the coming months did his attitude ever
change: he became more of an enemy than ever, opposed to
me and to implantology. He maintained this view zealously,
almost religiously, to the end of his career.

Which brings me to my 1993 visit to Zurich, expressly to
spend two days with my dear friend and colleague, Alfie.

Alfie was then about seventy-six years old. Unfortunately,
due to a series of illnesses over the previous decade, he was an
old seventy-six. He seemed to have shrunk several inches and
slouched in a walking posture so stooped that his head angled
well in front of his torso. A once vibrant dear friend had rapidly aged. Nonetheless we had a great few days together, for
the first time in years. On previous meetings our time had
been dominated by conventions and business.

On the second day Alfie took me to the fifth floor of the
Rococo or Baroque that landmark building he owned on
Bleicherweg in Zurich, there maintaining a magnificent office I had never before visited. I remarked how much I admired his building, to which he pridefully replied that an in-
vestor had recently offered him ten million dollars for it. Alfie
rejected the offer; he liked the building far more than the
money, for which he no longer had much personal use.

Entering his spacious office I spotted two photographs. One,
of us, taken about twenty years ago on a small Zurich bridge,
and another of me on a mock "baseball card"–a souvenir of
the injury-plagued Million Dollar Dream Week I had spent in
Florida. The room was bereft of any other photos.

A small side room served as an alcove. Alfie indicated that
I should sit opposite him in a plush leather chair. He dropped
into a smaller chair. The short walk had fatigued him. He
looked old and sickly. I could see that the life force was ebb-
ing. But he remained regal, truly a lion. He related the signifi-
cance of the fifth floor, and I was shocked and then consider-

ably depressed by his words. "Lenny," he began, "the room we are in now is the room where I first started practicing dentistry. That was before I bought the building. This room is where I choose to die." This remark brought an instant lump to my throat. I tried to make light of it. "Alfie, only the good die young, so you're going to live forever."

I hated to bid adieu. At my age, and the ages of my dearest, most enduring friends, any time could be the last. Giorgio proved that to me with a thunder that still roars in my ears. Best to leave happy, brotherly, to freeze that image in the mind, to supersede all the others.

The next morning I departed for France. Arriving at Charles de Gaulle airport in Paris, my friend Professor Emanuel Chanavaz picked me up and drove us to Rouen, a journey of about two hours. I was to stay in his home with him, his wife Claire and their children Isabelle, Charles and Peter. All three children of this brilliant family at the time were in medical school. Two became doctors and at this visit the third was on the verge. Chanavaz heads the oral and maxillofacial implant department at the University of Lille, which boasts the largest medical university in France and one of the biggest in Europe, admitting fourteen hundred freshmen every year. Incredible! Several years prior, through Professor Chanavaz and his confident recommendation of my implant expertise, I was made an associate professor of Lille Medical University by French government officials. On many occasions over the years, Chanavaz has flown me from Rouen to Lille in his private two propeller plane, at times flying his craft blind, without instruments, for the challenge. What a hell of a way to shorten one's life!

From Rouen it took over two hours via highway, hurtling at 150 km/h or more, to reach the University of Lille. I was to lecture there for an entire day; it had become an annual custom. I certainly enjoyed this time in the car with a respected colleague. It was a golden opportunity for good conversation from which grows mutual learning, respect, and understanding. Zooming through the provinces of Somme and Artois, I realized that Emanuel is the most brilliant and knowledgeable academician in the field of head and neck surgery and bone physiology, as well as sinus lifting and grafting. Asking him a question is comparable to opening the very latest and very best, encyclopedia; his answers always have the ring of authority.

Because of his friendship I left France a richer and a happier man. But that trip–to Zurich, and then in France–was an emotional roller coaster.

# Twenty-one

## BAD BUSINESS

$G$enuine mutual trust is a rather rare commodity, like platinum or gold. But unlike those precious metals, valued for their great durability, trust tarnishes instantly on the revelation of poor or unethical business management among partners.

In 1991 I became entangled in a skein of events which has cast a long shadow over my work and, more than any divorce decree or any other legal decision I have been party to, feeds my disgust towards lawyers and the legal system. And operate they do, like vultures, picking with ugly and indiscriminate behavior over the carcass of the case or their client.

I had to sue to protect my rights and what was left of my practice after I entered into a partnership, of sorts, with a group that purchased the business end of my practice. I was, in effect, an autonomous employee. In addition to their own practices they would administrate my accounts, an arrangement I welcomed so that I could attend exclusively to writing, surgery, new implant applications, and lecture travel. That was the goal.

Once again, my hopes and the reality of the situation were moving in different directions.

I had sold my practice to a dental group that looked upon me, Dr. Leonard Linkow, as an investment commodity. Like a well-trained dog, I could do all sorts of tricks, including teach them implantology. Linkow Associates, we called it, but my "associates" worked at odds with sound business and practice management, using methods they kept hidden from me. After a while they flubbed some cases and alienated a number of patients. For instance, temporary bridges were often required prior to affixing teeth to new implants. But these bridges were not to be attached with hard cement, as had been done a number of times. The patients were traumatized when the bridge had to be knocked off, usually causing the implants to loosen. This was counterproductive! I asserted repeatedly that this was an improper method. A dental student could have known better! Arguments occurred over procedure and simple, common sense management. Their arrogant response was the equivalent of saying that if necessary a square peg could be forced into a round hole. The patients, that is, would have to accustom themselves to the ways of the office rather than the office adapt to the patients' needs. On one such occasion, when I was out of town, two of my patients (who would be seen by other members of the group) had traveled several hours from Pennsylvania to keep an appointment–but were asked to return on another day because the office was "behind time." My patients have always been treated like first-class travelers, like they were on the Love Boat; on this instance they had come in, needing care, to find themselves reduced to passengers on the Staten Island Ferry. My "associates" were off the wall!

To cut costs they laid off most of the experienced staff and hired lower class, unmotivated dregs. Patients naturally became unhappy; the quality of service had declined, but the fees had not. (I heard the monster called Profits At Any Cost rising from the water like Godzilla.) The practice deteriorated. As a consequence, so did mine. And, given my extensive travels and commitments, I was slow to learn of it. One day, the receptionist, making a mistake she had evidently been warned against by others in the group, put me on the phone with an exasperated, screaming man.

"Linkow, you son of a bitch! We'll get you . . . !"

"What the hell are you talking about?"

"You owe us $75,000 in payment you've been ignoring."

"Wait a minute. It's not my practice."

"Don't you tell me it's not your practice! They call it The Linkow Associates!"

I soon discovered that my "employers" also owed $77,000 to the landlord and $10,000 to the phone company. I, too, was owed money. Sitting in the hot seat, technically and legally liable, I immediately contacted my attorneys to inform them of this latest debacle. They asserted that I should have the bank note on the sale of the practice brought forward. The purchasers had breached the terms of the contract in several ways, not least of which was sullying my name and reputation with their unethical or even corrupt management. I presented the note with every intention of seeing it was paid, in full, and immediately, before they went bankrupt. I would collect outstanding monies owed me and prevent or cut my losses in this circus.

I was leaving the very next day, the last week in June, 1991, to lecture at a university in Hungary. My daughter Sheree called me in Hungary, sounding rather uncomfortable, to inform me that my employees had fired me. Well, they were not legally entitled to such a tactic. This itself was a breach of contract. They could not simply fire me. It was my option that every three years I could renew the contract, or not, at my discretion.

For the time being my practice was gone. Returning from Europe I found a padlock on my door. I had no access to patient charts, no office from which to practice, nothing. My "employers" were playing hardball. The news traveled fast. One of my generous colleagues, Dr. Bonk, who with a partner ran a small practice on 57th Street, offered space in his office for as long as I needed it so that I could retain some of my patients.

But in effect, without charts I had no certain way to render treatments to many of them. Moreover, the characters who had ruined the business and fired me began telling the patients who phoned to consult me or set their next appointment that I had gone to Europe and my date of return was unknown. Many patients saw through this nonsense; the Leonard Linkow they knew didn't behave like that. They came to the office demanding their charts, and learned from a few employees still loyal to me what had happened and where I was. I kept my head above water by treating a few patients, but I took a tremendous beating.

The landlord eventually evicted the bastards for nonpayment of rent. Rather than suffer the loss of such fine offices, I made a deal with the building owner to pay the back rent. The outlay burnt me up, but I availed myself of the legal system with the intent of punishing my tormentors.

They sued me first; I countersued. The case went to arbitration. The frequent sessions cost up to $1,800 each, with me picking up half. $200,000 in legal bills later, I successfully severed myself from these "employers," regaining what had rightfully been mine all along, and winning a substantial judgment. I also won the privilege of paying $75,000 in late payments to Healthco Dental Company. By the summer of 1995, the decision was still tied up in the knots of judges and interim decisions, suits and legal fees . . . a fetid swamp of claims and counterclaims where I should never have been thrown. The judge finally signed a "move to consent" order, and although I was awarded a large amount of money I had to settle for less than half. Otherwise, the defendants would plead for bankruptcy, which one in fact already had. I had been disrupted, dismayed and disrespected. Once again, I let my disdain for business administration get the better of my judgment. Seeking relief from the courts was tantamount to visiting a boxing ring to get cured for a headache.

\* \* \*

As of this writing, several years have passed since I last invested time in this manuscript. It merely sat on a shelf. Why? Because I was never able to have the book published; always tinkering to make it better so the market would like it, it was an on-again, off-again love affair. Furthermore, who in this crazy world and business would want to publish a book about a dentist? If my name was O.J. Simpson, or a lawyer connected with that travesty, no problem; I would have been a popular tab on the Rolodex of agents and publishers even if I had written hardly more than a word.

As I look back over the years and decades, I can honestly say that the good Lord has been wonderful to me. He has afforded me good health and tremendous drive, a fervent desire to create and the ability to see it through, and the courage to oppose virtually an entire profession single-handedly for over four decades.

Since the mid 1990s I have traveled to countries and universities that I had never dreamed of seeing, much less teaching there and doing live surgery.

Twice I have lectured and performed surgery in St. Petersburg (formerly Leningrad and Petrograd), Russia, which from 1712 to 1918 was the capital of Russia. I have similarly visited Moscow and the university there. A special session was held in the grand hallway for me, during which a plaque was hung in commemoration: "On this very day, September 15, 1998, Professor Leonard Linkow has performed surgery in our university clinic . . . "

I made two long trips to Manila, Philippines, to perform surgery and lecture in their largest university. About seven thousand students (mostly girls) work six days a week from 7:00 a.m. to 7:00 p.m. in the dental school. They are very friendly and appreciative people, and my stay there was especially gratifying.

In fact, as of 1995, the Professor of the Linkow Chair at New York University College of Dentistry, Dr. Rachael Le Geros, was from the Philippines.

I also made a great hit in one of the universities in Shanghai, China, a vast and teeming city where many are eager to learn current and efficient implant techniques.

And I received a PhD as a doctor of medical science from the University of Bucharest, in Romania.

Naturally, each country has its own idiosyncrasies. Japan is very dissimilar from Italy which is very much unlike Romania that bears scant resemblance to Germany that is a universe removed from the Philippines. In each culture, however, I have met and enjoyed time with and helped to guide fine minds eager to know as much about implantology as I could put before them. I could travel the world forever and never be bored.

But I have noted some strange customs. Perhaps it is my Western man view of life. After all, that is my only frame of reference; I'm from Brooklyn, not Budapest or Kobe. I do not and cannot have a completely open mind to, say, the penchant younger Japanese businessmen have for sitting on the floor in Geisha houses drinking sake and playing finger games with old women until two in the morning rather than spending these hours at home with their wives, or at least with beautiful young women. Several times I observed these shenanigans until the wee hours, certain I would lose my mind from boredom until my hosts at last departed with me in tow. Then let us not forget Italian business and media methods of wining, dining, and surreptitious videotaping; in one case, at least, the Danish method of destroying one of their own; and, of course, American technological and ethical, kiss-and-kill practices, which are in a league of their own.

This is part of the global human spectrum I have witnessed, what I might otherwise never have experienced had I pursued my lot in life as a baseball player.

I can say in all sincerity that through my frustrations I have to be extremely content over so many accolades that have been bestowed upon me over the years.

The Linkow Chair at the New York University College of Dentistry will remain in perpetuity. A street bears my name in Kappel-Graffenhausen, Germany. The Linkow Institute in Italy is the only Institute founded outside of Italy that was accepted by the Academia of all Italian universities, and they had a grand event in accepting it into the fold.

In Caserta, Italy–in the province of that name, north of Napoli–a post-graduate school of dentistry was named after me in 1998. My reputation was making the circuit.

I received the previously mentioned plaque in 1979 from His Holiness Pope John Paul. And the certificate of my knighthood to the Knights of Malta.

I was bestowed with a large diploma and acknowledgement from El Presidente de la Republica–Order de Andres Bello, Venezuela.

The students now at New York University College of Dentistry have requested me to give them hands-on surgery with the blade type implants.

My latest accomplishments can be seen on my web site: *www.linkow.com*. Dentists can take 52 courses on line on implants and acquire as much as 73 continuing education credits from the Academy of Implant Prosthodontics and the Academy of General Dentistry, which they need in order to maintain their dental license.

In November of 2001 in Berlin I received an extraordinarily long standing ovation at the conclusion of my lecture, and even a longer one in the same month a year later in New Orleans during the 50th Anniversary of the American Academy of Implant Dentistry. I felt like royalty or the president!

My only regrets in my four decades of practice was my chronic naivete and simplicity in the conduct of my business affairs. I trusted everyone. Consequently, many took advantage of me.

I could recount dozens of harrowing episodes, but I would only get aggravated or distressed. I will recount a few of especially trying occasions, mostly involving people who at different times worked for me. I thought of them almost as family. If you can't trust your colleagues and employees to play that role with some integrity, who can you trust?

In the 1960s, most universities declined my lectures on implants because they were not yet ready for the transition to new dental methods or technologies. But I had been giving lectures to the Institute for Graduate Dentists on West 67th Street in Manhattan. That audience was ready-made and receptive. On one occasion there I operated on a woman in her middle sixties, and it had ramifications more than three decades later.

The surgery was shown to 65 doctors via closed circuit TV. The woman already had a full lower subperiostal implant (the implant rests on top of the bone) that had been inserted in Austria. That procedure had been done incorrectly, in my opinion, but the implant had nonetheless lasted for fourteen years. The time had come for its removal, but part of the implant had sunk into the bone. For full extrication, it was necessary to drill through the bone to expose some of the underlying struts. Finally, after at least two hours of delicate work I managed to remove the implant, though I had to cut it into pieces to facilitate the task. I then inserted four of my blade implants directly into the bone, sutured the tissues together and made her a temporary fixed acrylic set of teeth with which she left the operating room. During the next three weeks she called me almost daily complaining of great pain and begging me to take the implants out. I kept reassuring her that the pain was coming from the removal of the old subperiostal implant and not from the new blades.

Finally, after the pain subsided, I completed her permanent bridge. She was thrilled.

Five or six years later (she was now about 70 years old) she said she would like to "will" her jaw to me for science because she was so very satisfied with the results, and she wanted to provide proof that implants were highly effective. She noted that her daughters did not concur in this decision, but she would make sure that her wishes were observed.

Several years later I was delighted to receive a document written by Mrs. Gergely's lawyer stating that the "will" gave me the right to send her jaw for histologic and pathologic sections once she expired. Of course, this being such a rare gift, I thanked her and called her many times in the coming years. I assured her that she would be making an important donation to medical science. She reached 90 years of age and resided in a senior citizen home. Mrs. Gergely was thrilled when I would call her there. I wanted her to live a good long life–she was certainly doing that–but I was also anxious to obtain her jaw, the one with the proof that implants were long-term solutions and had no ill-effects of any kind on human jaws.

Now, as an aside, during these years I had unfortunately hired a few half-wits and disorganized types to help run my office. In my non-stop routine of travel, seminars and surgery, I hadn't contacted Mrs. Gergely for several years. One day I realized that she may no longer be alive. At once I called her daughter. She wasn't home, but I spoke with her husband, and he told me Mrs. Gergely had died three months ago, at the age of 97. I said I was very sorry and didn't mention that I was to have received the decedent's jaw. How odd or silly might that have sounded? A short time later the daughter called back, apologizing for the evident mix-up and delay in notifying me. She told me that two years previously the person in charge of all patients at the senior citizen center had called my office requesting that, if I was still interested in receiving Mrs.Gergely's jaw when she passed on, I should write a letter stating so. But the office cretin who took the message never related it to me!

Her daughter told me they had cremated the body. I had waited *thirty-three* years for that jaw bone, now ashes. The implants would have provided a histological autopsy of the longest functioning implants and, with the paper I published, would have been milestone in the worldwide dental profession: incontrovertible proof against those who had claimed for years, and were still claiming, that implants caused many problems.

It is too often the lowest man in the chain who will drag the leaders down. One cannot raise them to your level. Such a simple task it was for an "educated" man: mentioning a phone call. I had fired this character about two years prior to hearing this sad news. At that moment I briefly wished he were still in my employ so I could give him an immediate and heartily profane parting gift; that is, a swift boot in the ass and my profound ingratitude.

The same goes for another clown whom I was foolish enough to hire. He had periodontal training. But, in retrospect, I have come to believe that this man, in his early 30s, was so smooth and corrupt he could sell cheap beach front in Miami and make you believe you were the beneficiary of a real and bona fide transaction.

While he worked in my office he had a method of pulling away a good number of my patients. Soon after I completed the implants and the reconstruction, he would tell them–secretly–that in order to maintain the work they needed him to take care of their gums. He talked me into letting him use the office on weekends, which of course was when he had arranged for my bamboozled patients to arrive for their "extra care." The scoundrel treated my well-tended patients as his own, but poorly. He went in over his head with phony and unnecessary bone grafts. Adding insult to injury, he charged $5,000 to $15,000 for a procedure involving materials that cost $60 a tube, *and he never used more than two tubes!* Consequently, he could never get the tissues to heal completely. When the suffering patients complained, he would resort to underhanded tactics, telling them to sue *me* because the tissues *he* opened–on his own, obviously without my advice or consent–were not healing. For one, critical thing, he didn't know how to separate the tissue from the subperiosteal implants. A great deal of skill–which he did not possess–is required, if it has to be done at all. He was charging thousands of dollars–for unwarranted work! And then he was brazenly blaming his greed and incompetence on me! He was an evil no good scumbag!

I never saw most of these patients again; even worse I was hit with a number of law suits brought on by his inept work and conduct. He diverted (that is, he stole) many of the patients who did not sue to other offices he worked in. This opportunist never opened an office of his own, instead sponging off the good will of once-trusting colleagues like myself. A used car salesman, an ambulance-chasing lawyer, even a drug dealer has more scruples!

This pond scum of a dentist, a fungus that prospers on rotting timber, is the most evil son-of-a-bitch I had the misfortune of affiliating with in 50 years of ethical practice and leadership in implant dentistry. The low life will probably live forever, as it seems that only the good die young.

\* \* \*

When I was a young dentist, one of my few idols, besides the great baseball player Ted Willliams, was Mario Lanza, the magnificent tenor. I would play his records eight hours a day in my first office in Queens, six days a week. One of his songs was "Summertime in Heidelberg." The beautiful melody, written by Sigmund Romberg for his operetta "The Student Prince," conjured the alluring frauleins of that classic German city. I had traveled the world widely, but until 1991 I had never visited Heidelberg. Still, for some strange reason I believed that one day I would find my way there. And then I had my chance!

The German Society of Implantology (DGZI) had scheduled a summer seminar in Heidelberg. I was invited to be the main speaker. Nestled on the Neckar River, not far from the Rhine, Heidelberg was a most beautiful and romantic city. Nine centuries of history were bound up in its vibrant streets and buildings. Germany's oldest university (established in 1386) presides here. The city of about 130,000 people has long been a center for the manufacture of precision medical and scientific instruments. No wonder that it regularly plays host to gatherings of accomplished professionals in a variety of related fields.

It was like coming home again. I saw many German colleagues whom I had taught in the past and who had been so kind to me. Always glad to see me, ever so courteous, they would help haul my huge bags of slides to my hotel after the lectures, interpret questions in languages in which I had not a word of fluency, and, when in New York, lavish me with thoughtful gifts.

The first evening they held a huge dinner party at a majestic medieval castle. There is no shortage of such edifices in Heidelberg or many other German cities, but this one was especially impressive for its ornate stonework and exquisite gilded woodwork, plaster painted in bright pastels, massive mirrors, marble, chandeliers, and sheer size. Huge!

The elegance of German culture is immediately noticeable in the manner of dining and service. Every course, every dish, the very dining ware, are works of art. The soft music—played by superb classical musicians from across the ballroom—would move to uptempo at the end of each course. The neatness and mannerisms of every staff member, from servers to management, is unsurpassed. One feels enthralled and very special to attend such a gala, and such happy gatherings in these historic settings have always been a highpoint for me.

Cecilia, myself and Dean Edward Kaufman during one of these gala events. Dr. Kaufman was instrumental in creating the Leonard I. Linkow Professorship Chair in Implantology in perpetuity at New York University, College of Dentistry.

My son in-law Nathan, little Jennifer and my beautiful daughter, Sheree.

# Twenty–two

## THE MOUNTAINS OF MY IMAGINATION

There are some people who retain a hold on you even after many years have passed. And often in more ways than one. I've found that in assuming a responsibility one isn't necessarily free to forget about it, or abandon it if you want to, or are justified, or feel all obligations have been fulfilled. Rosita, for instance; I'm still paying alimony decades after our divorce. But, as much as I loathe the burden, it is an obligation mandated by the courts. There are other imperatives that are matters of the heart.

During the summer of 1990, in the middle of a sweltering New York heat wave, one of Wiesia's friends called me with urgent news. Wiesia, she said, was very sick and I should go to see her as soon as I could. From the little I could gather, the emergency sounded mysterious, and beyond that, worrisome. Wiesia, it seemed, had regressed into chronic neurosis and depression.

When I arrived at Wiesia's Upper East Side apartment she refused even to admit me. I soon found out from her friends that she had the unsettling habit of roaming Carl Schurtz Park near Gracie Mansion, the traditional home of New York City mayors–late at night. The thought of any woman–or man for that matter–taking a solo nighttime stroll in a park in this city is alarming enough. But for a woman who had become mentally unstable, the danger was far more pronounced. Fearing for my ex-wife's safety I went to the park on subsequent nights to look for her. Wiesia's erratic behavior turned me into a benevolent stalker, a guardian angel, one making an honest although guilty effort to protect her.

It's not a big park, and not many minutes passed before I saw her. I couldn't believe my eyes; Wiesia's condition and behavior was pitiful. She was holding a rolled piece of paper in her hand as if it were a candle, muttering what sounded like garbled prayers to the Virgin Mary and John the Baptist. Wiesia saw me and smiled, but it was a peculiar smile. She looked horrible, her eyes were wild and she smelled like she hadn't washed in a month. She looked right through me, seeming not to recognize me in the least. Wiesia ran off like a frightened animal the moment I began speaking to her.

I persisted, returning time and again to the park, all but certain she would end up raped or possibly murdered. One rainy night I searched the area for hours, to no avail. I had left my phone number with the superintendent of her building, and not long afterwards he called me, urging that I come at once. Wiesia was in desperate need of help.

However, I had no more luck in breaking through the blank wall of her mind than on my previous visits. The psychiatric consultations I had arranged had apparently failed. Having no clear idea about other options–does a psychiatrist make house calls?, should I call Emergency Medical Service?–I contacted the police. They said nothing could be done unless I substantiated my claim that Wiesia was ill, likely to harm herself or others, and therefore required intervention. How could I come up with this evidence? Get her to sign an affidavit? By this time I was quite beside myself.

Very early one morning about 2:30 a.m., on a day that I was to play golf (a sport I attempted about once a year) with friends, I hit upon a plan. I called the police in the precinct with the claim that I was afraid that Weisia would commit suicide and that I needed assistance in breaking into her apartment. This time the NYPD responded, meeting me at her apartment on Third Avenue and East 66th Street at about 4:30 a.m.

But we didn't need to break in. The door, without a lock, was wide open. Wiesia had lost the key and somehow removed the useless lock. We could see at once that there was a real problem. The apartment was a squalid mess. It was a stifling summer morning; Weisia was sitting on the couch, wearing a fur coat and nothing else. The floor was covered with Indian nut shells. Roaches were rampant on the floors and flies buzzed in squadrons through the air. The officers kept brushing them away the entire time they were there. Wiesia clearly resented our intrusion. What were we doing in her home? she demanded to know. I gently explained that she wasn't well and we were there to help her. We got no rational response. The officers removed her to Memorial Hospital. There she was housed in a ward for the insane, inhabited mostly by indigent black and Hispanic patients. Memorial was the last place I wanted her to be. For the next two weeks I worked on getting Wiesia admitted to Cornell Medical Center in White Plains, where conditions were more similar to a country estate than to a scene from Dickens or Kafka. Finally I succeeded.

Déjà vu again. A wife, ex-wife, woman in my life, on the verge of a breakdown. Or actually in the grip of one.

Wiesia received adequate attention at Cornell. Her condition was diagnosed as bipolar syndrome. Manic depression. This was a blast of thunder to me: I had lived and slept with this woman and now learned that she had expertly hidden her symptoms from me, and others, for years. No stray pill vials. No extreme behavior. No unmistakable syndrome. I was heartbroken.

She later admitted that this wasn't the first time she had suffered from this crippling affliction. Episodes had occurred in Poland when she was much younger. Perhaps fearful of frightening me away, she had never told me about the illness.

The earlier bouts had been precipitated when, like this one, she had ceased taking her antidepressive medication.

Wiesia had been diagnosed with multiple schlerosis after we divorced. The diagnosis, by a world renowned doctor at Columbia Presbyterian Hospital, proved to be mistaken. (Her symptoms were later diagnosed as a "subclavian Steele syndrome" which can mimic symptoms of MS.) However, the intense panic that this faulty opinion had set off in Wiesia may have been responsible for her decision to forego the medicine, triggering yet another psychotic event. About a month after her admission to Cornell the doctors pronounced that her symptoms were under control. Wiesia was released with a good prognosis, provided she maintained the regimen of medication.

Any notion that Wiesia was home free was dispelled the following summer when again she went off her medicine (for whatever reason) and suffered a relapse. Again I summoned the police. This time they detained her on the street. Again they took her to Memorial, and once again I got her admitted to Cornell. I was considerably relieved when, over a span of years, she suffered no recurrence. But these incidents gave me quite a scare. Not married, not in love, not intimate, but still linked. This time bode trauma for me as well; during these two stressful episodes my cluster headaches recurred with a vengeance.

Sometimes love is just around the corner or has been staring in your face like an invisible reflection. It is reciprocated or freely given, just for its own sake. If there is any woman who has proven this to me it has been Cecilia. Over the years she has suffered through my lovesick episodes and suffered in silence, all with great resilience. Part fantasy, part lust, part asynchronous desire to love and be loved without a quid pro quo—with none of the terms and conditions that men and women tacitly or implicitly convey to each other in an affair or a marriage—I sought success on my terms in romance and marriage with many of the same criteria that I sought triumph in my profession. "My terms"–a great line from the great movie "Citizen Kane" affirms I think quite rightly that those are the only terms anyone ever knows. Think about it. I do, quite often. I was, am always willing to discuss, to reason, to compromise, to admit mistakes, to learn. But never to enter territory where I sacrifice my integrity merely to curry someone's favor. This includes colleagues, wives, women, partners, patients. That demeans all parties concerned. So when it comes to romantic love, well, I'm not a pushover. Perhaps because I'm afraid of it. Perhaps I distrust the surrender it requires, the willingness, even the desire, to accept a relationship, blemishes and all, simply to be with a "significant other." I'm sure that this is a root cause of the storms that have battered my relationships. And why fantasy has sometimes won out over reality, a dream that the next or greatest love was out there if only I kept seeking it/her out. Sure, there are millions of magnificent looking women in the world, but few, I deduced long ago, would have the flexible persona to blend with mine. Moreover, I am convinced that unless someone is deluded or deranged or a megalomaniac or some wholly hateful person that the world would be better off without, we must be who we are, let all friends and lovers know that this is very much all that we have to give and to share, that a prospective lover's half of the relationship will make or break us because I am all I have and can't make-to-order another aspect of my personality. My strengths and limitations should be or should have been known at the beginning of the affair or marriage. Do not underestimate the resistance of a proud man to efforts to remake him. Painful as it has often been, I have always maintained a "take it or leave it" position.

I have no doubts about Cecilia's devotion in class, intelligence, honesty or integrity. No one could be more caring. Cecilia probably loves me more than anyone has ever loved me, constantly doing things that make my life easier and less stressful. How many others would work like a demon for a man like me, who writes books, articles, prepares for lectures and courses, is on an airplane to or from, traversing another city or another country? How many would selflessly type manuscripts, plunge into research–to the point of discovering facts I did not know about my own profession–or just listen to me? Or would they spend much idle time shopping, painting their face, gossiping and socializing? Many gorgeous women, unfortunately, invest too little time expanding their inherent intelligence; perhaps because they fear the "right man" will not want them if they do, or that it requires too much effort, or they will not be rewarded for their efforts. (Nonetheless, knowledge is there to be gotten for its own sake.) These women are damned if they do, damned if they don't. When an astute woman wants to expand her horizons, she forms a threat to an insecure mate; a shallow woman can't give more, so she bores hers. These seeds of romantic conflict are everywhere. Instead of germinating a lovely garden where two people are delighted to live, these emotions too often sprout wild growth and weeds that choke off the blossoms. Beautiful people feel unloved, to great misfortune. From my time, Marilyn Monroe is a classic example. Rita Hayworth, too. Tragedies that could possibly have been avoided with more true commitment and fewer expectations.

Cecilia was very different. There was no conflict in her soul. She was bright. Lovely. Brilliant. Pretty. Self-assured. She would watch me like a hawk, looking out for my interests before I even knew what some of them might be. Cecilia, nurturing, patient and compassionate by nature, in time became wise as well. I long ago came to understand just how precious she is. I am so very proud of her.

On her trips with me to Europe she is admired and respected by all the doctors. She speaks several languages, most fluently Italian, Romanian, French and Spanish. Many times she has done near-instantaneous translations for me from English to Italian and from Romanian to English, all in the role of main translator during my rigorous journeys. Her knowledge of world history is deep and passionate. She is an opera aficionado, divinely fond of *La Traviata, Tosca, Rigoletto, The Marriage of Figaro, The Bartered Bride* and more. She is thrilled by the ballet, too. At last I found a truly cultured and inspiring woman to be my assistant and companion. And I truly love her.

Would I consider getting married yet again? Given my previous experiences, it would be quite a risk. To use a baseball analogy: three marriages, three strikes, I'm out.

As I reflect, I've come to believe that the break-ups—the failures—of the marriages were due to me. They all loved me, and I loved them, but not as much. My work came first. I was tied to a treadmill, set at an incline, and there was a price to pay in my daily strivings to be one of the best in a terribly competitive business. We are doctors of dentistry, yes, but also businessmen protecting territory, ideas, inventions, and reputations. Here as in any other profession, business is a form of warfare.

As a consequence, whether due to guilt that the marriages had ended or to an assumption that my very attractive ex-wives would all remarry soon, I had neglected to hire a lawyer. I consulted with their lawyers and consented to what in retrospect were outrageous demands. They have it virtually written in stone: I must pay to my dying day. To be the loser in a lawsuit would perhaps have been better: a payment, a penalty, and the matter is settled. But, in these cases at least, there is no final settlement to the covenant of marriage.

My third wife, Wiesia, was the nicest of all, and the most in need of my support. As she prepared to return to Poland in 2002, Wiesia sold the Manhattan apartment which I had bought for her many years ago. I gained $40,000 from the proceeds toward the unpaid balance of the mortgage, which helped me a great deal. I even drove her to Kennedy Airport to catch the flight to her homeland. Since then, we have spoken by phone several times, and I am gratified that she is happily living there with her family.

As for Jean, despite the good nature she would display, she was covetous of money and loved to spend it. That is easy to do when its appearance is guaranteed, without effort or sacrifice. Heaven forfend the check should be just one day late; my accountant and I would receive a flurry of demeaning phone calls demanding its immediate delivery. So much for her faith that I would fulfill my legal obligations. At the least, she could have granted me that honor.

My disaffection at this, however, is somewhat assuaged by fond memories. For a number of years Jean worked very hard for me and with me in my office, and was a wonderful cook, too. During the years while my practice was growing we had many friends and very often Jean grandly played hostess to our parties in Cedarhurst, Long Island home. Yes, she did like to spend money; but some of that compulsion can be attributed to her desire to be more attractive for me.

Surely, if there were such a thing as marriage insurance, no company would sell me a policy at anything less than a huge premium! Could a woman's love and devotion and understanding transcend the legacy of my past? Would our personal chemistry, like good wine, improve with time? Would love bind us together? Or would the excitement ebb and the passion between us weaken and die, almost as if it were a bad habit impossible to break? And what if once again I had to confront the prospect of a failing marriage? Could I again endure the ordeal of separation and divorce? Is it a self-fulfilling view that would take me from the intoxication of new love to the hangover of dissolution? Where does fantasy leave off and reality begin? I can't be sure. All these questions are part habit, part expectation, part imagination.

Napoleon once said that imagination rules the world. I wholeheartedly agree. Imagination offers a glimpse of life's coming attractions. It is not just for the invention of stories or paintings. It is a vision, sometimes a clairvoyance, that may indeed someday become reality. But is it because the imaginer made it real by sheer will and ingenuity, or that he/she simply saw solid evidence in life of what would someday inevitably come to pass? Da Vinci, for instance, conceived of (and built) the first flying machines–a helicopter *and* an airplane–nearly four hundred years before the first one was manufactured. I recently read that some prototype computers were built, as one might expect, in America, 1941-1944, but also in England of the *1820s* (using mechanical gears rather than electronic tubes, of course, but in basic operating principal remarkably similar). Imagination and hard work leads to new discoveries that surpass the predecessors, that improve on the function and utility, and sometimes become classics in their own right. Each advance becomes a new building in the city of knowledge. Older citizens like me try to guide the new professionals, university students on the threshold of career, the children trying to decide what to do. That is why the best strive with such perseverance, so they have a legacy that is truly worth passing on.

Without imagination and the discipline to see it become reality I would never have pioneered implantology and influenced modern dentistry. Without imagination I might have settled for a comfortable but rather unfulfilling domestic life and never sought perfect love, despite the storms that search brought upon my head. Lord knows I might have been happier that way, or at least more content. Then I would never have had to endure the calumnies and envy of an entrenched dental profession or fight so hard to be accepted and respected. And it's possible that I might have stayed married to one woman. Happily ever after. Till death do us part. But in truth, I regard my imagination as a great blessing despite the misfortunes that sometimes have resulted from my attempts to exercise it.

Go ahead. Make yourself a genie. Come into my office and grant me a wish to start over again, but on the condition that I agree to dream less and conform more, abandon argument, relinquish the pursuit of perfection and settle down to a life of little challenge. I'll likely escort you to the elevator.

* * *

I nearly made that compromise on the fateful day when Giorgio Gnalducci appeared in my office and took the offensive (literally and figuratively) as the point man for Dr. Scialom, whose pin implants were then the rage in Europe, particularly in Italy, where he and his cronies were making fortunes hawking systems that my own soon surpassed. Little wonder Scialom wanted to co-opt me, to entice me with money, or intimidate me into avoiding his turf. But everything changed after that second day in my Queens office, when Giorgio pored over my slides as if he were a novice student come to the academy for a lesson. From there, I began to build an empire of reputation on deeds that Giorgio was so crucial in promoting. We were each other's mentor. I shared my technical expertise, and he his business acumen. If not for him, I may never have seen La Scala or the art treasures of Italy, the Alps or Rome, Zurich or Paris, been on a Mediterranean cruise, or been briefly discussed as a candidate for the Nobel Prize. Much came from my association with him.

Giorgio's passing was a psychological setback to my ventures, as if I had gone to sleep on a pleasant mountain day and woken up in a dark rain squall. The fifteen years I had known him was far too short. We had so much left to do and experience. Dental methods to be taught, practitioners to be convinced, money to be made.

It is appropriate, somehow, to segue from the issue of money, ultimately of limited consequence, to the death of someone who both coveted money and, in effect, had little regard for it. Gnalducci, you will recall, lived the high life: jewelry, yachts, condos, the finest cuisine, luxury cars. I understood why he was so acquisitive. Giorgio knew that he was destined to live a short time. So he determined to live some of it in the fast lane. As they say, a candle burning twice as bright burns half as long.

Always eager to show me a good time, to offer moral support and share his wisdom, Giorgio was very much like the brother I never had, or would have wished for. His generosity knew no bounds. It wasn't enough that Wiesia and my younger daughter Sheree were his guests aboard his yacht for a two-week cruise off Ibiza and the coast of Spain. No, next summer, he said, we must spend a full *month* with him on the boat. I had never taken a vacation that long in my career, but it was impossible to resist Giorgio's entreaties—he was that persuasive! Alright, I said, remembering the lovely time spent aboard (but with some workaholic guilt nearly a year in advance of the sin), I'll commit myself to a full thirty, blissful, sun-drenched, no-stress days sailing around the Mediterranean!

But I would never get to take that cruise. Just before Thanksgiving Day, on November 23, 1978, less than three months after the vacation in Ibiza, his elder son Marco called me. There was a sad, terrible urgency in his voice. "Dr. Linkow," he said, "Father *morteo*. Please come immediately to Milano."

I asked my secretary to call Alitalia Airlines to reserve my seat on the evening flight to Milano, and to contact Giorgio's office and inform someone on his staff that I would be on it. I left the office at once. I didn't even take the time to go home to pack. The only clothing I carried was the suit on my back.

The plane arrived at Malpensa airport early the next morning. It was not unusual that rain was drenching Milano. The airport almost always seems to be under a sea of rainclouds, which if they turned violent could cause a diversion of planes to other cities. Thankfully, not this time. When I deplaned someone from Giorgio's office was waiting to take me to the church.

About an hour later we arrived at the Church of San Pietro in Sala, a Milanese neighborhood. Giorgio's body was lying in state. Now I was overcome with grief. I realized that the day he died was also the date he had been born. It struck me that this would be the last time I would look at my friend. True friendship is so precious. Life is so fleeting. I had lost my best and most trusted colleague. Those sentiments together weighed on my heart like a cold, black mass. While I had certainly known that sooner or later Giorgio would fail from his poor health, I never dared to expect it would happen at his age. He was only fifty-two years old.

The church was so crowded it was almost impossible to move, but other than his technicians and his close associate Dr. Mongeri, I saw only a few whom I knew from my wide travels with Giorgio. While I stood by the coffin, transfixed by the sight of his body, I felt a tap on my shoulder. I turned to see Marco, now a pre-med student with the goal of following in his father's footsteps as a dentist. He threw his arms around me and we both wept together.

His wife Titi, from whom Giorgio had been separated the last three years of his life—making way for the Russian girl, who spent his money, with his consent, as if the Warsaw Pact might invade at any time—then appeared at my side with her younger son, Massimo. Dressed in black, her face was obscured by a dark veil which wasn't so opaque that it could hide her tears.

As if I were immediate family, and the most aggrieved, the three of them led me toward the doors of the church and the limousine at the curb. I sensed that we were being observed by a thousand eyes. Finally we were outside. We climbed into the limousine behind the hearse that bore Giorgio's body. I was already drenched by the relentless rainfall.

Giorgio had always wanted to be buried in the hills near the small town of Montepoulciano, on the Arno River, in the lovely province of Toscana, very near the border with Umbria. He had lived there as a young boy, and his younger sister and her husband owned a hotel—the Marzocco—just a few hundred yards from the cemetery.

Suitable to the sorrowful occasion it rained hard all day, not once relenting during the two and a half hour drive to Montepoulciano. Titi sat in the front of the limousine with the driver while I sat in the back with Marco and Massimo. She cried and wailed and grieved the entire trip. Titi really took

Giorgio's death hard, even though she had been fighting with him terribly during their years of separation.

At last we arrived. The rain had become a deluge. Soaked to the skin, we were made even more uncomfortable by a sudden chill at the higher elevation. The cortege proceeded a block or so to the small cemetery, Santa Chiera. I and several men from the village served as pall bearers. We gathered around the solid, cement-lined crypt. Giorgio's mother, his sister and Titi were clustered together, a tableau in black, while his father, brother-in-law, and others from the village stood to one side. What happened next was almost like a scene from an Italian comedy, although a very wry and macabre one.

We surrendered the casket to the men of the cemetery staff, who with rope began to slowly lower it to its resting place inside the cement crypt. But the rite stopped short. Everyone was puzzled. We realized why. The casket wouldn't fit! It was at least three inches too long! This catastrophe brought even more weeping and anguish from the women. And near-panic among the men. A sudden death. Dismal weather. The body of a beloved one that could not be interred. How tragic! Quickly conferring, two of the cemetery fellows ran off, leaving the casket perched obliquely over the crypt. They soon returned–not with a shovel to somehow enlarge the grave–but with a two-man lumber saw! What, exactly, were they going to shorten? More screams echoed over the headstones as they sliced hastily into the rich wood. I stood there, stunned and disbelieving. After some minutes of vigorous, rain-soaked activity before our silent, suffering huddle, enough length was removed from the casket, at the foot end. I thought they were going to cut off Giorgio's toes!

The casket, crudely but finally reduced to the proper size, was once more lowered into the crypt. It fit snugly but without a problem. Then the men began to shovel wet earth over it. Thump! Thud! The image and sounds conveyed the finality of the ritual and of life even more than the funeral at the church.

We straggled away from the cemetery, a solemn group if there ever was. My clothes and shoes felt as if I had just emerged from the nearby lake. Every thread clung to my wet body so tightly that it was difficult to move.

We next entered a very small church, located several hundred yards from Giorgio's final resting place. It was named Saint Agnese, after the martyr who lived during the fourteenth century. When Saint Agnese died she was beatified by Caterina de Siena–who herself was proclaimed a saint after she died in 1380. Caterina was proclaimed patron saint of all Italy together with San Francesco, or St. Francis of Assisi.

I sat near the back of the tiny church, recalling the unforgettable and happy times I had enjoyed with Giorgio. That was my instinct, to dwell on the joy, because death is a part of life and the person we choose to celebrate is best memorialized as they were when most engaged in living. The priest began his sermon. There were only about ten rows of seats and I had a good view of the altar and chapel wall behind the priest. I noticed a peculiarly shaped structure there, covered with what looked like a purple curtain. This probably would otherwise not have attracted my attention but for an event which almost shocked me and my clothes into instant dryness. As the priest concluded his sermon he either banged the podium with his hand or yanked a chord which activated a mechanism of some kind. It set off a heavy echo. As if on cue the curtain rose to reveal a glass structure housing what appeared to be a woman's body. This was strange theatre. As the congregation knelt to pray I edged closer for a better look. Yes, it was definitely a female form, dressed in a lacy gown; her face was darkened to almost the color of mahogany. She had been dead and preserved for a very long time. The most unnerving aspect of this grotesque sight was the position of one of her legs, which was elevated and stretched out at an angle of at least thirty-five degrees. She/it appeared to be frozen in motion. Death had been animated.

I later heard the explanation for the mummy's contortion.

According to legend, Caterina visited the remains of Saint Agnese and paid homage to her by prostrating to kiss the saint's feet. But in honor of Caterina's own saintliness the spirit of Saint Agnese actually raised the foot of her corpse's leg to spare Caterina the need to stoop. Since then, the foot of the remains of Saint Agnese has remained perpetually extended.

The service concluded, I joined the family members as they proceeded to the small hillside hotel owned by Giorgio's sister. By now I was frozen stiff, shivering unbearably, and couldn't wait to take a hot bath and go to sleep. It was only seven in the evening, but it was already a dark, wet November night.

For the time being, I banished my memories of lavish evenings in Milano and Rome, feasting and laughing and talking teeth and culture with colleagues. Giorgio was almost always among the cast, and I couldn't bear to think of life without him.

As soon as I got to my room I turned on the tub faucet—and made the unhappy discovery that there was no hot water! I panicked. I was frigid to my core; my fingers and toes were numb. I felt vulnerable and went in search of someone who could help, but the hallway and tiny lobby were dark and desolate. Everyone had retired. It seemed like time had warped to 3:00 a.m. At this time of year the hotel was usually closed, and had opened only for Giorgio's family. There were few or no staff members on the premises. I was reluctant to disturb anyone, in their private grief, over the relatively trivial matter of no hot water. I realized that this would be a miserable night. Plodding back to my room and its cold white marble floor, absent even a throw rug for my bare feet, I made do with two thin bathroom towels. But there was nothing at all to be done about the bed; upon it was one white sheet. No blanket. I looked in all the drawers, and again padded into the hall in search of a closet, but had no luck. I felt uncomfortable poking around in someone else's home, so I returned to the room, removed my damp, rumpled suit and fell upon the bed. Sleep would not embrace me. I tried to conjure up the rigors of my Army days, of weapons training and long marches in the heat, of parachuting from a plane and KP. Mind over matter, I thought. But the discomfort was insurmountable; I felt I must have been a lot colder than my poor friend Giorgio. Sleepless all night, I could hardly wait for daylight.

At dawn, zombie-like, I donned my cold clothing. To warm up, I ran back and forth in the early sunshine. In the lobby I found the chauffeur hired by Giorgio's family. No one was around to bid me arrividerci. I prevailed upon the man to drive me to Rome, where I could catch the next flight to Kennedy Airport and resume the momentum Giorgio had helped me attain. I never had a chance to purchase a new suit. At no point in the journey did my clothes ever dry. It was a minor miracle that I did not contract pneumonia. But this torture probably was of some use, after all; at least for a time it distracted me by so focusing my attention on the distress that I wasn't overwhelmed by grief for my dear friend.

Me, happily surrounded by (l to r) Jennifer, Michael, Steven and Stephanie

\* \* \*

For my disappointments, some of them grave, I have many wonderful gifts to show for the blood, sweat and tears. (Sorry,

Winston.) First and foremost are my two daughters. I have often asked myself that without my marriage to Rosita, would I have anyway been destined to be their father? Such a question crosses into the realm of philosophy, and is unanswerable in this life. Robin and Sheree have brought into the world four grand and delightful children. Robin has three children–Stephanie (who prefers to be called Steph), Steve and Michael (Mike).

Steph is beautiful, breathtaking, lovable. A brilliant student, she always wants to participate in everything going on around her. What a love of life! Such energy! A prodigy, she has assisted me in office surgery when on vacation from school and traveled with me to seminars. In 1993 on the fabulous Mediterranean isle of Capri, she watched me place an implant in a dried mandibular bone specimen, and then performed the task as if having practiced it many times before. Steph at the time was but nine years old.

Steph is also an incredible athlete, competitive with boys in soccer, touch football and street hockey. In 1993 she was the only girl in the entire Little League baseball championship, getting at least one hit in every game and receiving a trophy at season's end. When she first joined the team none of the boys would even talk to her. Baseball, it's a man's game! The boy's club! I attended a mid-season at which she had a turn at bat with two teammates on base. A hit would win the game. "Don't worry," I heard one of her mates confidently state to another, less positive player, "Steph will get a hit." It was a clutch moment, and there I sat in the stands, as I often did, with my heart racing in anticipation of her success. Pow! She rapped a solid hit and her nine won the game!

And she, a daughter in a family deserted by a cowardly father who seldom if ever had the minimum decency to phone his children, on their birthday or at any other time. I took over the role of father, irregular and surrogate as it may be, guiding Steff to the consideration of career interests. Perhaps because of her family experience, at an early age she pondered becoming a divorce lawyer. I talked her out of throwing in with such lumpen lowlifes and counseled her to weigh a field in medicine. Mercifully, dermatology has caught her interest.

Little Mike is quite a guy. When he was three, four and five years old, he had difficulty pronouncing words and we thought he had a speech impediment. But apparently the brain neurons designated for that task eventually connected. Now Mike speaks the Kings English. And he can hit a baseball.

When he was still a wee one I took Mike to a batting cage just like I did with Steph and Steve. I started him at the slowest speed, about 35 miles an hour. One rule is that all batters must wear a helmet. Mike was just a tyke; the smallest helmet rested over his ears and nearly obscured his vision. The very lightest bat was still lumber to his little muscles. I positioned him just off the plate so he could reach the ball. Batting in tandem, I guided his wrists and arms in the proper swing. He had never swung a bat before. Most novices swing either too late or too early. To miss by an inch is the same as a mile, so timing is everything. Mike, however, had the knack first off. I believe there is a strong case for genetic behavior, and Mike would be a fair example. He swung the bat and connected. His momentum repeatedly knocked him off balance and the helmet wobbled off his noggin. He would get right back up, resume position and hit it again. I admire such perseverance in a lad, whether he is my grandson or someone else. Soon after I nicknamed him "Mr. Foist," because he so often got the hang of a task or a skill the first time out, and because that is how he originally pronounced first. Mike gets annoyed when I call him by this moniker, although he usually doesn't say so. But "Mr. Foist" still sticks, because Mike excels in sports and nearly everything else. He is an independent young guy, doing naturally on his own what many other youngsters need to be shown. When he wants to participate in something he will not quit until the goal is met. Many times I have taken him to my upstate New York home in Ulster County. As a youngster, he was a landscape artist, diligently helping me plant trees, plants and bulbs. In his teen years, he has become a budding computer genius. Such traits say he is going to get somewhere in life. I am certain of that.

Steve is the middle youngster, sixteen years old in May of 2002. He is a very sensitive, humane young man with deep feelings. He loves animals and children and has reflected on the pros and cons of life as an architect or a pediatrician. Demonstrating an early and masterful flair of the ingenuity required of an architect, Steve built his small dog, a Maltese, a nine-room condo. Out of cardboard boxes. With an upstairs and downstairs, a bedroom, even an exercise room. Unbelievable. Who but a budding genius would do such a thing? Too bad the dog hasn't got any money, Steve could charge Manhattan rents. When he wasn't devising such schemes, Steve's athletic interest embraced soccer. Moreover, he displayed great talent as a comedian, a dancer and a music composer. This is perfect material for a Hollywood career! A brilliant drummer, he has won competitions against 75 other players. He was the star in all of the school's orchestras–brass, jazz, philharmonic–and his own five-piece band. Steven has followed his real dreams and will start a music business career at one of the most prestigious universities in the nation.

From childhood into his teens, Steven had been somewhat intimidated by his older sibling. To be sure, Steph was a tough act to follow, and the devil in disguise when it came to annoying her brother.

Jennifer, my granddaughter through Sheree, turned eight years old in March 2001. She was and is so adorable I cannot look away from her. Whenever she would want something from you or was compelled to show off some of her toys, dolls or books she came up to you, took your hand in hers and guided you rapidly to her interest. On each of my visits she would wait until I enter, flash her brilliant smile and scoot into the bedroom until I come to get her. She is flowering into a strong and delightful personality. I nicknamed her my little "Petunia Fly."

The attention children need and deserve fills me with joy to be part of their lives. It amazes me that by two or three years of age they have many of the traits–expressions, gestures, acuity, likes and dislikes–that help to form their identity for life. You can't help but wonder what mysterious and numerous factors of environment and spirit come together to create a personality.

We live for many reasons, I believe, but one of the most important, certainly the most sacred, even one of biological imperative, is to pass on what we know and believe to subsequent generations. That transfer begins most intimately with our own blood. Some will succeed. Unfortunately, many will not. But that is life.

Looking back through these decades I have come to realization, however cliched it may sound, that we are all candles in a wind over which we have little or no control. We are born, we grow and mature and contribute. And then it's over, snuffed out like Giorgio's, or it flickers for a while, slowly diminishing. While we are here, some give sixty minutes of every hour, ever seeking what is out there to share. These lucky few have the ingenuity, skills, creativeness, belief and fortitude to strive on against imposing odds in the attempt to invent or create something that one day will prove to have significant value: a new device or method, an opera, some profound insight. They can give those sixty minutes from each hour to create something that can prove to have lasting value, to make society better, whether it is in medicine or any other walk of life. How greatly or for how long they will be appreciated, if at all, is part of the equation. If their contributions are to have any effect, ideally while they are alive, there has to be a degree of acceptance among even those groups that may be inclined to resist. Often those groups are comprised of souls who give too little to the profession, but expect a lot–influence, prestige, money–in return. Some of them get it, but they remain disappointed that life was not better for them. This may come from a suspicion that they were not all they believed themselves to be, that much of the gratification they received was in trying to deny others what they could not attain themselves.

No striving is done without cost. To turn the huge wheel requires great effort, especially in this complex and competitive world we have created. Straining against forces who refuse to concede, the strivers find that much of their energy is spent just fending off the jabs and criticisms of their self-appointed adversaries. At each point of the wheel burns a candle with a delicate flame. The small fire needs to be carefully nurtured with spirit, discipline and determination. These qualities are vital, but not easily maintained or applied. It shouldn't be taken for granted that they will come to us at all, or remain once they arrive. They are gifts, but they are not free. We must climb the mountains to take them, and climb still others to prove we are worthy of them.

So, how green were my mountains? I have had my days of glory, my thrills and memories. I have a few left to enjoy. But at this point, looking back down the years, I ask myself if it was worth it. Giorgio Gnalducci and Gustav Dahl and Jack Wimmer and many other friends and colleagues notwithstanding, I plowed this field myself. Writing books at a breakneck pace, traveling city to city, continent to continent loaded with cases and duffel backs stuffed to capacity with slides, maneuvering through a schedule jammed morning to evening with patients and lectures and . . . well, I'm being redundant. But I gouged the rocks out of the soil, leveling the earth for the sowing I set myself to do. Few made the task easier by at least pointing out the costly mistakes I was about to make. How could they? I have found that when one is successful, many want to share the rewards, like the sunlight pouring through one window in a darkening roomful of people. But during the rough periods, many loyal and once generous allies seem to recede into the shadows, apparently feeling their energies are best directed elsewhere if they are to get appropriate recognition. That is why many of the implantologists practicing today, even though they know of me, can be so quick to denigrate my methods, and would not know me in the street. They have spent their time going where the pastures are greener. They don't go out on a limb, don't risk the disapproval of their peers, and have not frequently called to ask my advice. I'm "old fashioned." The pendulum has swung with me, and now, they think, away toward them. A two-week course, a couple of cases, and abracadabra, they're experts. I, bunk. Nothing ventured, nothing gained. There is little that is respectable in taking the easy way out.

Many in my profession have vacillated between the methods I have propounded, and the alternatives. Subperiosteal, or screws! Blades, or osseointegrated implants! Often the dentist offering his version of what is the best method bases his judgment on what will bring him the profit. He knocks whatever stands in the way of a patient with pockets, even if, or especially if, that patient has enjoyed Linkow implants. The rationale: these "old-fashioned" methods have to be exposed for what they are. They proclaim it is excessive technology; their simpler approach will suffice. Well, this family of implants is well-designed, like a Swiss watch, or the Empire State Building.

Was it all worth it, to butt heads with the naysayers, the know-it-alls, the resentful and envious? On principle, yes. But practically speaking, given frequently cynical and self-serving human nature, well, I don't know. Erich Fromm wrote, "There is perhaps no phenomenon which contains so much destructive feeling as *moral indignation,* which permits envy or hate to be acted out under the guise of *virtue.*" I have met dentists determined to hold me in contempt, or at least suspicion, no matter the array of scientific, clinical and empirical evidence marshaled in my favor. As if I have questioned *their* integrity. And they will go to great lengths to prove me wrong. Like prevailing upon a patient of mine to have the implants removed and replaced with something better, even if those implants have functioned successfully, comfortably, for years. Other patients sorely in need of a remedy, for whom implants are the perfect answer, are instead tossed into the hospital for a bone graft from the hip that will give them enough tissue in their jaw to accept screws. So what if the patient must walk like a penguin for several weeks and so what if the wearer must first suffer an ill-fitting denture over the sore bone grafts until the implants are finally inserted–only to be burdened for several more months before they can be affixed with teeth, which takes another few months to fit properly. And my procedure? Several hours over several visits, no hospitalization and little pain to insert systems that in the great majority of cases last for years. Ladies and gentleman, if these were political candidates, how would you vote?

Ahh. So how green were my mountains?

I have climbed many mountains during my career thinking that with each success I would be happy at the achievement. But at the summit I have often found myself alone and either too tired to continue or too consumed with explaining why I had to be first, or why someone else didn't get the chance, or defending myself against those who simply didn't and don't realize that I am not their proper adversary. To my mind, in the end, the color green is beautiful because it signifies the attempt, the journey, and not the summit. But many of the hills I climbed were anything but green. Barren or water-deprived, rocky or steep, not always hospitable to the wayfarers like myself trying to rise above the din below.

I guess the time has come for me to stop climbing and to smell the flowers.

I wrote this book as honestly as I could. It is all truth and rightfully because it has been about my life. The only truths omitted were more of the women who crossed paths with mine. To continue more on that subject would risk sounding boastful or foolish, and I would repeat myself.

I have received many letters over the years from patients who praise me for restoring them to the pleasures of life. And living without pleasure is not much of a life, they imply, so benefitting from my work is for them often a kind of epiphanous experience. I can't help but be moved by their splendid gratitude, and be grateful myself that with the right skills, armamentarium and interpersonal chemistry I have been able to positively affect so many. They do everything but call me a miracle worker! I offer this one letter from a Manhattan patient, the widow of a dentist to whom I had also taught implantology, that bears proof of a refrain I have heard in my decades of practice:

10/26/93

Dear Lennie,

It is so rare to find a doctor with total dedication, meticulous attention to detail and extensive, deep knowledge of your profession, combined with kindness, compassion and humour.

You are truly a humanitarian spreading knowledge around the world.

Thank you so much for all the care you have given me. I lucked out when we became friends and I became your patient.

You are a great man and may you live forever.

With Love and Eternal Gratitude,

Martha

It is strange how certain events or dreams remain in the mind and heart throughout our lifetimes, long after others have turned to haze or fallen into the void. One such event has haunted me from the age of eleven years old, when I spent my summer at Camp Ta-Ri-Go.

Often I would gaze at one of the several distant mountaintops that overlooked the campsite. How exciting, I thought, it would be to climb to the summit and gaze down into the valley below. What, in my daydream I wondered, would it be like?

One morning all the campers in our group were scheduled to go on an all-day hike. We were not told where we were going. It was a mystery destination. First we piled on a bus for a slow-motion drive that seemed unduly long (but in fact was only a couple of miles). Finally the bus stopped and we filed out. Led by the adults, about twenty children began to walk up a gently sloped path. It occurred to me that the landscape looked familiar. Then I realized we were climbing up the very same mountain that had caught my eye from camp. The venture was like waking up from a dreamy sleep to enter a new reality that was exactly as I had imagined it to be! I was thrilled!

At last we came to the end of the road which marked the summit. Peering down the steep undulating hill that seemed to me as big and as wondrous as the day of its creation, I saw a small house with a white fence and patches of multicolored hollyhock flowers growing all around. Like out of a fairy tale. What a beautiful view the people who live there must have, I thought enviously. My gaze wandered and I beheld a magnificent view of the valley. Extending for miles in all directions, it was as vast as I had imagined. What made for an even more breathtaking sight was the checkerboard pattern of the terrain. Farmhouses of various colors dotted the valley like jewels on broad swatches of green velvet interspersed with fields of corn and other crops. And with the sun high in the sky shining so brightly, the many lakes below had taken on the aspect of melting pots of gold. It was a sight that I will never forget.

It seems to me that I have lived my whole life trying to get to the top of the mountain and discover what is on the other side, to find what is hidden beyond the next hill, and the next, to attain greater achievements, no matter how impossible they may have turned out to be. In many ways I am still that young man setting out for the summit, eager to discover whether the vision I hold in my imagination will be equal to the sight that finally greets me when I arrive there.

# EPILOGUE

No works, major or minor, exist in a vacuum. They are influenced, inspired, shaped and promoted by many others, some of whom remain unknown but who believed in the spirit of new methods and have guided their careers accordingly. But there are many that I do know, and I have much gratitude to them for their steadfast faithfulness to the mutual causes of progressive techniques, honest business, and plain old hard work. They have integrity, forthrightness, talent. I have been and will remain proud to call them my colleagues and my friends.

Ronnie Cullen—London, England
Giordano Muratori—Bologna, Italy
Isaiah Lew—New York, NY
Aaron Gershkoff—Providence, Rhode Island
Gerhard Heim—Berlin, Germany
Raymond Gerard—one of my dental technicians from the 1950s
    through the 1980s.
Gerry Reed—Dallas, Texas
Jack Wimmer—Park Dental Research, NY
Ken, Judy and Herb Gross, who were greatly responsible for
    the impetus for the Linkow Chair at NYU.
Gustav Dahl—the first to do subperiosteal implants. He has given
    me tremendous confidence all these years, calling me

numero uno de mondo. Number one in the world. He is
now 97 years old

Eiichi Kojima—Tokyo, Japan

Yana Yanagisawa—Tokyo, Japan

Shumen Otobe—founder of one of the earliest implant societies in Japan

Bue Inada—President and my "son," from Nara, Japan

Sheldon Winkler—Temple University, Philadelphia

Margarita Roumeletti—President of the implant society of
Greece

Amilka Ariza, Bogota, Colombia

Charles Mandel—Florida

Marty Altman—Florida

Raul Mena—Florida

Sebastian LoBello—Trento, Italy

Stefano Tramonte—Milano

Ugo Pasqualini—Milano

Ric Ricciardi—USA

Antonio Pierzzini—Massala, Italy

Franceso Mangini—Bari, Italy

Holger Burkel—influential in naming the street after me in
Kappel-Graffenhausen, Germany

Bruce Fischl—long-time friend since we were both eleven years
old in Brooklyn

Frank La Mar—Rochester, NY

Carl Misch—Detroit

Dr. George Anastassov, brilliant scholar and excellent surgeon,
who purchased my practice with a group of his doctors
from Mt. Sinai

Jean Sirbu—Bucharest, Romania

Hans Grafelman, Bremen, Germany

Charlie Weiss, New York, NY

Anthony Rinaldi, Philadelphia, PA

Arthur Lieberman—we played softball together many times in
Kelly Park in Brooklyn.

Sid Berger—New York, NY

Irwin Smigel—my very dear friend from N.Y. City - Father of Cosmetic Dentistry.

Arthur Kogan—my dear friend goes way back to Cunningham Junior High School in Brooklyn

Norman Cranin—created the first and most popular implant maxi-course at Brookdale Hospital in Brooklyn.

Robert Miller—Del Ray Beach, FL.

Norman Goldberg—one of the earliest pioneers in subperiosteal implantology, R.I.

David Hoexter—New York, N.Y.

Alain Claret—Paris, France.

Eugene Joffe—New York, N.Y.

Jerry Lynn, New York, N.Y.

Maurice Valen—President of Impladent, LTD., Queens, N.Y.,

Jack Hahn—Cincinatti, Ohio.

*Leonard Linkow Seminars*

World Implant Congress, Paris
Nihon University, Tokyo, Japan
Loma Linda, California
University of California, Los Angeles, Los Angeles, California
University of Zurich, Zurich, Switzerland
Howard University, Washington, D.C.
Academy of Osseointegration, Philadelphia, PA
Lille University, Lille, France
Manila University, Manila, Philippines
Universities of Milano, Bari, Torino, Pisa, Podova and Bologna
George Eastman University, Rome
University of Munich
European Academy of Oral Implantology, Rome, Italy
Hebrew University of Jerusalem and Haifa
Tel Aviv University, Tel Aviv, Israel
University of Alabama, Birmingham, Alabama
Bucharet University, Bucharest, Romania
Graz University, Graz, Austria
Hamburg Univ., Hamburg, Germany
Germany Academy of Oral Implantology
University of Shanghai, China
Universities of Mississippi, Oregon, Indiana, Detroit, Boston,
    Albert Einstein, New York, Emory (Atlanta), Ohio State,
    Buffalo, Washington (St. Louis, MO), Tennessee, Medical
    School of South Carolina, School of Dentistry and Medical
    School of Virginia

I will always feel indebted to Dr. Carl Misch, who, during my
three months recuperation, unselfishly spent two days a week
keeping my practice alive. He had to travel from Detroit with
his dental assistant taking him away from his own practice and
incuring more expenses. Moreover he refused any compensation. God bless you, Carl.

Some of Leonard Linkow's patents

1. Ring-type implant for artificial teeth—patent # 3,465,441, filed March 20, 1968; date of patent September 9, 1969

2. Intra-osseous pins and posts and their use and techniques thereof—patent # 3,499,222, filed Aug. 17, 1965; date of patent, March 10, 1970

3. Template for Implant Denture—patent # 3,624,904, filed May 10, 1968; date of patent, Dec. 7, 1971

4. Bridge Stabilizing System—patent # 3,660,899, filed Sept. 16, 1970; date of patent: May 9, 1972

5. Oral implant—patent # 3,729,825, filed Aug. 2, 1971; date of patent May 1, 1973

6. Bone adapting tissue packing post system—patent # 3,849,888, filed Oct. 19, 1973; date of patent Nov. 26, 1974

7. Device for facilitating the taking of an impression of bone portions of the mouth, and method of using same—patent # 3,916,527, filed June 30, 1973; date of patent, Nov. 4, 1975

8. Wide Vent dental implants – patent # 4,024,638, filed Feb. 24, 1969; date of patent, May 24, 1977

9. Symphyseal Rami Endosteal implants – patent # 4,044,467, filed June 28, 1976; date of patent, August 30, 1977

10. Symphyseal Rami Endosteal implants – patent # 4,062,119, filed June 28, 1976; date of patent Dec. 13, 1977

11. Oblique oral implant – patent # 4,420,305, filed Sept. 14, 1983; date of patent, Dec. 13, 1983

12. Oral implant for oversized support openings – patent # 4,521,192, filed July 21, 1983; date of patent, June 4, 1985

13. Osseous integrated submergible implant – patent # 4,600,388, applied for Feb. 23, 1984; date of patent, July 15, 1986

14. Detachable post for an osseous implant – patent # 4,531,917, filed April 2, 1984; date of patent July 30, 1985

15. Dental implant patent DES 282,580 – date of patent, Feb. 11, 1986

16. Movable plate implant — patent # 4,661,066, filed Nov. 25, 1986; date of patent, April 28, 1987

17. Prefabricated partial subperiosteal implant—patent # 4,702,697, filed Feb. 14, 1986; date of patent, October 27, 1987

18. Adjustable sinus lift implant—patent # 4,682,951, filed May 28, 1986; date of patent, July 28, 1987

19. Improved submergible screw-type dental implant and method of utilization—patent # 4,713,004, filed Sept. 4, 1986; date of patent, Dec. 15, 1987

20. Submergible screw-type dental implant and method of utilization—patent # 4,842,518, filed December 29, 1987; date of patent, June 27, 1989

21. Method of manufacturing synthetic bone coated surgical implants—patent # 4,908,030, filed April 29, 1987; date of patent, March 13, 1990

22. Method of Manufacturing Synthetic bone coated surgical implants—patent # 4,944,754, filed April 26, 1988; date of patent, July 31, 1990

23. Submergible dental implant and method of utilization—patent # 4,915,628, filed Dec. 14, 1988; date of patent, April 10, 1990

24. Asymmetrical bone drill—patent # 4,943,236, filed Dec. 22, 1988; date of patent, July 24, 1990

25. Neckless blade implant—patent # 5,102,336, filed Jan. 30, 1989; date of patent, April 7, 1992

26. Submergible screw-type dental implant and method of utilization, patent # 4,932,868, filed March 6, 1989, date of patent, June 12, 1990

27. Neckless Blade Implant—patent # 5,116,226, filed Oct. 4, 1990, date of patent, May 5, 1992

28. Neckless Blade Implant – patent # 5,110,293, filed Sept. 30, 1988, date of patent, May 5, 1992

29. Neckless blade implant—patent # 5,165,892, filed Oct. 11, 1990; date of patent, Nov. 24, 1992

30. Dental Implant Method of Installation – patent # 5,427,527, filed May 25, 1993; date of patent, June 27, 1995

31. Apparatus and Method of Closing a sinus opening –
patent # 5,547,378, filed Oct. 21, 1994; date of patent,
August 20, 1996

32. Apparatus and method for closing a sinus opening
during a dental implant operation – patent #
5,685,716, filed June 7, 1995; date of patent Nov. 11,
1997

33. Submergible Screw Type dental implant and method
of utilization – patent # RE35,784, re-issued, date of
patent May 5, 1998

34. Immediate Post-Extraction implant – patent #
6,413,089, filed Feb. 10, 1999; date of patent July 2,
2002